An Errand of Mercy

An
Errand of Mercy

The Evangelical United Front   *1790-1837*

By Charles I. Foster

Chapel Hill
The University of North Carolina Press

To

ARTHUR MEIER SCHLESINGER

PREFACE

WHEN QUEEN VICTORIA ascended the British throne in 1837, the ideas, attitudes, and social practices later associated with her name were already established. The mental furniture of which the household furniture of the period became so apt a symbol had been constructed, and British prestige was spreading the vogue throughout Western civilization, particularly in the United States.

The power of American Victorianism as a conservative counterpoise to native radicalism is obvious to any thoughtful observer of the American scene in the nineteenth century. The equally obvious lack of historical treatment is due to the amorphous nature of this influence: its subtle, pervasive character has frustrated analysis.

This book is a case study in the rise of American Victorianism, the transmission of British ideas to the United States and their adaptation to American purposes. Although the study is of religious enterprise, it may serve to illuminate the process as a whole.

Although the United States began its national career in the anti-Christian atmosphere of the Enlightenment, it received during its most formative years an intensive, systematic indoctrination in the ideology of Evangelical Protestantism. The indoctrination was not the work of Protestant sects but of an Evangelical united front operating through societies quite free of denominational control.

The united front arose in Great Britain to conduct ideological warfare during the Napoleonic Wars. Its organization penetrated the Continent as well as the United States, where the movement eventually became naturalized to serve American purposes.

Such is the story of these pages. Part I deals with the rise of the Evangelical united front in England, its work in bringing the home front under control, and its activities abroad; Part II treats its career in the United States to the collapse of the movement in 1837.

A few words of definition and explanation may be useful. The term "Evangelical" is capitalized here to designate a clearly defined religious party exhibiting at times the potential of becoming a political party as well. Dictionary treatments of the word focus on the Evangelical conviction of man's depravity and his consequent need for salvation. The focus is entirely correct but not sufficiently discriminating to be helpful here. Three characteristics distinguished the Evangelicals from other Christians. In the first place they considered the emotional paroxysm of the revival to be crucial to redemption. They valued Christian nurture and discipline as leading to grace but not in themselves effective. Stemming from this attitude was an informality of worship, a disregard or disdain of rigid ritual and symbolism. The Evangelical's relations with God were immediate, warm, and intimate. Finally, Evangelical conversion carried with it the personal commitment to proselyte.

Another expression, "united front," was not known during the time of this movement, but today it would describe such a situation. Since it is the duty of an historian to interpret the past in terms meaningful to his own generation, he may plead the necessity of such liberties. This practice applies also to "ideological warfare."

A word as to italics in the numerous quotations reproduced here: they are, without exception, those of the sources. It was an age of italics.

ACKNOWLEDGMENTS

IN THE PREPARATION of this work over an extended period of years I have received competent assistance from many institutions and individuals. Any expression of appreciation here is inadequate but nonetheless genuine.

A grant-in-aid from the Social Science Research Council assisted research. I am indebted to The Faculty Research and Professional Development Fund of North Carolina State College for generous aid in the publication of this book and to the Ford Foundation for a grant under its program for assisting American university presses in the publication of works in the humanities and the social sciences.

The staffs of a number of libraries were co-operative beyond the call of duty: the public libraries of Boston, New York City, and Philadelphia; the Library of Congress; the college libraries of Harvard, Princeton, and North Carolina State College. Specialty libraries were particularly cordial, always ready to tax their resources in my behalf: the Andover and Princeton Theological Seminaries, the American Antiquarian Society, New York Historical Society, Church Historical Society, Presbyterian Historical Society, American Bible Society, American Tract Society, and American Sunday-School Union.

Several individuals have been of particular assistance. My

regard for Professor Arthur M. Schlesinger I have indicated else-where. Good friend, wise counselor, high priest at the altar of history, I trust he will accept this tribute from one of his less promising students. He introduced me to the study of history as a professional discipline; his criticism and editorial correc-tions of the manuscript were invaluable, a purifying chastise-ment in that literary woodshed so familiar to all Schlesinger men.

On those counts the book is his and has been from the start; for the ideas and attitudes expressed here he has no responsi-bility whatever. That burden, not a light one in this case nor thoughtlessly assumed, is wholly mine.

For guidance in studying the British background I am much indebted to Professor David E. Owen, also of Harvard, always ready with a sympathetic ear and good suggestions.

A peculiar difficulty of this story is the generous canvas re-quired for its picture, a liberal freedom in time and space with the peculiar insights of several disciplines. To the degree that I have mastered this problem I owe much to Dr. George A. Gullette and my other colleagues of the Department of Social Studies in North Carolina State College.

To the department secretary, Mrs. Marjorie Randolph, I am particularly grateful, not only for her typing but for enthusiasm and interest in the book. To bring her a new chapter has been a happy event beyond the just deserts of any writer.

Finally, I wish to thank Vivian, my wife, for her companion-ship in this long task. At this point, language, or my command of it, is quite inadequate to praise her patience, careful reading, good criticism, and helpful pencil marks. Most of all I wish to tell her I remember clearly those days when encouragement required a high courage, which never failed.

North Carolina State College
Raleigh, N.C.
November, 1959

CONTENTS

THE RISE OF THE EVANGELICAL
UNITED FRONT

In all that is done or begun by the Americans towards right thinking or practice, we are met by a civilization already settled and
overpowering. The culture of the day, the thoughts and aims of
men, are English thoughts and aims. A nation . . . has, in the last
centuries, obtained the ascendent, and stamped the knowledge,
activity and power of mankind with its impress. Those who resist
it do not feel it or obey it less.

RALPH WALDO EMERSON
English Traits

I

COMMON PROBLEMS OF GREAT BRITAIN AND AMERICA

AT THE END of the eighteenth century the British faced problems they had to solve if they were to survive as a nation on terms which permitted continuity in working out their peculiar destiny and did not involve catastrophe in the form of political revolution, invasion, and defeat. England was in a state of flux, intellectually, socially, and politically, under the simultaneous impact of the scientific and industrial revolutions. Many of the old ideas, attitudes, and assumptions underlying British institutions were openly challenged at the deepest level. A new outlook on life permeated the British people, new notions of man's relationships to his environment, to his fellow man, to God.

In this new outlook the scientific revolution played a fundamental part. It had turned the universe into a vast machine operating under self-enforcing mechanical laws. Vanished was the small, tidy, medieval world of God's purpose. God, a master-mechanic, had created the universe, set it going under His natural laws, and was now technologically unemployed. Man could understand these natural laws and through them manipulate his environment for his own benefit; he was no longer bound to pious acceptance of circumstances but could manage his affairs on a rational basis—change his life, change his government, change his religion.

This was heady stuff. Christianity, the most conservative force in Western civilization, had tied itself to Aristotelian cosmology and seemed destined to share its fate. Christianity was not designed for an indifferent mechanical universe but for a highly personalized world operated continuously by an anthropomorphic God. The function of Christianity was to adjust relationships between man and God. Man was continually committing offenses against God for which atonement had to be made. The offenses were not merely arithmetical errors in figuring things out; they were terrible affronts to an insulted deity. They were "sins." An adequate supply of sin was absolutely necessary to the operation of the Christian religion. For this supply, Christian doctrine drew upon two sources: overt offenses again God's law and, to assure that no human should escape the need of salvation, "original sin," a corruption inherited by all mankind from that first offense in the Garden of Eden.

By creating a mechanical universe, the scientific revolution reduced overt violations of God's laws to the status of mathematical errors, a trend culminating in Jeremy Bentham, who made all morals a business of arithmetical computation. This concept left no room for sin. As a New York preacher exclaimed in some dismay, "A sinner is a monster unknown in the religion of nature."[1]

To the undermining of overt sin the *philosophes* of the Enlightenment, both French and British, fused a long and devastating attack upon the notion of original sin. They changed to suit their taste the character of that mythical being, the "natural" man. Pictured in Christian doctrine as hopelessly and helplessly corrupted by the transgression of his most remote ancestors, he emerged now as the "noble savage," a very clever fellow overflowing with generous sentiments. If civilized man seemed somewhat less admirable, that was be-

1. John H. Livingston, *Two Sermons Delivered before the New-York Missionary Society* (New York, 1799), 14-15.

cause he bore the oppression of "two settled slaveries,"[2] religion
and monarchy, which developed out of man's contact with the
natural elements:

> Hence rose his gods, that mystic monstrous lore
> Of blood-stained altars and of priestly power.
> Hence blind credulity on all dark things,
> False morals hence and hence the yoke of kings.[3]

An age of reason declared all irrational institutions enemies
of mankind, barriers to progress. The intricate web of interlocking relationships which derived from the sacred society of
the Middle Ages and was sanctioned by immemorial custom
seemed to be falling apart. The core of medieval unity was
the Christian faith which infused all of life and gave its sanction to work, to government, and to social order as expressions
of God's will. Christianity was rational as long as it had a world
of sinners to save. In a world without sin it became empty
ritual. Great Britain of the eighteenth century had made
considerable progress toward getting along without sin (or
perhaps without "a sense of sin"?) in spite of the Wesleyan revival. To many a shaken, conservative soul it seemed quite
possible that Great Britain might now try to get along without
its monarchy and aristocracy.

To the general disruption of settled ideas stemming from
the scientific revolution, the industrial revolution was adding
strong forces of social disturbance. With industrialization,
population increased rapidly; opportunities opened, with a
corresponding shifting from one class to another. Adding to
the instability was the emergence of several new, distinct groups
to confuse the traditional social order. There appeared an
entrepreneur middle class, especially active in cotton and steel,
to challenge the older merchant bourgeoisie. Skilled workers
provided a new social level from which many were elbowing
their way into the middle class. Below them, the ordinary
working people were gaining self-esteem, and they resented
being referred to as "the poor." They were now the "lower
orders" or "working classes." There was trouble near the top,

2. Joel Barlow, "The Columbiad," *The Panoplist*, X (1814), 69, l. 85.
3. *Ibid.*, lines 157-60.

too. Attorneys, excisemen, directors, government pensioners, usurers, stockjobbers, and country bankers were assuming the airs and demanding the perquisites of a new aristocracy.

Altogether, in the mind of the British conservative, everything was a horrid mess. Life was coming apart at the seams, and across the Channel stood that terrible Bonaparte. Traditional values were under attack, and they had to be saved. If monarchy and aristocracy were to survive, then the Christian religion which supplied the sanction for this social order must survive. But a new relationship between religion and government was necessary. With 25 per cent of the people dissenting, the old order of church and state was hopeless and had been for a long time. There must be better contact between the classes, with some cordial sense of common purpose. And there was the war to win. It was a new kind of war, not the familiar dynastic squabble nor even a fight for territory. With massive armies of conscripts, Napoleon was bent on world conquest, and he embodied, however falsely, the ideas disrupting the British nation. Order at home and victory abroad demanded that a rather brilliant ideological warfare go hand in hand with foreign diplomacy and military effort.

The situation facing the British was more pressing but not in the long run more serious than that which the Americans contemplated as they sought such comfort as they could find in chewing tobacco and drinking amazing quantities of rum. Basically, their problems were the same—ideological division and social disintegration. They differed in degree: the danger of conquest by a foreign foe was probably less, while the internal difficulties were greater.

In many ways the United States simply reflected the total picture of the Western world, as John Bernard noticed: "It is curious to observe how America has been the general battlefield of principles, an epitome in her progress of so much that is interesting in the history of man. . . ."[4] Certainly the battle between French radicalism and British conservatism was bitterly fought. In his mellower years John Adams said, "Jefferson

4. *Retrospections of America, 1797-1811*, Mrs. Bayle Bernard, ed. (New York, 1887), 9.

and Rush were for liberty and straight hair. I thought curled hair was as republican as straight."[5] But it was more serious than that. Especially during the years from 1797 through 1800, fear repeatedly swept the country, fear that one might wake some fine morning to find the young republic something else, subverted by secret agents of the French or captured by a Federalist army.

When the Federalists met political defeat in 1800, the issue of foreign domination seems, in a political sense, to have been settled. The ideologies of the British and French factions worked their way into the native pattern of antagonisms: town against country, rich against poor, East against West, the wise and the good against the disreputable. But as the political crisis receded, the social crisis became more intense. Americans turned to the serious work of subduing a continent. Morris Birkbeck remarked in 1817, "Old America seems to be breaking up and moving westward."[6] In 1790 the trans-Allegheny population was about 100,000; by 1820 it had jumped to 2,250,000.

A nation on the move can carry little baggage in the form of settled customs. The American family, in the European sense of a stable organization in which each member had an assured place, ceased to exist: "A Yankee will sell his father's house like old clothes or rags."[7] All he needed was a few supplies, his wife at his side, and his dream in his head. Any American of consequence carried the prospectus of his pet speculation in the lining of his hat. Everyone was in a hurry to make the most of opportunity: the national symbol became Uncle Sam, that gaunt, haggard figure, victim of the ten-minute dinner on pork and beans.

Even if we discount the zeal of professional howlers and viewers-with-alarm who saw their people romping over the mountains into the "Valley of the Shadow of Death," the west-

5. *The Selected Writings of John and John Quincy Adams,* Adrienne Koch and William Peden, eds. (New York, 1946), 165-66.
6. Quoted by F. J. Turner, *Rise of the New West, 1819-1829* (Albert Bushnell Hart, ed., *The American Nation: A History,* XIV [New York, 1906]), 79.
7. Michael Chevalier, *Society, Manners and Politics in the United States,* T. G. Bradford, tr. (Boston, 1839), 298.

ward movement certainly disrupted values dear to the conservative heart: family life, law and order, property values, social status, education, and religion. From the conservative point of view, there was unquestionably a retrograde movement in American culture. As individuals and families left the cultivated country to enter the wilderness, years passed before they managed even comfortable dwellings, and more years before they were again part of a settlement. By the time they were able to support schools, churches, and other institutions, they had learned to get along without them. At least it appeared so in 1818: "The manner in which population is spreading over this continent has no parallel in history. The first settlers of every other country have been barbarians, whose habits and institutions were suited to a wild and wandering life. As their members multiplied, they have gradually become civilized and refined. The progress has been from ignorance to knowledge, from rudeness of savage life to the refinements of polished society. But in the settlement of North America the case is reversed. The tendency is from civilization to barbarism."[8]

So loose and flowing did American social order become under the impact of the westward movement that foreign observers considered the country a "tabula rasa," a clean slate, on which anyone was free to draw the pattern of the future.[9] People in peculiar garments roamed about promoting outlandish utopias of all kinds, many of them communist. No idea was too wild to lack supporters.

Under all this confusion there was, as in Great Britain, a basic shifting of values. Christianity was at the lowest ebb it had ever reached in the United States. Government lost the character of a divinely sanctioned order to become a strictly secular contract. As John Adams described it in the preamble to the Massachusetts constitution in 1779: "The body politic is . . . a social compact, by which the whole people covenants with each citizen, and each citizen with the whole people, that

8. M. N., "Retrograde Movement of National Character," *The Panoplist*, XIV (1818), 212-13.

9. *Home Missionary*, XXI (1848), 106, quoted by C. B. Goodykoontz, *Home Missions on the American Frontier* (Caldwell, Idaho, 1939), 30.

all shall be governed by certain laws for the common good."[10]
The federal constitution adopted in 1787 failed to mention
God, and secularism showed clearly in the early Presidents.
Although a Christian nation has since thrown a cloak of piety
about George Washington, it is doubtful that he wore it much
in real life.   Only the loosest construction of the term could
make a Christian of John Adams, and Jefferson was an outright
deist.   As state after state disestablished its Episcopal or Congregational Church, government became a secular thing,
another "speculation" to be exploited for power and profit.
Public office was no longer a public trust for which one accounted occasionally to the people but always to God.   The
essential unity between religion and government, upon which
conservatives depended for the solid core of social equilibrium,
split asunder in a world without sin, a world in which Tom
Paine could picture Christianity as a "strange fable," absurd,
blasphemous, and rather funny, a fable which many good men
had believed only because they were educated to believe it.[11]
It was the "Age of Paine," as John Adams wrote in 1805: "I
know not whether any man in the world has had more influence on its inhabitants or affairs for the last thirty years than
Tom Paine.   There can be no severer satire on the age.   For
such a mongrel between pigs and puppy, begotten by a wild
boar on a bitch wolf, never before in any age of the world was
suffered by the poltroonery of mankind to run through such a
career of mischief.   Call it then the Age of Paine."[12]

To be sure, the conservative cause in America needed a
renewal of vital interest in Christianity.   The years 1797 and
1798 saw marked revivals in some parts of Canada, New England, and the middle states; wholesale conversion by convulsion
soon occurred at camp meetings on the frontier.   But these were
not the answer to the need, as the conservatives saw it, for solid
characters formed by Christian nurture, for conformity to an
approved body of ideas and attitudes enforced by social pres-

10. *Selected Writings,* xii.
11. *The Age of Reason: being an Investigation of True and of Fabulous
Theology* (2nd Am. ed.; New York, 1794), 17.
12. Letter to Benjamin Waterhouse, Quincy, Oct. 29, 1805, *Selected Writings,*
147-48.

sure, for a body politic pervaded by the Protestant Christian ethic in substance if not in form.

Thus in both Great Britain and the United States the essential problems confronting conservatives were fundamentally much the same, although the environments in which solutions were to be worked out differed. And there was the factor of time. The British felt more immediate pressure; they had to solve their problems in 1790-1815 to win the war. In America the situation was different. Of course there was an early political crisis, but the central government was not of great importance in the lives of citizens who confronted it only at the post office and, some of them, at the polls. The social crisis, critical to the life of the country and its future political development, reached most serious proportions in the years 1815 to 1835.

This time lag appears to have been a most fortunate thing, at least from the conservative viewpoint. The British with their far superior culture were forced to think things out, to formulate ideas, and to originate institutions to put their ideas to work. With communication in such relatively fine condition and the prevailing influence of the British such as it was, Americans needed only to follow British experiments closely, absorb the prevailing ideas, and copy British institutions with such adjustments as American conditions and prejudices might suggest. In a general way, this seems to have been what happened.

II

CONSERVATIVE TERRORS

THE FIRST PHASE of conservative reaction to the Enlightenment as embodied in the French republic and French military power was an era of strong emotion marked by waves of terror in the years 1791-1806.[1] The fears were, for the most part, unfounded. Probably not one in five hundred Englishmen was interested in changing the existing order.[2] In trembling before the threat of revolution, the British were no more justified than were Americans in believing that Thomas Jefferson had sold out to the French for cash. But it was not the reality of objective fact which shaped men's thoughts; rather, it was the fact as they interpreted it, the reality of their hopes and fears.

This highly emotional period was of importance not only because of its intensity and duration, but more for the character it gave to the conservatives' long-term reaction. It was then that they rationalized, evaluated the meaning of the attack, measured its true essence to their satisfaction, and began to accept the challenge. It was then that they identified Christianity as the crucial issue in ideological warfare and associated the winning

1. Philip Anthony Brown, *The French Revolution in English History* (London, 1918), 169.
2. Bernard N. Schilling, *Conservative England and the Case against Voltaire* (New York, 1950), 178 ff.

of the war and the preservation of social order and of government itself with the triumph of the faith.

Emotional seizures began with the opening of the French Revolution, which the English-speaking world greeted at first with enthusiasm and lively hope. French admiration for the British constitution warmed English bosoms, while Americans saw in beloved France a confirmation and vindication of their own revolution, an acknowledgment of American political leadership.

In the United States, enthusiasm ran without serious check for several years, a period known as the "French Frenzy" and associated with the American tour of Genêt. As William Cobbett remarked, "The Carolinians had cut the strings of their culottes, and the Citizen pulled them down about their heels."[3] A network of secret societies known as "democratic clubs" flourished throughout the country, and antislavery societies blossomed in the Southern states. The names of streets changed: Royal Exchange Alley in Boston became Equality Lane; New York's Queen St., Pearl St.; King St., Liberty St. The colleges went French with fury; at the University of Pennsylvania Dr. Rogers altered the famous rallying cry of Shakespeare's Henry V to read:

> Follow your spirit, and, upon this charge,
> Cry—God for Freedom! France! and Robespierre![4]

All this feeling began to cool when the French beheaded their king in January, 1793. Americans had looked upon Louis XVI with considerable affection and gratitude for his help in their war of independence, a feeling warmly expressed at the war's victorious close: "Nor let our great and generous ally, who afforded an early and vigorous aid, be forgot—but let every American lip pronounce a 'Vive le Roi,' and every heart conspire, 'long may his most Christian Majesty, Lewis the Sixteenth,' long may he live, a blessing, and blessed on earth; and late resign an earthly crown, to shine in brighter glory. . . ."[5]

3. (Peter Porcupine, *pseud.*), *History of the American Jacobins* (Edinburgh, 1797), 9.
4. *Ibid.*, 40-41.
5. George Duffield, *Sermon preached in the Third Presbyterian Church,*

Whatever might be Louis' heavenly reward, the French sent him off to it with a violence profoundly shocking to Americans. As the Revolution entered its phase of terror, the French Frenzy came to a close in the United States. The democratic clubs lost popularity as President Washington added his official condemnation to popular revulsion against the French. By 1796 the tide had turned sufficiently to enable the Federalists, representing the British point of view, to squeeze John Adams into the presidential chair.

As the American conservative mind emerged shakily from this ordeal, it retained a residue of uneasiness. It had seen America's capacity to go the limit in pursuit of a social fad. It had seen the loosening of traditional ideas; the colleges remained hotbeds of revolt. It had feared the tricks and plots of twenty-four secret political societies, well organized and well distributed from Maine to South Carolina and to Kentucky in the West.[6] To be sure, the societies were disbanded, but there remained the notion of a secret, subversive, underground movement subject to the orders of a foreign power, ready to strike with deadly effect at a critical moment.

The fears of conservative Americans found confirmation and reinforcement as they followed avidly the course of affairs in England, where the early enthusiasm and hope for France speedily gave way to conservative riots and repression of every liberal thought. Under the impact of the "Burke Terror" the British plunged into a wave of violent reaction quite as undignified and unworthy of a civilized nation as anything which happened during the same period in America.

Since the spokesman and prime agitator of this terror was Edmund Burke,[7] it is profitable to give some attention to his *Reflections on the Revolution in France and on the Proceedings in Certain Societies in London Relative to that Event*, first published in 1790. This pronouncement not only furnished the

---

Philadelphia, Thursday, Dec. 11, 1783, day appointed by Congress as day of Thanksgiving for the restoration of peace (Philadelphia, 1784), 20.

6. Vernon Stauffer, "New England and the Bavarian Illuminati," *Columbia University Studies in History, Economics, and Public Law*, LXXXII (1918), 105, 107.

7. Schilling, *Conservative England*, 178 ff.

rationalization for the first phase of reaction but provided the ideas fundamental to conservative ideological warfare throughout the whole period, ideas which subsequent leaders developed, clarified, sentimentalized, but left essentially unchanged.

Burke's main concepts were simple enough; the power of his words lay in the fact that he was able to state clearly the British status quo and defend it resolutely. He would tolerate no adjustments of any kind: "We are resolved to keep an established church, an established monarchy, an established aristocracy and an established democracy, each in the degree it exists, and in no greater."[8] These, in Burke's mind, were part of a divine order; God was the "institutor, and author and protector of civil society."[9] Indeed, "We know, and what is better we feel inwardly, that religion is the basis of civil society, and the source of all good and all comfort."[10] And again, "He who gave our nature to be perfected by our virtue, willed also the necessary means of perfection—He willed therefore the state— He willed its connexion with the source and original archetype of all perfection."[11]

Possibly rationalizing notions derived from the medieval "Chain of Being" interpretation of biology, Burke presented inequality as an order of nature, a divine order, a necessary order. Inequality was the characteristic essence of property. As property was by nature sluggish and timid, the state must protect it from aggressions of ability. The greater the mass of property, the more especial must be its protection in order to safeguard lesser property by example.[12]

Along with the essential inequality of property went the equally divine and necessary inequality of social rank. There must be a wealthy and idle aristocracy to do the thinking for the busy and ignorant poor. It is leisure which produces wisdom, an idea Burke could readily bolster from scripture: "The wisdom of a learned man cometh by opportunity of

8. *Reflections on the Revolution in France* . . . (9th ed.; London, 1791), 135-36.

9. *Ibid.*, 146.   10. *Ibid.*, 134.

11. *Ibid.*, 146.   12. *Ibid.*, 75.

leisure: and he that hath little business shall become wise.
—How can he get wisdom that holdeth the plough, and that
glorieth in the goad; that driveth oxen; and is occupied in
their labors; and whose talk is of bullocks?"[13] Of course such
words, abhorrent to Protestant morality, would have to come
from a Catholic Bible; but they carried the ring of familiar
authority, and Burke could expand the idea in his own prose:
"The occupation of an hair-dresser, or of a working tallow-
chandler, cannot be a matter of honor to any person. . . . Such
descriptions of men ought not to suffer oppression from the
state: but that state suffers oppression, if such as they, either
individually or collectively, are permitted to rule. In this you
think you are combatting prejudice, but you are at war with
nature."[14] Here Burke is restating the relationship between
religion and government in terms suited to his argument and
the times in which he lived. The state served God's purposes
not in the old order of divine consecration of theoretically
absolute rulers but through the new order of the law of nature.
Nature was mechanical, to be sure, but God was the great
designer of a universe still essentially teleological.

Burke gave to religion not only the duty of explaining the
necessity of things as they are but the task, too, of serving as a
lubricant, oil in the social gears. He described with obvious
relish the opportunity that France had lost, the chance to
have "a protected, satisfied, laborious, and obedient people,
taught to seek and to recognize the happiness that is to be
found by virtue in all conditions, in which consists the true
moral equality of mankind."[15] He was referring to that mythical but highly necessary and peculiarly blissful class, the "contented poor." Happy in their superior chances of heaven, they
could meet any crisis by opening their worn and tattered Bibles.
But the rich, whom Burke called "the great," could use the
consolations of religion, too. They needed something to soothe
brows furrowed with gnawing anxieties, to fill the "gloomy

13. Ecclesiasticus 38:24-25, as quoted in *Reflections,* 73.
14. *Reflections,* 72-73.
15. *Ibid.,* 53.

void" of minds which had nothing to hope or fear, to ease the "killing languor" of those who had nothing to do.[16]

Certainly, as Burke warmed to his subject he described not so much the status quo as a conservative utopia, the England of his dreams, an England in which emotion attained a validity far surpassing reason. It was for this utopia that "we have consecrated the state, that no man should approach to look into its defects or corruptions but with due caution; that he should never dream of beginning its reformation by its subversion; that he should approach to the faults of the state as to the wounds of a father, with pious awe and trembling solicitude."[17]

All this opinion was indeed moving, and it voiced in rolling prose the conservative feeling of the time, an emotion composed of fear and pride—fear of the "lower orders" and pride in the wisdom and institutions of ancestors who had made England the envy of the world for her wealth and security.[18] But it was hardly something to start a riot. The disorders for which Burke is held as accountable as anyone else stemmed from that part of his discussion which was the occasion for all of it. He put his finger on two supposedly subversive British organizations, the Constitutional Society and the Revolution Society. The latter had sent an address to the French National Assembly; Burke claimed that it was under the direction of that body and that it acted as a committee in England to extend its principles. He also suspected that it had been infiltrated by new members who had altered its character and that it had intimate relations to British politicians.[19] As proof of subversion, Burke pointed to Revolution Society sponsorship of a "new and hitherto unheard-of bill of rights." These were the rights of the British people "1. 'To choose our own governors.' 2. 'To cashier them for misconduct.' 3. 'To frame a government for ourselves.' "[20]

Both of these societies were, to be sure, revolutionary ones, and everything Burke said about them was true except a mere

16. *Ibid.*, 152.
17. *Ibid.*, 143.
18. Brown, *French Revolution*, 166.
19. *Reflections*, 4, 5.
20. *Ibid.*, 20.

trifle, that one of them was under the direction of a foreign power. These societies were dedicated to commemorating and preserving the principles of England's Glorious Revolution of 1688. This fact Burke acknowledged, although he labeled it all a mistake. To an overheated public, the idea that it was a different revolution probably would not occur.

The passion Burke aroused presently had more to feed on. Tom Paine wrote a prompt reply to Burke, his famous *Rights of Man*. Part I appeared in a few months; the British bought 50,000 copies while Paine was completing Part II. In all, about 200,000 copies sold in England during the period. Joel Barlow did nothing to quiet things when he published his *Advice to the Privileged Orders in the Several States of Europe Resulting from the Necessity and Propriety of a General Revolution in the Principle of Government*. It contained such gems of moderation as this: "Mr. Burke, in a frenzy of passion, has drawn the veil; and aristocracy, like a decayed prostitute, whom painting and patching will no longer embellish, throws off her covering, to get a livelihood by displaying her ugliness."[21]

Conservative reaction was vigorous and violent. A scurrilous attack on Paine promptly appeared as *The Life of Thomas Paine, Author of the Rights of Man,* under the nom de plume of Francis Oldys. Evidently it was written by George Chalmers, a Tory refugee from Maryland reputedly hired by friends of Burke.[22] Paine became the symbol of everything the essentially conservative Englishman hated and feared: riots flared, especially in Birmingham; *Rights of Man* was burned in bonfires; Paine suffered in straw effigy as he burned at the stake on village greens and at crossroads. Medals and beer mugs ridiculed him and everything he stood for; people had his initials, T. P., lined in nails on their heels so they could stamp him symbolically into the ground with every step.[23] The hunt for subversives was on. It was time for anyone engaging in un-British activity to scamper for cover.

21. (London, 1795), Part II, 14.
22. William E. Woodward, *Tom Paine, America's Godfather* (New York, 1945), 209.
23. *Ibid.,* 217, 218.

The emotions sweeping through England in the early 1790's were quite as intense as those in America and they prepared the ground for the terror of 1797 which raged through Europe, Great Britain, and the United States. Ideas implanted in the conservative mind in the early 1790's became absolutely fixed by the end of that decade.

One of these ideas was that religion, government, and social order as the British knew it were all interdependent, all under attack. Of these, the Christian religion, the basis of civil society, was the focal point of attack; it had to be saved if anything was to be saved. Necessary corollaries were the ideas that all good conduct had to be Christian if it was to be truly good and that conduct motivated by any other principle was suspect; rationalism, skepticism, liberalism, loose morals, and licentious living were all the same thing, all Frenchy stuff inimical to the state. Emotion had been gaining ascendancy in British minds for many years;[24] now it began to attain a validity surpassing reason. As Burke said, "We know, and what is better we feel inwardly. . . ."[25]

The nature of the attack under which Western civilization trembled was another concept firmly imbedded in the conservative mind. Military action was only part of this war; a real danger lay in the penetration of hostile principles and a secret fifth column of subversion. The enemy's motto was "strike but conceal the hand." Such British inclination to look under the bed laid a good foundation for the panic of the Illuminati conspiracy. Indeed, England was psychologically well prepared to receive it and believe its story. There have been bad years in British history but 1797 was one of the worst, perhaps more difficult than 1940. The war was going badly. Negotiations with the French toward peace had failed completely by the end of 1796; Prussia was doing nothing; Austria was folding up and capitulated in April; Spain had declared war. England faced the prospect of sustaining alone a contest against the combined might of France, Spain, and Holland. There was a French fleet

24. Cf. Hoxie Neale Fairchild, *Religious Trends in English Poetry* (New York, 1939-42), I, 538 ff.
25. Above, note 10.

bound for Ireland, where open rebellion awaited it. In February a report flashed across the country that the French had landed in Wales. There were hunger riots.

If the British had confidence in anything, they relied on the British navy and the Bank of England. In February, specie in the Bank hit the lowest point in many years, only £1,272,000 left. The British had spent about 25 per cent more in subsidies on the Continent than for their own army and navy combined—and all for nothing. In May, mutiny broke out in the navy at the Nore and at Spithead.

Such an England then heard the story of the conspiracy of the Bavarian Illuminati, an organization which performed the astonishing feat of doing its most effective work ten years after it was dead. Two versions of the conspiracy appeared almost simultaneously in 1797. John Robison, an English scholar and Freemason, published in Edinburgh his *Proofs of a Conspiracy against All the Religions and Governments of Europe carried on in the Secret Meetings of the Free Masons, Illuminati, and Reading Societies;* and the first of a four-volume edition of Abbé Barruel's *Memoirs pour servir a l'histoire du Jacobisme* came out in London.

Of these the Abbé Barruel's work was the more important, because he was already an international figure. His *History* with its juicy content of French atrocities had appeared in London in 1793 and had run through four English editions by 1801. Aside from numerous editions in French, of which only one was printed in France, fifteen other editions of the *History* were published in Spain, Portugal, Italy, and the United States.[26] So throughout Western civilization there was a large audience ready to read another of the Abbé's stories, to believe that the cause of all of its troubles was a huge international plot of secret societies conspiring constantly to reduce and destroy organized government and religion. The fact that two revelations of the conspiracy appeared simultaneously, independently, and in essential agreement was convincing proof.

The conspiracy theory of the French Revolution had a long, although not very useful, life; it received scholarly support as

26. Schilling, *Conservative England*, 262, 263.

late as 1906.[27] Its appealingly simple explanation of a highly
complex era had, of course, some foundation in fact. The story
seems to have arisen from a struggle of secret societies in
Bavaria, the German states along the Rhine, Austria, and
Switzerland. The Order of the Illuminati, devoted to promoting the principles of the Enlightenment, arose in 1776
under the leadership of Adam Weishaupt, a professor of canon
law at the University of Ingolstadt. The order expanded by
capturing Masonic lodges, with strong assistance from a Masonic
leader, Baron Adolf Franz Friederich Knigge. In taking over
the Masons, the Illuminati ran into stiff competition from the
Rosicrucians, who had been strengthened by infiltration of
Jesuits after the Society of Jesus was repressed in 1773.

The Bavarian government outlawed the Order of the Illuminati in 1787. There is no evidence that it was active in
any guise after that year, but its ghost refused to be laid and
continued to haunt Europe. Several circumstances were responsible. The Jesuits, evidently thriving on reaction against
the Illuminati, were convinced that the Order had simply gone
underground and that it was still working through Freemasonry. They could readily believe this, since they had
done the same sort of thing themselves. They persuaded King
Frederick William II of Prussia that this underground was the
state of affairs, and they probably influenced the Bavarian
government, which continued to take action against the Illuminati, thus convincing itself and everybody else that the
Order was still alive. Contributing to this impression was the
fact that a new secret society, the German Union, obtained a
list of former Illuminati members and was trying to make
some money by selling them books. The result was a continuing deluge of printed attacks on the Illuminati in Europe
on the assumption that the Order was still active.[28]

So John Robison and the Abbé Barruel simply extended
and embellished a scare already well established among simple-
minded Protestants in Europe. In their version, Voltaire was,
of course, primarily responsible for all of the trouble which

27. Stauffer, "New England and the Illuminati," 199n.
28. *Ibid.*, 189-95.

afflicted conservative Europe. This devil let loose from the pit had planned the *Encyclopédie,* with the assistance of D'Alambert, Diderot and others, as "the grand arsenal of impiety."[29] The *philosophes* had gained control of the French academy, the attackers believed, in order to admit only infidels and to make the organization the central operation of a vast plot to destroy all the nations of Western civilization so that Christ and His religion should no longer be remembered on the face of the earth. In pursuit of this hellish objective, Voltaire first persuaded Frederick to encourage Berlin booksellers to print impious books. By 1770 Voltaire, it was alleged, had formed a network of influence in high places all over Europe. In Prussia he had enlisted Frederick the Great and throughout Germany a host of lesser nobility. In Russia he had Count Schouvallow and even Empress Catherine. He had seduced Joseph II of Austria, Prince Gallitzen at The Hague, the King of Denmark, the King of Poland, the Queen of Sweden, and her son, Gustavus III.[30]

It remained for Mirabeau, so went the story, to build on Voltaire's foundation and to crown his villainous work. He encountered the Illuminati in Berlin when he was there in 1786-87 and brought two members back to Paris with him. In France the Illuminati continued their policy of capturing Masonic lodges; they presently swung all French Freemasonry to their principles. They, in turn, worked through political clubs to inspire Jacobism.[31] The final congregation of this triple conspiracy of Illuminati, Masons, and Jacobins took place in Mirabeau's Jacobin Club in Paris. Readers were assured that numerous branches were at work in Europe, several in the United States.

The essential burden of these stories was that the whole revolutionary convulsion arose out of a preliminary war on the Christian faith and that it was not merely Catholicism under attack but Christianity as a whole, all sects, all organized expressions of Christian belief. Orderly government and religion

29. Abbé Augustin Barruel's *Memoirs pour servir a l'histoire du Jacobisme,* quoted by Schilling, *Conservative England,* 250.
30. Schilling, *Conservative England,* 254, 255.
31. Stauffer, "New England and the Illuminati," 195.

appeared to be utterly dependent on each other, and either could be vitally attacked through the other.

England received the story with avidity; believers were much more numerous and influential than doubters. There were plenty of opportunities to know about it. The *Memoirs* of Barruel speedily ran through three editions, one French and two English, as well as two abridgements. The plot against Christianity received special emphasis in digests with long quotes in the *Gentleman's Magazine* and the *British Critic.*

Of course this was meat for the clergy, who spread the panic in their warnings from the pulpit. Bishops hammered at the dread conspiracy in their *Charges;* preachers in their sermons trembled before the enemy who struck but concealed the hand. Not content with vocal warnings, they burst into print. The year 1799 saw three such publications: the Rev. Lewis Hughes's *Historical View of the Rise, Progress, and Tendency of the Principles of Jacobism;* the Rev. Francis Wollaston's *A Country Parson's Address to his Flock;* and the Rev. Henry Kett's *History the Interpreter of Prophecy.* The *Universal Magazine* supported the cause with an anonymous article, "Jacobism Displayed."[32]

Naturally the panic had marked effects on the British attitude toward the war. Piled on top of Edmund Burke's *Reflections* and the ensuing conservative riots, the panic had a serious, long-range impact on the British Christian's notion of the relationship between his church and his government and between himself and Christians of other sects. The government was no longer related distinctively and exclusively to a certain denomination; its welfare was indissolubly linked to the survival of the faith. All religion was patriotic, whether it issued from chapel or church. Jabez Bunting could shout with the rest of them, "Methodism hates democracy as it hates sin."[33]

And, reciprocally, government was religious, not in the old order of divine right and ordination but in a new sense. Government was an instrument of God's will in an essentially teleological universe, and since divine guidance was necessary

32. Schilling, *Conservative England,* 262-70.
33. Maldwin Edwards, *After Wesley* (London, 1935), 156.

to good government, officials should be good Christians of some socially acceptable denomination. The secularism of the Enlightenment failed at this point to penetrate British culture and was rejected in favor of a new version of the ancient medieval unity.

Another aspect of unity was the changing attitude of British Christians toward each other. In the face of a dangerous foe, denominational tensions eased. There was a loyalty transcending sectarian differences and calling for all Christians to march shoulder to shoulder in a common cause. The loyalty laid the foundation for a new British institution, nonsectarian Christianity.

All of these impulses the United States would accept, adopt, and adapt in its own way, in its own good time. Some ideas and techniques took fifteen or twenty years to cross the Atlantic; some traveled faster. As a rule they found acceptance in America when conditions there had developed to a point when British experience and leadership were obviously useful.

Of all ideas, panic traveled the fastest. The English translation of Barruel's *Memoirs* published in London in 1798 was reprinted the next year in Hartford, Conn., New York city, and Elizabeth, N.J. By then the terror of the Illuminati was rather old stuff in the United States, generally accepted even by heads which should have been steady: Oliver Wolcott, Timothy Pickering, John Adams, George Washington.[34] As in England, the terror struck at a time when the country was psychologically keyed to receive it. An inexperienced government was trying to lead a people torn by belligerent factionalism in a highly complicated international situation. A succession of events in the spring of 1798 made the arrival of the Illuminati panic a highly effective climax. In March, President Adams received dispatches from Marshall, Pinckney, and Gerry in what is known to history as the XYZ affair. It seemed that what Americans considered to be simple justice was to be obtained from the French only as a cash transaction. John Adams sent a spirited address to Congress and on March 23 issued a

34. Stauffer, "New England and the Illuminati," 11.

proclamation setting aside Wednesday, May 9, as a national
fast to "be observed throughout the United States as a day of
solemn humiliation, fasting, and prayer; that the citizens of
these States, abstaining on that day from their customary
worldly occupations, offer their devout addresses to the Father
of Mercies."[35]

Popular emotion reached a new pitch with the publication
of the XYZ dispatches in April; when the day of the national
fast arrived, the Illuminati terror had arrived, too. A few days
before the ninth of May, someone flung into President Adams's
house three anonymous letters telling of a plot to burn Philadelphia to the ground on the day of the fast. As Adams made
known the contents of the letters, many of the city's more
respectable citizens hurriedly packed their valuables in preparation for quick departure.[36] However, the nonexistent conspiracy created no disorder; the national fast was well observed,
and the clergy played a leading part. The editor of Philadelphia's *Columbian Centinel* complimented them on their
zeal: "Within the sphere of our information we can say, that
on no occasion were there ever exhibited more moral patriotism, and more ardent devotion."[37] In New York and Philadelphia the preachers apologized for bringing politics into the
pulpit, but that was unnecessary in New England, where
Jedediah Morse hammered away at the Illuminati in the New
North Church at Boston in the morning and repeated his performance at Charlestown in the afternoon. The Illuminati had
precipitated the "awful events" upon the distracted world and
were now working secretly among the American people.[38]
The story presently was echoed by the Rev. David Tappan at
Harvard and Timothy Dwight at Yale. In New York the Rev.
William Lynn of the Reformed Dutch Church took his text
from Joshua: "There is an accursed thing in the midst of thee,

35. Proclamation, in *A Compilation of the Messages and Papers of the
Presidents 1789-1902*, James D. Richardson, comp. (Washington, D.C., 1907),
I, 269.
36. Stauffer, "New England and the Illuminati," 138.
37. May 12, 1798, quoted by Stauffer, "New England and the Illuminati," 239.
38. Stauffer, "New England and the Illuminati," 10, 11.

O Israel: thou canst not stand before thine enemies, until ye take away the accursed thing from among you."[39]

Conspiracy was by no means the sole theme of orations on the day of the national fast. The relationship between government and religion received even more attention. In apologizing for bringing politics into his sermon, the Rev. Lynn admitted that to espouse a particular party in the pulpit was wrong. "But if they [possible critics] mean, that the love of country, the duty of citizens, and obedience to lawful government, have no connection with religion, and that a Preacher ought not to inculcate these, *I have not so learned Christ.* Religion, morality, and obedience to government are inseparably connected."[40] This idea found more forceful expression in a note of warning as his oration reached a spirited climax: "No army need invade, if licentious principles abound. These will do the fatal business, and blast, by an untimely death, the American Republic, the last and noblest work of God."[41] The concept of government as a divine institution found expression also in the Presbyterian Church at Alexandria, where James Muir proclaimed, "A good government is the center of union. . . . This is the bulwark which Providence has set around our property and lives. . . ."[42]

On every hand rose the call to forget party differences, to unite in the face of the foe. It was the principal theme of the Rabbi Seixas in the synagogue at New York.[43] Out in Washington, Pa., where there was no church or minister to lead observance of the national fast, a layman, Alexander Addison, took the stand to plead, "As they [the French] rest their hopes of injuring us on the belief that there is a party among us devoted to their will; let us shew them there is no such party."[44] The same theme brought Lynn's stirring appeal to

39. Joshua 7:13, quoted in *A Discourse on National Sins delivered May 9, 1798* (New York, 1798), 1.

40. *Ibid.,* 14. 41. *Ibid.,* 28.

42. *A Sermon preached in the Presbyterian Church at Alexandria, May 9, 1798* (Philadelphia, 1798), 7.

43. G. Seixas, *A Discourse delivered in the Synagogue in New York, May 9, 1798* (New York, 1798).

44. *An Oration on the Rise and Progress of the United States of America to the Present Crisis* (Philadelphia, 1798), 41.

its close: "Unnatural children are we, if, when the country which holds all that is dear to us is threatened, we do not breathe one spirit, and exert one strength; if we do not renounce all partialities to this or to the other nation, be they who they will; and if we do not banish all party dissensions for the name AMERICAN."[45]

It seems clear that the crisis, compounded with the experience of the past several years, brought to conservative minds in the United States approximately the same idea of the relationship between religion and government as that which prevailed in England. Americans would disestablish churches in several states during the next twenty-five years, but the secularism of the Enlightenment stopped there. The ideas of government and religion as utterly interdependent, of government as a divine institution, of religion as the foundation of good government and social order, were not to be disestablished.

A foundation was laid, too, for the institution of nonsectarian Christianity in the United States. In the light of the crisis, all Christians could consider themselves fellows in a common cause without regard to denominations. Government itself appeared to be a nonsectarian religious enterprise: John Adams had called for the religious support of the entire nation in terms to which even the Jews could respond. Catholics, too, hated as they were by many Americans, were fellow-sufferers and fellow-soldiers in the general battle to save Christianity. As the Rev. David Osgood announced at Medford, Mass., the French republicans were not bringing the millennium by "stripping the whore of Babylon, pulling down the man of sin, destroying popery."[46] They were devils let loose from the pit of hell to seduce other nations and destroy them so that Christ and his religion should no longer be remembered.

The general enthusiasm for unity had its hour: Philadelphia marched to "Hail Columbia," and the national fast proved so successful that the administration used it again the next year. But the panic had its baleful effects, too. In the summer of

---

45. *Discourse*, 37.
46. Sermon delivered May 9, 1798, quoted by Stauffer, "New England and the Illuminati," 98-99.

1798 John Adams, convinced that American cities swarmed with French spies,[47] signed the Alien and Sedition Acts, later characterized by his son as "two engines which the Federalists borrowed from the British government and put into the hands of their adversaries to be used with extraordinary power and efficiency against themselves and against the administration."[48]

But as the United States plunged into another era of factional strife and as Federalism disappeared as a national force, there remained in conservative thought ideas to serve admirably as a basis for borrowing further from the British, borrowing to better advantage than the Federalists did when they copied the Treasonable Practices and Seditious Meetings Bills of 1795 for their Alien and Sedition Acts.

47. *The Selected Writings of John and John Quincy Adams,* Adrienne Koch and William Peden, eds. (New York, 1946), xxiv.
48. *Ibid.,* 329.

III

THE BRITISH PATTERN OF CONSERVATIVE ACTION

WHILE REPRESSION in America brought a political explosion, in Great Britain it was doing very well indeed. There were, of course, several reasons for the different effects of similar measures in the two countries. The political climate was not the same; divergence of American ideology had already caused the Revolution. An agrarian country would not respond in the same way to a stimulus as one being rapidly industrialized, and the social structures were by no means identical. But a far more important factor in success with repression was British superior skill in social organization, called into action in the early phase of the Burke Terror, when Justice John Reeves organized in 1792 the Association for Preserving Liberty and Property against Republicans and Levelers. Within a year the Society had two thousand branches and was fully equipped with spies to hunt out subversives as well as propaganda to counteract liberal ideas.[1]

But Reeves had not had to think up anything new. In 1787 William Wilberforce had already organized his Proclamation Society, which later became the Society for the Suppression of Vice. Some spoilsports hinted that it was the pleasures of

---

1. Maurice J. Quinlan, *Victorian Prelude* (*Columbia University Studies in English and Comparative Literature*, No. 155 [New York, 1941]), 71 ff.

the poor that were to be suppressed, not the vices of the rich. The occasion for Wilberforce's organization was George III's *Royal Proclamation against Vice and Immorality*, issued June 1, 1787. The Prince of Wales was playing around with Mrs. Fitzherbert, and His Majesty felt the impulse to go on record against sin. However, Wilberforce's inspiration came from his earnest reading of Josiah Woodward's *History of the Society for the Reformation of Manners in the Year 1692.*[2]

It is interesting to examine the Society for the Reformation of Manners, for it set a clear pattern for the activities of the Wilberforce and Reeves organizations in their efforts to hunt down subversives, suppress hunger riots and peace demonstrations, block efforts of workers to combine, and keep the poor in sullen silence. The Society for the Reformation of Manners rose in 1692 in answer to the English desire to turn over a new leaf after the Glorious Revolution, clean up Restoration morals, and present to the new dynasty the scrubbed countenance of decency. The Society formed a voluntary police and spy system. The duties of its members were to expose and procure the closing of bawdyhouses, obtain the arrest of all blasphemers, drunkards, and vagabonds, smash shops found open on Sunday, and see that all violators of the Sabbath were put in jail.[3] Parliament made the work more interesting by paying informers. Membership with its arduous duties proved so popular that the Society, centered in London, soon had branches all over England and Ireland. Of course the movement reached America. According to Lyman Beecher, one of these moral societies appeared in Maryland about 1760; others were formed in various places as civil magistrates needed assistance.[4]

Evidently the work of the righteous in the Society required divine reassurance, for it led to a revival of interest in religion. This revival took the same form of social organization as the

2. R. Coupland, *Wilberforce* (Oxford, 1923), 54.
3. Maximin Piette, *John Wesley in the Evolution of Protestantism*, J. B. Howard, tr. (London, 1938), 189 ff.
4. *A Reformation of morals practicable and indispensable* (2nd ed.; Andover, Mass., 1814), 13. Records of American moral societies are difficult to find, as they did not publish.

Society for the Reformation of Manners, with the organization
of the Society for the Promotion of Christian Knowledge
(SPCK) in 1698, followed by the Society for the Propagation of
the Gospel in Foreign Parts (SPGFP) in 1701. There was considerable interlocking of membership and an appropriate division of functions: the Society for the Reformation of Manners attended to legal prosecutions; the SPGFP, stimulated by
the work of John Eliot in Massachusetts, carried the faith to
the heathen; the SPCK attended to domestic propaganda with
such tracts as *A Caution against Drunkenness, a Persuation to
Serious Observation of the Lord's Day, A Kind Caution to
Profane Swearers.*[5]

Although there were a few non-Anglicans among these
storm troopers of Christian decency, all three groups came under the firm hand of the Church. Their rules for meetings
forbade any discussion of theological or political concerns in
church or state and confined their reading to such parts of the
Book of Common Prayer as were not reserved to the clergy.
Members were to pray seven times daily, think holy thoughts,
and examine their consciences each evening.[6] Up to about
1714, these societies with their numerous branches interested
many young men and were vigorously active. They did not
confine their efforts to repression and reformation but founded
charity schools for the teaching of religion, provided for poverty-
stricken clergy with Queen Anne's Bounty, repaired old
churches, and built St. Paul's and twelve other new churches
in London and its suburbs.

By 1735 the Society for the Reformation of Manners had
started to collapse, after compiling a record of 99,380 arrests in
London and Westminster alone,[7] and among its good works
sent many vagabonds to the colonies. The SPGFP and the SPCK
lingered on without vitality. In the career of the movement
was a certain pattern of British conservative action. The elements of the pattern were repression with the use of spies and

5. Quinlan, *Victorian Prelude*, 17, 18.
6. Piette, *Wesley*, 188.
7. Fortieth annual report of the Society for the Reformation of Manners,
cited by Piette, *Wesley*, 189.

some physical violence, a revival of interest in religion, foreign missions, domestic religious propaganda, and benevolence toward the poor, not in the form of the physical comfort of beef and blankets but rather the eternal comfort of religious education. The same pattern emerged again one hundred years later. In meeting the emergency of 1787-1815, the British took out of moth balls social machinery which had proved effective in the years 1692-1714. Conditions were different and there were new elements to add to the old pattern, but from the perspective of time the parallel is too striking to be overlooked.

In the early 1790's the first, purely repressive phase of the pattern developed only negative characteristics. Burke was its spokesman and leader. His attitude was one of petrified terror: he did not want to move in any direction; he simply wished to freeze the status quo. Under his sponsorship Justice John Reeves played a part made famous later in the United States by Senator Joseph McCarthy. The role of J. Edgar Hoover today fell then to Henry Dundas of the Home Office. As usual when subversives are in great demand but in scant supply, the definition of subversion proved extremely elastic. Booksellers went to jail for handling proscribed literature; spies worked their way into meetings of the Constitutional Society and the London Correspondence Society and its branches; subsequent arrests suppressed these organizations. After the Combination Act of 1799 reinforced the Seditious Meetings Bill of 1795, any gathering of workingmen was subversive.

The propaganda issued by the Association for Preserving Liberty and Property against Republicans and Levelers showed the same negative characteristics. John Bowles, barrister and pamphleteer, was in charge of this phase of the work. His product was rather grim, calculated to frighten rather than to inspire, quite in tune with other aspects of the society's work. He printed and distributed extracts from Blackstone on treason and definitions of libel from Coke, Blackstone, and other authorities. Similar unhappy thoughts appeared under other titles: *Plots found out, Cautions against Reformers, Words in Season, Hints on Levelling, Antidotes against French Politics.*

The work of this society was not without effect. A survey of British propaganda in 1802[8] described the British press, especially the booksellers, as extremely patriotic. More than one hundred placards were up, and a generous supply of tracts and pamphlets poured forth in prose and verse. All of this output was calculated to depict the repulsive character of the enemy. It was rather rough stuff, full of the most bitter execration, coarse invective, and profanity. It directed its vituperation against the French as a nation, with no distinction between a misled people and the leader who had betrayed them.

Obviously the situation required a more positive approach. The frozen conservatism of such men as Burke, Reeves, and Dundas was not enough to serve in the long run to assure British victory in the war of ideas at home and abroad. Leadership in aggressive ideological warfare fell to a different group, the Evangelicals, "the praying section of the Tory Party."[9] It was not the Reeves organization which played the leading repressive role in the early decades of the 1800's but Wilberforce's Society for the Suppression of Vice.

The shift to Evangelical leadership was the logical consequence of two factors. In the first place, the sequence of events in the 1790's had made abundantly clear in the conservative mind that the war was the culmination of a long, persistent attack on the Christian faith. If this idea needed confirmation, the French outlawing of Christianity was ample. The war on religion was basic in the war on the British government; the interests of government and religion were inseparable, indeed indistinguishable. Conservatives felt religion to be the core of the contest; if the challenge in ideas was to be met, religious people had to meet it.

The second factor assuring Evangelical leadership was the character of the Evangelical movement. Ecclesiastically it was in the right spot—within the Church but quite sympathetic with dissent, especially Methodism. In fact it stemmed from the

8. "Literary and Philosophical Intelligence," *The Christian Observer*, II (1803), 507, 508.
9. Maldwin Edwards, *After Wesley* (London, 1935), 148.

same impulse as Methodism, the Wesleyan revival of the 1730's, but it represented the Whitefield faction, which remained within the Church, confined ministrations within parochial limits, and did not adopt itinerancy. Its mild Calvinism provided a doctrinal distinction whenever either body felt that it needed one. The main difference was social: Evangelicals belonged to the upper and upper-middle classes, while Methodism favored the lower and lower-middle classes. In this respect the two bodies moved closer together during the industrial revolution as Methodism rejected its opportunity to become the religion of the poor and turned solidly middle class.

Like the Methodists, the Evangelicals regarded the Church of England as simply one of many Protestant bodies.[10] In fact they sometimes spoke of themselves as the Anti-Sectarian Sect. This lenient attitude toward fellow Christians of different views did not arise from secularism, latitudinarianism, or any good-natured doctrinal laxity but rather from the concept of a central, essential core of Christian faith. Excessive scrupulosity, sectarian bickering, and division they considered evidence of human corruption. A firm belief in the natural depravity of man was part of that necessary core of doctrine. Granting that, the Evangelicals recognized as hopeless the task of reducing all varieties of sinful men to one model. Much as they wanted unity, it was better to honor piety wherever they found it and to treat all with "forbearance, candour and brotherly love."[11] Thus the Evangelicals were in an excellent position to organize and lead the united Christian effort which successful ideological warfare required. They were specially qualified to speak for Christianity by the utter simplicity of their faith. They were ready to discard jargon, cant, shibboleths, and quibbling, but on essential doctrines, attitudes, and conduct they were firm. They knew what they wanted and they were ready to insist upon what they regarded as necessary discipline not only for themselves but for everyone else, too. As one of them put it, "In short, it is their constant aim

10. John Henry Overton, *The Evangelical Revival in the Eighteenth Century* (London, 1886), 154.

11. Viator, "The Anti-Sectarian Sect," *The Christian Observer*, I (1802), 712.

to watch over themselves and others, with respect to the *whole* of Christianity."[12]

The excellent ecclesiastical position of the Evangelicals would have been of no service to the British without their desiring to assert leadership, but the desire was present in abundance. In demanding that all people conform to their ideas, the Evangelicals did not feel that they were proselyting a sectarian creed; they were performing a patriotic duty, a public service. They were simply doing what was right. And they were in a position to make themselves heard, to guard themselves from that most deadly of British social sins, "insignificance." Within the Church they formed the most definite party as well as the most influential, active, and aggressive one. Although their clergy did not hold many high posts, there were bishops such as Porteus in London to speak for them. They were strong where strength counted—in fashionable watering places and proprietary chapels. At court, Lords Dartmouth and Teignmouth represented them, in Parliament, the incomparable Wilberforce, close friend of Pitt. In the arts Hannah More picked up where William Cowper left off. Her wide circle of intimates included Garrick, Johnson, Burke, and Reynolds.[13]

Together with social position, influence, and wealth, a necessary factor in Evangelical success was leadership. It came from the "Clapham Sect," an informal group of powerful Evangelicals living in Clapham. Their common bond was an interest in philanthropy, with a strongly religious bias. Typical was John Thornton, an Evangelical of the first generation. He was a merchant with connections all over the world, a banker, and a member of Parliament. His hobby was the purchase of advowsons and presentations for Evangelical clergy, who would indulge in good works which he supported with funds. He also had printed at his expense large quantities of Bibles, prayer books, and other religious material for wide distribution through trade channels.

The group often met to mature its pious schemes in the garden or oval library of Henry Thornton, John Thornton's

12. *Ibid.*, 715.
13. Overton, *Evangelical Revival*, 92-96, 158, 159.

son. Like so many of the second generation of Evangelicals, Henry was treading urgently on his father's heels in good works. When he was burdened with only a bachelor's cares he gave six-sevenths of his income to charity, which in one year came to more than £9,000. After his marriage he was obliged to retain more to meet expenses: he gave away only two-thirds.

A good "front" man was John Shore, first Lord Teignmouth, friend of Warren Hastings, who had joined the Clapham Sect after his term of office as an innocuous and commonplace governor-general of India. With Teignmouth in the chair, the most meticulous Britisher could attend an Evangelical meeting without the slightest suspicion that he was engaging in a bit of slumming. Another East India Company man was Charles Grant, chairman of the company's court of directors. His foreign service led him to an intense interest in missions.

Venerable and respected dean of the Sect rather than leader, Granville Sharp had cut his niche in history by fighting through the Somerset case abolishing slavery in England. He was particularly fitted to give the proceedings of the Clapham group a nonsectarian flavor. Born the son of the archdeacon of Northumberland, he was indentured to a Quaker linen draper. Death or retirement of masters brought him to serve in turn under a Presbyterian, an Irish Catholic, and finally an atheist, where he lodged with a Socinian and a Jew. His continued struggle against the slave trade brought him close and friendly contacts with Quakers on both sides of the Atlantic. The American Revolution found him holding a job in the Ordnance Office, which he resigned rather than purchase munitions to shoot at Americans. A rather early senility troubled Sharp, who was inclined to millennial babblings inspired by the Book of Revelations, but there were younger members of the group who supported his interest in the Negro: Zachary Macaulay, manager of the Sierra Leone colony for free Negroes, and the wealthy lawyer, James Stephen.

Another father and son combination effectively watched over the spiritual concerns of the Clapham Sect. Henry Venn, curate of Clapham, and John Venn, the rector, both owed their appointments to John Thornton. As occasion arose they proved themselves capable of able and fairly independent leadership in the enterprises launched by the group.

Perhaps we should not rank William Wilberforce as the leader of the Clapham Sect, since he was one of the younger members and showed a proper deference to his distinguished elders, but he was brilliant and aggressive; he came to be most generally known as the parliamentary guardian of religion and public morals. He was a close friend of William Pitt in his younger days, but later Pitt chose Henry Dundas as his favorite comrade. Need for a majority in Parliament may have been a factor in this shift. Wilberforce vied with other members of the Sect in good works. His practice was to give one-fourth of his income to charity. In one year he depleted his capital by £3,000 for such donations.

For the most part the objectives of all this generosity were in the traditional Evangelical line—charity schools and colleges, Sunday schools, distribution of pious printing, and relief of the cases of destitution and disaster which continually came to their attention. The most ambitious activity of the Sect had been a drive to push through Parliament a law abolishing the slave trade. The Quakers had long been working toward this law in both England and America. The Clapham Sect came to their support, Granville Sharp headed their organization, and Wilberforce led the movement in Parliament.

In the late 1780's it seemed that success was assured, but then the antislave-trade drive ran into the reaction against French ideas. All liberal and humanitarian movements, like all attempts at political reform, fell under the suspicion of republican subversion. The antislavery societies in America had linked themselves to the ideals of liberty and equality; this taint carried to England, and by 1793 the antislave-trade movement was dead on its feet. The suspicion of equalitarian subversion affected the other Clapham Sect charities in much the same way. Any attempt to improve conditions among the poor was obviously republican leveling. What was the point of gathering poor children in Sunday schools and teaching them to read, if they read Tom Paine?

So the Clapham Sect found itself frustrated in its accustomed humanitarian efforts at precisely the moment when conservatism, religion, and patriotism fused into one common, holy cause. The pressures of military disaster, mutiny, threatened invasion, financial stringency, panic of subversion, and social upheaval, perhaps revolution, pushed other interests aside. Men of power, resources, and energy could not stand idly by while the forces and ideas of the French Revolution threatened the England which had given them so much, the social order in which they had gained such an advantageous position, and the religion so dear to them.

In retrospect it seems that the Clapham Sect was sluggish in leading the Evangelicals into effective ideological warfare at home and abroad. But it was a new kind of war—not the old dynastic scuffle or merely a contest for colonies and territory— war of an aroused nation striking for mastery of the world in the name of new ideas and for men's minds as a necessary part of the struggle for lands, peoples, and resources. This basis the French had recognized very early. In fact their propaganda had paved the way for military conquest. That it had done so was probably inadvertent. It seems doubtful whether the *philosophes* and Encyclopaedists foresaw the wars which followed in the wake of the Enlightenment. British authors had contributed substantially to the movement, and they would hardly have contributed had they seen in their works any national peril. Therefore, inadvertently or not, the French had the initiative before the wars started and held the advantage during the early part of the struggle.

Certainly the British were slow in recognizing the nature of the contest in which they were involved and the need for a massive and positive propaganda campaign at home and abroad if they were to achieve lasting victory. Quite possibly they never did recognize the situation in these terms. Perhaps, again, they simply did what was right in their eyes. But by the end of the Napoleonic Wars they were operating a propaganda machine of marvelous efficiency in nearly all the countries of Europe, in America, and, with remarkable intensity, at home. The British had defeated the French decisively in the warfare of ideas.

An anonymous American ally in the British effort did not believe that the victory was in the least inadvertent; he summarized it: "The splendid talents of Voltaire were never employed against Christianity with so much effect, as when they were devoted to the writing of small tracts, of licentious tendency, for gratuitous dispersion among common people. A respectable writer . . . affirms, that the industry and efforts of a few infidels, directed to this object, was a prime instrument of producing those terrible convulsions, which have since shaken the civilized world. The British Christians, taught by the zeal and enterprize of infidels, resolved to 'foil the enemy at his own weapons.' "[14]

So effective were these British Christians in foiling the enemy with his own weapons that they fixed their peculiar cast of thought, their ideas, and their attitudes upon much of the Western world, especially their own land and the United States. The Clapham Sect provided the leadership.

14. "To the Friends of Religion in New England," *Proceedings of the First Ten Years of the American Tract Society* (Boston, 1824), 8.

IV

CONFLICTING IDEOLOGIES

HOWEVER HAPHAZARD and inadvertent the French propaganda may have been, it played its part in creating the situation the British were obliged to meet. Repression and repressive propaganda had served a certain purpose but their usefulness was limited. Simple negation would not arouse a national effort; the crisis demanded a positive approach. Offering this opportunity, the Evangelicals proceeded to promote their ideology with such vigor and ingenuity that they took command of the field. So effective were their techniques that even their most bitter critics at home among the High Church faction were obliged to adopt them as a matter of self-preservation. In effect, for the duration of hostilities the Evangelical story became the British story.

What the Evangelicals believed was as well suited to the task at hand as their sincerity in believing it. Their insistence upon religious experience as an intimate, personal, emotional adjustment nourished a glowing sentimentality which blurred doctrinal differences and made them insignificant compared with the scalding tears of joyful assurance which might flow from the eyes of any true Christian. Thus the Evangelicals could lead a united religious front, and they did.

No less suitable to the purpose was the Calvinist element

of their religious tradition. Doctrinal laxity tended to soften the personal application of the more severe aspects of Calvinist thought, leaving a vague Augustinian piety, but Calvinism was there, ready for use as a social and political philosophy if not as a personal religious creed. What the British needed was a counter to French rationalism, an answer to the Enlightenment; Calvinism provided that answer. For every French "yes," Calvinism had its "no"; for every negation of the Enlightenment, Calvinism had its affirmation.

The most fundamental controversy had to do with the nature of man. In the doctrine of the Enlightenment, man was essentially good, moral, and reasonably bright. He was, in the natural state, the noble savage guided to goodness, truth, and beauty by "reason," natural law in its human aspect. This doctrine was one of the most powerful, dynamic ideas ever to arise in civilization. But the Evangelicals had their answer ready: the human race was degenerate, hopelessly depraved. Probably their Richard Baxter very early put it as well as anybody ever did: "When Christ comes with regenerating grace he finds no man sitting still, but all posting to eternal ruin, and making haste towards hell: till by conviction, he first brings them to a stand, and then, by conversion, turns their hearts and lives sincerely to him."[1]

Different notions of the nature of man colored every idea of man's relationship to his environment and produced conflicting approaches to all human problems. If man was a rational creature, as the advocates of the Enlightenment asserted, then reason was the ultimate sanction of order in human affairs; relationships in society, as in nature, were alike subject to critical examination. This spirit produced such men as Locke and Paine and such documents as the American Declaration of Independence. Here the moral order and the rational order were the same thing. But if man was essentially corrupt and depraved, his mind so disorganized as to be quite unreliable, then his reason could lead him only to confusion and ruin. Against the rational approach which was creating such

1. *The Saints' Everlasting Rest,* abridged by Benjamin Fawcett (New York, *c.* 1830), 19.

havoc with British institutions the Evangelicals strove to rein-state the divine order of the Middle Ages. The problem of reason they solved in the Thomistic manner: reason could be reliable when it was rightly used. There was a twofold path to truth, reason and revelation, but both of these were subordinate to faith. The essential condition for the proper use of reason was piety. Against the methodical doubt of Descartes they offered the belief of Aquinas.

In relating their divine order to morality, the Evangelicals probably went further than Thomas Aquinas would have ventured: they asserted that the true nature of any act de-pended not at all on its objective consequences to humanity or on the intent of the actor, but rather on his emotional, re-ligious condition. Wilberforce led the way in asserting that good qualities of character were neither genuine nor durable except as they stemmed from religion;[2] Gardiner Spring of New York put the principle more forcefully in his efforts to capture an American charitable society for the Evangelical forces: "Many an action appears liberal and humane; it is dictated by the 'social principle'; it is the effusion of a noble and a generous spirit; but when compared with the great stand-ard of human action, and weighed in the balance of the sanctuary, it is found wanting. . . . *the moral quality of every action lies in the disposition of heart with which it is per-formed.*"[3]

Not without reason has a critic remarked of the Evangeli-cals that the God above became more shadowy than the God within.[4] They did not seek the truth for which the children of the Enlightenment tortured nature with probing reason and experiment. To them the universe was not a rational order but a divine order in a very literal sense, and the truth

2. William Wilberforce, *A Practical View of the Prevailing Religious System of Professed Christians in the Higher and Middle Classes, Contrasted with Real Christianity* (American Tract Society, *The Evangelical Library*, II [New York, c. 1835]), 189 ff.

3. *A Sermon preached April 21, 1811, for the benefit of a society of ladies instituted for the relief of poor widows with small children* (New York, 1811), 7-8.

4. Hoxie Neale Fairchild, *Religious Trends in English Poetry* (New York, 1939), I, 546.

was a divine truth revealed in its full glory only beyond the grave. The Evangelicals conducted their own scientific experiments in their own way. They persistently endeavored to catch glimpses of the great unknown through the eyes of the dying, doggedly badgering the last moments of those who hung on the threshold. As lingering death by tuberculosis was most convenient for this purpose, it became highly prized. And we cannot deny the Evangelicals a certain amount of success in their explorations. The writhing agony of the infidel freethinker catching his first glimpse of the fires awaiting him was very convincing. So also was the smile of blissful content on the countenance of the expiring believer as he responded to carefully formulated questions and declared his complete willingness to leave his earthly home and his loved ones to enter upon the blissful eternity so close at hand that he could feel its glowing presence and see its dawning glory. For the Evangelical probing into the unknown, children in their innocence proved the most suitable subjects, and the high infant mortality rate presented many opportunities. So popular did such "happy and pious deaths" become in the United States that they gave rise to the popular saying, "the good die young."

In all fairness to the Evangelicals we must admit that they did not create the gushing tide of sentiment which engulfed Western civilization in the nineteenth century. It was not their doing that woman became a creature of such sensitivity that she would faint at the slightest contact with reality or that strong men found comfort and a certain glory in public weeping. The validity accorded to sentiment in what is known as the Romantic reaction seems to have had its roots in the material success of so many persons in the industrial revolution, which gave them such a feeling of inward virtue, strength, and goodness that their swelling bosoms could not contain themselves without occasional overflow. A theoretical assertion of Calvinistic worthlessness and depravity was a small price to pay for "the glorious liberty of the children of God";[5] what the orthodox Catholic would damn as the deadly sin of pride seems to

5. *Ibid.*, 545-46.

have become an Evangelical virtue confirmed by a sentimental interpretation of Calvinistic election and predestination. On every hand, wealth, power, and success supported God's good judgment. This belief was what one student has described as "Protestant Christianity in a more or less delightfully phosphorescent state of decay."[6]

Although the Evangelicals did not create the wave of sentimental romanticism which swept Great Britain in the years 1780-1830, they did give it voice and organization. Without it they could not have done what they did. Sentiment provided both the atmosphere and the sanction for their energetic counter to the rational ideology of the Enlightenment. Nor did they permit their atmosphere to be disturbed by those most vicious enemies to sentiment, wit and humor. The Evangelicals viewed themselves with an incredible sobriety:

> . . . Tis pitiful
> To count a grin when you should woo a soul:
> To break a jest, when pity would inspire
> Pathetic exhortation; and t'address
> The skittish fancy with facetious tales
> When sent with God's commission to the heart![7]

Equally antagonistic was the attitude of the Evangelicals toward change. To be sure, the world was treating them well with things just as they were, but they had theoretical support for their resistance to change as well as a possible disinclination to disturb a comfortable arrangement. The notion of orderly, rationally directed change was one of the strongest components of the French ideology. The concept of progress, quite unknown to medieval thought and to antiquity, for that matter, was a principal product of the Enlightenment. This concept, in turn, arose out of the success of the scientific revolution in constructing an astonishingly successful, mechanical interpretation of natural law. At the same time the industrial revolution and the opening of the Americas offered convincing justification. The result was a surging exuberance, an unbounded optimism in the future of the human race.

6. *Ibid.*, 535.
7. Extract from a letter of M. Fenelon to the French Academy, quoted by Ebenezer Porter, ed., *The Young Preacher's Manual* (New York, 1829), 130.

Against the doctrine of inevitable progress the Evangelicals rallied the full power of Calvinism. Since man was by nature a contemptible degenerate, the only direction in which he could progress was toward hell. Change was only the substitution of a new set of miseries for an old set of miseries, and sinful man richly deserved all the pain and trouble which were his natural lot. In essence the Evangelicals reverted to the medieval notion that the traditional order was God's order and that perfection was already achieved, at least that degree of perfection which God chose to achieve. Mixed with this medievalism was a certain patriotic complacency: because of its special friendship with God, England embodied all of the virtues in their highest degree, another argument against change.

Mixed also with medieval rigidity was a dash of science, the concept of the Great Chain of Being. God had constructed all life in a chain of orderly degrees from lowest to highest. The French naturalist Lamarck had blurred the distinction between degrees and introduced the idea of progress through evolution, which the Evangelicals denied. God had made each unit of the chain as perfect as its nature would permit; the chain itself was perfectly complete and perfectly dependent upon each unit. Furthermore, since each link of the chain was perfect, the link was as full as its nature would permit. The application of this idea to the hierarchical structure of British society was easy. It led to an obvious conclusion: one had better be satisfied with the station in life in which he finds himself, for there is no other place for him—they are all filled up. Furthermore, any rebellion against existing conditions was really rebellion against God, not only damning in itself but utterly hopeless.[8]

To persuade those at the top of the Great Chain of Being to accept its implications did not seem impossibly difficult; the persuasion of those lower down was a tribute to Evangelical ability. Their opponents, the restless advocates of rational experiment and progress, optimistically offered to solve all human problems in the not too distant future. They invited

8. Cf. Bernard N. Schilling, *Conservative England and the Case against Voltaire* (New York, 1950), 18-51.

Englishmen to throw off oppressive institutions and join their freewheeling pursuit of happiness. The Evangelicals had to show that misery was not only inevitable but really beneficial and desirable. The necessity of misery received strong support from the Rev. Thomas R. Malthus' *Essay on the Principle of Population* in 1798. Whether the Rev. Malthus derived his dismal thesis from the Evangelicals we cannot say, but his work was a rugged piece of propaganda, fitting nicely into the Great Chain of Being scheme. The Rev. Malthus published at the right time, and his cordial reception was assured.

But the Evangelicals were not dependent upon the intellectual support of the Rev. Malthus. However comforting they found it, his line of thought did not offer convincing material for popular consumption. The Evangelical attitude toward poverty and misery contained two directly conflicting aspects. It presented poverty as a peculiarly blessed state practically guaranteeing entrance to heaven, but poverty was also evidence of wickedness, sin, and vice, the stigma of those bound headlong to hell.

At times these attitudes were mixed and the poor caught it both ways, but the emphasis seemed to change with conditions. When the country was in trouble and the working classes were rioting with hunger, as often happened during the Napoleonic Wars, poverty was a truly blessed condition; anyone's failure to enjoy it was cause for astonishment. On the other hand, when no critical difficulty but an uncomfortable social dislocation among the lower orders made the poor laws a burden, wretchedness and vice became synonymous. The general idea was adequately expressed by the Boston (Mass.) Society for the Moral and Religious Instruction of the Poor, which decided that its work was "to impress on the minds and hearts of the rising generation the great truth, that *godliness is profitable unto all things, having promise of the life that now is* as well as of *that which is to come,*" and the obvious corollary, "Nine tenths of the pauperism in one country [England] is occasioned by vice."[9]

But appealing as was the association of sin and misery and

9. *Third Annual Report* (1819), 3, 22.

of virtue and well-being to the Evangelicals, who found such convincing evidence in their own experience, poverty as a blessing was the leading doctrine in those years of trouble and pressure, when the lower ranks of British society were under severe strain and badly needed reassurance that all was well in a world which had little to offer them.

The Evangelicals did not create the large, highly useful although highly mythical class, the contented poor. They developed a central idea of Christian doctrine, whose strength lay in its essential truth. Christianity taught that spiritual values were more important than material things; peace of mind and contentment were to be found in a religious assurance independent of material contingencies. Christianity was thus a spiritual insurance against physical disaster. Under the influence of St. Augustine, Christianity committed itself further: spirit was not only above matter but the two were antagonists. The spirit and the flesh had to fight it out. In the Middle Ages this idea took the form of the consecration of poverty, the essential concept of monasticism. St. Augustine's prejudice against the flesh and everything which nourished it entered Protestantism with John Calvin and flourished again in the Evangelical revival of the eighteenth century.

Thus the doctrine of the contented poor, so irritating to Marx and Engels, was ready at hand for Evangelical exploitation just when it would do the most good. The Evangelicals tried without success, at least in England, to avoid implying that the Christian religion, with all the advantages it had to offer, was the sole property of the lower classes.

The British focus on the lower orders of society often disturbed Evangelical colleagues in America. The Rev. Robert Hall of the American Tract Society complained that Miss Edgeworth's highly moral writings made no use of religion. After reading one of her books he was so upset he could not preach comfortably for six weeks.[10] When he called Miss Edgeworth to account for her betrayal of religion as the source of all morality, she replied that if she had been writing for the lower

10. American Tract Society, *Eleventh Annual Report* (1836), 40.

classes, she would have recommended religion, but she had written for a class to whom religion was less necessary. Far from mollified, the Rev. Hall concluded, "She seemed to think that the virtues of the higher order needed no assistance from religion, and that it was only designed as a curb and muzzle for the brute."[11]

But it would be a mistake to assume that the Evangelicals were promoting their doctrine of contentment in any worldly sense of advantage. It may at times have been calculated, but it stemmed from a metaphysical optimism to them eminently sincere and true. The optimism was a deeper and stronger conviction than complacency, directly in conflict with the rational optimism of the enemy. Evidently a happy outlook was in the air, shared by both sides, but they still could fight over why they felt that way: the child of the Enlightenment because man could conquer all his troubles through rational mastery of nature; the Evangelical because he trusted that God was good. Man was so degenerate and corrupt that he was incompetent to judge good from bad. What seemed bad was really very good; evils were necessary; everything was for the best; since God was good, whatever was, was right. Partial ill was universal good.[12]

Probably the most systematic exposition of Evangelical optimism appeared not in England but in the United States when Samuel Hopkins of Newport, R.I., published his *System of Doctrines Contained in Divine Revelations Explained and Defended* in 1793. Hopkins, the middle man in the Edwards-Hopkins-Channing teacher-student sequence, was the most popular Calvinist theologian of American Protestantism in the early part of the nineteenth century. Since nearly all American Protestantism was Calvinist at that time, his impact on American thought was correspondingly great. The vigorous support that the British Evangelicals gave to Hopkinsian optimism probably had much to do with its success.

In the Hopkins retort to the Enlightenment, God preferred that evil exist, that it be introduced into the system. Other-

11. *Ibid.*
12. Cf. Schilling, *Conservative England*, 33.

wise it would not have happened. Now, nothing could be more dishonorable to God than to imagine that the system which He made for His pleasure and glory was not wisely contrived. One must conclude, then, that the introduction of sin and misery was for the general good. In fact, the existence of moral evil so much the better disclosed the perfection of God's nature. As to the mechanics whereby God kept a beneficial amount of devilment going on in the world, Hopkins used biology to give a scientific twist to the old doctrine. God did not transfer Adam's original sin to each human being; rather, He saw to it that Adam's tendency to sin persisted through the processes of ordinary generation. Men were born sinners by inclination through heredity.[13]

The whole structure of this metaphysical optimism rested upon two assumptions or acts of faith: in the first place, the order of the universe was a divine order, not chance or the rational order of the Enlightenment; secondly, God was good, even if His goodness included evil. For his crucial statement of God's goodness Hopkins borrowed again from his enemy, the Enlightenment. The French *philosophes* had taught that man could be happy only if he worked for the happiness of others, so that "fraternity" took its place with "liberty" and "equality." Hopkins simply extended this characteristic to God himself. Nathanael Emmons marked it as the first of the distinguishing tenets with which Hopkins modified the Edwards picture of divine wrath: "That all true *virtue,* or real *holiness* consists in *disinterested benevolence.* The object of benevolence is universal Being, including God and all intelligent creatures. It wishes and seeks the good of every individual, so far as is consistent with the greatest good of the whole, which is comprised in the glory of God and the perfection and happiness of his kingdom."[14] Here Hopkins borrowed not only the spirit of the Enlightenment but one of its favorite catchwords, "benevolence." In France, the eighteenth century of the *philo-*

13. For this treatment of Hopkinsianism I have relied on the statement *Hopkinsian Calvinism* which the Rev. Nathanael Emmons, D.D., of Franklin, Mass., composed and furnished to Hannah Adams for her *View of Religion.* The statement bears no date (*c.* 1810).

14. Emmons, *Hopkinsinian Calvinism,* 1.

sophes was an era of benevolence. Charity, inspired by the love of God and reinforced by love of one's fellow man, had made human welfare a public concern.[15] As early as the sixteenth century the French had started to take the administration of relief from the clergy and to make it the responsibility of the laity. M. Babeau in his *Paris en 1789* symbolized French spirit by depicting "Benevolence" rising in a hospital ward amidst the beds of patients.

If the eighteenth century was the era of French benevolence, the nineteenth century was the age of Anglo-American benevolence. But as the word changed its nationality, it also gradually changed its meaning. With the French the term had indicated charity, with certain warm emotional overtones, but by the end of the Napoleonic Wars Anglo-American usage had changed "benevolence" to a specialized meaning it still carries, the organized promotion of the Evangelical faith.

In this transformation of benevolence, everyone still wanted to do good; as an ardent Methodist remarked, "the way to get good was to set about doing good."[16] But the idea of doing good was changing. In England the spirit of benevolence became increasingly colored by the desire to keep the poor subservient. The Evangelicals took the lead in this kind of benevolence, using their religion of contentment. As with the moral societies of the 1690's, this form of doing good became immensely popular. By 1813 the Evangelical fashion was a social fad, and membership in one or more benevolent societies was practically a social requisite.[17]

American Evangelicals naïvely took British benevolence at its face value. The contented-poverty angle baffled them somewhat. One Yankee skeptic remarked that poverty in Europe might be to a great degree contented poverty, but it was not contented in the United States. "Something better, something higher is forever in the view and the subject of

15. M. Roustan, *The Pioneers of the French Revolution*, Frederic Whyte, tr. (London, 1926), 277, 278.

16. "Class Meetings Formed into Tract Societies," *The Christian Advocate and Journal*, II (1828), 81.

17. Maurice J. Quinlan, *Victorian Prelude* (*Columbia University Studies in English and Comparative Literature*, No. 155 [New York, 1941]), 120-21.

discussion. And the characteristic of American poverty is everywhere discontented poverty, aspiring poverty, and must be dealt with as such."[18]

Overlooking the social pressure which was such an influence in British benevolence, Americans simply accepted the fad of their Evangelical cousins, this new, better, cheaper way of doing good: "But if charity to the mortal part of man be so excellent, how superior is that which confers on him an immortal benefit, a relief which will last to eternity."[19]

The Evangelical ideology made a more positive and permanent contribution to Western thought than its doctrine of benevolence. This positive contribution of Evangelicalism was a readjustment of the relationship between church and state, religion and politics, to bring these institutions abreast of the changes which the Reformation, the Enlightenment, and the growth of capitalism had introduced. Current practice had broken almost entirely from the traditional coalition of church and state in a national religion, and it was high time to bring doctrine into closer alignment with reality.

The traditional position of a national religion is implied in St. Paul: "Let every soul be subject unto the higher powers. For there is no power but of God: the powers that be are ordained of God. Whosoever therefore resisteth the power, resisteth the ordinance of God: and they that resist shall receive to themselves damnation."[20] However, by 1800 the doctrine of fused religious and governmental power was rather well exploded. Revolutionary France had disestablished the Catholic Church and seized its property; it presumed to operate a strictly secular government under the benign smile of that secular goddess Reason. England had given the old doctrine a bad jolt in the Glorious Revolution of 1688; furthermore, dissent had developed to the point where it embraced about 25 per cent of the population.[21] An indifferent formalism

18. Stephen H. Tyng, *Forty Years' Experience in Sunday-Schools* (New York, 1860), 161-62.

19. *An Address of the Bible Society to the Public* (Philadelphia, 1809), 18.

20. Romans 13:1-2.

21. Cf. John Henry Overton, *The Evangelical Revival in the Eighteenth Century* (London, 1886), 156, 157.

seems to have captured a larger percentage than that. Meanwhile the United States was getting along on a strictly secular constitution without even a pagan goddess to bless it. All of the component states had disestablished their churches except for a few in New England under severe pressure.

What the conservatives desperately needed was a new, positive concept of the relation between religion and government which would not only tolerate dissent but include it and use it; this viewpoint the Evangelicals provided. It was probably their most positive contribution to Western civilization, and it still endures. The Evangelical solution stemmed from a doctrinal lenience permitting a common denominator of belief among all Christians, Catholic and Protestant, to serve as a ground of understanding and action. The modern extension of this common ground to all religions as well as to all Christian sects is merely an expansion of the Evangelical position.

The Evangelical political ideology which triumphed with the allied triumph in arms is generally expressed in the principles of the Holy Alliance, formulated by Alexander I of Russia and proclaimed at Paris on September 26, 1815: the principles of Christianity, not of any particular church, formed the foundation of government.

What the Holy Alliance expressed in general terms the Evangelicals of England and America had worked out in particulars. But the gradual process met frequent and vigorous criticism, especially in the United States, where the spirit of the Enlightenment was stronger. A particular difficulty in America was the popularized Cartesian mode of thought which divided experience into compartments: the legislative, executive, and judicial functions of government had to be separate; business was business and the Sabbath was the Lord's day; spirit was distinct from matter; religion was to be kept apart from politics and never the twain should meet.

The issue came strongly to the front in the presidential election of 1800, in which the people of the United States had to choose between the deism of Thomas Jefferson and the rather dubious Christianity of John Adams. In New York the Rev. John M. Mason met the issue head on:

Yet *religion has nothing to do with politics!* Where did you learn this maxim? The bible is full of directions for your behavior as *citizens.* . . . You are commanded *"in all your ways to acknowledge him"* (Prov. iii, 3). *"In everything, by. prayer and supplication, with thanksgiving to let your requests be made known unto God"* [Phil. 4:6] *"And whatsoever ye do, in word or deed, to do all in the name of the Lord Jesus"* [Col. 3:17]. . . . But you are afraid that to refuse a man your suffrage because he is an infidel would *interfere with the rights of conscience.* This is a most singular scruple, and proves how wild are the opinions of men on the subject of liberty. Conscience is God's officer in the human breast, and its rights are defined by his law. The right of conscience to trample on his authority is the right of a rebel, which entitles him to nothing but condign punishment.[22]

The Federalist party went down to defeat, and so did such efforts as the Rev. Mason's to link religion to government through religious authority and the power of the clergy. But defeat did not solve the problem: the issue went down only to bob up again presently in different guise. By the end of the Napoleonic Wars American conservatives, much stronger in numbers and more confident, were relating religion to politics at quite a different level.

Of great assistance was the thinking and writing of the British Evangelicals on the same problem in their efforts to maintain a united home front in the face of a war which was not going at all well. William Wilberforce made the most substantial contribution with *A Practical View of the Prevailing Religious System of Professed Christians in the Higher and Middle Classes in this Country Contrasted with Real Christianity.* Wilberforce was a busy politician and would not have undertaken this laborious work had he not considered it a necessary part of his business.[23] But it was worth the trouble: the tract-style book reached the public at the right time, considerably influencing contemporary thought on the relationship of religion to government and to society in general. *A Practical View* ran through six British editions before 1837; it was translated into French, German, Italian, Spanish, and Dutch. Free

22. *The Voice of Warning to Christians, on the Ensuing Election of a President of the United States* (New York, 1800), 25-27.
23. Cf. R. Coupland, *Wilberforce* (Oxford, 1923), 237.

from copyright restrictions then, Americans reprinted the book twenty-five times[24] to form a substantial part of Evangelical thought in the United States.

When it is read today, much of *A Practical View* presents a rather disorganized assortment of stilted piety; but it had something meaningful to say in its time, and portions have an authentic punch of urgency and sincerity. Such was its concluding appeal to all true Christians:

Let them consider as devolved on them the important duty of serving, it may be of saving their country, not by busy interference in politics (in which it cannot but be confessed there is much uncertainty), but rather by that sure and radical benefit of restoring the influence of religion. . . . It would be an instance in myself of that very false shame which I have condemned in others, if I were not boldly to avow my firm persuasion that *to the decline of Religion and Morality our national difficulties must, both directly and indirectly be chiefly ascribed: and that my only solid hopes for the well-being of my country depend, not so much on her fleets and armies, not so much on the wisdom of her rulers or the spirit of her people, as on the persuasion that she still contains many who love and obey the gospel of Christ; that their intercessions may yet prevail; that for the sake of these, Heaven may still look upon us with an eye of favour.*[25]

But there was much more depth and purpose to Wilberforce's *Practical View* than his call for Christian unity to save the nation. He wanted to change the level of British thinking about Christianity in its relation to national welfare. He took it for granted that any decent person in the middle and upper classes was ready to admit that religion was the only instrument for cultivating a satisfactory conduct and temper in the lower orders of society;[26] he wanted them to know that Christianity applied equally to the practical working of the entire social structure. That was his "practical view."

The new concept of the relationship of religion and government began to emerge, a concept broad enough to include all Christian sects and eventually all the principal religions. It

24. *Ibid.*, 237-44.
25. Wilberforce, *Practical View*, as quoted by Coupland, *Wilberforce*, 241.
26. *Practical View*, 189 ff.

stemmed out of the usefulness of religion in keeping the working classes in their place, contentedly poor, quietly subservient. If religion could do that for the lower classes, it could do as much for all classes, to the immense benefit and smooth performance of the entire society.

Upon reading Wilberforce, Madame de Stael murmured, "C'est l'aurore de l'immortalité,"[27] and in a sense she was probably right. The book was his challenge to the upper and middle classes of British society to overlook doctrinal differences in Christian unity and to rise to the occasion. He demanded that they impose restraints upon themselves, encourage virtue and discountenance vice, enforce the laws against infractions of morals, and fortify the political community by restoring the prevalence of Evangelical Christianity.[28]

A Practical View supplied a working blueprint of ideas for the organized effort of the British Evangelicals. It also strongly influenced American thought, but because of social and economic conditions peculiar to America it was rarely possible to apply a British idea successfully there in its raw, unmitigated condition, as the failure of the Alien and Sedition Acts testified. In the adoption of the fruitful idea of unified Christianity as a powerful and necessary social force, American conservatives gave the idea a more precise formulation and, eventually, a more definitely political application. The Americans were more self-conscious and articulate in political matters than the British; problems of lawless violence, sectionalism, and social disintegration threatened the political experiment which was their pride. Finally, as American conservatives began to apply successfully the propaganda techniques of the British Evangelicals, there appeared the opportunity to achieve political ends outside of party politics and thus to redeem the defeat of the Federalist party.

However, Americans did not fail to stress the obvious application of Christianity to society through the identity of religion and morals familiar in Wilberforce's *Practical View*. There was the Rev. William S. Plumer in Virginia to remind

27. Coupland, *Wilberforce*, 349.
28. *Practical View*, 279-321.

them that a servant who did not believe in hell would steal the silver.[29] Plumer blamed all social ills on the infidel free-thinkers Voltaire, Paine, Rousseau, Bolingbroke, and Hobbes. And in Boston the Rev. Joseph Tuckerman found the "ministers of infidelity and sin" generating and perpetuating a debased pauperism with their infidel publications, gambling houses, brothels, and dram shops. In Tuckerman's opinion, the police, the laws, and the courts had failed to do more than keep society from being swamped and overwhelmed. The only effective remedy was Christianity.[30]

But among the responsible leaders of the Evangelical movement in the United States there was much thinking at a deeper and eventually a more fruitful level. The first stage brought them a realization of the politics implicit in the popular Hopkinsian Calvinism. God was ruling the universe even if He did mix evil with good in proportions which pleased only Him. So there were two levels of government, "God's government" and secular politics. The first of these had a universal application and corresponded in scope to the "natural law" of the Enlightenment but employed religious rather than rational sanctions. Secular politics could be good insofar as it was attuned to divine politics. The connection could not be direct, because American political theory insisted so strongly upon the separation of religion and government. But the separation did not rule out the Ciceronian type of relationship between divine and civil law, a sort of field theory. God's government could provide a field or conditioning environment within which secular politics could operate in terms agreeable to the conservative disposition. In its full development, divine government constituted an invisible, nonsectarian, Protestant Church. Furthermore, there also arose the idea of a compensation between God's government and secular politics. If secular government was to be weak, loose, and divisive, as in American conditions of freedom, so much the stronger must be the

29. *The Bible True and Infidelity Wicked* (American Tract Society [New York, *c.* 1830]), 71, 72.

30. *The Principles and Results of the Ministry at Large* (Boston, 1838), 28-30.

uniting power of God's government if the United States was to survive.

The development of the American concept of a new relationship between religion and politics was gradual over the years between the election of Jefferson in 1800 and of Jackson in 1828. As the 1840's approached, the idea of God's government, under which American liberty prospered, fused naturally with the more nationalistic notion of manifest destiny. God's government served best as a vague, general assumption because of its conflict with the secularism of the founding fathers and its threat to freedom. Whenever it found explicit expression and application it caused trouble.

It is not too difficult to trace the development of American thought along these lines. There is little, for example, in Thomas Dunn's treatment of religion and politics in 1794 to suggest later developments: "Religion is a great system of benevolence; it disposes us to consult and promote the interest and happiness of the whole of mankind. —So far Religion and Politics are connected together."[31] A much stronger idea was developing in the mind of Lyman Beecher, that Evangelical stalwart and leading exponent of Hopkinsianism. By 1807 he had formulated "the government of God": "The sole object of the government of God, from beginning to end, is to express his benevolence. His eternal decrees, of which so many are afraid, are nothing but the plan which God has devised to express his benevolence, and to make His kingdom as vast and as blessed as His own infinite goodness desires."[32] Seven years later Beecher was ready to bring God's government down to earth in a practical way by launching what was to become the American Education Society. "The integrity of the Union demands special exertions to produce in the nation a more homogeneous character and bind us together with firmer bonds"[33] but did not require the consolidation of state govern-

31. *A Discourse . . . before the New York Society for the Information and Assistance of Persons Emigrating from Foreign Countries* (New York, 1794), 1.

32. *Autobiography, Correspondence, Etc., of Lyman Beecher, D.D.*, Charles Beecher, ed. (New York, 1864), I, 165.

33. *Address of the Charitable Society for the Education of Indigent Pious Young Men for the Ministry of the Gospel* (Concord, Mass., 1820), 20.

ments into a despotism. There was another way to get the same result, and here both the American field theory and the compensating device appeared clearly for the first time: "But the prevalence of pious, intelligent, enterprising ministers through the nation, at the ratio of one for a thousand, would establish schools, and academies, and colleges, and habits, and institutions of homogeneous influence. These would produce a sameness of views, and feelings, and interests, which would lay the foundation of our empire upon a rock. Religion is the central attraction which must supply the deficiency of political affinity and interest."[34]

Beecher's proposal aroused bitter opposition as the American branch of the Evangelical movement grew in strength and proceeded to carry out his ideas. There was resentment against the emergence of "an extended combination of institutions, religious, civil and literary."[35] The people of the United States were not going to be caught "by these *combination* trappings; not all the hypocritical pretensions to religion, the prayers sounding *long* and *loud,* the addresses, the forming of societies, with specious names."[36]

But if Beecher stirred up sharp opposition, he also aroused genuine and durable support among his conservative countrymen. The more clearly they saw their control of secular politics slipping, the more strongly did the idea of double government appeal to them. A leading Evangelical of New York, Dr. Gardiner Spring, proposed in 1820 a very general political formula: "Liberty without godliness, is but another name for anarchy or despotism. Let philosophers and statesmen argue as they please—the religion of the gospel is the rock on which civil liberty rests. You have never known a people free without the Bible; with it, they cannot long be slave."[37]

General acceptance of the double government notion and rapidly growing Evangelical strength were sure to bring, sooner or later, a test of how far the idea could be carried in practical politics. That test came in 1827, when the Rev. Ezra Stiles

34. *Ibid.*
35. A Layman, *A Letter to the Rev. Lyman Beecher* (undated), 3.
36. *Ibid.,* 7.
37. Ed., *Memoirs of the Rev. Samuel J. Mills* (New York, 1820), 106-7.

Ely of Philadelphia attempted to rally the Evangelical vote behind Andrew Jackson for President. At this time Ely was moderator of the General Assembly of the Presbyterian Church and a leading power in the American Sunday-School Union, two organizations feeling their oats rather strongly. He had satisfied himself of the general's religious position as early as 1823, when Jackson had called for his assistance in the case of the Rev. Thomas B. Craighead of Kentucky, whom the General Assembly was about to try on doctrinal charges. On that occasion General Jackson wrote Ely a letter neatly grooved to the Evangelical party line: "Disunion is evil in both Church and State; and the present is a period, when every means, consistent with the principles of true religion, ought to be employed to restore harmony and union to the Christian cause."[38]

Ely became generally known as a Jackson man when he defended the general from a sharp Baptist attack in June, 1823. In vindicating his execution of six militiamen to quell a mutiny at Fort Jackson in 1815, Jackson stated that the leader of the mutiny was a Baptist preacher. In his published response to the anguished Baptist outcry, Ely said there were all kinds of Baptists; he had heard a Baptist preacher near the Hermitage "who was a Socinian, and which is rather remarkable for a Socinian, a downright blockhead."[39] So there was no question in anyone's mind about Ely's position when he mounted the pulpit of Philadelphia's Seventh Presbyterian Church on July 4 to deliver his discourse, "The Duty of Christian Freemen to Elect Christian Rulers." He wanted to bring God's government down to earth: "I propose, fellow citizens, a new sort of union, or, if you please, *a Christian party in politics.* . . ."[40] Ely did not propose a formal political organization but rather an agreement among orthodox Evangelicals to effect the union "by adopting, avowing, and determining to act upon, truly religious principles in all civil matters,"[41] a precise statement of the Holy Alliance formula.

Ely was no more disposed than the Alliance to be tolerant.

38. Nashville, April 21, 1823, quoted by Ezra Stiles Ely, *The Duty of Christian Freemen to Elect Christian Rulers* (Philadelphia, 1828), 31.
39. *Duty,* 16-17.   40. *Ibid.,* 8.
41. *Ibid.*

He claimed that public officials were bound to be orthodox: "They may no more lawfully be bad husbands, wicked parents, men of heretical opinions, or men of dissolute lives, than the obscure individual who would be sent to Bridewell for his blasphemy or debauchery."[42]   Although he mentioned neither presidential candidate by name, his statement ruled out John Quincy Adams with his unenthusiastic Unitarianism as compared with the equally vague but more amenable orthodoxy of Andrew Jackson.

Getting down to cases, Ely believed that if the Presbyterians, Baptists, Methodists, and Congregationalists acted together, the country would never have an *"avowed infidel"* in Washington in any official position.[43]   At that time American Evangelicals considered the Unitarians to be infidels, unfaithful to Christ.   Carrying his calculations a little further, Ely thought that if the Episcopalians would join the Evangelicals, they "could govern every public election in our country."[44]   The German and Dutch sects would fall in line, and the various denominations would take turns at holding office.

The fusion of divine and secular politics suited General Jackson, since he hastened to write Ely from the Hermitage on July 12 that he was educated and brought up under the Presbyterian discipline and had always had a preference for it.[45] However, there were many Americans not quite so well pleased. In fact, there was quite a rumpus as Ely's speech and some rather strong statements from the American Sunday-School Union brought the issue to a point.   Ely did not help matters when he published his speech with an appendix "designed to vindicate the liberty of Christians and of the American Sunday School Union," in which Ely included all correspondence as well as his endorsement of Andrew Jackson.

Although there is no evidence that the Ely incident seriously damaged Jackson's candidacy or the Evangelical movement, American theory of the relationship between government and religion did not again attain this extreme position.   The united Evangelical front which made Ely's idea a possibility had

42. *Ibid.*, 6.
44. *Ibid.*

43. *Ibid.*, 11.
45. *Ibid.*, 32.

begun to crack; in another ten years it had split wide open, and that threat to political liberty in the United States was past. The theory of the two governments persisted in more general form. Even children became familiar with such exhortations as this: "Young Americans! as you grow up to manhood, and enjoy the great blessings of freedom from all unjust and oppressive laws of man, beware of wishing to be free from the just and righteous laws of your creator."[46]

But political theory was only one aspect of the conservative pressure the Evangelicals brought to bear against the dynamic and disruptive forces of the Enlightenment represented in their political form by the French offensive. The strength of the conservative counteroffensive we can measure by its obvious results—the Victorian era of pious propriety in Western civilization. And equally obvious is the fact that the conservative forces could not have achieved their massive power without appropriate social machinery.

The Evangelical machinery is of particular interest because it contributed to the ideology it promoted. The means can never be so distinct from the ends that they do not become, to a degree, ends in themselves.

46. *The Life of George Washington,* American Sunday-School Union (Philadelphia, 1832), 209.

V

THE EVANGELICAL MACHINERY

IN ITS COMPLETE DEVELOPMENT, the organization which conducted ideological warfare for the British and successfully imposed the Evangelical point of view on the Western world was a highly complex machine typical of those of modern ideologies. For example, the Evangelicals had foreign missions, although they did not confine international activity to those missions. Cash subsidies for the support of foreign Evangelical organizations conducting ideological warfare against the French constituted a routine practice during the Napoleonic Wars. For the production and distribution of printed propaganda at less than cost prices, the tract and Bible societies were fairly successful in exerting price pressure as well as social influence to force competing literature from the market. At a time when reading matter was scarce, this pressure was a peculiarly effective tactic, one the communists much later used in Asia.

To apply their propaganda to the young, the Evangelicals captured the Sunday-school movement, at that time a secular charity, and converted it to an effective educational system. With the Sunday schools, numerous societies of young people contributed to a vigorous youth movement which afforded an unfailing source of energy. All types of Evangelical organizations linked together with interlocking directorates, and all brought their pressure to bear on the home front. In this work the Evangelicals developed those techniques of systematic coverage by trained teams now familiar in house-to-house campaigns for any purpose. For this and for fund-raising in general, they were the first to organize the energies of women on a large scale. For circulating information and concentrating energy upon a designated aspect of the work the Evangelicals developed the "concert of prayer," a system of prearranged meetings for the promotion of a particular project. At an agreed moment, groups gathered at convenient points over an extended area to receive information and unite in prayer. Under this arrangement a message from the head organization received careful attention, with the powerful psychological effect of mystical union.

As for sanctions, the application of psychological pressure for conversion was routine. In politics, while there was no direct connection between the Evangelicals and the government, the same people functioned in both, and they often managed to convey the impression, particularly in Great Britain, that their visits were official. The use of economic sanctions was fairly general in some aspects of the work. To complete the picture, Evangelical organizations also devoted their energies to the development of the professional branch of the service, training not only missionaries but agents highly skilled in promotional techniques.

Such was the over-all character of the regime that the Evangelicals created for the successful prosecution of ideological warfare. The techniques did not appear overnight but were the product of some fifteen years of strenuous effort on the part of the British Evangelicals, who did a great deal of earnest, experimental fumbling in attempting to meet the situation. Americans adopted the British machinery with little or no changes in its essential character. An extreme example was the Society for the Encouragement of Faithful Domestic Servants in New York, which organized in 1826 and then had to write to London to find out what it was supposed to do next.[1]

1. Cf. *First Annual Report* (New York, 1826).

As time passed, Americans polished and adjusted British methods to suit their peculiar needs, but as with the more complicated industrial machinery imported then, their social machinery was British-made.

The initial effort toward united-front organization came in foreign missions, oddly enough, it seems, until we grasp the relationship of missions to a movement of this sort. Stated in the simplest terms, no ideology with pretensions to world conquest could survive without such pretensions. It was not necessary that world conquest be achieved, but it was necessary that it be always in view. If the vision of universal dominion was permitted to fade, the penalty was loss of vitality on the home front, a veritable fracture of the psychological backbone. By 1838 the British were spending a total of about £500,000 per year to conquer the world for Christ.[2] The significant question is not how it was spent, how many souls found their way to a Christian heaven, or even what part the effort played in British imperialism. Much more significant is the fact that the raising of this considerable sum was the devoted work of nearly the entire British population. It not only demonstrated the British nation to be solidly and earnestly Christian, but it went far toward creating the condition it demonstrated.

Needless to say, Evangelical writers rarely argued this aspect of foreign missions, but it did crop out now and then in emergencies or in the shoptalk of professional operators. For example, in 1831 when the American Board of Commissioners for Foreign Missions came under attack on the ground that sending so much money out of the country would ruin the nation financially, Lyman Beecher of Cincinnati and D. T. Kimball of Ipswich, Mass., collaborated in writing a statement directly to the point. They did not bother to count the converted heathen: "The direct and powerful effect of foreign missions has been to give estimation and extent to the institutions of religion in our own land. . . ."[3] They showed that

2. Saxe Bannister, *British Colonization and Coloured Tribes* (London, 1838), 169-71.

3. *Missions will not Impoverish the Country, Missionary Paper No. XI* (Boston, c. 1831), 9.

since the start of foreign missions, efforts to evangelize the United States had increased a hundredfold.

With equal penetration the Rev. Henry Mandeville discussed the place of foreign missions in talking with a group of students at a theological seminary in New Brunswick, N.J. The title of his lecture explains itself: "The Reflex Influence of Foreign Missions." Mandeville described how foreign missions carried the banner for the whole church; they were to the church what Columbus was to Europe. They demanded vision, sacrifice, and piety absolutely essential to the vitality of religion at home.[4]

Mandeville failed to mention one contribution of foreign missions to the domestic scene: excitement. The Evangelical sermons on foreign missions were stirring: they carried the roll of drums, the rhythm of a marching host, the fire of defiance, to a foe already shaking in his boots, and the confident promise of victory under command of a glorious Leader. Returning missionaries enthralled congregations with their tales of heathen horrors; sometimes they brought exotic strangeness to drab lives with their living exhibits of converted savages. Excitement helped to make the wheels go round. Calvin Colton, suffering from an Evangelical overdose, was a little bitter about it: "But the secret of the whole matter, when scrutinized, will be found in the convenience of such excitement to keep in motion certain machineries which have been formed, and which must have a needful supply of power."[5]

Foreign missions were the primary power factor of the whole Evangelical movement. Essentially a domestic phenomenon rather than a foreign venture, foreign missions were not only logical but necessary to lead the Evangelical front on both sides of the Atlantic. They raised the Evangelical flag and shouted the Evangelical challenge to the whole world: "IN THE NAME OF OUR GOD WE LIFT UP OUR BANNERS."[6] Although the New York Missionary Society issued this battlecry, it had

4. An Address on the Reflex Influence of Foreign Missions (New York, 1847), 14-16.

5. (A Protestant), Protestant Jesuitism (New York, 1836), 34.

6. New York Missionary Society, The Address and Constitution of the New-York Missionary Society (New York, 1796), 8.

no immediate plans to carry the banners any farther than Long Island, where there was a settlement of Indian heathens. However, the Evangelical flag went up in the United States in 1796 in response to stirring news from abroad:

Events have recently occurred which deeply interest every genuine Christian. We learn, from sources the most direct and authentic, that exertions of uncommon vigour are now making, beyond the Atlantic, for extending the kingdom of our Lord Jesus Christ. A spirit of jealousy for his name, not less decisive than universal, actuates our brethren in Britain. . . . Large Societies, founded on evangelical principles, and embracing various denominations, have already been formed, and are rapidly forming, for the purpose of propagating the gospel among the unhappy Heathen. . . . Unwilling to restrict their efforts to their own immediate connections, it is their noble design to produce if possible, "a general movement of the church upon earth." It was their generous piety which gave rise to the New York Missionary Society.[7]

The generosity of British piety here included not only a good example but probably also some funds. Evangelicals who voted cash subsidies in Parliament to support the military front fell into the habit of doing the same in their societies to support the ideological front. It would have been most impolitic for the New Yorkers to advertise such grants at that time; there is only the implication of their statement and the general pattern into which such a grant would fall. Such support, together with directions for organization, would have come from the London Missionary Society. The name, the inclusion of assorted orthodox denominations, and the large representation of laity on the board of directors all marked the New York Missionary Society as the first American example of the new Evangelical impulse, the reflected image of the first British organization of its kind.

The formation of the London Missionary Society was the culmination of a mission movement started in 1790 when the Clapham Sect gave its support, typically, to some missions established by the Methodist Society. The group rarely, if ever, originated an idea; the members examined carefully the numerous proposals which came to their attention, selected one

7. *Ibid.*, 3.

appealing as not only good in itself but practical, and then backed it not merely with funds but with personal effort as well.

The next move centered around Nottingham. William Carey, a Baptist preacher, had for some years contained with difficulty an ambition to carry the gospel to India. He published his ideas at Nottingham in 1792 both orally and in type; with Baptist support he sailed for India the following spring. The *Evangelical Magazine,* established in 1792 to disseminate the Evangelical views, picked up the foreign-missions ball with an enthusiastic review of Melville Horne's appeal to all Protestant ministers in Great Britain. The review stressed the need for united effort in a task of such magnitude.[8] William Carey's first letter home aroused a great deal of interest, and the *Evangelical Magazine* followed up the excitement by publishing in its issue of September, 1794, David Bogue's appeal for action on the part of all non-Baptist Evangelical dissenters. The outcome was a general meeting in the old Spa Fields Chapel, led by the Congregationalists. The Calvinist Methodists joined, and the Clapham Sect, represented by the Rev. Henry Venn, led a faction of the Established Church to support the formation of the London Missionary Society.

The Clapham Sect did not dominate this organization, which retained its essentially Congregational leadership. Although the Clapham people, especially Wilberforce, continued to give friendly interest and support, they became a little unhappy about it all. In 1799 Henry Venn withdrew to form the Church Missionary Society for the Evangelical faction of the Established Church. Eventually the moribund official Anglican organs, the SPCK and the SPGFP, challenged both competitors, a typical example of the snowballing aspect of Evangelical energy.

But the Clapham Sect learned much from its experience with the London Missionary Society, especially about operating its favorite type of venture, the nonsectarian religious organization. Some experiments passed muster. The London Society imposed no religious test, and that hurdle was behind. More

8. Richard Lovett, *The History of the London Missionary Society, 1795-1895* (London, 1899), I, 11.

important was the grouping of several denominations with some semblance of unity. But from the Clapham point of view there were failures, too. Although election to office and to the board of directors was without restriction, the ministry predominated. Clerical influence could entrench itself, since the organization of the board was of the closed-corporation, self-perpetuating type common to English local government at that time. And the precisely religious nature of the Society's objective, foreign missions, aggravated both clerical control and sectarian disputes. If churches were to be founded, just what churches would they be? If missionaries were to be trained, who would teach them and precisely what?

For these reasons, neither the London Missionary Society nor its counterpart in the United States, the American Board of Commissioners for Foreign Missions, could ever be truly nonsectarian. For a genuinely united Christian front, the Clapham Sect needed a religious objective sufficiently vague and general to bring in the Methodists, Baptists, Quakers, and perhaps even Roman Catholics, not as denominations but as Christians.

Another lesson that the Clapham Sect seemed to have learned from the London Missionary Society could rate no higher than as a stratagem, but a most successful one. A mass communion featured the London Missionary Society's annual assembly of 1803. Clergy of the several denominations by the hundreds administered the cup to the gathering of five to six thousand people. In the midst of the rather sober ceremony, a German Jewish Protestant minister seized the cup in his hands and ventured to stammer to the assembly, in such English as he could muster, his confession of Christ. It brought down the house.[9] Piety in broken English, especially if the break be in the German direction, proved to be a tearsqueezer no loyal Englishman could resist. And this event was not to be forgotten.

Perhaps it was another lesson for the Clapham Sect. The presence of the German symbolized a shift in the London

9. Missionary Society of Connecticut, *Communications from the London Missionary Society to the Missionary Society of Connecticut* (Hartford, 1803), 6.

Society's focus of attention. At its foundation in 1795 the Society was intent on capturing for the Evangelical faith the new world in the Pacific discovered by Captain Cook's explorations,[10] and in 1797 it had twenty-nine missionaries working in the South Sea Islands. But by then interest was already shifting to the good that could be done much nearer home—on the Continent, especially in France and Italy. Since the Pope was having a hard time, the temptation to jump on him while he was down was irresistible: "The entire abolition of papal authority in France and its appendages, the overthrow of that system of superstition, which, in the judgment of Protestants, constituted the corruption of Christianity . . . are events of transcendent importance to the cause of religion. . . ."[11] And the Evangelicals could argue that Roman Catholicism was the mother of infidelity as well as of those destructive principles of rationalism causing all the trouble.[12] In their opinion, the Pope had created his own difficulties by his corruption, and if Evangelical benevolence added to the difficulties, it was no more than he deserved.

The London Missionary Society was working vigorously on the large numbers of French and Dutch prisoners of war who formed a captive audience in a very literal sense. In 1802 the Society voted to spend £848 on Bibles, texts, and catechisms in French for export. It decided to start a publication in France similar to the *Evangelical Magazine* and voted to send the Rev. Samuel Tracy to Paris for six months as the Society's agent. One of his duties was to send home six suitable Frenchmen to be trained under the Society's patronage for the Protestant ministry in France.[13]

So when the German Jewish minister caused the scalding tears of pious benevolence to roll down the cheeks of that devoted assembly in 1803, the group viewed itself not as fighting the heathen gods of the Pacific but as challenging "the

10. Lovett, *History*, I, 20.
11. London Missionary Society, *Report* (1800), as quoted by Lovett, *History*, I, 92.
12. Lovett, *History*, I, 92, 93.
13. London Missionary Society, *Report* (1802), as quoted by Lovett, *History*, I, 94, 95.

vaunts of infidelity in all lands, the impious fêtes of reason, falsely so called, and the reviving struggles of superstition [Roman Catholicism]."[14] Although this attack upon the Pope was not in line with Clapham Sect thought and policy, the London Society had demonstrated how religious benevolence could join the war effort in a direct and practical way, a Clapham objective of prime importance.

While the foreign-missions drive was getting under way, a positive, domestic propaganda, another Clapham enterprise, to replace the negative, dismal warnings of the Reeves-Dundas campaign was being developed. Hannah More, the Sect's able writer, struggled at the task while the Rev. Venn was busy with his missionaries. Her first effort came in 1792 when she met the call to counterrevolutionary propaganda with considerable trepidation. At the moment Tom Paine and his adherents were very busily spreading their printed matter in cottages, workshops, on the public roads, even at the bottoms of coal mines and pits. Hannah More sent *Village Politics* anonymously and secretly to a publisher with whom she had had no previous dealings. The tract was in the form of a dialogue between Jack Anvil, the blacksmith, and Tom Hod, the mason. Poor Tom was miserable because he had been reading a book which told him how unhappy he was. The situation gave Hannah More a nice play for her wit, and *Village Politics* went like hotcakes.[15] Its success did nothing toward relieving Miss More of such duties. She rallied some of her friends, and from 1794 her Cheap Repository Tracts, designed primarily for use in Sunday schools to teach poor children to read, enjoyed a tremendous general vogue. Some of them carried the rough wit of *Village Politics* in such passages as the remark of Clark, one of the *Two Soldiers:* "The soldier's best headquarters was the head of a beer barrel." But since Hannah More sold these tracts at such low prices that their popularity threatened to ruin her, she gave up the job in 1798.

Miss More had shown what could be done, and the financial pressure under which she suffered pointed the need for sub-

14. Missionary Society of Connecticut, *Communications,* 6.
15. Cf. Annette M. B. Meakin, *Hannah More* (London, 1911), 308-10.

sidized propaganda on a systematic basis. The London Religious Tract Society organized in 1799, with Clapham Sect blessing, to fill the gap left by Cheap Repository Tracts with material for sale at less than cost. Membership fees and donations would make up the difference. But in its first few years the Religious Tract Society failed rather miserably to replace Hannah More and her friends. It issued only doctrinal warnings and exhortations of no general appeal. There were several reasons for this state of affairs. The two Evangelical enterprises of 1799, the Church Missionary Society and the London Religious Tract Society, were in direct competition with organs of the Established Church, the SPGFP and SPCK, and were quite sensitive about it.[16] To avoid criticism, the Religious Tract Society took its lead from the SPCK[17] rather than from Hannah More. Another factor may have been the changing nature of the Sunday school, the market for which the tracts were primarily designed. The British Sunday-school system was originally a product of the Enlightenment, a secular charity designed to teach reading and writing to children who had no other opportunity to learn. At the turn of the century Evangelical pressure was converting the institution to an Evangelical nursery, and although the *Two Soldiers* with their beer-barrel headquarters had been ideal Sunday-school literature in 1792, it did not meet the changed requirements of 1799. And, finally, in 1799 Evangelical propaganda had achieved neither a confident sense of direction nor a suitable vehicle.

The situation changed radically in 1805. At that time the most famous of the Clapham nonsectarian enterprises, the British and Foreign Bible Society, was fighting tooth and nail with the High Church faction. The Religious Tract Society, under the same leadership, cast off restraints to go about its business in a more serious fashion. It determined to broaden its field and secure a monopoly of British reading matter. Therefore it cleaned up and brightened its line of tracts.

16. Cf. John Henry Overton, *The Evangelical Revival in the Eighteenth Century* (London, 1886), 138 ff.

17. Maurice J. Quinlan, *Victorian Prelude* (*Columbia University Studies in English and Comparative Literature*, No. 155 [New York, 1941]), 123.

Throwing out the SPCK approach, the Religious Tract Society changed to simple, forceful, brief stuff of wide appeal enlivened with narrative, dialogue, and illustration.

With this equipment and with increasing financial support, the London Religious Tract Society opened its price war on secular literature. It enlisted the help of bookshops and hawkers by selling to them at prices assuring them a much greater return than from sales of any other printed material. Booksellers not connected with the Society often bought tracts in bulk, added some colored prints, and bound them neatly in hard covers for sale at a nice profit. The Society also sold tickets for the convenience of Evangelical gentlemen accosted by beggars. Instead of giving the beggar a copper for his pint of bitter, one could slip him a ticket redeemable with any hawker for twelve tracts. By selling the tracts the beggar would get his pint and win a victory for piety at the same time.[18]

Another innovation was the introduction of Evangelical broadsides and posters in 1814,[19] a distinguished contribution to advertising technique, which were tacked upon walls of cottages, pubs, passenger stations, and ships. At first the broadsides were regular tracts printed on large sheets, but later they carried specific and pointed challenges, such as "Why are You an Infidel?"[20] More important than these techniques was the market provided by the rapidly expanding Sunday school as an Evangelical institution. Most helpful of all was the development of tract distribution as a social fad. Tracts came to form part of the habitual Evangelical wardrobe; a gentleman would no more venture into the street without his pocketful of tracts than without his trousers. And this volunteer distribution became highly organized as well as casual and routine after the British and Foreign Bible Society had provided a systematic pattern.

Behind the development of this expanding program stood the quality of the Religious Tract Society's product. After

18. American Tract Society (New England), *Proceedings of the First Ten Years of the American Tract Society* (Boston, 1824), 180, 181.

19. *Ibid.*, 132.

20. London Religious Tract Society, *Twenty-first Annual Report* (May 11, 1820), xiv, xv.

the break with SPCK influence in 1805, Evangelical propaganda hit its stride. It learned to serve several themes straight or mixed, seasoned to the popular taste. One of these was the warning against "infidelity" or freethinking from the days of Justice Reeves and Henry Dundas. An infidel was anyone who entertained an opinion not strictly orthodox. Infidelity and freethinking were French activities, degenerate and corrupt. Constant repetition of this idea was probably one source of the American suspicion that the French were corrupt by definition and that anything from Paris must bear the taint of some exciting irregularity.

But such warnings did not carry the Evangelical load. That was the job of four other concepts: Evangelical benevolence, conversion, contented poverty, and happy death. Benevolence usually got the story under way; conversion might involve an exotic heathen to hook into the foreign-missions interest, perhaps a French Roman Catholic for patriotism, or a child for sentiment; contented poverty hammered home the lesson of orderly, subservient conduct; and happy death offered the reward.

A series of extremely successful tracts developed each of these themes and made them the Evangelical arsenal to be used time after time with such variations and combinations as ingenuity might suggest. The sole addition of American enterprise was the tale of "mother murder": a child who misbehaved in effect murdered his mother. The story always had a temperance message in line with America's contribution to Evangelical institutions, the temperance society.

One of the tracts most successful in shaping Evangelical policy was Hannah More's *Shepherd of Salisbury Plain*. Not only did she trot out the contented-poverty myth in its most persuasive aspect but in her delineation of Mr. Fairbanks, a benevolent gentleman, she set a flattering pattern for Evangelical conduct in relation to the lower orders of society. It is a tribute to Hannah More's genius that she could write such a cerebral product as *Village Politics* and this story. But as a tearjerker, Hannah More was a rank amateur.

Perhaps more popular than *The Shepherd* was Mrs. Sherwood's little effort, *History of Little Henry and His Bearer*, tapping the foreign-missions, benevolence, double conversion and happy, pious child-death themes. The scene of this touching story was India. Little Henry was a sickly child of Anglo-Indian parents. Apparently unable to walk, he had a native bearer, Boosy, to carry him about. He was confused by the number of gods around the place, but benevolence appeared in the form of a pious young lady visitor who gave him a Bible and taught him to read it. Henry figured out that he must believe in Jesus Christ or go to hell. Not only did he believe and attain salvation for himself, but he also converted Boosy before he died a lingering and happy death at the age of eight.

Evidently this little work embodied the elements of a successful tract: brevity, exotic setting, piety, and enough emotional punch to suit the most avid sentimental appetite. It was the first book to be accepted for publication by the Sunday-School Union in Philadelphia, among the first to be endowed for perpetual circulation by the American Tract Society of New England, and when Little Henry reached New York state he almost brought the ordinary business of life to a halt.[21]

Equally popular and perhaps more important in setting a style not only for tract writing but for benevolent behavior was Legh Richmond's *The Dairyman's Daughter*, published by the London Tract Society in 1809. It sold two million copies,[22] and the Rev. Richmond is said to have received information of three hundred conversions effected by his story. Its impression upon American readers led the Rev. David Kimball to observe, "The humble piety of the Dairyman's Daughter . . . will tell upon the destinies of immortal beings, until time shall be no more."[23] The popular American version abridged the story to thirty-two pages. Its essential ingredients were two protracted deathbed scenes, two funerals, and five conversions, one of them at the graveside. The emotional tone which ac-

21. Cf. American Tract Society (New England), *Tenth Report* (1824), 141.
22. Maldwin Edwards, *After Wesley* (London, 1935), 131.
23. The General Association of Massachusetts Proper, *Minutes* (Boston, 1834), 20.

counted for the book's immense popularity was that overripe sentimentality often associated with romanticism. Richmond gave full vent to his "many pleasing yet melancholy thoughts" connected with burying the dead, the "sweet" and "profitable" meditations which "fill the heart with pleasing sadness."[24]

In several respects the Dairyman's Daughter set a theme to be played with variations by subsequent Evangelical authors. It opened directly with the Evangelical social gospel, appealing to the poor as "God's real children," representing riches, polished society, worldly importance, and high connections as obstacles and encumbrances of which the poor were free: "Let us bless the God of the poor, and pray that the poor may become rich in faith, and the rich poor in spirit."[25] Richmond found occasion to present contented poverty as pious, neat, clean, and orderly, the stereotype. In his concluding paragraph Richmond left no doubt of what his audience was to gain from reading the book: "My poor reader, the Dairyman's daughter was a poor girl, and the child of a poor man. Herein thou resemblest her: but dost thou resemble her, as she resembled Christ? Art thou made rich by faith? Hast thou a crown laid up for thee? Is thine heart set upon heavenly riches?"[26]

In the body of the book Richmond raised deathbed questioning to the art of a third degree, immensely popularizing this form of Evangelical entertainment. He represented himself as badgering with amazing persistence a girl dying of tuberculosis. During one visit little Elizabeth lost consciousness while delivering a sermon to her mother. Typical of the romantic anti-intellectualism which the Evangelicals promoted was the notion that while they were in a state of grace, children could and should instruct their elders. Rather than attempt to revive Elizabeth, the Rev. Richmond used the interval to continue Elizabeth's sermon to her mother until he could return to his original objective. Richmond obviously wanted to extend this gruesome practice, as he pointed out to his readers

24. The Dairyman's Daughter, American Tract Society, Elegant Narratives, I (New York, c. 1830), 27, 28.
25. Ibid., 8.
26. Ibid., 32. The italics are the Rev. Richmond's, or possibly those of an American editor.

the many glowing opportunities: "I have often thought what a field for usefulness and affectionate attention on the part of ministers and Christian friends, is opened by the frequent attacks and lingering progress of consumptive illness. How many such precious opportunities are daily lost, where Providence seems in so marked a way to afford time and space for serious and godly instruction!"[27]

Emphasis on infant mortality seems to have been regular practice with the Rev. Richmond, to judge from this exchange during the deathbed questioning:

Question: "What made you first think so seriously about the state of your soul?"

Answer: "Your talking about the graves in the churchyard and telling us how many little children are buried there. . . ."[28]

It is difficult to see why this sort of thing should appeal to the British, and it is even more puzzling to understand its great popularity among Americans, usually pictured as practical, energetic, materialistic, intent upon the mastery of a continent, and rather optimistic about it all. But there can be no question about the popularity. A striking example occurred in 1831 during a joint meeting of the London Religious Tract Society with representatives of the American Tract Society and the American Bible Society. Dr. James Milnor, president of the American Tract Society, toured the Isle of Wight, scene of the Rev. Richmond's most famous stories, *The Dairyman's Daughter, The Young Cottager,* and *The African Servant.* Tracts in hand, he visited the grave of the young cottager and saw the jutting rock under which Richmond had conversed with the African servant. Then he went to the cottage of the dairyman, met the brother of the dairyman's daughter, and reverently examined the daughter's Bible as well as "the chamber where the soul of Elizabeth ascended to its rest." From there he followed the route of her funeral procession to her grave in Arreton churchyard, reading the tract descriptions of the scenery through which he was passing. During this solemn journey Dr. Milnor was sometimes so overcome by his

27. *Ibid.,* 13.
28. *Ibid.,* 11.

emotions he could no longer read the pages before his blurring eyes.[29]

Such was the literature with which the British combatted the disturbing rationalism of the Enlightenment, a rationalism they increasingly identified with the public enemy. Contented conformity to a sacredly ordained social order brought priceless rewards in the form of a happy death which was only an introduction to eternal bliss. Injustice, sickness, hunger, and cold were not the fault of the social order: they were precisely that degree of evil which God ordained for the greatest good in the best of all possible worlds. And in the perspective of this propaganda, temporal discomforts were of negligible importance. Of those who conformed and made no trouble for their betters, one could say with Legh Richmond, "Whether they were rich or poor, while on earth, it is a matter of trifling consequence; the valuable part of their character is, that they are now kings and priests unto God."[30] Conversely, anyone who rebelled against conformity to the existing order of things was not rebelling against human power but against God, who had ordained the existing order. Punishment came not from man but directly from God. The rebel met all manner of misfortunes, culminating in a most unhappy death which sent him to the hottest imaginable hell.

Confronting their public with the uncomfortable choice between a happy life followed by eternal agony on the one hand and a miserable existence with happy death on the other, the Evangelicals had the unanswerable argument—death lasts longer. And they were not reluctant to press their advantage. From a low point in 1804 when the sales of tracts totaled only 314,613, production of the London Religious Tract Society rose rapidly. In the year 1808, sales through the bookstores alone went to 1,400,000 copies, and the Society found satisfaction in the thought that putting its product into commercial channels at less than cost price had forced out of circulation about 300,000 "profane" books. By 1814 the Society's annual production of tracts had risen to 3,100,000 and ten years later

29. American Tract Society, *Sixth Annual Report* (New York, 1831), 20.
30. *The Dairyman's Daughter,* 8.

went over the ten-million mark.[31]   These figures did not include the Society's large output of the standard Evangelical
authors, Doddridge, Baxter, and Alleine, as well as Pike's
Persuasives to Early Piety and Bunyan's *Pilgrim's Progress.*
Broadsides also swelled the total.

In promoting tract distribution, the London Tract Society
enjoyed the help of auxiliaries numbering 207 by 1824, but
quite as important was the effect of this energetic work upon
friendly imitators and competitors.   For example, the Liverpool Tract Society started publishing in 1814 the same material
as the London Society.   Haddington started in the same line
in 1805.   Edinburgh, Glasgow, Bristol, and even Dublin followed.   The Established Church responded with two efforts,
the Prayer Book and Homily Society, founded in London in
1812, and the Church of England Tract Society, started in
Bristol the year before.   The Methodists also made a separate
effort in Sheffield.[32]

At a time when reading matter was relatively scarce and
expensive, the mass production and distribution of Evangelical
propaganda was unquestionably successful in making a deep
impression upon British minds.   It would be a mistake, however, to believe that the whole effect of this activity, or perhaps
even the major effect, was upon the lower classes.   As distribution of the tracts became a fad among the more respectable
elements of the population, they must have come to believe
quite sincerely in the persuasion they administered to others.
Or at least they must have believed quite sincerely that it was
suitable for them to promote the doctrines among the lower
classes.   Perhaps it all comes to the same thing, considering the
nature of the doctrines.   At any rate, the London Tract Society
could feel in 1820 that it had indeed made some progress in its
battle for the British mind: "the devouring flame which threatened destruction on every hand, is indeed checked and confined
within narrower limits; but we are still proceeding upon embers
as yet but half extinguished, and glowing beneath our feet.
The minds which have been tainted with infidel principles,

31. American Tract Society, *Proceedings,* 180, 181.
32. Quinlan, *Victorian Prelude,* 124.

still retain their hostility toward Christianity, although the outward manifestation of their enmity may be in some measure repressed."[33]

Although the Sunday-school movement provided a steady market for tracts, that was incidental to its principal function. Control of public education is a prime factor in the policy of any ideology aspiring to national status, but the Evangelicals faced a situation in which there was no public education to control. Of course there were the great public schools, but they were for the rich only. For the middle class there were a few crumbling grammar schools. After 1779, nonconformists could lawfully teach, and a number of private schools for dissenters opened, but they were not important.

As for the poor whom the Evangelicals wanted especially to reach with the doctrine of Christian contentment, the vast majority were wholly illiterate. It was to the credit of the Clapham Sect and the Evangelicals on both sides of the Atlantic that they realized the necessity of a radical measure for the preservation of their ideology. Suppression might subdue the adult working class, but future stability required that their children be taught the Evangelical story and accept it as the natural order of things. Thus the Evangelicals mustered strength to defeat the extreme conservatives of the Burke and Reeves type and eventually to establish the foundations of public education in both Great Britain and the United States.

There was not much to start with. In the years following 1698, the SPCK had fostered some charity schools which put poor children into uniforms and taught them to read. They apprenticed the boys to handicraft trades and sent out the girls to menial service. With typical English stodginess, these schools never changed the style of their uniforms; in the course of a century or so they became distinctively charming to everyone but the wearers. For a few years these schools throve, but by 1800 they had declined badly in numbers and strength.

More promising to the Clapham Sect was the Sunday-school movement. Although several parishes had started such free schools for the poor before 1780, Robert Raikes advertised his

33. London Religious Tract Society, *Twenty-First Annual Report*, xvi.

Sooty Alley school in his *Gloucester Journal* and thus identified himself with the origin of the movement.[34] It began to gather headway when a Baptist, William Fox, with help from the Clapham Sect, organized the London Sunday-School Society in 1785 as a nonsectarian charitable enterprise.

During the next ten years the Society established more than one thousand schools, but it was moving too slowly to suit Evangelical ideas. One handicap was the inability of the London Sunday-School Society to break loose from traditional methods of school operation. Hired rooms, paid teachers, and donated supplies made these schools too expensive for rapid expansion. But a more serious effect was undoubtedly the same shift of public opinion which killed the antislave-trade legislation and labeled as subversive any liberal activity. The Church fought Sunday schools as hotbeds of vice and sedition; the conservative right wing claimed that the education of the poor savored too much of French equalitarianism and that these schools turned out servants who were supercilious, demanded higher wages, and generally embarrassed the upper classes. Curates persecuted teachers and charged Hannah More with fomenting sedition.[35] In general the extreme conservatives took the position that children who learned to read the Bible were now reading Tom Paine. Illiteracy of the poor was the best guarantee of domestic peace, they thought.[36]

In the face of these discouragements the London Sunday-School Society was losing ground when the London Sunday-School Union organized in 1803 to give new life to the movement. The main contribution of the Union was to capture the Sunday-school movement for the Evangelical cause, to shift it out of the role of Christian charity into that of Evangelical benevolence. The Union took the essential step in that direction by changing from paid teachers to volunteers. Then Sunday-school teaching became one of the recognized benevolent activities at a time when benevolence was attaining its status

34. Quinlan, *Victorian Prelude*, 45, 46.
35. Edwin Wilbur Rice, *The Sunday-School Movement, 1780-1917, and the American Sunday-School Union, 1817-1917* (Philadelphia, 1917), 19, 20.
36. Quinlan, *Victorian Prelude*, 82.

as fad. The Union was not slow to realize and organize this
potential. In 1805 it published a plan for organizing Sunday
schools and also a guide for teachers, two essential helps to
enthusiastic amateurs, and by 1811 it had a regular periodical,
The Repository or Teachers' Magazine, to give circulation to
the latest ideas.

That there were new ideas was evidence of new vitality.
Since England was so backward in educational techniques, far
behind all Protestant countries on the Continent, there was
ample room for experiment. The London Sunday-School
Union tried out the Lancaster system of student monitors
without much success, then a Scotch method, another British
plan, and three European systems, all with indifferent results.
In the meantime its American cousins were doing much better,
and the London Union settled on a program of reprinting the
material of the American Sunday-School Union, a return of
compliment long overdue.[37]

On the whole the British continued to lack imagination in
their conduct of Sunday schools. In most respects they reflected current secular practice. To organize a school they
hired a room, ranged it with benches on either side, one for
boys, the other for girls, and filled these benches on Sundays
with poor children from the streets, using such inducements as
seemed necessary. There was a chalk line in the middle of the
floor; when called upon by the teacher, a child "toed the mark"
to deliver his memorized lesson, usually a few verses of scripture,
to spell, or to read. Instruction in spelling was to assist reading, not writing. Strong opposition to teaching children to
write came from the very people who were so intent upon
teaching them to read.[38] These children were in training for
their stations in life as servants and laborers, and writing was
an upper-class accomplishment. This outlook suggests that
the main purpose of the Sunday schools was not education but
indoctrination.

In addition to bringing its work within the scope and

37. Rice, *Sunday-School Movement,* 36.
38. Cf. Maldwin Edwards, *After Wesley* (London, 1935), 106, 107; Bernard N.
Schilling, *Conservative England and the Case against Voltaire* (New York, 1950),
79.

purpose of Evangelical benevolence, the London Sunday-School Union adopted the Evangelical system of auxiliary societies with considerable success. They carried the Union's work into the manufacturing towns, such as Liverpool, Manchester, Birmingham, Leeds, and Sheffield, so vigorously that London activity comprised only about 10 per cent of the total. By 1818 there were 5,463 Sunday schools operating in England and Wales, most of them within the Union. The total enrollment of children was 477,225.[39] Eventually, Sunday-school enrollment far exceeded the combined total of all other schools of all varieties.

On the whole the Sunday-school structure formed a substantial youth movement to support the nonsectarian Evangelical front. Not only did it bring conservative pressure to bear on that segment of society causing the most trouble but it provided a useful and socially popular outlet for the patriotic enthusiasm of the younger set of Evangelicals.

However, it is doubtful whether the missionary, tract, and Sunday-school societies could have attained the strength they achieved without the leadership of the greatest of the Evangelical ventures, the British and Foreign Bible Society. This organization fought the battle of nonsectarian unity against the vested interests of the Established Church; it made the Evangelical cause socially acceptable; it developed methods of organization and techniques of operation widely and successfully copied throughout Great Britain and the United States. Many of these are still in use today.

39. Rice, *Sunday-School Movement*, 37.

VI

THE BRITISH AND FOREIGN BIBLE SOCIETY

IN 1804 CIRCUMSTANCES enabled the Clapham Sect to complete and weld together its machinery for ideological warfare with a national, nonsectarian organization for printing and distributing Bibles. The Sunday-school, tract, and missionary societies were all discovering, developing, and creating needs for Bibles. The SPCK enjoyed a monopoly but failed to meet the growing demand—at least, those interested could make out a case that the SPCK failed to meet the demand, and since the objection arose from nonsectarian and dissenting sources, there is some probability that the SPCK could muster a certain amount of indifference. The only existing societies interested in Bible distribution were those of the Established Church, exclusively devoted to the armed forces.

In addition to creating the need for Bibles, the Clapham Sect had demonstrated that organized, nonsectarian action was possible, and conditions were ripe for a major effort in that direction. The British were sufficiently frightened in 1804 to make a united front not only possible but welcome. The French empire was established; it embraced Europe to the left bank of the Rhine. Napoleon was across the Channel, building flat-boats. Business was bad. The British working classes were sufficiently distressed and disorderly to suggest the possibility of simultaneous invasion and revolution. The time for the major Clapham enterprise was at hand:

The *"signs of the times"* appeared . . . portentious—*"Men's hearts failing them for fear"*; and something was required that should erect a secure mound against the tide of infidelity and the waves of licentiousness. Of what materials *could* that safeguard be composed, if the BIBLE proved insufficient to stem the torrent? What voice *could* lead the poor man to the path of peace and safety, if that of sympathy and kindness from the lips of his superiors proved ineffectual? What footsteps would be welcome at his humble door, if those of Mercy and Gentleness and Benevolence were repelled?[1]

The Clapham Sect had been exploring the Bible idea for more than a year before it put the idea to the test of organization. Late in 1802, the Rev. Thomas Charles, minister of the Established Church who was active in promoting Sunday schools in Wales, appeared at a meeting of the London Religious Tract Society to complain of the lack of Bibles in Wales. The Tract Society decided that Wales was not alone in its needs; it requested the Rev. Joseph Hughes, a Baptist, to prepare an address bringing the subject to the attention of the public. Hughes took his problem to Clapham, where Wilberforce and Charles Grant went to work on it in a most modern, businesslike fashion. They formulated a questionnaire designed to give them the information they required to evaluate the Bible idea:

1. Can the poor in your neighborhood read?
2. To what extent are they furnished with the Holy Scriptures?
3. Do they discover a solicitude to read them?
4. What has been done towards supplying this want?
5. Are there persons in your neighborhood willing further to encourage the distribution of the Holy Scriptures in our own and in foreign lands?[2]

The Rev. Hughes circulated the questionnaire through the United Kingdom and Ireland while the Rev. C. F. A. Stein-

1. C. E. Dudley, *An Analysis of the System of the Bible Society* (London, 1821), 214-15.
2. John Owen, *The History of the Origin and First Ten Years of the British and Foreign Bible Society* (New York, 1817), 10.

kopff, pastor of a German Lutheran church in the Savoy, undertook similar inquiries on the Continent. Joseph Hardcastle,
treasurer of the London Missionary Society, carried the questions to France. He reported that it took four days to find a
Bible in the Paris book stores; he could sell five thousand copies
there at a profit.[3] The London Missionary Society thereupon
voted an appropriation of £848 for Christian literature to be
distributed in France and Italy.[4]

Hardcastle, a wealthy merchant, was also a member of the
executive committee of the London Religious Tract Society,
which held a meeting in the spring of 1803 where he could talk
with the Revs. Steinkopff and Hughes about the Bible problem.
In the meantime the Clapham Sect had decided that the distribution of the Bible offered great possibilities for united action
of all Christian sects and that as a basis of unity it had best be
kept free of all other propaganda activities. The difficulties in
nonsectarian missionary, tract, and Sunday-school operations
had taught the Sect something.

So when the Rev. Hughes spoke not for another activity of
the Religious Tract Society but for a wholly new society, he
must have carried the Clapham word and the Clapham promise
of massive support. He met with no opposition, only enthusiastic assent. And when the Religious Tract Society held its
general meeting in May, 1803, it was to endorse the formation
of a new nonsectarian Bible society whose constitution had
already been drafted.[5]

This proposal left the Rev. Hughes free to write his essay
advocating the "first Institution that ever emanated from one
of the nations in Europe, for the express purpose of doing good
to all the rest."[6] The Clapham Sect gave the essay wide distribution and condensed its essential points in a circular calling
a meeting for organization. The circular showed some careful
composition: "The projected Society, not refusing to cooperate

3. Missionary Society of Connecticut, *Communications from the London
Missionary Society to the Missionary Society of Connecticut* (Hartford, 1803), 12.
4. William Canton, *A History of the British and Foreign Bible Society*
(London, 1904), I, 8.
5. *Ibid.*, 9-11.
6. Owen, *History*, 16.

on the same ground, would traverse scenes which the other Societies are, by their regulations, forbidden to occupy; and, presenting nothing but the inspired volume, would be sure to circulate the truth, and truth alone; hereby avoiding the occasions of controversy, and opening a channel into which Christians of every name might, without scruple, pass their charitable contributions."[7]

In a further attempt to mollify inevitable opposition, the Clapham Sect sent letters with plans for its proposed British and Foreign Bible Society to the SPCK and to the Association for Discountenancing Vice and Promoting the Knowledge of the Christian Religion in Dublin. The latter replied cordially, as it should have to another Wilberforce enterprise, but from the SPCK there was no response.[8] However, through the Rev. John Owen, rector of Paglesham, Essex, the Sect managed to enlist in advance the support of Bishop Porteus of London, a maneuver of considerable importance.

About three hundred men of various denominations attended the meeting for organization in a London tavern on March 7, 1804. Granville Sharp presided, and there was a generous sprinkling of his antislave-trade friends. The project threatened to fall flat on its face while this odd assortment of chronic enemies sniffed each other like a pack of strange dogs. The four originators of the Bible Society idea spoke without any effect except cold assent. But then Steinkopff rose to give the group the broken-English treatment, and everything changed: when he sat down there was not a dry eye or a hard thought in the house.[9]

Much moved, the Rev. Owen offered the resolution for organization, which passed handily. It set the scale of membership dues and established a committee of thirty-six members to conduct the Society's business. There was enough enthusiasm to produce £700 in contributions on the spot.

But the essential difficulties were still there when members of the committee met five days later to shape a going organization. It looked for a while as though they would follow the

7. *Ibid.*, 19.   8. *Ibid.*, 57, 58.
9. *Ibid.*, 21-25.

London Missionary Society into the hands of dissent, for the committee wanted to appoint the Rev. Hughes, Baptist, its secretary. The Rev. Owen fought stubbornly for the interests of the Established Church, so they made him secretary, too. For good measure they added the Rev. Steinkopff as foreign secretary. That brought the balance of power into the open where the committee could deal with it, but only by reorganizing itself. The resulting settlement reduced friction by providing a wholly lay committee on which fifteen seats were to go to members of the Established Church, fifteen to dissenting sects, and the remaining six seats to foreigners. Re-election was open to the twenty-four with the best attendance records.

With lay control assured, the committee soothed clerical pride by extending a seat and a vote to any clergyman who was a member, but balancing this concession was the same provision to anyone who would give fifty guineas in a lump sum or five guineas annually. However, as board membership for both of these classes was a privilege rather than an obligation, attendance would be infrequent; the practical effect which was intended and achieved was lay control, with clerical staff and clerical guidance. Lack of a religious test for membership was also significant in lay strength.

This compromise and balance of power found approval at the second meeting of the Society in May, 1804, and cleared the way for businessmen and politicians to show what they could do in the promotion of an adventure in patriotic religion.

A first and an abiding concern of the lay committee was to give the Society a social position above challenge. Public opinion was not to consider this effort to be the effervescence of religious fanatics: "it became an object of serious attention with the Committee, to look out for such patronage as might shield their undertaking from the charge of insignificance, and stamp it with the recommendatory sanction of some 'high' and honorable name."[10] In this need, the Clapham strength was helpful. Zachary Macaulay, member of the Sect, author, and governor-general of Bengal, joined with Bishop Porteus in persuading their mutual friend Lord Teignmouth of the East

10. *Ibid.*, 36.

India Company to serve as president. Teignmouth signed the Society's prospectus before it was printed; this good start helped to line up four more bishops as well as four well-known lay aristocrats to pay membership dues of five guineas and to assume vice-presidential posts.

The British and Foreign Bible Society therefore had no cause to blush for the names heading its first prospectus: for the numerous members of the British upper classes who were intent upon doing the proper thing, joining became distinctly the proper thing to do. And as the work of the Society progressed, the advantages of membership became increasingly clear. As one who was perhaps a little critical of the Society's work remarked, "Though its *splendor* is derived from the operations abroad, its *influence* depends on the operations at home. It *there* provides for *temporal,* as well as *spiritual* wants. It gives *power* to the dissenter, *popularity* to the churchman, and *interest* to the politicians, which is useful at *all* times, and especially *at the approach of a general election.*"[11]

The social machinery which opened such opportunities to the British gentry throughout the United Kingdom developed experimentally but rather rapidly. The first auxiliary to the British and Foreign Bible Society appeared in London in 1805. Its purpose was to organize those who wished to share in the Society's work but could not afford the minimum membership fee of one guinea. A second auxiliary developed in Birmingham the following year with a businesslike procedure which must have impressed the committee in London. The promoters seem to have been a group of laymen who joined with the clergy and the magistrates to canvass the city thoroughly. They divided Birmingham into twelve districts, appointing a collector for each, while the clergy worked on their congregations. The proceeds went to London as a "united contribution" with a list of subscribers entitled to purchase Bibles at the 20 per cent discount which the Society granted its members.[12]

But the true auxiliary idea appeared for the first time when

11. Herbert Marsh, "Inquiry into the Consequences of Neglecting to Give the Prayer Book with the Bible," *The Pamphleteer,* I (1813), 150-51.
12. Canton, *History,* I, 48.

Reading organized its Bible Society in 1809 on a permanent basis with commitments to send half of its funds to the parent body and retain the other half for expenses, including the purchase of Bibles. In that year the machinery began to roll: four more auxiliaries formed in 1809, and by 1814, when every county in England had one, the total number had risen to 161.[13] According to the official history of the Society, its rapid growth greatly surprised its founders.[14] However, to unfriendly observers on the spot it appeared that the members of the British and Foreign Bible Society "have accurately calculated the power of every part of their apparatus."[15] Quite possibly both of these statements are true: the leaders of the Society moved with skill and precision, while the rising fad of benevolence swept their efforts to success far beyond their expectations.

In a typical drive for a new auxiliary, the successive steps in organization followed quite precisely those of the parent body. The first move was to line up patronage. Auxiliaries were high society, aimed at the top social and economic levels. As the Society's centennial historian remarked, "but if there had been no Auxiliaries, the Society would never have secured the brilliant *cortège* of nobility and gentry which these local bodies enlisted for it in all parts of the kingdom."[16] The next task was to secure a meeting-place, perferably a church; often this was a difficult task, for the High Church faction controlled many. However, once one was finally secured, the promoters erected a platform before the reading desk and finished arrangements for the public assembly. The meetings were protracted: they started at eleven in the morning and did not complete their business until tea-time at five. Probably there was a break for refreshment. A local gentleman of standing, usually a member of the nobility, was called to the chair to get proceedings under way. The chairman then presented in turn three members of the parent Society to describe its purposes. These

13. *Ibid.*, 65.
14. *Ibid.*, 62.
15. *A Practical Exposition of the Tendency and Proceedings of the British and Foreign Bible Society,* H. H. Norris, ed. (London, 1813), 292.
16. Canton, *History,* I, 65.

earnest expositions led to the climax: Dr. Steinkopff rose to express the gratitude of Europe; his broken English never failed to open tearducts and purses. When business called the Rev. Steinkopff to the Continent, a Swede, Dr. Brunmark, filled this crucial spot on the program effectively and in the same way.[17]

After the meeting of organization, the new auxiliary printed an eight-page circular containing its proceedings, constitution, and address to the public for distribution throughout the parish. Follow-up of this circular enlisted the interest of those who failed to attend the meeting and produced membership dues and donations amounting to several hundred pounds. In areas within its domain but beyond the distance of convenient attendance, the auxiliaries established branches[18] which operated in about the same relationship to the auxiliaries as those bore to the parent establishment in London.

Such was the organization of the gentry in London and the United Kingdom, a hierarchy topped by a lay group of considerable power in the metropolis, extending its influence over the land with a vast network of auxiliaries and branches. It exhibited distinctly the genius of veteran businessmen accustomed to achieving results with precision and speed. But the network was only a preliminary step in the design of the British and Foreign Bible Society: the organized gentry constituted a working force to achieve a fundamental purpose, the indoctrination of the lower orders of society in Christianity, with its lesson of blessed contentment in things as they were.

Procedures became standardized in 1811 when Richard Phillips, on behalf of the parent Society, investigated the activities of existing auxiliaries and drew up a code of rules for their operation.[19] Sharp criticism by the High Church faction evidently moved the London committee to control more closely the work of its auxiliaries. Supporters of the right-wing SPKG charged "that Bibles are profaned to the basest purposes, being

17. Norris, ed., *Exposition*, 292, 293.
18. Owen, *History*, 580, 581.
19. Data for the procedures described here are from Norris, ed., *Exposition*, 322.

hawked about by Jew Boys amongst their contemptible mer-
chandize, being in use at Cheesemongers to wrap up their
articles of traffic, and being bartered at the Gin Shop for the
means of intoxication."[20]

It was the job of Richard Phillips to bring order out of
chaos among the auxiliaries, to convince them that their task
was not to throw Bibles around but to organize and manage the
poor and to discipline them by making them buy their own
Bibles. Phillips drew together tested ideas from several sources,
one of which was very probably the "Hamburg Experiment,"
familiar to the British through a pamphlet published in London
in 1796, *An Account of the management of the Poor in Hamburg since the year 1788.* Two years later the Rev. Malthus
gave the Hamburg work further publicity in his book on
population.

The essence of the Hamburg idea was the subdivision of
each poor neighborhood into small districts with systematic
investigation and visitation of each district under the supervision of a central bureau to prevent overlapping.[21] Phillips
apparently added to the system the penny-a-week financial
method developed by the Methodists for their classes. Fusion
of these two concepts gave Phillips his code of rules for the
performance of auxiliaries adopted by the London committee
in 1811. Under the code, the first move was the division of
the auxiliary committee, constituted along the same lines as in
London, into subcommittees. Each of these assumed responsibility for its allotted district in the territory to be worked. The
program of each subcommittee contemplated a series of weekly
meetings of the lower classes resident in its district. Monday
was the favorite day, since the previous week's pay was still
unspent and the poor were often idle on the last day of the long
week end typical during the transition from village industry to
the urban factory system. The purpose of these weekly meetings was to organize Bible associations among the poor on a
permanent, self-sustaining basis.

20. Letter V, Norris to Freshfield, Norris, ed., *Exposition,* 47-48.
21. Daniel T. McColgan, *Joseph Tuckerman, Pioneer in American Social
Work* (Washington, D.C., 1940), 112-14.

It was essential to the Society's aims that attendance at the meetings be good. It could hardly be otherwise if the sponsors followed the procedures prescribed on the folio sheets which the parent society supplied, *Hints on the Constitution and Objects of Auxiliary and Subordinate Societies.*[22] The first step in assuring attendance was to distribute through the district a handbill with such messages as these:

Appeal to Mechanics, Labourers, and others, respecting Bible Associations.

. . . . .

THE British and Foreign Bible Society is a treasury, open to receive not only the gifts of the rich, but the mites of the poor.

. . . . .

The poor are as deeply interested in the success of the Bible Society as any other class of people,—and in the promotion of this great work, perhaps THEY CAN DO MORE THAN THE RICH. How?—A penny a week subscribed by every poor person in this kingdom, who really could afford it out of his earnings without hurting his family;—for how little food can a penny purchase!—would exceed, on a very moderate calculation, *half a million annually*. And who can *not* afford a penny a week for such a noble end?[23]

With the handbill went a questionnaire requiring a positive answer whether the recipient would attend the scheduled meeting:

Bible Association among the Poor, connected with the Hackney and Newington Auxiliary Bible Society.

The object of this Paper is to inform you of the design, and to ask you to promote it. You will be so good, therefore, as to consider the subject, and to give an answer to the following questions:—

*Place for
Answers*

How many Bibles or Testaments have [you] in your family, and how many are you in family?

Are you ready to join in supplying yourselves and others with the Word of God, by subscribing a Penny a Week?

A General Meeting will be held in July, to which you are invited: will you attend it?

Your answer to the above enquiries will be called for.[24]

22. Norris, ed., *Exposition*, 324, n. K.
23. *Ibid.*, 328, 331.
24. *Ibid.*, 340-41.

At a time when the questionnaire technique was new, these documents, often bearing the names of magistrates, hit the lower orders with the impact of official citations;[25] when the members of the subcommittee entered the poor man's dwelling to receive his answer, there was little likelihood of anything but a co-operative response.

Convened at its Monday meeting under the guidance of the auxiliary subcommittee, the Bible association organized with a membership of all those pledged to the penny-a-week, shilling-the-quarter formula. These chose a secretary and treasurer of the association and then divided into classes of not more than twenty-four members. Each of these classes elected its collector, who became also a member of the association committee. An example of an early organization of this nature was the Willow Walk Bible Association, formed in 1812. Its members were chiefly journeymen weavers, although the chairman of its committee was a chimney sweeper and old-rag merchant.[26] In operation, the collectors of the classes turned over their weekly contributions to the treasurer of the Association, who used the money to purchase Bibles from the auxiliary until the territory was supplied. Then all funds went to the auxiliary for its use.

Such was the rather crude structure of the early Bible association. There was an obvious weakness in the great reliance upon the poor to enforce their own discipline. By 1811 a new element of strength entered into these activities, one changing the nature of Bible association operation to put it on a much more effective basis. The gentlemen of the auxiliaries did their patriotic and religious duties toward the poor, but their wives and daughters were the ones to pick up the burden and build the success of the British and Foreign Bible Society.

The ladies did not win their freedom to voluntary association without a sharp struggle, and they could hardly have done so at that time had not the Evangelical leadership been with them all the way in the face of the sharpest criticism from the High Church faction. The Evangelicals did not admit women

25. *Ibid.,* 322, 323.
26. *Ibid.,* 327n.

to membership or attendance in their parent societies,[27] but in preparing for meetings to launch Bible society auxiliaries they advertised, "Seats will be provided for the Ladies."[28] Even this offer was apparently a bold move at the time, for it brought scathing comment.

Eagerly accepting the invitation, the ladies then had to find some outlet for their benevolent enthusiasm. They seized upon the system formulated by Richard Phillips in 1811; in that year female Bible associations started blossoming spontaneously in all directions to take up the work of distributing Bibles to the poor. In defiance of the indecorum of young ladies' entering cottages of the poor alone, at the risk of having their feelings hurt by improper language and their delicacy wounded by unpleasant scenes, the girls of Manchester and Salford issued a proclamation of female freedom. They claimed that "the sickly refinement, fastidious delicacy and helpless dependence of females which was the idol of former years, has been exploded by the better taste and sense of the present age."[29]

With some uneasiness, Evangelical leadership went along with this development. At the main office in London, Secretary Owen wanted to use overflowing female energy in his holy cause if he could do so in a manner "comporting with that delicacy which has ever been considered as characteristic of the sex, and which constitutes one of its best ornaments and its strongest securities."[30] A compromise cleared the way to everybody's satisfaction: the ladies could meet and organize, provided that a gentleman always presided at such gatherings. This system would satisfy I Timothy 2:12: "But I suffer not a woman to teach, nor to usurp authority over man, but to be in silence." Such a sop to male egotism did not discourage the girls; it only made the meetings the more exciting. In fact the popularity of male attendance led eventually to another important innovation, the professional agency system.

27. Ladies were first permitted to attend meetings of the British and Foreign Bible Society in 1831. See Canton, *History*, I, 59.
28. Norris, ed., *Exposition*, 272.
29. Canton, *History*, I, 58.
30. *Ibid.*

Naturally the Atlantic was no barrier to this war of the sexes and although, as the history books say, there was a war between the countries, the girls were not fighting. In 1814 ladies of Philadelphia timidly inquired of Bishop White whether it would not be more proper for them to contribute their money simply and quietly to the Philadelphia Bible Society than to form female societies of their own. The bishop replied quite boldly that they would contribute more and do better work in distributing Bibles if they had their own societies; they need not be apprehensive of exceeding the bounds of modesty as long as such associations were among themselves.[31] Bishop Hobart of New York had other ideas. Representing the High Church point of view in the United States, he supported the Rev. Norris' scorn "of *females* laying aside the delicacy and decorum, which can never be violated without the most *corrupting* effects on themselves and public morals,"[32] to invade private households in the absence of the owners, soliciting contributions for Bible societies from children and servants.

The battle for American female freedom was not confined to the Episcopal Church but rapidly spread northward to New England for decision by Congregational potentates.[33] On all sides Bishop White's position prevailed by a wide margin; female Bible societies and "cent societies" blossomed in profusion over the American landscape. And American girls seem to have won more handsomely than their British cousins, since they were free to associate without the presence of a male presiding officer. Doubtless a local clergyman contributed whatever excitement a pair of trousers could lend to such gatherings, but his presence was not a requirement.

In the meantime, the enthusiasm of the British ladies was at work with truly marvelous efficiency, not so much because of superior female talent, a quality no writer would venture to

31. Female Bible Society of Philadelphia, *Constitution and Address* (Philadelphia, 1814), 5-8.
32. John Henry Hobart, *A Pastoral Letter to the Laity of the Protestant Episcopal Church in the State of New York on the Subject of Bible and Common Prayer Book Societies* (New York, 1815), 11.
33. Cf. *The Panoplist*, XII (1816), 256-60.

question, as of the genius of C. S. Dudley, known by his critics as "the Society's Sergeant Major in the female department."[34] Dudley was one of those inconspicuous workhorses, like the Rev. Samuel Mills in the United States, who made the dreams of great men come true. Although he never attained greatness for himself, his work has had a far-reaching influence in Western civilization.

Dudley started devoting himself to the Bible society cause in 1815 in a purely voluntary capacity, aiming his efforts exclusively for the benefit of the ladies. He drew up a code of rules and bylaws for their use and busily traveled around getting them straightened out.[35] Through experience he perfected his procedures, finally publishing them in 1821 under the title *An Analysis of the System of the Bible Society*, a work his enemies labeled, with more accuracy than grace, "Bible Society Craft, made easy to the meanest capacity."[36] The book became a general guide to American practice in 1827.

In the meantime, Dudley had done a great deal of work. Aside from highly organizing the labors of existing female Bible associations, he started 180 new ones in the course of his first five years at this task. During 1817-18, he traveled 4,500 miles, attended 107 auxiliary committee meetings and 128 general meetings which founded 59 new organizations, and he had done all of it at his own expense. Such a schedule obviously afforded Dudley little time for his own affairs, and business reverses brought his work to a halt. Thereupon the British and Foreign Bible Society promptly hired Dudley as its first accredited home agent, whom it could well afford. Receipts from auxiliaries had risen from £5,945 in the fiscal year 1809-10 to £61,848 in 1814-15, almost solely because of the work of the ladies in their associations,[37] and Dudley was to carry the total to £83,707 by 1824.

The appointment of Dudley as a full-time professional agent created a precedent of great importance. Other appointments followed, and the promotion of social organization came to be

34. William Jay (A Churchman, *pseud.*), *A Letter to the Right Reverend Bishop Hobart* (New York, 1823), 75.

35. Canton, *History*, I, 352.   36. Jay, *Letter*, 73.

37. Canton, *History*, I, 53.

the vested interest of a professional class. That success without paid agents was improbable or impossible became the accepted idea on both sides of the Atlantic; by 1837 in the United States agents were said to swarm "like the locusts of Egypt."[38]

During the post-war years, Dudley's system was hard at work in England. In effect it took Bible association membership away from the laboring classes and gave it to the ladies of Dudley's organizations. This transference rendered the role of the lower orders entirely passive except for the weekly penny contribution. Aside from providing an outlet for frustrated female energy, this move possibly stemmed from two other sources. Elected officers of the laboring classes were probably inefficient and unenthusiastic. Also, any meeting of workers at that time was presumptively subversive. Dudley's plan increased the pressure on these people but did not bring them together.

Dudley said it was easy to start a female Bible association; all one need do was to introduce the subject at an annual meeting of an auxiliary or branch society. At the appointed time the ladies gathered with a gentleman to preside over their deliberations. They first chose a patroness of sufficient quality to render their proceedings socially respectable, a step their American cousins often neglected. Next they elected of their own number a president, two vice-presidents, a treasurer, and three secretaries. Each of the remaining members bore the title of "collector." On the following Monday a committee of the members met at a schoolhouse and divided the association's territory into districts of about fifty houses each. To each district the committee assigned three collectors, who were to work in pairs, with an alternate available to ease the inevitable inconveniences. To each district with its team the association committee also allotted certain supplies: six copies of the rules and bylaws, visiting book, collecting book, collecting bag, form of monthly report, twenty Bible subscriber cards, twenty transfer tickets, and a supply of printed information for distribution.

Thus equipped, the collectors went to work each Monday,

38. Calvin Colton (A Protestant, *pseud.*), *Protestant Jesuitism* (New York, 1836), 132.

recording in the visiting book rather full accounts of their interviews. Instructions asked them to note much information besides contributions received: number in family, ability to read, possession of Bible, condition of the family, relief indicated, and other items. This sort of inquiry naturally developed into a recruiting effort for Sunday schools. If the family moved, the transfer ticket enabled it to carry credit for contributions to another district or Bible association. The Bible subscriber cards gave holders the right to claim their Bibles at public distribution, another publicity feature.[39]

By 1821 there were more than one thousand Bible associations operating in this pattern in the United Kingdom under the guidance of about 650 auxiliaries and branches of the British and Foreign Bible Society.[40] To a degree one can judge the intensity of coverage by examining the work of one of the more successful auxiliaries at Southwark, a city of 150,000. That auxiliary must have enlisted almost the total population of upper and upper middle-class ladies in its work, for it had twelve Bible associations with a total membership of 650.[41] In eleven and one-half years of operation, this auxiliary issued 31,722 Bibles and Testaments, of which 28,478 went out through these associations. Of the £18,786 that the Southwark Auxiliary managed to raise, £12,589 came to it in the collecting bags of the ladies. It seems clear that the poor paid generously for their own indoctrination.

As this form of doing good to the poor became a fad with the upper classes, enthusiasm could not confine itself to the pattern of association districts. Employers signed up their workers in mechanics' associations to collect at the rate of one penny to sixpence per week. For example, in 1812 the 125 employees of Storr & Co., Dean St., Soho, London, formed such an association, putting their names to rules drawn up by their employers. Whether these rules included deduction of dues from pay is uncertain. During the next eight years, members of this association paid in £271.10.6, for which they received 304 Bibles and 26 Testaments at a cost of £129.11.8;

39. Dudley, *Analysis,* 415, 416.   40. *Ibid.,* 1.
41. Canton, *History,* I, 56.

the balance went as a contribution to the British and Foreign Bible Society.[42]

Employee activity extended with less success to the crews of ships. Sailors, viewed by Evangelicals as prospective self-supporting missionaries, proved disappointing to benevolence. More successful was the extension of the penny-a-week idea to Sunday-school classes and private schools, especially the seminaries for young ladies. Dudley himself developed still another opening. As secretary of the Guardian Society for the reformation of prostitutes, he discovered that out of 200 of these "wretched females," 150 had been domestic servants. To attack the evil at its source, he pushed the formation of female servant Bible associations under the care of his energetic ladies.[43]

The manifold nature of Bible activities presented the obvious problem of keeping these thousands of enthusiasts in touch, enabling each to benefit from the ideas and experience of all. So in 1817 there appeared a British and Foreign Bible Society house-organ or news bulletin under the title *Monthly Extracts*. As the title suggests, the sheet contained clippings from the Society's correspondence; it served its stimulating purpose very well.

Inevitably such widespread and intensive activity on the Bible front affected kindred social activities, especially in the organization of feminine energies. One effect was the capture by the Evangelicals of the old benevolent society movement, which had been primarily philanthropic in the tradition of the Enlightenment. In 1803 these societies were making three hundred calls per week on the poor, spending about £150 per month for relief. The Royal Benevolent Society, founded in 1812, directed the energies of the ladies toward religious proselyting rather than physical relief. Rather belatedly, in 1828 the High Church faction offered its counter to Bible association activity in its General Society for Promoting District Visiting, which organized and operated chapters similar to Bible associations in every respect but one: it did not sell Bibles.[44]

42. Dudley, *Analysis*, 259-62.   43. *Ibid.*, 365-67.
44. Maurice J. Quinlan, *Victorian Prelude (Columbia University Studies in English and Comparative Literature*, No. 155 [New York, 1941]), 134-36.

Another transfer of the Bible association techniques was the adoption of its house-to-house plan by the London Religious Tract Society with its 124 auxiliaries in 1815. Three years later this Society introduced a tract loan system, providing the purpose for frequent, intensive visiting in poor districts.[45]

At the close of the Napoleonic Wars, the organized activities of missionary societies, tract societies, Sunday schools, and Bible societies, with the allied and competitive work of other groups, was subjecting the British population to an intellectual, emotional, and moral pressure such as Western civilization had not seen before. Probably the pressure had its major effect upon those who applied it, the ruling classes. For evidence, one notes the Victorian attitudes which dominated British society for a century and still prevail in some measure. But the pressure had its effect, too, in counteracting the disintegrating forces at work upon British life. The movement brought all segments of the social order into frequent personal contact in a massive co-operative effort. They learned to know each other not as symbols but as human beings.

And although the social doctrine of the new benevolence was not the most liberal imaginable, it did preach order resolutely and at the same time managed to ease tensions with the assurance that the troubles of any group were the concern of all. There seems to have been a conscious recognition among more thoughtful Britishers that industrialization, combined with intellectual movements of the seventeenth and eighteenth centuries, had dissolved old relationships, and new must be established.

In this situation, Christianity did not emerge as a corrective force in the doctrine of Evangelical benevolence. The dominant idea was still the one Wilberforce expressed in his *Practical View:* Christianity was a social palliative, a soothing unguent for social sores. The Evangelicals wanted no changes in the social machinery; they would grease the gears. As one Bible society explained, the poor had formerly been taught to regard their superiors with suspicion and dislike. Driven to desperation, they believed their troubles "were wantonly entailed upon

45. *Ibid.,* 124.

them by the great." They wanted revenge for "imaginary wrongs." "At a period like this, when the minds of the lower orders have been exasperated by the heavy pressure of calamity, the peaceful influence of the Bible Society is peculiarly needed."[46] Although there was no hint of social reform in the Evangelical air, there can be no question that their activities were creating an atmosphere for future action in that direction. Only the most dismal mind could picture so much talk of Christianity with no trace of the Christian ethic. A paragraph from the report already quoted is remarkable in combining several themes: the pressure exerted upon the poor, the possibility of social reformation, and the unifying effect of personal contact between classes: "Such an intercourse with their superiors is calculated, at once, to soften and humanize the manners and sentiments of the lower orders, to discover their wants and distresses to those who are able and willing to relieve them; and, what is a point of no small importance, to form a bond of union, a connecting link, between the higher and lower classes of the community."[47] On the other hand, in minds still tainted by the Enlightenment, the "connecting link" was far from wholesome. Contemplating the approach of Christmas, one critic remarked that the poor would receive not the beef and blankets of the old days but Bibles and tracts. "A groveling prostitution of body and soul among their inferiors, effected by half-starvation and driveling, enervating cant of censurers of other peoples' enjoyments is most acceptable in the sight of the upper classes. Whether this be sheer hypocrisy or sour puritanism we will not decide."[48]

46. Ladies Branch of the Manchester and Salford Auxiliary Society, *Third Annual Report* (c. 1814), as quoted by Dudley, *Analysis,* 349.

47. Ladies Branch, Manchester and Salford Auxiliary, *Third Report,* as quoted by Dudley, *Analysis,* 348.

48. *Morning Chronicle* (Dec. 22, 1827), quoted by Quinlan, *Victorian Prelude,* 137.

VII

EVANGELICAL ACTIVITY ABROAD

WHEN NAPOLEON entered Moscow in 1812, agents of the British and Foreign Bible Society were among those who fled before him.[1] There was nothing unusual or remarkable in finding them there. In whatever direction Napoleon might turn, the Baltic, the Lowlands, the German states, Italy, Greece, or the Near East, he would find the British rallying conservative forces in their holy crusade against the infidel. From the start the Evangelicals aggressively carried the ideological war to the enemy, a testimony to the quality of Evangelical leadership.

By 1821 the British and Foreign Bible Society had established more than six hundred Bible societies outside the United Kingdom and had promoted the printing or distribution of the Scriptures in 130 languages and dialects, in eighty of them for the first time.[2] In support of its foreign societies, during the war it had spent in cash subsidies and material grants more than £100,000.[3] Partially as a by-product of Bible activity, tract societies also flourished over the Continent and the United

1. John Owen, *The History of the Origin and First Ten Years of the British and Foreign Bible Society* (New York, 1817), 383.
2. C. S. Dudley, *An Analysis of the System of the Bible Society* (London, 1821), 1.
3. British and Foreign Bible Society, *Report of the British and Foreign Bible Society for 1814-1815*, Section LXXXI, 503-14.

States to spread the British story in its simplest, most appealing form.

The work abroad was not in the least a by-product of Bible activity at home. In fact, a careful reading of the early reports of the British and Foreign Bible Society leads to the conclusion that the situation was quite the reverse: activity in foreign fields was the principal intent; success at home was the inadvertent by-product caused chiefly by the enthusiasm of the ladies. Almost the entire *First Report* dealt with activities in Europe; to a lesser degree all of the early reports carried the same emphasis. The world situation gave the Society its reason for being, in the minds of its founders: "The *reasons* which call for such an Institution, chiefly refer to the prevalence of Ignorance, Superstition, and Idolatry, over so large a portion of the world; the limited nature of the respectable Societies now in existence, and their acknowledged insufficiency to supply the demand for Bibles in the United Kingdoms and Foreign Countries; and the recent attempts which have been made on the part of Infidelity to discredit the evidence, vilify the character, and destroy the influence of Christianity."[4]

The chief agent for the British and Foreign Bible Society on the Continent was the Rev. C. F. A. Steinkopff. It was he whose broken English had played a conclusive part at the meetings founding the Society and its principal auxiliaries. And it is worth noting that the content of this broken English was an appeal on behalf of the Continent to tap the emotional drives of foreign missions and war effort at the same time.

The Rev. Steinkopff devoted most of his work to the German states, where he felt at home, but he held a roving commission as well, since the war years found him on Continental tours of six months or more, allotting funds here and there to struggling Bible societies. Other agents were the Scottish Revs. John Paterson and Ebenezer Henderson, who started working the Scandinavian countries in 1805. Also Scottish was the Rev. Robert Pinkerton, laboring in northern Europe, especially

4. British and Foreign Bible Society, *First Report* (1804-5), 32.

Russia, and in Greece. Covering the Near East were W. Jowett and C. Burckhardt.[5]

During the war the Bible Society made common cause with the Roman Catholics on the Continent as it recognized in Catholicism a conservative force, a fellow foe to French rationalism. There were four agents working for the Society among the German Catholics. Professor Leander Van Ess of the University of Marburg with the help of his brother distributed 339,488 copies of his Catholic New Testament and 287 Catholic Bibles without his notes. Also laboring among German Catholics were M. Gossner of Munich and Regeus Wittman of Ratisbon.[6] This Evangelical-Catholic alliance endured until the Apocrypha controversy of the 1830's, when the Society established a policy which estranged its Catholic supporters. The American Bible Society followed suit in its dealings with Latin America.

For penetration into France proper the British and Foreign Bible Society established a base of operations in a society at Basel, Switzerland. From there it endeavored to supply Bibles to Protestants in the interior of France.[7] There is no evidence that British agents succeeded in organizing societies within the national boundaries of France during the war.

Switzerland also provided a center for the distribution of tracts. Societies appeared in Basel and Bern as early as 1802 and then spread to Zürich, St. Gallen, Schaffhausen, Lucerne, and Lausanne. But most of the tract societies organized on the Continent during the war were products of those industrious Bible Society agents Paterson and Henderson, with the help of occasional small subsidies from the London Religious Tract Society. Following their footsteps, tract societies flourished in Sweden, Denmark, various German states, and Finland. In Russia they managed to interest many dignitaries of the Church, as well as a princess of the royal family, in the translation and printing of the London Society's tracts. When Napoleon's army retreated from Moscow these people managed to rush through a special French edition of *To The Afflicted*, "which

5. Dudley, *Analysis*, 24-32.   6. *Ibid.*
7. New Hampshire Bible Society, *First Report* (1812), 5.

proved a most seasonable and unexpected comfort to the poor sufferers."[8]

There is no record of the London Sunday-School Union's joining the Continental labors of Bible and tract societies during the war. Later efforts proved unsuccessful, as strong clerical authority among Europeans of all sects would not permit so much lay leadership. Throughout the struggle the most successful British effort went into Bible societies.

In the promotion of its Continental organizations the British and Foreign Bible Society used methods which its diplomatic and military procedures had long made familiar. As early as 1703 in the War of the Spanish Succession, the British had paid cash subsidies for European support of their military objectives. By 1794 Lord Grenville could observe to Lord Malmesbury that "German Princes think England a pretty good milch cow."[9] Since this was the accepted way of doing business both at home and abroad, it was easy to make the transfer from the diplomatic-military application to the ideological front, especially since the same people were making the grants in both cases. For that matter, the same people were receiving the grants. As in England, the organizing technique was aimed at obtaining the sponsorship and support of the court and the nobility to assure the highest possible social prestige. The relationship between military and ideological subsidies does not extend much further. The military subsidies were a flat failure. Although they helped to provide the materials of war and secured agreement to fight, they could not supply the will to fight. It cannot be said for the Continental Bible and tract societies that they were remarkably successful in meeting the deficiency. But certainly the British got more for their modest expenditure of money and energy on the ideological front. In an alliance badly weakened by divided and competing interests as well as by military disasters, the Bible and tract societies continued to propagate and sustain the single moral and emotional

8. American Tract Society, *Proceedings of the First Ten Years* . . . (Boston, 1824), 192-93.

9. Jan. 17, 1794, quoted by John M. Sherwig, "Subsidies as an Instrument of Pitt's War Policy, 1793-1806," unpublished Ph.D. dissertation, Harvard University (1948), p. 44.

commitment which could form a common bond of union—and this commitment finally carried the day on the Continent. Although, for political reasons, Great Britain did not join the Holy Alliance, its proclamation of Christianity as the foundation of government was to a considerable degree the product of the British ideological campaign.

The campaign did not confine itself to the Continent but extended to America, where a military front developed in the years 1812-15. Concern for public attitude in the United States was secondary but genuine; we find the British employing no agents in this country and spending here less than 5 per cent of the total outlay of subsidy funds. The expenditures were wholly those of the British and Foreign Bible Society; they began with a grant to the Philadelphia Bible Society in 1809 and continued throughout the War of 1812 to a final donation to the Rhode Island Bible Society in 1817. All told, there were twenty-five cash grants of £50 to £500 totaling £3,400.[10]

Donations of Bibles and Testaments as well as of stereotype plates raised the total of British help to about £5,000. This sum was indeed modest, but it was successful out of all proportion to its size. The subsidies began in the years of tension preceding the outbreak of hostilities; the year of 1812 saw an interruption probably because of genuine estrangement and early American naval success. Then in 1813 the subsidy payments started again and continued in increasing measure through the peace settlement.

People did not relate Bible activity to the war. This fact seems quite clear, for example, in the origin in 1813 of the Bible Society of Nassau Hall. In a prank not perhaps typical of Princeton students, one of the boys cut out the middle of the chapel Bible, leaving the margin entire. For the entertainment of the college president and the student body at chapel service, he filled the hole with playing cards. The result was all one could expect, but in a reaction of mortification and re-

10. British and Foreign Bible Society, *Annual Reports* (1808-9 through 1816-17), *passim*. Also refer to William Canton, *A History of the British and Foreign Bible Society* (London, 1904), I, 248, 249.

pentance, the students formed a Bible society to replace the chapel Bible[11] and wrote at once to the Rev. John Owen, secretary of the British and Foreign Bible Society, to tell him of their action. To believe that these pious youths hoped for nothing more substantial than the Rev. Owen's blessing would be an insult to the intelligence of Princeton men of all generations. In a letter dated Fulham, December 15, 1813, the Rev. Owen compared their Society to those in Cambridge and Oxford. He said that even in the existing state of unpleasantness he did not believe that either government would object to the donation of £50 his organization was sending.[12]

By protesting too much, Rhode Island did better than Princeton at the "milch cow" of Europe. In a letter of November 18, 1813, to the Rev. Joseph Hughes, the other secretary of the British and Foreign Bible Society, Rhode Island announced the formation of the twenty-ninth Bible society in the United States. Requesting all of the British annual reports to date, the Rhode Islanders denied they wanted money: "We wish not to divert the attention nor the funds of your Society from the glorious cause. . . ."[13] Evidently the Rev. Hughes thought the cause in Rhode Island was glorious enough, as he sent more literature than requested and he placed £100 at its disposal.[14] Later Rhode Island secured another £100.

There were other aspects of co-operation during the war. The Louisiana Bible Society announced in 1813 that its sole object was "to distribute the Scriptures, without note or comment, in the English, French and Spanish languages, in the versions circulated by the British and foreign Bible Society."[15] "Emulous of contributing to the success of the great scheme that has been adopted in both Europe and America," it offered religion as the only genuine security "for property, for reputation, for life."[16] To this purpose the British supplied materials

11. New Hampshire Bible Society, *Second Report* (1813), 8.
12. Bible Society of Nassau Hall, *Semi-Annual Report* (April 2, 1814), 7, 8.
13. Bible Society of the State of Rhode-Island and Providence Plantations, *Statement* (Providence, 1814), 25-26.
14. *Ibid.,* 26.
15. Louisiana Bible Society, *Constitution and Address,* a broadside dated 1813.
16. *Ibid.*

to the value of £603.[17] At the same time near the battle front
in New York state, the Oneida Bible Society complained, "War,
like the pestilence, is destroying the morals of our citizens,"
but rejoiced that the work still continued: "The Parent Society
in England has already issued 431,939 Bibles and Testaments."[18]

Of course American privateers captured some shipments of
British Bibles. In June, 1813, one brought into Portland, Me.,
a lot consigned to Nova Scotia and auctioned it off with the
rest of the captured cargo. Raising twice the sum needed to
replace the books, the Bible Society of Massachusetts sent them
to their original destination. It repeated the performance the
following year. On another occasion the owners of the priva-
teer delivered the Bibles free of all charges, shipping them on
to Canada.

The general attitude of the time placed Bible activity on a
plane above and apart from political and military conflict.
Like the British, American Evangelicals were simply doing
good. As Charleston, S.C., expressed the idea with a degree
of understatement, "The United States of America, with the
rapidity of her Eagle pursuing the nations of the old wor[l]d,
in the splendid career of learning, of science, and of art, was
not an indifferent spectator of their zeal in the cause of heaven
and of human nature."[19] But it is hard to escape concluding
that the British cause and the cause of heaven became a little
confused, and the British were quite willing to pay a little
money to encourage this effect.

The Bible movement spread in the United States with remarkable speed during the War of 1812. By 1814 there were
sixty-nine Bible societies representing all of the original thirteen
states as well as Ohio, Kentucky, Tennessee, Mississippi Territory, Louisiana, and the District of Columbia; there were also
seven ladies' Bible associations of record.[20] By 1815 the number
of societies had swelled to 108.[21] At the same time the tract

17. Canton, *History*, I, 248.
18. *Constitution, Address and Report for 1813* (Utica, N. Y., 1813), 10.
19. Bible Society of Charleston, *Constitution and Address* (Charleston, S.C.
1810), 15.
20. Canton, *History*, I, 244.   21. *Ibid.*, 247.

idea was also making some progress. By 1815 there were twelve
tract societies scattered from Vermont to South Carolina, which
were growing rapidly in strength as well as numbers, and they
were all busy reprinting and distributing the output of the
London Tract Society.[22]

Another weapon in the Evangelical arsenal, the Sunday
school, was much more successful in America than on the Continent. By 1815 it had become a fairly general institution in
the United States, with centers of real strength in Philadelphia
and New York.[23] Also, it was well along in the process of transition from enlightened charity to Evangelical benevolence, a
process that the Sunday school eventually completed much more
thoroughly in the United States than in England, where the
general illiteracy of the poor forced emphasis on elementary
education as a prelude to indoctrination. The net result in
terms of ideology was that scores of Sunday-school organizations
joined the missionary, tract, and Bible societies in looking to
the British for leadership and in spreading the British message
in the United States.

Peace brought a renewed and clarified vigor to Evangelical
progress on the American front. In addition to easier British
relationships, the Evangelical idea enjoyed the world prestige
accompanying military victory. The British cause and the
cause of heaven both triumphed in Europe, and the warming
glow of success extended to the United States. On August 3,
1816, the Rev. John Owen could write another draft on the
funds of the British and Foreign Bible Society, this time for a
generous £500, and hail the American Bible Society as "a powerful Auxiliary in the confederated warfare which is now carrying on against ignorance, evil & sin."[24]

The British had been pushing the idea of an American
national society for six years. As early as 1810 they had
broached the project with offers of aid first to the New York
Bible Society and then to Philadelphia, but both turned it

22. American Tract Society, *Proceedings*, 208.
23. Circular addressed to Mathew Carey, Esq., by George Boyd, General
Agent, American Sunday-School Union (Philadelphia, Feb. 20, 1825).
24. John Owen to Elias Boudinot, Brighton, Aug. 3, 1816.

down.[25] The idea had not lacked consideration by Americans. Upon its founding in 1809, the Philadelphia Bible Society had weighed the prospect of starting as a national organization in the British pattern. Difficulties of travel and communication as well as anticipations of sectional jealousies discouraged the suggestion. Instead, Philadelphia proposed a decentralized pattern of independent state societies located specifically at Boston, New Haven, New York, Baltimore, Richmond, Savannah, and Lexington, Ky.[26] This design promptly materialized, but that was not the end of the original idea. National leadership in Bible activity passed from Philadelphia to New York by way of New Jersey. The dynamic force in this transition was Elias Boudinot of Burlington, N.J., a lawyer and businessman with connections in both Philadelphia and New York. His influence and interests ranged widely as trustee of the College of New Jersey at Princeton, director of the Bank of the United States, and member of the corporation of the General Assembly of the Presbyterian Church. With religious zeal of a rather feverish, millennial variety, he helped to found the New Jersey Bible Society at New Brunswick in 1809 as an auxiliary to the Philadelphia Bible Society and became its first president.

Inspired with the vision of a national Bible society, Boudinot found an answer to the problems of a national organization in his experience of nearly twenty years with the Bank of the United States. The stockholders of the Bank lived in every state in the Union and they chose directors from every part of the country, but the majority of them lived in or near Philadelphia. For that reason a meeting of the board with adequate attendance presented no serious difficulties.[27] Since he viewed the formation of a national Bible society as both practical and advantageous, Boudinot began to push the idea vigorously

25. Gardiner Spring, ed., *Memoirs of the Rev. Samuel J. Mills* (New York, 1820), 95, 96.

26. Philadelphia Bible Society, *An Address of the Bible Society to the Public* (Philadelphia, 1809), 5-8.

27. Elias Boudinot to the Rt. Rev. William White, President, Philadelphia Bible Society, Jan., 1815, as quoted in his pamphlet, *An Answer to the Objections of the Managers of the Philadelphia Bible Society against a Meeting of Delegates from the Bible Societies in the Union* (Burlington, N.J., [1815]), 10.

through a committee of the New Jersey Bible Society in 1814. To his dismay, an appeal to more than one hundred Bible societies met with approval by fewer than twenty.[28] Bishop White, president of the Philadelphia Bible Society, had been equally busy circulating the same societies with his objections to the scheme as unreasonable, unprecedented, useless, injurious, and impractical. Boudinot replied at length to Bishop White in a pamphlet of his own, citing the British and Foreign Bible Society and the Bank of the United States as examples and precedents.

Boudinot claimed some results for his argument, but the difference between failure in 1814 and success in 1816 was undoubtedly Samuel J. Mills, who returned from his Evangelical exploration of the Mississippi Valley to report that some of its population had never seen a Bible or heard of Jesus Christ. Mills was busily painting his picture of the "Valley of the Shadow of Death," one destined to color Evangelical thinking for years to come. According to Lyman Beecher, "It was by personal conversation, I doubt not, with thousands of the most influential men all over our nation, and addressing, when he had opportunity, ecclesiastical bodies, that he had prepared the way for a harmonious concurrence in favor of organization when the Convention met."[29] Beecher himself was one of those most impressed. In 1814 he joined other orthodox stalwarts of New England in founding the American Education Society to strengthen the ranks of the clergy. He gave his prescription for America: *A Bible for every family, a school for every district and a pastor for every thousand souls.* "The press must groan in communication of our wretchedness; and from every pulpit in the land the trumpet must sound long and loud."[30] Clearly, John E. Caldwell of the New York Bible Society was one of Mills's converts, as he wrote to Boudi-

28. Henry Otis Dwight, *The Centennial History of the American Bible Society* (New York, 1916), 16, 17.

29. As quoted by W. P. Strickland, *History of the American Bible Society* (New York, 1856), 26-27.

30. On the Importance of Assisting Young Men of Piety and Talents in Obtaining an Education for the Gospel Ministry (2nd ed.; Andover, Mass., 1816), 10.

not that a bare statement of facts about conditions on the western frontier would be enough to raise money for "supplying the deplorable wants of these famishing fellow men."[31]

But the controversy of 1814 and 1815 brought home to Boudinot a more serious evaluation of the difficulties confronting him as he wrote to William Jay in New York, "I am sorry to say from experience of the most unreasonable opposition I have rec'd. from those who I depended upon, as the surest supports in this great Cause, & that as far as I can discover arising from an ill founded Jealousy, that it was originated in the wrong section of the U.S. and that the Clergy would soon be excluded from any great share in this important work. . . ."[32]

Boudinot encountered the problem of dealing with the clergy in a more acute form than confronted the Clapham Sect in England when it organized the British and Foreign Bible Society, because there already were more than one hundred Bible societies in the United States under clerical leadership. The pattern of the Evangelical united front required lay control and the subordination of the clergy, with their denominational preoccupations, to the role of expert advisers and assistants. In England, where the industrial revolution had already shifted the balance of social power to the laity, subordination was troublesome enough; in America, still essentially agrarian, it amounted to a social revolution possible only because the secularism of the Enlightenment had hurt the American clergy severely in prestige.

To please the clergy and ease them out at the same time was a difficult task, but it was Boudinot's. He had it in mind in writing to William Jay, with whom he was collaborating on a draft of a constitution for the national society: "But especially would I leave out the clause excluding the Clergy—they would raise the whole Body as a formidable Phalanx agt us. We had better conciliate as much as possible. Experience will be our best Teacher. Very few of them can ever attend, and will not willingly en[?] themselves to the Labour that may be required."[33] As a further precaution, Boudinot suggested to Jay

31. To Elias Boudinot, New York, Sept. 22, 1815.
32. Burlington, April 4, 1816.   33. Ibid.

in the same letter that it would be better to withhold publication of the proposed constitution in order to give the opposition nothing to take hold of. They would present it to the convention and meet objections there.

In reply to Boudinot's letter, William Jay believed he had solved the dilemma:

So far from excluding the clergy, I propose to give to every clergyman on the continent, if he chose to accept it by subscribing to the Society, an equal vote in its management, with the President himself, and in order to prevent *invidious distinctions,* I propose that no clergyman in particular should be *selected* for managers but that all should possess the powers and privileges of managers. I regarded this as the most important feature of the whole constitution—as the article best calculated to obviate objections & to ensure the success of the Society. This article alone is sufficient to prevent the Society from becoming a sectarian institution—at the same time it invites the support of the clergy by making them *ex officio* managers. This article is the prominent feature of the constitution of the British Society & the success of that wonderful institution is the highest eulogium on the wisdom of the constitution, & it is probably by means of this very article that it has achieved what has never before been effected,—a friendly and zealous cooperation among the most discordant members of the christian family.[34]

Quite clearly, opposition involved not only clerical and sectarian jealousy but sectional jealousy as well. It did not stem from New England, where the leadership and national vision of Lyman Beecher had its effect. John E. Caldwell, corresponding secretary of the New York Bible Society, told Boudinot that he could expect considerable resistance from the South and West.[35] Also involved was the contest for social and economic leadership of the nation between Philadelphia and its rising rival, New York city. Circumstances left Boudinot no choice. The opposition of Bishop White made Philadelphia an impossible location for the national society. The Episcopalian bishop of New York, John Henry Hobart, stood ready to fight the whole Bible society idea, but he was younger than Bishop White and not nearly so influential. And there was

34. New York, April 23, 1816.
35. April 9, 1816.

strong support in New York, even among Hobart's Episcopalians. The New York Bible Society rallied to Boudinot,
even to the point of urging an independent national organization in New York.[36]

Encouraged by increasing enthusiasm, the Boudinot forces
ventured to issue the call for a convention. With such formidable obstacles, only expert management and showmanship
could make the convention a success. To Boudinot's great
disappointment, severe illness kept him at home, and he asked
Joshua M. Wallace to act for him. Everything went well until
the committee on the constitution met under Wallace's chairmanship in the home of the Rev. John M. Mason on Thursday,
May 9, 1816. Evidently Boudinot and William Jay had decided
that the experience of the British and Foreign Bible Society
had more than symbolic value and had abandoned attempts
to write their own constitution. It was the British document
they placed before the committee as a model.

Suddenly there arose the same type of situation which had
confronted the launching of the British and Foreign Bible
Society. There was a sharpness in the air; feelings began to
rise and tangle. And there was no Rev. Steinkopff to dissolve
them in tears with his broken English. But perhaps even he
would have done no good in New York. It was an American
crisis, to be met in the American way. The Rev. Mason, rough,
talented, a "Master in Israel," rose to address the chair: "Mr.
President, the Lord Jesus never built a church but what the
devil built a chapel close to it; and he is here now, this moment,
in this room, with his finger in the ink horn, not to write your
Constitution but to blot it out."[37] As a roar of laughter cleared
the air, Mason continued, "There, there! he has gone already
to his blue brimstone!"

In an easier mood the committee spent the rest of the day
tinkering with the constitution of the British and Foreign Bible
Society to preserve all essential features, yet give it an American
appearance: "Yet to avoid *servile* imitation we have in several

36. *Ibid.*
37. Lyman Beecher's account, as quoted by W. P. Strickland, *History of the
American Bible Society* (New York, 1849), 26-27.

particulars so far departed from the terms of the instrument as to give *our* constitution an air of peculiarity suited to our national views & circumstances."[38]

Preparations for the convention had been thorough. Twenty-nine Bible societies sent representatives. A number of societies could not send delegates but forwarded letters of greeting and approbation. The only sour note came from Philadelphia, which disapproved and could not join. In a generous glow of enthusiasm the convention admitted the Quakers to their number and advised the Roman Catholics that they were not excluded.[39]

With the drafting of the constitution completed on Thursday, the convention could conclude its principal business on Saturday. Since the opposition chose not to attend and the various interests had been reasonably satisfied, everything went smoothly. The delegate from the New Jersey Bible Society described the scene to his wife in touching terms: "I do not think you ever saw such an impression in the Countenances of any assembly as appeared on this when after the Question was put Does this convention determine that it is expedient to form a National Bible Society the Answer *Yea* with loud acclamation was followed by a most solemn & *total* silence when the Chairman desired if any Person present disapproved of the Measure he would say *nay*. Tears of Joy and Exultation were the Expression of the General Sentiments."[40]

The public launching of the American Bible Society received as expert staging as any other part of the proceedings. The leaders apparently made the arrangements well in advance, in anticipation of success. Monday was the chosen day, the day the British had dedicated to Bible work because the poor would still have some of last week's wages. On this occasion the day was quite as suitable for another reason: it gave the churches their Sunday opportunity to advertise the work of the convention and to rally attendance at the meeting. They did well at advertisement in the Presbyterian and Associate Re-

38. Samuel Bayard to Elias Boudinot, New York, May 11, 1816.
39. Elisha Boudinot to Elias Boudinot, New York, May 11, 1816.
40. J. M. Wallace to Mrs. Wallace, New York, May 11, 1816.

formed churches, probably in the Methodist churches, and in some of the Episcopal churches.[41]

These efforts brought more than one thousand of New York's leading citizens to the public meeting in City Hall at five in the afternoon of Monday, May 13, 1816. The place was neutral; like its British parent, the American Bible Society kept strictly clear of identification with any church. And the atmosphere was of lay leadership in a religious enterprise. The chief justice of the state of New York introduced the business of the meeting, then appointed as its chairman Justin Platt, mayor of New York. Although the Rev. Dr. Nott, an eminent Presbyterian, was one of the speakers, two of the eloquent laity, counsellors P. A. Jay and George Griffin, rather over-balanced his divinity.[42]

Thus amidst much enthusiasm the American Bible Society started its long career. An examination of the convention's work shows, too, that the convention marked the true launching of the Evangelical united front in the United States. The importance of the event rested in the fact that it opened a pattern of social organization which spread through the middle and northern areas of the United States with great rapidity and vigor. It operated in religion, generally of interest to Americans, but, unlike the earlier Bible, tract, and missionary societies, was free of clerical domination and therefore free of any religious test expressed or implied. Such a form of organization opened social activity to a wide range of impulses, an opportunity accepted by American conservatives with great enthusiasm.

The Evangelical united front thus came into being in the United States after it had accomplished its main purpose in Europe, helping to make the world safe for the conservative. Sunday schools and Bible, tract, and missionary societies had developed possibilities of united effort realized for the first time in the American Bible Society. And this organization in turn launched a movement which conditioned American social thought and action for the following twenty years, finding ex-

41. J. M. Wallace to Mrs. Wallace, New York, May 13, 1816.
42. Samuel Bayard to Elias Boudinot, Princeton, May 14, 1816.

pression in Bible and tract publication and distribution, the financing and education of foreign and domestic missionaries, promotion of Sunday schools, enforcement of Sabbath observance, temperance, anti-Catholicism, antislavery, colonization of free Negroes, and conversion of Jews. Americans discovered that they could apply the organizational techniques to the servant problem, to juvenile delinquency, to prostitution, to the care of orphans and immigrants, and to poor relief. Organization itself became an American passion; hardly could two Americans meet without one calling the meeting to order. Wherever a moral purpose could be brought to bear by any twist of the imagination, the Evangelical united front presented the mode of attack. Its implications and ramifications extended into the political and business life of the American community to set the pattern of approved social conduct.

The leaders, for the most part wealthy merchants and lawyers of New York, Philadelphia, and Boston, decided upon policies and objectives; as in England the clergy served as expert staff. The American experiment in the voluntary system of religious support had made the clergy peculiarly dependent upon the wealthy of their congregations. Not that the clergy were consciously sycophant, but without the independence of relatively secure political office they would naturally find the most favorable prospects for effective ministry in close co-operation with the existing economic power.

This alliance of wealth, energy, and intelligence devoted itself to the inculcation of certain attitudes and values in American society. Genuine religious conviction was, of course, one of them, but it had to find its expression in conformity to a pattern of behavior. And even without the conviction, conformity would serve. The pattern was one of American Victorianism. It insisted that life was a most serious business to be conducted with sobriety, industry, and, above all, dignity. One had to observe the proprieties. There was a place for everything, and the place for levity and relaxation was well hidden from public view. When a gentleman was exposed to social or business contact, a stiff attitude was as necessary to him as his stiff shirt—and if he could not afford a shirt he might at least present a starched bosom and a pair of cuffs. But beneath that rigid exterior there was a heart brimming with the warmest sentiments. The favorite gesture of the American Victorian was his "errand of mercy," his benevolent exercise. The errand might take him to the humble dwellings of the poor, to the home of a sick employee, to a meeting of one of his numerous Evangelical societies, to a saloon for the rescue of a fallen friend; but wherever it led him, he was doing good. Sunday he set apart exclusively for the concerns of eternity. The morning would find him teaching in Sunday school; at the hour for divine worship he and his entire family would be in their pew, where his business associates expected to see him.

The Victorian's relationships with God were frequent, sincere, and usually nebulous. They were as personal and confidential as his relations with his bank. Religion was the peculiar concern of the Victorian woman, whom the Victorian male exalted to the status of an angel at the same time that he debased her to the level of servant in practice. She provided the energy of benevolent activity while her husband provided the funds. Like her husband, the Victorian lady had to present a front of decency and decorum. She could do arduous, mean, and dirty work when it had to be done, but when there were males in attendance she could prove her sensitivity by swooning at the slightest indelicacy.

Conformity to the model of conduct and attitude which came to be known as Victorian was the work of the Evangelical united front in America as in England. The enforcement of conformity brought into play pressures probably stronger than any that the United States has seen before or since. Interlocking Evangelical organization enabled the conservative, respectable element of the community to act with united power in a subtle coercion. In this atmosphere, nonconformity meant the loss of social, business, and political credit. The concept of religious freedom lost an essential element, the freedom to disbelieve, and became the freedom to belong to any one of a number of Evangelical churches. At the same time the choice of a church became subject more and more to nonreligious factors.

However, in 1816 these developments lay hidden in the future. It was a momentous year when the Evangelical forces in the United States turned to new objectives with the promise of power in unity born with the American Bible Society. There was some reason for confidence. These forces could already chalk up one victory: the tide had turned away from the Enlightment; the infidel was on the run.

PART

II

THE EVANGELICAL UNITED FRONT IN THE UNITED STATES 1816-1837

The wolf shall dwell with the lamb, and the leopard shall lie down with the kid; and they shall not hurt nor destroy in all my holy mountain: for the earth shall be full of the knowledge of the Lord.

AMERICAN SUNDAY-SCHOOL UNION
Motto, 1824

VIII

CHARACTERISTICS OF THE EVANGELICAL UNITED FRONT IN THE UNITED STATES

THE INCOME OF THE principal benevolent societies of the United States in the fiscal year 1826-27 totaled $361,804.54.[1] The rapidly growing, chiefly agrarian nation had a population of about eleven million. From its foundation to October 1, 1828, the republic had spent $3,585,534.67 for internal improvements; over the same period the revenue of the thirteen leading benevolent societies came to $2,813,550.02.[2] At that time the Evangelical effort was still expanding, and by 1830 the income of its organizations was well past the half-million mark. But of particular interest is the distribution of financial support for the promotion of the Evangelical cause in the United States. The fourteen leading benevolent societies, listed in order of income for the fiscal year 1826-27, were these:

American Education Society
American Board of Foreign Missions
American Bible Society
American Sunday-School Union
American Tract Society, New York
American Home Missionary Society
American Colonization Society

1. *The Christian Almanac for New York, Connecticut, New Jersey and Pennsylvania,* American Tract Society (New York, 1828), 32.
2. *The Quarterly Register of the American Education Society,* III (1830-31), 63.

American Baptist Board of Foreign Missions
American Tract Society, New England
Presbyterian Education Society
Missionary Society of Connecticut
Reformed Dutch Missionary Society
Western Domestic Missionary Society
American Jews Society[3]

Of these Evangelical organizations, only four were under denominational control, and none of those were among the leaders. The other ten societies, accounting for more than 91 per cent of the total receipts, were quite independent of any ecclesiastical bodies. One should qualify the estimate somewhat by the fact that the compiler of the records did not consider the Methodists with their Book Concern as constituting a benevolent society. Although the Methodists were not then the potent force they later became, their system was essentially missionary in its scheme of operation. At the same time, the Methodists were not united in support of their Book Concern. As with all of the other Protestant denominations, a large portion of Methodist energies was going into the independent societies, and Methodists were using the propaganda materials and techniques which those organizations provided.

The picture which one can construct from the information at hand is clear enough in its broad outlines: the Evangelical movement which restored the prestige of religion and gave the United States its Protestant character was not, at this stage, a denominational effort. The financing of education for the ministry, the organization and administration of missionary effort both foreign and domestic, the promotion of the Evangelical youth movement in its various aspects, and the production and distribution of propaganda in its numerous forms, as well as the general direction of lay activity and, to a degree, the formulation of doctrine, were all the work of societies requiring no test for membership other than a small fee. Societies were a central fact of the country's religious life during its most formative years, clearly recognized by Thomas S. Grimke in 1833: *"The Christian History of Society has never*

3. *Christian Almanac* (1828), 32.

yet been written. . . . When the pen of some future Luke shall record its eventful scenes, that Christian History will be founded, not so much on the annals of Churches, as on those of social institutions, whose spirit is regenerating the nations, whose influence is pervading, with life-instilling energy, all the classes, and the very depths and recesses of society: 'whose sound is gone out into all lands, and its word into the ends of the world.' "[4]

At once certain questions demand clear answers. To what extent was the Evangelical effort a united front of Protestant denominations? To what extent was it a fusion of like-minded sects? What degree of identity and integrity did the church bodies lose, and how much did they retain?

The most sweeping generalization that the history of the movement will justify is that it was a united front supported by American Protestants to achieve ends far beyond the powers of their separate denominations, a united front of individual Christians and of those who, for some reason or other, wished to identify themselves with the Evangelical cause. It was not a united front composed of assorted ecclesiastical bodies. Some denominations endorsed all united-front work; some blessed certain ventures but withheld the nod from others. In each sect there were some clerical leaders who devoted their principal energies to the general societies, while others jealously guarded the prestige and power of their particular persuasions.

A certain impulse toward fusion was inevitable in these circumstances. At the core of the united front lay a cordial co-operation among the Presbyterians and Congregationalists, who formed their Plan of Union in 1800 for operations in New York state. There they encountered kindred spirits in the Reformed Dutch, and membership in these churches became quite interchangeable. The informal alliance thus attained a geographical coverage of the eastern United States. It included many leaders in business and professional life ready to supply both energy and guidance to benevolent societies; these men had influential friends among the Episcopalians, Baptists, and

4. *The Temperance Reformation* (Charleston, S.C., 1833), 34-35.

Methodists.   Around them could rally a host who for various reasons would not want to be left out.

Once underway in their holy endeavor, the people in these organizations would naturally focus on what was common to all.   And the societies, like churches, built up loyalty and devotion to their united effort.   Not only did the benevolent societies absorb money and energy to which the separate denominations might have some claim, but they tended to exercise church functions.   They did not administer sacraments, unless preaching is considered a sacrament.   With this exception there was little that the churches had to offer which did not find duplication in the ritual of society meetings.   The American Sunday-School Union was explicit: "when there should not be public worship and preaching, it should be the duty of the Superintendent so to arrange the closing exercises of the school, as to supply the place of it, and to preserve something of a similar form."[5]   What is here explicit for Sunday-school operations was implicit in the meetings of other benevolent groups, which were, after all, religious organizations conducting their proceedings in a religious atmosphere.   In such circumstances it was inevitable that societies should share with the churches the emotional experience of revival and conversion. At an evening meeting of tract distributors in New York city,

. . . the Superintendent, distracted with the cares of the business of the day, entered the room, fearing that the Spirit of God was withdrawn.   He confessed his own spiritual deficiencies and stated how just he thought it would be of God to depart from them.   After prayer and singing, he took up the Distributer's written reports, as they had been laid on the table promiscuously; and the first gave delightful evidence of *two souls converted to God.*   The meeting paused and blessed the Author of conversion.   His presence seemed to fill the room.   Breathless silence prevailed, interrupted occasionally by sounds of weeping.[6]

There is abundant evidence that the Evangelical united front was more than a co-operative effort of Protestant denominations or of individual Christians with their assorted sectarian prejudices.   Some claimed that the movement con-

5. *Third Report* (1827), 17.
6. American Tract Society, *Fourth Annual Report* (1829), 16-18.

stituted a suprachurch embracing particular churches but not owing its existence to them: "The church, in her benevolent movements, seems to be circumscribed within no limits save those of the habitable globe."[7] The foundation of the supra-church rested on a ground that its membership would have repudiated violently had they been aware of it—the deism of the Enlightenment. Deism espoused a basic, "natural" religion of which all formal religions were faulty human variants. And to the deists, as to the Evangelical suprachurch, the most valid expression of true religion was "benevolence."

However, the active expression of "benevolence" as Evangelical propaganda by a mystical, universal "church" was possible only in an era of good feelings which paralleled in religion a similar aspect of politics. This era in American Protestantism found encouragement in the progressive disestablishment of churches. As the principle of voluntaryism swept through the country, placing all sects on a par before the law, it relieved a situation such as Lyman Beecher wryly described in Connecticut in 1811: "So the democracy, as it rose, included nearly all the minor sects, besides the Sabbath-breakers, rum-selling tippling folk, infidels, and ruff-scuff generally, and made a dead set at us of the standing order."[8]

Along with the elimination of legal discrimination with all its bitterness came the general impact of the Enlightenment, of which disestablishment was only one aspect. With its attack upon revealed religion and its promotion of natural religion, the Enlightenment was stressing what was common to all at the expense of peculiarity. That is, even those who fought the Enlightenment in its political and social aspects were imbued with its philosophy.

Into this relaxed atmosphere the Evangelical united front moved as a positive force to advance the concept of Protestant unity. In 1816, the Rev. J. M. Mason of New York wanted to go as far as "a sacramental communion on catholick principles." He noted: "Within a few years there has been a manifest re-

7. The General Association of Massachusetts Proper, *Minutes* (1829), 16.
8. *Autobiography, Correspondence, Etc., of Lyman Beecher, D.D.,* Charles Beecher, ed. (New York, 1864), I, 342. See also, I, 452, 453.

laxation of sectarian rigour in several denominations. And the spirit of the Gospel, in the culture of fraternal charity, has gained, upon a respectable scale, a visible and growing ascendancy. This happy alteration may be attributed, in a great degree, to the influence of Missionary and Bible Societies."[9] There was much the same spirit in Philadelphia, where the Sunday and Adult School Union at its first anniversary in 1818 heard the Rev. Parker voice identical sentiments: "The primitive spirit of harmony and union is reviving; and I believe that Missionary societies, Bible societies, and Sabbath school societies are to be honorably instrumental in bringing about that enlarged, cheerful and universal co-operation in the work of the Lord, which is so devoutly to be wished."[10]

On every hand there is abundant evidence of the good temper of those years. In 1819 a society for promoting the gospel among seamen opened a mariners' nonsectarian church on Roosevelt St. in New York near the East River docks. A Presbyterian minister presided at the dedication, which treated its audience to three sermons delivered in turn by Protestant Episcopal, Reformed Dutch, and Methodist Episcopal clergymen.[11]

A considerable factor in this genial era of good feelings, one affecting both politics and religion to subdue factional differences, was the rising tide of nationalism. The Evangelical united front was one expression of this general emotion and probably could not have prevailed without it. A disgruntled Methodist, writing tongue in cheek to the editor of his religious journal, stated the case clearly enough:

Mr. Editor: —I am a national man, and therefore cannot understand what you mean by complaining of *national societies.* Sir, it is the order of the day to be national. We have our national theaters, national lottery offices, national hotels, national steam boats, and national grog shops. We have our United States shoe

9. *A Plea for Sacramental Communion on Catholick Principles* (New York, 1816), v.

10. Speech at the Philadelphia Sunday and Adult School Union, 1818, as quoted by E. W. Rice, *The Sunday School Movement, 1780-1917, and the American Sunday-School Union, 1817-1917* (Philadelphia, 1917), 64.

11. Nathan Bangs, *A History of the Methodist Episcopal Church* (3rd ed.; New York, 1853), III, 305, 306.

blacks, U.S. corset makers, U.S. infirmaries, and U.S. manufactories of every kind, from our match makers up to our carpet factories. I see no reason why we should not have national societies, since this character gives those societies a popularity and influence they could not otherwise sustain. Besides, sir, to be an officer in a national society, sounds abroad like being an officer in a national government, and will, by and by, give those societies an influence with the national government; and if this be a good thing, the sooner the better. We have already our American Bible Society, American Tract Society, American Missionary Society, American Temperance Society, American Sunday School Union, American Prison Discipline Society, American Jews' Society, &c. &c. and we are in a fair way to have an American Sabbath Society, and I know not how many more. . . . The fact is, sir, it is time that some national effort was made to create some religion as the law of the land; and unless you Methodists become "national" too, you will stand a poor chance among so many American Societies.[12]

In this situation the threat of an enforced Protestant uniformity was, perhaps, something more than a joke. The most aggressive of the united-front societies was unquestionably the American Sunday-School Union. It managed repeatedly to blurt out fighting words, confident of general support. In 1830 it acknowledged, "the more recent forms of Christian effort were not designed to supersede the division of Christian effort into different communions. . . ." But "The Churches of Christ have slumbered for ages over the miseries of the world; and now, while individuals are associating to relieve these miseries, the Churches, with here and there an exception, are slumbering still. . . ."[13]

To the extent that a genuine revolution threatened American Protantism, it was not so much the danger that the independent lay societies would replace the multidenominational structure as that they might absorb it. The individual churches were the working units of the societies; agents in ever greater numbers demanded and received pulpit time for their causes. With increasing skill the agents organized congregations for their own purposes, diverting energies and money to the bene-

12. Uncle Sam, "National Societies," The Christian Advocate and Journal, II (1828), 143.
13. The American Sunday-School Magazine, VII (1830), 131.

fit of their independent societies. They used church property for their meetings, usually for a two-dollar fee. The agents also worked at the highest level: at every ecclesiastical assembly there was a line of them waiting to present their pleas.

Within the churches themselves a number of factors operated in favor of the work of the united front. As in Great Britain, benevolent activity was the only way open to American women for participation in public affairs. The churches were not providing outlets for tremendous energies at their disposal. At that time, too, there was political trouble in practically all of the denominations. The clergy, extremely conservative in their bias and intent upon ministerial dignity and authority, were holding the line against an earnest attempt on the part of influential laity to obtain a voice in policy-making at ecclesiastical assemblies. Probably this effort was one expression of American pride in political maturity. There were republican movements of one sort or another in the Methodist, Presbyterian, and Congregational Churches, and in the American Catholic Church, too, for that matter. The spirit was in the air. At the price of a few small schisms, the clergy stood fast, yielding nothing to the laity. But there was a hidden cost for the victory of clerical pride. Business leaders had power and money at their command, with a healthy appetite for good works and public recognition. The Evangelical united front welcomed them with open arms, took what they had to offer, as shown by the statistics at the beginning of this chapter, and gave them what they wanted. Agents and missionaries knew that the independent societies not only paid better wages but really paid them.

Clerical conservatism in the highly organized denominations and the limitations of parish activity in those more loosely constructed affected the relationships between the churches and the benevolent societies. After all, it was a time of change, a time for speculation, a chance to get ahead. In the ministry a goodly number of energetic, ambitious clergymen either had no place to go or no chance of getting there. Some denominations such as the Baptists and Congregationalists offered no ladders at all. In others, the path to power seemed barred by unbearably stodgy denominational politics. For these frustrated clergy, the united-front societies opened the door to nationwide activity and fame. Lyman Beecher of Connecticut was an example of both effects at work. The Congregational Church had no more structure than its general associations. Real power stemmed from "Pope" Dwight at Yale and a conservative faculty at Andover, positions Beecher could not hope to challenge. He tried Presbyterianism, only to find himself too far from the center of influence at Princeton, but in the united front he found release for his tremendous enthusiasm as well as a path to national fame: missions, Bibles, tracts, Sunday schools, temperance, and education for the ministry. Another example was the Rev. James Milnor, Episcopal clergyman of New York city. He came late to the ministry; he was not in the line of succession or in favor with the young and vigorous Bishop John Henry Hobart. His progress blocked on the ecclesiastical front, he achieved national renown as the leading spirit of the American Tract Society.[14]

Clearly there was much in the Evangelical united front to threaten the existing order of American Protestantism and with it the separation of church and state, but not enough to justify the hopes of the fusion radicals, such as the Rev. Ezra Stiles Ely, or the fears of sectarian stalwarts, such as Bishop Hobart. Several causes, however, operated to make the total scheme complementary and co-operative in its nature rather than competitive. In the first place, the various denominations could not do the massive job of revitalizing American Protestantism. They were too weak, divided, conservative, and lacking in imagination to make the Evangelical faith the important force in American culture which it later became. And, just as obviously, the denominations grew in strength with every advance of the united front. The object of the united front was the conversion of every American and, beyond that, of every non-Evangelical person in the entire world. Those conversions could be signed, sealed, and delivered only in the sacraments of some Evangelical sect. The united front

14. John S. Stone, *A Memoir of the Life of James Milnor, D.D.,* American Tract Society (New York, 1849), 270 ff.

might have the power and the glory of battle in the great cause, but when the dust settled, the denominations were in possession of the field.

So it was with the general prestige of religion in America. Right and left the united front fought for Bible-reading, prayer, sobriety, Sabbath observance, and church attendance as the only respectable American ways of life. It raised the prestige of Christianity to the point where belief or at least the pretense of belief was the norm of American behavior. The direct beneficiaries of that prestige were the denominational churches.

Sectarian identity also asserted itself in varying degrees within the united-front societies, especially in the control of propaganda. For example, on the publishing committee of the American Tract Society in 1830 were the Rev. James Milnor, Episcopalian, the Rev. Thomas McAuley, Presbyterian, the Rev. John Knox, Reformed Dutch, the Rev. Samuel Green, Congregationalist, and the Rev. Charles G. Sommers, Baptist. At their meetings the members of the committee were expected to "come to their work with the solemn and honest stipulation to be each the protector of his own peculiarities,"[15] which should find recognition but should not prevail; sufficient common ground existed to load each tract with "enough of Divine Truth" to save a person who had never seen or heard of a Bible.[16]

The same sort of arrangements prevailed in the American Sunday-School Union, which claimed its chief support from Episcopalians, Methodists, Baptists, Congregationalists, and Presbyterians.[17] In this society no clergyman could hold office or be a manager. At first the committee of publication consisted of five members of these denominations appointed by the board of managers.[18] Later the society increased this membership and formalized representation: "The Committee of Publication shall consist of eight members, from at least four different

15. American Tract Society, *Fifth Annual Report* (1930), 9.
16. *Ibid.*
17. Willard Hall, *A Defense of the American Sunday-School Union against the Charges of its Opponents* (Philadelphia, 1828), 11.
18. American Sunday-School Union, *First Report* (1825), 33.

denominations of Christians, and not more than two members from any one denomination."[19]

Similar provisions prevailed formally or informally throughout the united-front structure at the top level. Sometimes the nonsectarian balance of sectarian interests carried on through the intermediate or territorial associations to the local groups. This balance could and did happen in Sunday-school, Bible, and tract work. But more often it broke down somewhere along the line into a maze of denominational auxiliaries of nonsectarian societies, particularly in foreign and domestic missions as well as in temperance societies. For example, the Methodist Episcopal Sunday School Association of New York City belonged to the nonsectarian New York Sunday School Union Society, auxiliary of the American Sunday-School Union (Philadelphia). There were at the same time, the 1820's, nonsectarian Sunday schools in New York, but the tendency was for them to break up, not into denominational schools but into denominational churches fostering their own schools.[20]

Another reinforcement of sectarian interests at the local level was the custom of society agents to use the church congregation at its Sunday devotions, not the public meeting on neutral ground, as the focal point of attack. In this practice they differed from the British, probably because population in the United States was more scattered and the difficulties of special meetings were discouraging. At any rate, the auxiliary groups which the agents organized on such occasions would fall more or less under church auspices, and the natural impulses of a vigorous pastor brought them under church control.

There were degrees, too, in the sectarian orientation of the united-front societies. Probably the American Education Society had the narrowest allegiance, since it trained solely for Congregational, Presbyterian, or Reformed Dutch ministry. The American Board of Commissioners for Foreign Missions relied, too, on members of these three denominations, although it seems to have drawn in some degree upon other Calvinist

19. "Sunday School Books," *The Biblical Repertory and Theological Review,* VIII (1836), 110.

20. Stephen H. Tyng, *Forty Years' Experience in Sunday-Schools* (New York, 1860), 132, 159-66.

sects in its early years, especially the Baptists.[21]   While the
American Tract Society may not have been fully representative,
its pricing policies together with the lack of obvious bias in its
product were enough to assure it fairly general support; the
same conditions were true of the American Sunday-School
Union.   The American Bible Society stood at the head of the
group in the esteem of all American Protestants and in official
recognition by denominations.   For example, the Methodist
General Conference of 1820 struck out the word "Bible" from
its Missionary and Bible Society as a friendly gesture toward
the American Bible Society.[22]   Other united-front organizations rode the religious impulse which these leaders helped to
create but were not so oriented as to raise the sectarian issue.
Such were the American Temperance Society, the American
Colonization Society, the American Anti-Slavery Society, and
the General Union for Promoting the Observance of the
Christian Sabbath.

On the whole, the denominations steadily gained in strength
during the era of good feelings, but the united front managed
to maintain an atmosphere unfavorable to sectarian dispute up
to about 1828.   By that time it had attained sufficient mo-
mentum to sustain it in full power for some years.

More or less general Protestant support of societies pretending to national character would not be sufficient in itself to account for the results achieved.   The essential question remains
to be answered: just how united was the united front?   Geographically there were three main centers of activity: New
England, with Boston as the focal point, New York city, and
Philadelphia.   In each, a single, cohesive group of people operated the whole range of united-front organizations.   The membership of these groups represented the conservative elements
of those regions.   They were clergymen, merchants, lawyers,
judges, and politicians who seemed driven together by the necessity of doing something to protect conservative interests in

21. See statement of Central Union Association of Pennsylvania in I. M.
Allen, ed., *The United States Baptist Annual Register for 1832* (Philadelphia,
1833), 125.
22. Bangs, *History*, III, 150.

the dynamic social atmosphere of a rising democracy which was threatening to cast off all traditional restraints.

New England chose to meet the threat to its "standing order" with a moral-society movement. It does not seem to have been a reinvigoration of organizations stemming from the British moral societies of the 1690's but a new impulse rooted in Wilberforce's revival of the old line of attack in, the 1790's. The Connecticut Society for the Suppression of Vice and the Promotion of Good Morals, founded in 1812, took its name from Wilberforce's British organization. As Lyman Beecher said, "That was a new thing in that day for the clergy and laymen to meet on the same level and cooperate. . . . The ministers had always managed things for themselves, for in those days the ministers were all politicians."[23] In the good old days it was the custom for Connecticut clergy to meet for political purposes in the home of some colleague generous enough to supply unlimited quantities of rum, lemons, and sugar and goodnatured enough to mop up the mess after the pious deliberations. "And, fact is, when they got together, they would talk over who should be governor, and who lieutenant governor, and who in the Upper House, and their counsels would prevail."[24] But those days had gone forever in Connecticut by 1812; it was necessary for the conservative impulse to organize the wise and the good along broader lines to include the more powerful laity on a basis of equality. The standing order faced a dangerous situation, an attack on the established church and the political leadership of the ministry combined with the rise of the Republicans and a split in the Federalist party. Mixed with such problems was the general social upheaval marked with rapidly increasing drunkenness and violation of the Sabbath.

Moral societies of such mingled motives spread rapidly through Connecticut.[25] Not only did they bring the clergy and laity into co-operation on terms of equality but they tended to extend equality to others than Congregationalists. For ex-

23. *Autobiography*, I, 259.
24. *Ibid.*
25. There were thirty branch societies by Oct. 20, 1813. See *The Panoplist*, X (1814), 17-20.

ample, the Moral Society of East Haddam, Conn., included Presbyterians, Episcopalians, and Baptists.[26] Clearly, class interests rather than religious interests were primarily at stake: a new aristocracy was intent upon establishing social, religious, and political control in the pattern of the old, Tory aristocracy.[27]

These forces moved to the attack with the weapons provided by the British in about the same order as the British themselves deployed those weapons. First they applied coercion and maintained that pressure fairly consistently. This was a "law and order" crusade aimed at the acute discomfort of tithingmen and the other town officials until they enforced a lot of obsolete laws, distinctly bluish, concerned with Sabbath observance, profanity, gambling, intemperance, and general "frolicking." They damned all manner of fun in the mood of moral societies of the older tradition: "All diversions, whether more mean or more manly, are the grapes of Sodom and the clusters of Gommorrah. . . ."[28]

The same situation held true for Massachusetts, with some interesting variations. In Andover, Mass., home of Andover Theological Seminary and center of supralapsarian Calvinism, a group formed in apparently deliberate imitation of the Clapham Sect in England. The members were Ebenezer Porter, professor of homiletics and later president of the Seminary, Leonard Woods, another professor and leading spirit in policy-making at Andover, Moses Stuart, professor of sacred literature, Justin Edwards, pastor of Andover's South Church, Mark Newman, principal of Phillips Academy in 1810 and member of the Seminary's board of trustees, John Adams, a rugged revivalist who succeeded Newman at Phillips Academy, and John Farrar, a Seminary student who became Hollis professor of mathematics and natural philosophy at Harvard.

These men met on Monday evenings in Dr. Porter's study

26. *The Panoplist*, XIII (1817), 252.
27. Vernon Stauffer, "New England and the Bavarian Illuminati" (*Columbia University Studies in History, Economics, and Public Law*, LXXXII [New York, 1918]), 29 ff.
28. Nathanael Emmons, *A Discourse delivered . . . to the Society for the Reformation of Morals in Franklin* (Worcester, Mass., 1793), 14.

"for devising plans of doing good, and advancing the Redeemer's kingdom, at home and abroad, in every practical way."[29] The gathering had its finger in most of the benevolent projects centered around Boston. Leonard Woods was one of the founders of the American Board of Commissioners for Foreign Missions; Ebenezer Porter successfully promoted his American version of the British concert of prayer as a device for Evangelical unity. At their meetings they schemed for the foundation of the American Tract Society (New England), the American Education Society, the American Temperance Society, and the Association for the Better Observance of the Sabbath.

But underlying these successes was the group's promotion of the moral-society idea, which brought together throughout Massachusetts those people who would carry the burden for the full range of benevolent activities. Justin Edwards led an effort to make Andover a model moral community blessed with a model moral society. To this end Edwards organized seventy gentlemen into a cohort of righteousness on April 20, 1814, to "discountenance" immorality, particularly Sabbath breaking, intemperance, and profanity. The Society met quarterly but operated from day to day with a standing committee under Edwards' chairmanship, with special attention to the school system.[30]

In the meantime the ladies of Andover had not been idle. Within a year from the founding of the Moral Society they had started the Andover South Parish Charitable Society as its auxiliary, charged with raising money for the purchase of pious books for the school libraries. By 1818 the Sunday-school movement had arrived in Andover; its popularity and its demands upon the time, energies, and funds of the wise and the good began to absorb the moral-society impulse.

Much the same sort of thing was going on throughout rural New England. While the country squires engaged in the stern work of their moral societies, frowning industriously

29. John Adams, *The Testimony of a Veteran to the Value of the Labours of Sunday-School Missionaries* (Philadelphia, c. 1855), 3-4.
30. William A. Hallock, *Light and Love. A Sketch of the Life and Labors of the Rev. Justin Edwards, D.D.* (New York, 1855), 44 ff.

upon this and that, their ladies were proving that they, too, could read British periodicals and behave like British gentlefolk. Having no one else from whom to collect, they formed "cent" societies and collected from each other. This development was not as frivolous as it seems, since it provided the germ of feminine organization, the first to come to New England. The proceeds of the cent societies originally went to foreign and domestic missions, but as Evangelical organizations developed, the cent societies, like the moral societies, disappeared. They became female auxiliaries of the numerous specific Evangelical efforts. The support of education societies became a favorite cause of New England women. To their weekly meetings they brought not only such coppers as might escape their husbands' vigilance but cloth and other home produce to help finance the education of pious young men for the ministry at home or abroad. At that time a year in college cost about seventy-five dollars, and such efforts maintained nearly 20 per cent of the student body.

The Puritan heritage of rural New England extended its influence over New York state and ultimately Ohio; it differed only in degree from the Evangelical aspect of the rural areas farther south. The problems of Boston were quite different, more akin to those of New York city and Philadelphia than to those of its surrounding countryside.

In the years immediately following the War of 1812, these three cities awoke to the startling fact that the operation of a large community requires organization, energy, and money. Rapid expansion caught them all by surprise as a growing nation brought these centers of trade, industry, and finance under great pressure. Businessmen, mechanics, and unskilled workers crowded in to take advantage of so many opportunities and "speculations." Boston, New York, and Philadelphia each developed the same pattern of growth. There was little change in the old part of town, where the respectable element of the city maintained its staid, orderly way of life. Around the old town crowded the new city, a community quite different in its values and customs. The same pattern can still be traced in the old walled towns of Europe; in America the walls were not of stone but rather of social class and cultural background. This pattern was an invitation to violence and goes far to explain the riotous disorder, crime, and bloodshed characteristic of urban life in the United States during those early years.

New York city was probably in the worst condition of the three. In 1816 the resident population of New York was 120,000, to which one should add about 10,000 transients, sailors, and visitors. The old part of town extended from the Battery to about Spring St., perhaps a little above City Hall. There began the new town, a jungle of cheap, small, wooden houses huddled solidly together without yards. In these little houses, foreigners, Negroes, and native whites hived without distinction, two or three families in a room, four to twelve families in a house.[31] There was no running water, no sewage disposal, and quite possibly no dug privies. The plagues which swept American cities are quite understandable. But the town was not lacking in other essentials: there were 1,489 licensed dram shops. Sixteen churches graced the old part, but in the seventh ward, twice as large, there was only one. There the only other suggestion of religious life was the customary horseshoe under each doorstep to keep out evil spirits. According to one reckoning, the seventh ward gave employment to two thousand prostitutes operating out of innumerable "ballrooms." Hostility between the two parts of town was evident enough. When an early Bible distributor ventured across the line, his prospective converts beat him, stripped him, and left him naked and bleeding in the street.

The prevailing attitude in the old town toward the newcomers was indifference bolstered by ignorance. America was the land of freedom and opportunity; if anyone failed, the fault was his own. Failures and misfortunes were private and individual, not public. By 1834 New York was much more conscious of its responsibilities for its sick and broken people, but the attitude toward using public funds to help them was not much different: relief undermined character. In that

31. Ward Stafford, *New Missionary Field, A Report to the Female Missionary Society for the Poor of the City of New York and its Vicinity* (New York, 1817), 11-16.

year New York spent $14,841.81 to assist 29,726 of its citizens, degrading them at the price of about sixty-five cents per annum per degradation.[32]

The conditions of division and disorder brought by rapid growth to New York were not only unhappy and unwholesome but positively dangerous to the security of life and property. The same problem in less degree confronted both Boston and Philadelphia—wild and lawless chaos just beyond the boundaries of respectability. Remedy by governmental action was out of the question in that laissez-faire atmosphere. Conservative elements could control the city administration with little opposition from the "dirty shirts," but control was of slight help when the only obligations of government were to maintain order and enforce contracts. There was more enthusiasm for the latter of these functions, although imprisonment for debt was on the way out as uneconomical. Practically all other city services, including fire fighting and education, depended on free enterprise and voluntary association.

Clearly, the situations in each of the three principal cities called for concerted, organized effort by the wealthy and respectable old town to absorb and digest its chaotic and dangerous environment, to inculcate the entire city population with its attitudes and values. The effort had to be one of voluntary association. Since the virtues to be propagated in the newly arrived citizenry bore a one-to-one relationship with religion in respectable minds of the day, the aggression of the old town upon the new would be of a religious nature. More simply, the British had already done the job; why look further?

Leaders of the Evangelical forces in the cities were outstanding clergy, members of bench and bar inevitably associated with politics, and businessmen. Of the last the chief representatives were importers, such as Alexander Henry of Philadelphia and Divie Bethune of New York, and a rising group of wholesalers or jobbers. While American industry remained insignificant, imports swelled to meet the needs of the growing country and attained proportions far beyond the

32. George B. Arnold, *Third Semi-Annual Report of his Service as Minister at Large, in New York* (New York, 1835), 12, 13.

distributing capacity of the importers. This growth provided opportunities for wholesalers to collect stocks to supply the country's retailers and peddlers. At a time when brand names and standard qualities and prices were unknown, the operators could extract juicy profits by clearing the inventories of importers and domestic producers of complete items, or job lots, for sale in broken quantities to their numerous customers at sharp advances in price. This was the life of the "merchant princes," a class of extensive influence and power which dominated American business during the nineteenth century. The Tappan interests of New York and Boston were typical Evangelical representatives.

Importers and jobbers were the chief source of substantial financial support. In addition, they were the men with the widest range of relationships and connections to bring into the movement effective workers from all parts of the country engaged for all imaginable motives. Further, with their friends they served as a network of communication and information. The importers spent much time in England making their purchases. From their British connections they picked up firsthand Evangelical experience and returned to the United States loaded with ideas, documents, and literature. Of course the first to share this exciting material would be their customers, the jobbers. From that point the step to American application of British techniques was short.

It is not suggested that the transfer of British techniques to American shores was mechanical. These businessmen were smarter and better informed on the nature of the United States and its people than was the Federalist party in 1798 with its Alien and Sedition Acts. Probably their main contribution to the Evangelical effort was in method. It would be an injustice simply to say that they applied British methods to American problems, although they used every bit of information they could glean from British experience. And it would be an equal injustice to label their contribution as the application of their commercial "know how" to the production and distribution of Evangelical propaganda. These men were inspired by a driving faith, a vision. Their objective was not merely to produce and distribute religious material efficiently but to bring the Kingdom of God to the United States—by driving every other form of literature off the market with price competition. It was commercial war against sin, cutthroat competition with the devil. And to this notable project the importers, jobbers, and merchants applied methods nearly a century in advance of current business practices. It was undoubtedly the first American experience of mass production for a national market at the lowest possible price; it was not merely production at a low profit but at a deliberate, calculated loss to be made good by the faithful. Here was the first national brand, nationally distributed through geographical districts, each with its warehouse or "depository," district manager, and salesmen. It was the first American experience with a uniform, standard package, sold nationally at a uniform, standard price printed on the package, backed by a national campaign of advertising and sales promotion.[33] It is no coincidence that modern sales promotion is still sometimes called "missionary work."

Underlying and permeating the whole machinery was the buoyant spirit characteristic of the times. The movement was another "speculation," a speculation in immortal souls but still a speculation. This fact showed whenever an Evangelical united-front society slipped into financial difficulty. In those days the thing to do was to double commitments in every direction and rally the faithful, not to save a sinking venture but to launch a campaign so ambitious as to make present liabilities shrink to the dimensions of mere trivia. And invariably they so shrank.

As in England, the laity gave energy, method, money, wide social appeal, and prestige. But even more than in Great Britain the articulate element of the movement was the clergy. And, more than in Great Britain, the role of spokesman tended to merge with the role of political leader in the Evangelical united front, perhaps because of a greater fluidity in the society of the United States, a less clear separation of the clergy from the laity under the voluntary system of America, a less complete

33. See below, Chap. XIII.

dedication to a separate way of life than prevailed in England. For example, Samuel Bayard, a New York lawyer and judge, helped found Princeton Theological Seminary, the New York Historical Society, and the New Jersey and American Bible Societies, and he felt competent to publish a book, *Letters on the Sacrament of the Lord's Supper.*[34] Another of the middle ground was Zachariah Lewis, class of 1794 at Yale, who studied theology under the Presbyterian leader Ashbel Green, at Philadelphia, and then became editor of New York's *Commercial Advertiser* and *Spectator.* He continued his religious interests by serving as corresponding secretary and writer of annual reports for the New York Religious Tract Society and United Foreign Missionary Society.

An interesting character, perhaps more typical of the American scene, was James Milnor, Philadelphia lawyer and politician, later Episcopal clergyman and leading spirit of the American Tract Society in New York. Reared as a Quaker, he refused to conform to the discipline and was read out of meeting and disowned in 1799. He became a Universalist, but by 1809 he was attending both Presbyterian and Episcopalian services. Conservative constituents of Philadelphia sent Milnor to Congress, where in 1812 he became involved in legislation arising out of "the needless and calamitous war."[35] Two proposed bills were particularly distressing to Milnor. One would permit boys of eighteen to enlist without parental consent; the other would protect debtors after enlistment from arrest by their creditors. Milnor's comment was: "Two more scandalous violations of true policy, the civil rights of the citizen and the principles of religion and morality, cannot be conceived."[36] Unfortunately for Milnor, the politician pushing these measures was quite as resolute and vehement. His name was Henry Clay. Clay proposed to settle his differences with Milnor by a method which appealed to him as direct, simple, and conclusive: pistols at thirty paces. Since Milnor was far above the primitive brutality of such proceedings, he faced the choice of leaving his principles or leaving Washington. Quite properly

34. (Philadelphia, 1825).
36. *Ibid.*

35. Stone, *Memoir of Milnor,* 75.

he chose the latter course, returned to Philadelphia, and abandoned politics "because his soul was sick of its unprincipled demagogism."[37] Milnor then became deeply interested in Lindley Murray's little book with the long but relevant title, *The Power of Religion on the Mind on Affliction and Retirement, and at the Approach of Death.* Under the influence of this work Milnor rapidly completed his protracted conversion and applied through Bishop White for admission as a candidate for Episcopalian orders. For a year he studied, while he wound up his law practice, and was ordained in the summer of 1814. Two years later he received a call from St. George's in New York city to serve under his old friend but uncomfortable superior, Bishop Hobart.

Along with such men as Milnor, who helped bridge the gap between laity and clergy, a considerable number whose lifelong professional dedication to the ministry entitled them to British recognition as proper wearers of the cloth gave lively attention to the united-front program. Such were the Andover group in Massachusetts and the Princeton-Philadelphia Presbyterians Archibald Alexander, Ashbel Green, and Samuel Miller. In New York the united front found stout supporters in Gardiner Spring, pastor of the famous Brick Presbyterian Church, 1810-56, John Knox of the Reformed Dutch Church, and John M. Mason of the Associate Reformed Church. Of these, Spring was the most consistent worker in the American Bible, Tract, and Home Missionary Societies and Sunday-School Union, but Mason was a necessary tower of strength in the critical early days. He was a great scholar, orator, and spokesman for the conservative view; he showed no reticence whatever. He, like Milnor, entertained certain ideas about the proper course for America during the troubled times around 1812. Upon one occasion he opened his sermon with some appropriate blasts from Jeremiah and then launched into a prayer which was less supplication than a shouted ultimatum to divine power: "Send us, if thou wilt, murrain upon our cattle, a famine upon our land, cleanness of teeth in our borders; send us pestilence to waste our cities; send us, if it please

37. *Ibid.*, 72, 73, 171.

thee, the sword to bathe itself in the blood of our sons, but spare us, Lord God Most Merciful, spare us that direst and most dreadful of all thy curses—an alliance with Napoleon Bonaparte."[38] Mason's vehemence in his impassioned apostrophe was such that in the midst of it blood burst from his nostrils. Without pause Mason sopped his face with his handkerchief and continued, while waving the gory symbol of defiance in the face of a fascinated congregation.

In addition to the support of the united front given by such stalwarts as Mason and Spring, some clergy made their careers in the movement. Such were Lyman Beecher of New England and Ohio, Ebenezer Porter of the Andover group, Alexander Proudfit of Troy and New York city, and Thomas McAuley and Ezra Stiles Ely, Philadelphia Presbyterians. These were planners, writers, editors, and corresponding secretaries, who developed a vested interest in the success of the enterprise. Beneath them a host of lesser clergy found employment as agents and missionaries. At a time when few parishes could support their ministers in even approximate decency, part-time or full-time employment by a united-front society at the respectable rate of $400 to $800 per annum, plus expenses, looked good. These were earnest and competent workers, whose meticulously honest expense accounts might bring a blush of shame to many modern, tax-minded executives.

Such was the conservative coalition of lawyers, judges, politicians, businessmen, and clergy who operated the Evangelical united front. To describe the relationships between the various societies as interlocking directorates seems a little inadequate. The different societies were essentially made up from this same group in various aspects of conservative activity. Few outstanding Evangelicals belonged to only one or two societies. A leading interest in one or two with membership on the board of managers in five or six others was the norm for the leaders.

A peculiar evidence of common leadership, membership, and purpose was the transfer of funds between societies. For example, in 1833 when the Evangelical dream of world con-

38. *Appleton's Cyclopaedia of American Biography*, J. G. Wilson and John Fiske, eds. (New York, 1887), IV, 246.

quest was at fever pitch, the American Board of Commissioners for Foreign Missions received $10,300 from the Ameri-
can Bible Society and $6,000 from the American Tract So-
ciety.[39] The following year the American Bible Society proposed to raise $30,000 for the American Board, the American
Tract Society aimed its contribution at $20,000, and the Ameri-
can Sunday-School Union set a tentative, more modest mark of
$1,000 to $4,000.[40]

The solidarity of the Evangelical united front at its upper
levels found expression in a passion for merger, consolidation,
and monopoly such as swept the business world some seventy
years later under similar conditions. British example, supported by a succession of religious and social fads, had spattered
the American landscape with innumerable independent societies. The urgencies of the conservative position in the United
States and the natural drive for personal power supplied motivation, while the myth* of nationalism gave the necessary
emotional energy and patriotic sanction. The American Board
of Commissioners for Foreign Missions, founded in 1810, was
not truly part of this pattern of merger but rather an imitation
of the London Missionary Society, with a pretension to nationalism in its name. The same was true of the American Bible
Society of 1816 in its relationship to the British and Foreign
Bible Society, except that here the British example imposed an
American merger.

But for eight years Americans continued to use the foreign
instrument of combination without truly understanding its
possibilities. Probably they had accepted it before they were
ready for it. The monopoly rash did not break out until 1824,
with the formation of the American Sunday-School Union.
There followed in quick succession the same action in the
societies for tracts, temperance, domestic missions, and Sabbath
observance. As a Connecticut clergyman who had previously
opposed mergers wrote to an American Sunday-School Union
board member in 1825, "But I am now convinced that the

39. American Board of Commissioners for Foreign Missions, *Report Read at
the Twenty-Fourth Annual Meeting* (1833), 32.
40. American Sunday-School Union, *Tenth Annual Report* (1834), 72, 73.
* The word "myth" is used here and later in the sense used by Pareto and
Sorel, a symbol evoking emotional response without reflection.

principle of combination has powers in the advancement of every useful design connected with religion."[41]

The opening of the Erie Canal in 1825 and the rise of New York city to national leadership seem to have had something to do with all of this development. New York appears to have been a great magnet exerting an increasing pulling power in all directions, a natural geographic point of concentration. A fair example of this process at work was the organization of the American Tract Society in New York in 1825. An American Tract Society formed in Boston in 1814, following the example of the London Religious Tract Society, but its influence did not extend beyond New England. There had been a similar operation going on in New York city just about as long, the New York Religious Tract Society. Both of these groups were producing the same tracts written by the same British authors, and both had fairly extensive local affiliations for support and distribution. The chief arguments for merger into a national society located in New York were that city's growing population and prosperity, better communication by sea with foreign parts, and, with the completion of the proposed canal system, direct water communication with every village in the country west of the Alleghenies.[42]

A meeting in New York for final arrangements immediately preceded the annual assembly of the American Bible Society for the convenience of all concerned. The resulting merger left both component societies operating as before without changing their names but related them to each other as auxiliaries of the new national organization.

This sort of thing worked so well that in a very few years a pattern of procedure emerged which has been standard American performance ever since. A contemporary summarized the various steps in 1836:[43] "Whatever is started, a national society must at once be got up. . . ." The first move was to select an imposing name. Then one had to get a list of

41. American Sunday-School Union, *Second Report* (1826), 93.
42. *Address of the Executive Committee of the American Tract Society to the Christian Public* (New York, 1825), 12, 13.
43. Calvin Colton (A Protestant, *pseud.*), *Protestant Jesuitism* (New York, 1836), 42-54.

respectable and influential people to sign up as members and patrons. Funds collected in this process were sufficient to hire a secretary with his corps of assistants and to send forth a band of popular lecturers as agents. Then it was time to put the press in operation. These measures started the multiplication of subsidiary societies in a snowballing process no community could resist.

Such methods were effective in promoting organizations with national pretensions, but their realization required machinery of communication and cohesion. Concerts of prayer were an early and fairly effective device for this purpose, but the printed word did much more. Most of the societies made production and dissemination of publications a chief activity, which established a network for the dissemination of ideas which annual reports purposefully exploited. The reports were volumes of detailed information regarding the activities of the parent organization and all the auxiliaries of which it could gather news. Taking their cue from small-town newspapers, they mentioned as many names as possible and included massive sections of correspondence. They circulated directions, rules of procedure, suggestions for the successful solution of common difficulties, and exchanges of experience. They were as welcome in any Evangelical household as an almanac. For that matter, there were Evangelical almanacs, too.

Supplementing circulation of the printed word, an extensive and complicated machinery developed for bringing kindred spirits to meet in the flesh. As early as 1820 a convention circuit began to emerge. A principal feature was "Anniversary Week" in New York, an institution developing around the annual meeting of the American Bible Society during the second week in May. Since essentially the same people formed the nucleus of each successive "national" Evangelical enterprise, the best time to organize a new venture was when the Bible people got together. Any project believing itself entitled to Evangelical support took that time and place for its starting point and had an anniversary to celebrate.

The program in 1820 was quite modest. Tuesday was the anniversary of the Union Sunday-School Society. That morning twenty-five hundred of the city's nine thousand Sunday-school pupils with their teachers marched up Broadway from Battery Park nearly a mile to the Circus, where they ate cakes from the baskets they carried in the parade. There was another meeting for them in the evening at the Methodist church on John St. Wednesday went to the Union Foreign Missionary Society; the next day was for the American Bible Society, since it had moved its proceedings from British Monday to a more climactic Thursday. On Friday the Society for the Conversion of Jews gathered to report no converts for its colony in New Jersey. Their business in New York concluded, the leading spirits went on to "Ecclesiastical Week" in Philadelphia, where the attractions were meetings of the governing assemblies of the Presbyterian, Episcopalian, and Baptist communions as well as the Philadelphia Sunday and Adult School Union.[44]

These were promising beginnings. Full development of the national convention as an American institution came with the railroads, but the American Sunday-School Union could not wait for that. During the years 1820-25 there were numerous local Sunday-school conferences or conventions in the Eastern, Middle, and South Atlantic regions.[45] New Hampshire held the first Sunday-school convention at the state level in 1824. All the other states followed its example to form state Sunday-school unions. Delegates from state unions met at the American Sunday-School Union's anniversary celebrations during Ecclesiastical Week at Philadelphia in alternating years from 1824 to 1830. At the May meeting of 1830 the delegates of thirteen states took the bold step of planning a national convention in New York city that fall. They carried through with reasonable success—220 delegates from fourteen states and territories met for the occasion. The amount of energy the meeting required, at a time when the United States could boast only three hundred miles of railroad track, is a sincere tribute to Evangelical devotion.

44. Dorothy C. Barck, ed., *Letters from John Pintard to his Daughter, Eliza Noel Pintard Davidson, 1816-1833* (New York, 1940-41), I, 290 ff.

45. For development of this topic see Rice, *Sunday-School Movement*, 355 ff., and Marianna C. Brown, *Sunday School Movements in America* (New York, 1901), 53 ff.

But the convention ball really started to roll in 1832. Experience had taught the Sunday-school people that a successful national convention was a complicated and well-articulated piece of social machinery. That year the preliminary meeting at the home offices during Philadelphia's Ecclesiastical Week prepared a carefully worded, eight-page circular and questionnaire, printed three thousand copies, and sent them out. From 142 replies of schools and unions in twenty states, the central office constructed a convention agenda focusing on common problems almost everyone wanted to discuss:

(1) frequency and length of Sunday-school sessions (some were running up to six hours) ;
(2) importance and modes of pupil visiting by teachers;
(3) teacher preparation of lessons;
(4) training scholars to become teachers;
(5) influence of the personal habits of teachers;
(6) influence of the superintendent.[46]

These were truly wonderful topics for Evangelical shoptalk and buzzing gossip. The national convention of the American Sunday-School Union in New York on October 3, 1832, was an outstanding success; it not only established the convention as an American social institution but set the standard procedure in use today.

Undoubtedly the experience of the American Sunday-School Union contributed much to the entire Evangelical convention circuit, which was operating full blast in 1834, when a deputation from the Congregational Union of England and Wales crossed the Atlantic to see what was going on. The delegates started with Anniversary Week opening on May 5 in New York, went through Ecclesiastical Week in Philadelphia, and then on to Boston for the June wind-up with the American Board and the Congregational Association. The experience left them exhausted but not too tired to write a fairly coherent account of what they had witnessed.

The Britishers found New York well organized for Anni-

46. Andrew Reed and James Matheson, *A Narrative of the Visit to American Churches by the Deputation from the Congregational Union of England and Wales* (New York, 1835). The following account is from the material in Vol. I, written by the Rev. Reed, pp. 37 ff.

versary Week. Evidently a central committee of the Evangelical united front ran the whole affair. The operations of such a committee are clear although its organization remains obscure. Quite possibly it was informal, for the cohesion of this group would have permitted informality. Pastors of churches asked members of congregations who would entertain guests to submit their names and some details of accommodations, and this material went to the central committee. The three to four hundred out-of-town attendants sent their names and needs to the committee, which assigned lodgings in advance, with due regard to indicated friendships. Upon arrival each traveler reported to the desk of the central committee. There he signed in, was allotted his lodgings, and received a map of the city as well as a complete program of meetings. No poor and unknown preacher ever lacked entertainment; none ever needed to use a hotel or lodging house. Apparently those entertaining kept open house all week to encourage that general run of visiting characteristic of American conventions.

The main sessions all took place in Chatham St. Chapel, the suitable neutral ground required by the united front. Here the operations of the ghostly central committee again came into play. The Chapel was a theater which had been purchased as a free church for all denominations. A minimum of reconstruction placed a roomy pulpit on the stage, front center. Behind the pulpit rose banked seats for the ministers, to preserve their dignity and distinction. Before the stage was the familiar orchestra and two galleries, supposed to seat two thousand but often crowded to twenty-five hundred.

The schedule of Anniversary Week meetings which the British delegation preserved for its records was impressive:

Monday, May 5

American Seamen's Friend Society, at Chatham-street Chapel, half past 7 o'clock, P.M.

American Anti-Slavery Society; meeting of Delegates at Society's rooms, 130 Nassau-street, 4 P.M.

Tuesday, May 6

American Anti-Slavery Society, at Chatham-street Chapel, 10 o'clock, A.M.

Revival Tract Society, at Third Free Church, corner of Houston and Thompson-streets, 4 P.M., and in the evening.

Convention of Delegates, American Tract Society, 4 P.M., at Society's house.

American Peace Society, at Chatham-street Chapel, 4 P.M.

New York Sunday School Union, at Chatham-street Chapel, half past 7 P.M.

Children of the Sabbath Schools appear in the Park at half past 3 P.M.

Wednesday, May 7

American Tract Society, at Chatham-street Chapel, 4 P.M.

Delegates to American Bible Society, at Society's house, 4 P.M.

New-York Colonization Society, at Chatham-street Chapel, 4 P.M.

American Home Missionary Society, at Chatham-street Chapel, half past 7 P.M.

Delegates to American Bible Society, at the Bible House, 4 P.M.

American Baptist Home Missionary Society, at Mulberry-street Church, 7 P.M.

Thursday May 8

American Bible Society, at Chatham-street Chapel, 10 A.M.

Directors of American Home Missionary Society, at their rooms in the Tract House, 4 P.M.

Seventh Commandment Society, at Chatham-street Chapel, 4 P.M.

Presbyterian Education Society, at Chatham-street Chapel, half past 7 P.M.

American and Presbyterian Education Society united.

Friday May 9

Meeting for the Foreign Mission Board, at Chatham-street Chapel, 10 A.M.

New York City Temperance Society, at Chatham-street Chapel, half past 7 P.M.

New York Infant Sunday School Society in Canal-street Church, 10 A.M.

Morning prayer meetings will be held at half past 5 o'clock on Tuesday, Wednesday, Thursday and Friday, in Chatham-street Chapel, and in Mr. Patton's church, Broome-street, near Broadway.

Although the British visitors failed to note the unsuccessful attempt of the new American Anti-Slavery Society to displace the American Colonization Society as the Evangelical answer to the race problem,[47] they made some interesting observations on the week's program and a few pertinent comparisons with Evangelical proceedings in England. The early prayer meetings at 5:30 A.M. were popular and well attended. The morning gatherings at Chatham St. Chapel engaged the more important societies. They opened at 10:00 A.M. and closed about 2:00 P.M. Formerly they had been able to wind up their business by 12:30 P.M. but now needed the full four hours or more. Singers in the galleries supplemented the evening speakers. All meetings were later in the day than was the custom in England.

On the whole, the British found that their American cousins showed spirit and efficiency and that their meetings were not inferior, possibly superior, to those in Bristol, Liverpool, and Manchester. Among American speakers they heard fewer to be classed as formal, inappropriate, or turgid. There was less talent in New York, to be sure. No Englishman ever crossed the Atlantic expecting to find more talent. And there was less beauty of period. But these honest visitors admitted that they also met with less claptrap, trifling, and frivolity. Compared with the English, the American Evangelicals were grim and determined. They met to do serious business in a serious manner. They looked with wonder and pity on the impertinence of anyone who sought to amuse them with pun, humor, or prettiness of speech. From the deep sincerity of British comment, one can surmise that some member of their delegation tried to float a bit of pleasantry only to have it land with a sickening thud.

In action, American speakers showed they had used more time in preparation than was British practice, but they leaned less heavily upon their notes. Audience response was less active but not less interested. Only once was there a spattering of applause, quickly stifled. It was American custom to show approval by smiles and a higher degree of encouragement by tears. The greatest tribute an orator could evoke among his Evangelical listeners was a deep, sublime silence, sobbing muted.

47. See the author's article, "The Colonization of Free Negroes in Liberia, 1816-1835," *The Journal of Negro History*, XXXVIII (1953), 63 ff.

One cannot attribute the weeping in these sessions to the so-called "weaker sex." It was a solidly masculine audience; women were barred from such meetings at the time.

Andrew Reed, a member of the British deputation, rated the assemblies of the American Tract, Home Missionary, Bible, and Foreign Missionary Societies as creating most interest. Of these, the meeting of the American Board of Commissioners for Foreign Missions on Friday was the climax. Proceedings opened at 10:00 A.M., with the Honorable John C. Smith presiding over a packed house and stage. The Rev. Alexander Proudfit, an old blood-and-thunder warhorse of missions, opened with prayer. Then Dr. Wisner, secretary of the American Board, read the Board's report. The Rev. Winslow, just returned from Ceylon, gave an account of missionary work in India. Following him, Dr. Beman produced a punchy, argumentative speech for the cause. Then the Rev. Reed himself took the floor with a resolution and speech evoking great emotion. At that point the meeting threatened to fall apart. A certain tendency to go off the deep end was a fairly constant hazard to Evangelical enterprise, one to which the English were not immune. When the British and Foreign Bible Society was fighting out the issue of a religious test for its membership, a Baptist minister staged a type of sit-down strike for the test by kneeling on the platform, his hands folded on his breast, his face lifted in silent supplication. He refused to budge, and only a most forceful declaration by a powerful Quaker finally put the Society back on the track.

A similar situation arose in New York after Reed concluded his resolution. The Rev. Blayden gained the floor. He wanted to take up a collection on the spot and resolve into a prayer meeting. He thought that he could pick up $5,000 for the cause. There was a lot of argument: it was contrary to Evangelical custom to take collections at the sessions, and there was business to be done—four more speakers to be heard. A compromise finally gained the day. The chair overruled Blayden; a resolution to open two places for special prayer in behalf of missions on Sunday evening passed. The following speakers, Alder, Matheson of the British deputation, Bethune, and the famous Gardiner Spring, all suffered from reaction, but the meeting managed to wind up at two-thirty with some sense of accomplishment.

Reed and Matheson found the Sunday evening prayer meetings for missions crowded, "serious and interesting"; then they hastened on to Philadelphia's Ecclesiastical Week, where the Episcopal Church Missionary Society met on the night of their arrival. They decided that Philadelphia's performance did not suffer in comparison with New York's. The arrangements were much the same; Ezra Stiles Ely rather outdid himself with thirteen or fourteen houseguests. The General Assembly of the Presbyterian Church was the main show; meetings of the American Sunday-School Union and other ecclesiastical affairs crowded in between sessions of the Presbyterian government. The British visitors rated this body next in importance to the Congress of the United States, a judgment in which some Presbyterians would hardly concur.

The third week of May found the British continuing their Evangelical marathon in Boston, which wished to benefit from the discussions and decisions of New York and Philadelphia. Dr. Codman spoke to the Boston Missionary Society at Park St. Church. The following day belonged to the Pastoral Association, an organization of Massachusetts ministers. Then came the Society for the Promotion of Christian Knowledge, the oldest American missionary venture, and the Congregational Convention. The latter was a sort of widow's-fund society of orthodox and Unitarian membership. The orthodox majority appointed a speaker with the consent of the minority. There were two business meetings and then a public service where the orthodox preacher, aware of the condition of his appointment, pulled his punches notably.

A similar embarrassment afflicted the principal speaker at the Northern Baptist Education Society; the unexpected presence of Congregationalists from England forced him to pocket a hotly sectarian address. To make amends, the goodnatured British tossed a bait to the meeting. They would provide a twentieth scholarship to a Baptist school if those present could find the first nineteen. Such scholarships ran from sixty to seventy dollars. The enthusiastic response promptly mounted the total to forty-five.

Sunday climaxed Boston's week. Morning saw a three-hour service in Old South Church. The program contained seventeen items, including communion for four hundred. And the climax was the same as in New York, a final go with the American Board of Commissioners for Foreign Missions on Sunday evening in Park St. Church.

On the whole, the British visitors proclaimed the American Evangelical machinery to be in good working order, but they were perhaps not quite so keenly aware as some Americans that it was one vast engine of nicely articulated parts: "The American Board act not alone. . . . And if we take a view also of Bible, Education, Tract, Domestic Missionary, Sunday School and Colonization Societies, moving harmoniously on, forming so many parts in the grand whole, to the completion of that last command of our ascended Lord, 'Go and spread the influence of the gospel over every creature': we may truly say, never was the eye of man saluted with so magnificent a scene of moral grandeur."[48]

But other Americans were not quite so happy about it all. Calvin Colton saw that in less than a generation the social economy of the country had been formed on a model new to the United States, although not new to history—he had in mind the Society of Jesus. He found control assumed by a few at the head of the organizations. The public was simple, honest, confiding; it did not note what was going on or suspect that societies formed for such good purposes might contain the leaven of ambition. As he saw the operations of the mighty engine, "Most extraordinary measures are devised to obtain funds; itinerating mendicants are flying in all directions, traversing the country from east to west, and from north to south; every part of the complicated machinery is well contrived to answer the end; the system is thorough and perfect; and at the head of all sit a few eminent individuals, looking down upon and managing this work of their own hands, themselves inde-

48. Eastern Auxiliary Foreign Missionary Society of Rockingham County, *First Report* (1826), 5.

pendent and secure in their places by provisions which cannot fail while their influence lasts."[49]

Colton feared the mounting pressures to Evangelical conformity which this system was exerting upon Americans. To put his apprehensions in a few words, he found a quotation from *Spiritual Despotism: "The priest of superstition rides an ass; the priest of fanaticism—a tiger."*[50]

49. *Protestant Jesuitism*, 108.
50. *Ibid.*, title page.

THE NATURALIZATION OF THE UNITED FRONT

THE BRITISH DELEGATION making the tour in 1834 found American institutions serving American objectives. There had been no overt declaration of independence: the leadership, inspiration, and ideas of the mother country across the Atlantic commanded almost as much regard and respect as ever. But by 1834 the Evangelical united front in the United States had struck its roots deeply into American soil and was drawing from that source sufficient nourishment to flourish. It had solved a problem of great difficulty and importance.

The process of naturalization required general acceptance of the united-front concept and its successful use in solving American problems. British example was not in itself a sufficient incentive. Successful aping of the English gentry might bring social acclaim in some quarters, but it could also bring disaster. The initial impulse—the crusade against the infidel and the freethinker—petered out with the triumph of the Holy Alliance. That battle was supposed to be won in Europe. There were still many infidels in the United States, probably a majority, but their position was not vulnerable to frontal assault by a British party. A tag-end, guerrilla action would never energize Evangelical forces in the United States. By the time the American Bible Society was founded in 1816, the

Evangelical movement was already uncertain of its purposes. Native objectives were roughed out, to be sure, but native energy was missing.

The effect was to make some of the American societies rather tentative and diffident in conduct during their early years. For example, Bishop Hobart with his cohorts kept the American Bible Society in a state of trembling frustration for a decade. The Society met at intervals at the City Hotel on Broadway. For the most part it debated the question of whether or not it was a religious organization. Eventually it decided in the negative. The issues of prayer and preaching troubled the members severely; they voted against both of these encroachments upon church functions, an example followed by most early Bible societies.[1] One member, John Pintard, observed in 1820 that the Society refrained from publishing strong addresses lest it offend someone: "The fear of giving exceptions almost predominates over the duty of doing what is right."[2]

The first impulse to generate the kind of energy to carry the Evangelical united front was the Sunday-school movement. In the United States, as in Great Britain, a fad exerted power of such prevailing intensity as to leave a lasting imprint upon the fabric of society. A craze for voluntary teaching in Sunday schools started to rise in Philadelphia during the years 1814-15 and hit New York in 1816 and Boston and Charleston, S.C., in 1817. For each of these centers the Sunday school became the principal instrument of aggression by the old town upon its rapidly growing, chaotic suburbs. The Sunday school proved an effective means for the conservative element to digest and incorporate its radical environment.

The early Sunday schools in America, as in Great Britain, were essentially ventures in charity, in the spirit of love for one's fellow man characteristic of the Enlightenment. Such schools were religious in the same sense that all education was religious; there was no idea of secular education then. Bishop

1. Henry Otis Dwight, *The Centennial History of the American Bible Society* (New York, 1916), 62, 67.
2. Dorothy C. Barck, ed., *Letters from John Pintard to his Daughter, Eliza Noel Pintard Davidson, 1816-1833* (New York, 1940-41), I, 289-90; II, 263-64.

White's First Day Society, the initial effort of the sort, started in 1790.[3] When Bishop White returned from his ordination in England, he had brought the idea with him. He tried to introduce it as an ecclesiastical affair, but his parish offered too much resistance. So the bishop turned to such laymen of good will as he could rally without regard to religious persuasion, including Dr. Benjamin Rush, Universalist, Mathew Carey, Roman Catholic, and Dr. Benjamin Say, Presbyterian. Clearly, this operation was in the spirit of Benjamin Franklin, not of Lyman Beecher. The Society opened schools for boys who could afford no other means of education. It hired masters at £45 per year to run the system; classrooms opened on Sundays, 8-10 A.M. and 4-6 P.M. The pay for Sunday-school teachers in those days was thirty-three cents per Sabbath. By 1800 the First Day School system had taught more than two thousand of Philadelphia's boys.

In 1797 a similar venture started in Pawtucket, R.I., for the benefit of Samuel Slater's millhands. It was not of much importance; Slater brought the idea across the Atlantic as just another piece of textile-mill equipment. More highly organized attack on the problem continued to stem from Philadelphia, which put on a truly remarkable performance in 1808 when some of the city's ladies formed the Union Society[4] (the word "Union" indicated that they were of various Protestant denominations). The women persuaded the Superior Court to recognize them as citizens of Pennsylvania and they obtained a charter of incorporation from the state for the Society. At a time when a married woman had hardly more legal status than any other article of household furniture, this step marked a notable advance, far ahead of British precedent and conservative opinion, even in Philadelphia. The objective of the Union Society was to teach poor girls how to read, write, sew, and memorize Bible passages. The ladies soon had Sunday schools in operation, with more than three hundred girls in one of them. They advertised their good work with annual

3. Edwin Wilbur Rice, *The Sunday-School Movement, 1780-1917, and the American Sunday-School Union, 1817-1917* (Philadelphia, 1917), 42 ff.
4. *Ibid.*, 51.

public meetings for conducting examinations and awarding premiums.

In the same year, a corresponding male organization of assorted denominations, the Evangelical Society, began holding Sunday schools for both adults and children, devoted principally to the memorizing of scripture. The group expanded its operations and incorporated in 1812. So Philadelphia mothered a considerable number of Sunday schools, which varied in their attention to religion and were not attached to any religious sect. The extended visit of Robert May, British missionary, in 1811 served to give these schools the benefit of British experience and some degree of uniformity in practice.

The craze for voluntary teaching coincided with the capture of the whole Sunday-school movement for the Evangelical united front, and both seem to have been involved in the coalition of all these enterprises. The forces bringing a higher degree of organization to the Sunday-school movement were, in the first place, a passion for Protestant unity as a good thing in itself and, secondly, a need for printed material and supplies to be met efficiently only by a central agency.

The Male Adult Association of Philadelphia went to work on the problem in 1815. Possibly the name arose from a determined effort of the members to state what they had in common—sex and age—but probably the original objective was to specialize in Sunday schools for male adults. The principal instigator was Alexander Henry, an immigrant from Ireland who had become a successful importer and jobber. He had joined the Presbyterian Church in 1803 and he patterned his life thereafter according to current notions of Christian benevolence. Since he owned extensive woodlots, he donated firewood to the poor in winter. On his purchasing trips to England he picked up the current Evangelical fashion—he loaded tracts for distribution at home along with other items of British merchandise. He became interested in Sunday schools very early and served as president of the American Sunday-School Union for nearly thirty years. Another key figure was a fellow importer and friend of Henry's, Divie Bethune of New York. Bethune and his wife caught the Sunday-school fever on a buying trip to England in 1803. Bethune and Henry were typical illustrations of the prevalent notion that the ideal American gentleman was the closest possible approximation of his British counterpart. And the same was true of their ladies.

As Divie Bethune had business connections in Philadelphia, he chanced to be on hand to encourage the efforts of the Male Adult Association in working out its problems. The group managed to sign up ten of the local societies. But of the three female societies which subscribed, two had the audacity to send lady representatives, a cruel blow to the Male Adult Association. However, the enterprise survived the shock and managed to produce an acceptable constitution for a meeting in May, 1817, to form the Sunday and Adult School Union. The members tried to find a preacher to bless their efforts, but none would attend.[5]

This event seems to mark a major step in the absorption of the Sunday-school movement by the Evangelical united front. There were several causes involved. The drive for unity was one. It found expression in the preamble of the constitution adopted at that meeting, "To cultivate unity and Christian charity among those of different names,"[6] and again: "The comparative *fewness* of Christians calls for all practicable and profitable union amongst themselves. *Divide* and *conquer* is the maxim of their great foe: *Unite* and *triumph,* be then the motto of christians."[7] Another factor was the progressive acceptance in America of the British Evangelical doctrine of benevolence, the idea that true charity and philanthropy could find proper expression only in connection with the propagation of Evangelical faith. Along with this idea went the type of romanticism Gardiner Spring was promoting in New York: what really mattered was not the social consequence of one's conduct but the inner glow of conviction. A third element activated the intellectual and emotional persuasions of British propaganda. Benevolent enterprise, in its form as organized assault upon the poor, attained the popularity of a raging fad

5. *Ibid.,* 61.
6. Philadelphia Sunday and Adult School Union, *First Report* (1818), 27.
7. *Ibid.,* 3.

in Great Britain by 1813 and reached the United States in 1815. It found expression in distributing Bibles and tracts, to be sure, but Americans favored voluntary teaching in Sunday school as a fitting expression of their benevolent emotions.

Urging them on was still another British Evangelical influence, the literature of the happy, pious deaths for children. For some reason this theme made a deep impression upon American minds. Mothers joined "maternal associations" to consult with each other regarding the early conversion of their children in eager anticipation of some happy, pious deaths in the family. One way to make sure there were some prospects for this ending was to send the children to an evangelized Sunday school. The American Sunday-School Union cooperated by issuing warnings to watch carefully for happy, pious deaths among teachers as well as pupils and to report them at once to headquarters; Union publications recorded twenty-four such interesting cases, twelve boys and twelve girls.[8] The danger of shortening life expectancy, for themselves and for the children as well, did not stem the rush of Americans to become Sunday-school teachers; it only added spice to the venture.

The evangelizing of the Sunday-school movement by the united-front laity explains some odd aspects of the early reports. The utter indifference or hostility of most clergy was one. The clergy were not accustomed to thinking of Sunday schools as having religious significance. Besides, most of the pupils came from families which did not pay pew rentals or the minister's salary. When a preacher found one of the schools appropriating the cellar of his church, he naturally would complain about *"clamavi e profundis."*[9] And, for that matter, the united-front people did not consider Sunday schools to be primarily church nurseries. They were basic training units for the Evangelical united front. They would supply missionaries and devoted workers to all of the national societies: "They are coming into the action of life, a well-informed army of

8. George Hendley, *A Memorial for Sunday School Boys; A Memorial for Sunday School Girls* (Philadelphia, 1823).

9. Stephen H. Tyng, *Forty Years' Experience in Sunday-Schools* (New York, 1860), 154 ff.

soldiers for the Lord—'bayonets that think,' as Kossuth called his revolutionary soldiers."[10]

The conversion of the Sunday school to Evangelical purposes took at least eight years. As late as 1825 the union in New Jersey's Delaware County complained that too much swearing was impeding instruction in its schools but claimed some progress in making a Christian of the superintendent of school no. 3.[11] In the same year Massachusetts boasted that fifty-two of three hundred Sunday-school teachers were church members. If what took place in Carlisle, Pa., was at all typical, Evangelical strong-arm squads were occasionally useful. There, a group of muscular young Presbyterians simply moved into a Sunday school which they deemed was paying insufficient attention to religion and took over.[12]

With the Evangelical sweep and the voluntary teaching enthusiasm, the Sunday-school movement extended rapidly from its home base in Philadelphia. Divie Bethune sent his business associate, Eleazer Lord, from New York in 1815 to get the latest line on methods and experience. Upon his return they joined with Richard Varick to promote the New York Sunday School Union Society, which immediately started printing the London Sunday-School Union's lessons, alphabets, tickets, class papers, registers, and hints on how to establish Sunday schools. It also republished two English books, *The Young Cottager* and *The Orphan,* inspiring works which combined two popular themes, contented poverty and happy, pious deaths for children.[13] In the meantime, Mrs. Bethune and her friends were doing just as well with the Female Union for the Promotion of Sabbath Schools. By the end of 1816 there were more than seventy schools in New York with more than five thousand pupils.

As in Philadelphia, this development marked the invasion of New York's chaotic new town by the respectability of the old town. And there was nothing diffident about the activity. Competition for pupils among Evangelical enthusiasts was so

10. *Ibid.,* 67.
11. American Sunday-School Union, *First Report* (1825), 75-77.
12. *Ibid.,* 33 ff.
13. New York Sunday School Union Society, *First Report* (1817), 7-10.

severe that they had to spend an hour and a half or more each Sunday morning rounding up classes for the day. To a degree, the drive on the new part of the city was not a deliberate one but a result of the competition. In the old city, only a few servants were available to accept free instruction from a host of eager teachers. For instance, sixteen young Episcopalians of Grace Church could corral only twenty pupils, eight of them Negroes, in their neighborhood to start their school. They moved uptown and obtained a room in Rose St., to find that there was already another Sunday school in the building.[14]

News of what was going on in New York reached Boston through the striking report of the city missionary, Ward Stafford, in 1817.[15] Suspecting that Boston was in little better shape than New York, the town fathers called Stafford to address them, and from the meeting the Boston Society for the Moral and Religious Instruction of the Poor emerged. Boston chose to follow the Andover lead in forming a moral society, but its methods did not differ from those of New York and Philadelphia. The group gathered and disseminated information about British Sunday schools, already available in Stafford's report, passed out Bibles and tracts, and hired four part-time preachers to go to work on the city's poor.[16] Of these measures the Sunday school was the most successful; it rapidly became a New England institution.

In the same year, Boston's spiritual twin, Charleston, S.C., was going through the same experience, although its inspiration came directly from Philadelphia. To the west, Pittsburgh, on the way to becoming an Evangelical stronghold, was off to an even better start. As early as 1808, Pittsburgh had organized a moral society and started a Sunday-school system.

Probably the best evidence of the rapid development of the Sunday school under the drive of evangelization and voluntary teaching is in the records of organization. The Phila-

14. John Henry Hobart, *The Beneficial Effects of Sunday Schools Considered in an Address* (New York, 1818), 40-41.
15. *New Missionary Field, A Report to the Female Missionary Society for the Poor of the City of New York and its Vicinity* (New York, 1817).
16. Boston Society for the Moral and Religious Instruction of the Poor, *Report* (1817), and *Second Report* (1818).

delphia Sunday and Adult School Union tripled its size during its first twelve months, from forty-three schools of the original ten associations to 129 schools. During that year the First Day Society gave up running paid schools to devote its resources to the Union's cause; two years later the Philadelphia Religious Tract Society transferred its tract business to the Union and followed in 1824 with all of its assets. During the first six years the Union's growth is shown in these figures:

Year	Schools	Teachers	Scholars
1818	43	556	5,970
1821	313	2,724	24,218
1824	723	7,300	49,619[17]

By 1824 the Philadelphia Union had extended its connections to fifteen states and the District of Columbia; the time was ripe for a national union. The New York people, pointing to the experience of the London and Irish Sunday-school unions, had been urging the step since 1820. With further encouragement from Princeton and Charleston, the transition went smoothly. The only change was to pattern the constitution of the American Sunday-School Union very closely upon that of the British and Foreign Bible Society. Since Philadelphia intended to maintain supremacy over a structure of subordinate auxiliaries, the Union did not need to deviate from the master model as did the American Bible Society. The personalities remained about the same, with Alexander Henry continuing as president.

The expansion of scope stimulated the whole Sunday-school movement. The next year Massachusetts joined with eighty-one schools, and the fever of forming auxiliaries was on. The instructions issued from Philadelphia for founding auxiliaries were precisely those of the British and Foreign Bible Society, even to the designation of Monday as the proper day for board meetings, with the single addition of opening and closing prayers.[18] By the fiscal year 1827-28 the rate of growth was still a healthy 25 per cent per year. At that time the Union

17. Circular addressed to Mathew Carey, Esq., by George Boyd, General Agent, American Sunday-School Union (Philadelphia, Feb. 20, 1825).
18. American Sunday-School Union, *First Report* (1825), 96-101.

had 394 auxiliaries, with 3,760 schools, 32,806 teachers, and 259,656 students. The estimated total of children attending Union and non-Union schools was 345,000, or one-seventh of the age bracket of five to fifteen.[19]

Contributing to this remarkable development was the attitude of the people in the central office of the Union at Philadelphia. There was much religious enthusiasm around the place, to be sure, but the only yardstick for the success of the enterprise was sales. The Union was in business to produce Sunday-school printed matter in the greatest possible volume at the lowest possible price. Creating the market for the product was part of its job, and promotion received just as expert attention as did the editorial office or the pressroom. The Philadelphia Sunday and Adult School Union put an agent or "missionary" to work in its fiscal year 1821-22. He traveled twenty-five hundred miles in six states, reinvigorated twenty schools he discovered in trouble, founded six tract societies, four adult schools, and sixty-one new Sunday schools.[20] After that, the Union never lacked professional agents.

Quite as important to success was the democratization and generalization of the whole Sunday-school movement. Under the impulse of American pragmatism the social status of the Sunday school was a prompt and radical departure from British precedent. Lyman Beecher brought the children of his most prominent parishioners into his Sunday schools and claimed credit for overthrowing the British idea that these institutions were for the poor exclusively.[21] He should have some credit but by no means all. Boston's moral society concluded as early as 1819 that Sunday schools or any other special treatment for America's poor as "the poor" aroused too much antagonism and simply would not work.[22] Pittsburgh reported in 1823 that almost every class of citizens in town and every

19. American Sunday-School Union, *Fourth Report* (1828), viii, ix.
20. "Sunday School Missionaries," *American Sunday-School Magazine*, I (1824), 48.
21. Marianna C. Brown, *Sunday School Movements in America* (New York, 1901), 23.
22. Boston Society for the Moral and Religious Instruction of the Poor. *Seventeenth Annual Report* (1834), 10.

family, whether rich or poor, was sending its children to Sunday school.[23]

Obviously what was going on was the upgrading of the Sunday school to the level of middle-class respectability which some Americans had attained and the rest refused to admit that they could not attain. On Saturday night the poor scrubbed up. The next morning they dressed up and presented themselves at Sunday school to prove they were just as good as anybody else. It is a tribute to American society that they were received at face value—but that face had to be clean.[24] It is difficult to see how the American system of public education could have arisen without the foundation of social equality and mutual respect which the Sunday school provided.

The contribution of the Sunday school to the integration of American life in the cities and villages was considerable but not so heavy as its contribution to the Evangelical united front. It was the first genuine social success in America of the type which carried the movement to such heights of influence in Great Britain. It gave a lift of confidence and power to the whole front, especially to the laity, who, in this case, had taken religious leadership out of the hands of the clergy with outstanding success. The Sunday schools extended the scope of the united front in all directions and brought in new social classes and hosts of new people. Here was a great market for Testaments and Bibles; here were new readers and distributors of tracts, new nuclei for missionary societies. Furthermore, as a youth movement it gave the promise of immortality to the Evangelical effort and made the glowing goal of world conquest seem more attainable.

In method and technique, too, the Sunday school brought notable progress. In its attack upon the city frontiers it developed the essential approach to the winning of all frontiers—west, north, south, and those internal "waste places" of which Lyman Beecher spoke. It gave the missionary his most useful instrument. Unlike the modern missionaries of sales promo-

23. Philadelphia Sunday and Adult School Union, *Sixth Report* (1823), 7.
24. There are innumerable contemporary comments on this. See Joseph Tuckerman, *The Principles and Results of the Ministry at Large, in Boston* (Boston, 1838), 129 ff.; also, Tyng, *Forty Years*, 63-65.

tion, Evangelical missionaries never expected to convert anyone. They could not earn a living or justify expenses that way.
Theirs was a more genuine and fundamental concept of promotion: they reported results not in terms of conversion but of
organization. They prepared communities for the coming of
preachers who would do the converting. The missionary had
done a good day's work if he left behind him a settlement
equipped to proceed on the Evangelical course under its own
power. For this purpose the Sunday school was ideal. It did
not require a serious religious commitment; it made no distinctions of age, sex, nationality, or sectarian persuasion; it was
sociable and informal; and it appealed to the generally recognized need for cheap education. So great was the effectiveness
of this new American institution that one is tempted to suspect
that it could have carried the Evangelical burden alone. But
hardly had it fought its way to security when another impulse
picked up the united front to carry it in a dizzy dance and leave
a lasting, if not quite as wholesome, impression upon American society, the "Temperance Reformation."

The temperance movement did not come from the British.
It was an American phenomenon, and Americans have not
been known for temperance in much of anything. It was
precisely the departure from temperance to teetotalism in the
attack upon alcoholism that hooked it up with Evangelical
religion and started the Temperance Reformation. The pledge
to teetolatism became a sign and seal of Evangelical conversion.
The relation between teetotalism, which finds legal expression
in prohibition, and the Evangelical faith was and is psychological. Temperance was a rational discipline of moderation, an idea associated with the Enlightenment. Benjamin
Franklin preached this kind of temperance and so did Dr.
Benjamin Rush when he pushed the virtues of beer as
compared to rum for the soldiers of the Revolution. Teetotalism, on the other hand, was a romantic affair: it required
the same type of emotional upheaval as religious conversion,
resulting in a decision to lead a new life. The Temperance
Reformation of the 1820's and 1830's was a combination and
confusion of teetotalism with religious conversion. Forti-

fying the psychological tie was the general Evangelical susceptibility to ascetism, inhibition, and prudery.

In considering the evidence of this movement, the historian
has considerable difficulty trying to decide who is exaggerating
and how much. There were ardent feelings as well as ardent
spirits at issue, and as the temperance people did almost all of
the publishing, the evidence is heavily lopsided. For example,
they would lead one to conclude that the average American of
the day woke at dawn or before, yawned, stretched, and reached
for his rum. After a liberal wetting of his whistle he was ready
to fit his chew of tobacco in his cheek, pull on his cowhide
boots, and face the day's chores. This picture seems a little
prejudiced on the temperance side, but one wonders—after
hearing of a preacher's warning his congregation in 1805 that
when a man arises earlier than usual to get at his bottle, he is in
grave danger of becoming a drunkard.[25] There is plenty of
evidence, direct and indirect, to support a reliable picture of
the public attitude toward liquor in the United States during
the early years of the nineteenth century. The jug on the
shelf was as necessary to housekeeping as meat in the salt barrel,
and for sufficient reasons. Life in those days for most people
was rugged, housing was flimsy, diet was inadequate, and most
work involved severe exposure. Any source of warmth and
comfort was welcome: the rum ration of sailors at sea was only
the counterpart of the half-pint which land laborers considered
part of the day's pay.

In the common understanding, the human constitution
could not face the rigors of life in the United States without
alcoholic fortification. The rich drank French and Spanish
brandy; those moderately well off favored West Indian rum;
and New England rum kept the breath of life in the rest at the
price of 66⅔ cents per gallon. Workmen had it at meals and
again with a little water in the middle forenoon and afternoon.
Professional men and businessmen followed a similar custom:
today's coffee break was then a break for the bar, a half-hour

25. Ebenezer Porter, *Fatal Effects of Ardent Spirits*, New England Tract
Society, Tract No. 125 (Andover, Mass., 1822), 3.

for punch, hot or cold according to season, for a sling, a toddy, or a flip. The South seems to have favored whisky with a little mint for all ages and sexes on waking in the morning. And there were special mixtures for special conditions. A seasoning of cherries made rum a good protection against cold; peach-stones turned it into a confection; milk in the rum was good for nursing mothers. Lyman Beecher, preaching at the funeral of a young alcoholic, excused the youth's dissipation on the ground that he never had a chance, since "he was nursed on milk punch, and the thirst was in his constitution."[26] Without water, rum aided digestion and secured sleep. With herbs, it helped women and old folks bear their troubles: they drank Huxham's Tincture or Staughton's Elixir. With opium (paregoric), it quieted the baby.[27]

A fair check on the seeming bias of this picture is the fare in public institutions. One may assume that it was not luxurious; Bridewell, in 1810, was serving its customers a tub of mush and molasses twice a day, supplemented by meat and potatoes every other day.[28] The accounts of Philadelphia's almshouse for the year May 23, 1803–May 23, 1804, show that its management spent $594.69½ for wine and $472.88 for rum and whisky to maintain the health of 536 adult inmates.[29] This proportion was substantially below the level of national consumption but probably not more so than the rest of the diet. And, too, Philadelphia never faced the liquor problem which confronted New York. That city was issuing 3,500 liquor licenses in 1810 as compared with Philadelphia's 190.[30] In the same year a meeting of the Congregational consociation of clergy to ordain the Rev. Heart as minister of Plymouth lined up for its rum, water, and sugar both before and after the ceremony,

26. *Autobiography, Correspondence, Etc., of Lyman Beecher, D.D.,* Charles Beecher, ed. (New York, 1864), II, 34-35.
27. *Encyclopaedia Americana,* Francis Lieder, ed. (new ed.; Philadelphia, 1840), XII, 174-79.
28. Humane Society of New York, *A Report of a Committee of the Humane Society* (New York, 1810), 11.
29. *The Accounts of the Guardians of the Poor and Managers of the Alms-Houses and Houses of Employment of Philadelphia from 23rd May, 1803 to 23rd May, 1804* (Philadelphia), 5.
30. Humane Society, *Report,* 6-8.

an affair which exhibited "a considerable amount of exhiliration."[31]

The liquor expenditures of Philadelphia's almshouse were contained in the accounts of its medical department, good testimony that orthodox medical opinion of the day was in thorough accord with prevailing lay notions of the virtues of alcohol in its various potable forms. But an outstanding exception in the profession was Dr. Benjamin Rush, who hammered away relentlessly, warning Americans of the threat to health and welfare. He cautioned the public to watch carefully for his eleven ghastly symptoms of intemperance. The mildest of these was "A decay of appetite, sickness at the stomach, puking of bile or discharges of a frothy and viscid phlegm, by hawking in the morning."[32] With this promising start, he went on to discuss insanity. Dr. Rush's point of view began about 1810 to gain adherents in his calling and some clerical support. For example, the Congregationalists began to dry out official meetings after the affair at Plymouth, and there was mounting pressure to do the same for funerals. The two professions joined forces with a focus on temperance in the moral societies and other Evangelical associations of lay-clerical solidarity. For example, in 1812 Dr. Billy J. Clark was serving the town of Moreau, a community devoted to lumbering and heavy drinking in New York's Saratoga County. Having read Dr. Rush with keen interest, he noted with dismay the effects of rum upon his patients. The thought of forming a temperance society struck him so forcibly that he had to share it immediately with the Rev. Armstrong. "The visit was made on a dark evening, no moonshine, and cloudy. After riding on horseback about three miles through deep mud of clay road, in the breaking up of winter, the doctor knocked at his minister's door, and, on entrance, before taking seat in the house, he earnestly uttered the following words: '*Mr. Armstrong, I have come to see you on important business.*' Then lifting up both hands, he continued, '*We shall all become a community of*

31. Beecher, *Autobiography*, I, 245 ff.
32. *A Caution against Our Common Enemy*, New York Religious Tract Society, Tract No. 28 (New York, 1814), 2.

drunkards in this town unless something is done to arrest the progress of intemperance.' "[33]

The society arising from this conversation imposed a fine of twenty-five cents upon any member who drank hard liquor except for medical or religious reasons. It never set the world afire or appreciably reduced America's growing thirst, estimated at four and a half gallons of distilled liquor per capita in 1810 and nearly six gallons in 1830.[34] But such organizations somewhat modified public opinion of strong drink and prepared temperance to join with another rising preoccupation, concern for American health. Americans considered themselves as physically inferior to the peoples of many European nations, as a scrawny, sickly lot; half of the population belonged in the hospitals for mental or physical deficiencies, and the other half was not far from the door. Illness in the manual-labor schools, which was the special concern of the education societies, emphasized this point. The time was ripe for dietary fads, patent medicines, European systems of exercise, and other nostrums. Temperance could fuse with the health movement to become another cure-all.

Such was the situation which the Andover version of the Clapham Sect moved to organize in the familiar Evangelical pattern. Two fatal accidents clearly caused by drink and nothing else received considerable publicity and created an atmosphere favorable to such a move late in 1825. On January 10, 1826, the Andover group met with a select number of its Boston friends in the vestry of Park St. Church. The group came to a decision on two points: it would make more systematic efforts to restrain the intemperate use of intoxicating liquor and it would hire an agent. Out of this arrangement arose the American Temperance Society, with the usual Evangelical structure and trimmings. The top offices went to distinguished members of the bench, and the financial posts, to wealthy merchants. On the executive committee were the Revs. Leonard Woods and Justin Edwards of the Andover

33. Lebbeus Armstrong, *The Temperance Reformation* (New York, 1853), 18-19.
34. *Encyclopaedia Americana*, XII, 174-79.

group, John Tappan, Boston partner of New York jobber Arthur Tappan, and Judge S. V. S. Wilder to tie into the American Tract Society.

But there is no reason to suppose that even this auspicious start would have produced an organization of much more power than any of the numerous temperance societies already in existence, since the doctrine was the same: the temperate use of liquor. Justin Edwards had already formulated the doctrine which would provide the temperance cause with its myth, its emotional drive, but this conservative Boston assembly was not ready to subscribe to total abstinence for itself or for anybody else. In fact, the parent Society did not accept the pledge to total abstinence until 1831.[35]

The myth developed at the promotional level and surged upward to engulf the entire organization. Justin Edwards advanced the doctrine of total abstinence in 1825, when the American Tract Society published his story, *The Well-Conducted Farm,* as Tract No. 176. This tract reported an experiment on a Massachusetts farm proving conclusively that labor and liquor could part company entirely without fatal results. On the contrary, health, wealth, and happiness blessed Mr. B—— and every one of his hired hands. The appeal in Edwards' tract was to health and economy. It was rational rather than emotional; Edwards probably did not realize the power latent in his argument. Lyman Beecher, with his good nose for the dramatic, supplied the emotional punch to start the movement rolling. In Litchfield, Conn., he delivered six rousing sermons on total abstinence and there published them. Confronted in this way, the doctrine was a profound shock, a challenge to the American public. It put the issue in those beautifully black and white terms demanding an answer, be it "yes" or "no." It was a Calvinistic division between the elect and the unregenerate; like original sin it applied to all, the just and the unjust, the temperate quite as much as the inebriate. For example, Samuel Miller, the eminent Presbyterian divine at Princeton, had been taking one glass of wine daily for sixteen years upon the advice of his physician. He gave total

35. American Temperance Society, *Fourth Report* (1831), v.

abstinence a trial, with "strikingly beneficial" results. Suspecting that the demon in rum contaminated all fluids, he gave up water, too, except for a few teaspoonfuls, sipped slowly, when he was very thirsty.[36]

As the doctrine of total abstinence spread over the country, the movement attained a fervor wholly lacking up to that point. With the multiplication of auxiliaries came a flood of religious revivals directly associated with the temperance cause. To many observers the relationship between temperance and revival was baffling. As one put it: "What connection the temperance efforts in this place sustained to the revival, God only knows. . . ."[37] But they all agreed that temperance prepared the way, and they were probably right in a more subtle sense than they realized. It is well known among revivalists that the best prospect is one who has been revived before. The experience is not only contagious but habit-forming. In each case it demands a decision; it may be to enter the ministry, become a missionary, or change denominations. In those days there were additional issues: total abstinence, foreign missions, Sabbath observance, abolition of slavery. In the late 1820's and early 1830's, the conversion sequence in the North seems to have been: temperance, as total abstinence; foreign missions in the world-conquest aspect; and abolition of slavery, also in its immediate and total form. All three were varieties of teetotalism, with a common psychological content which may help to explain their often noted relationships.

New York state with its "burned-over district" was an extreme example of the succession at work. The impact of temperance there was huge. In 1832 the state auxiliary printed and distributed 350,000 circulars as well as 100,000 constitutions for family societies to paste in their family Bibles; in 1834 it reported 1,652 temperance organizations in the state, with 320,427 members, but it was uncertain about the figures. Returns were coming in as at election time; there were 111 cities and towns yet to report. The parent body, equally un-

36. Letter from Samuel Miller to Justin Edwards, Jan. 1, 1836, quoted by Justin Edwards in *Letter to the Friends of Temperance in Massachusetts* (2nd ed.; Boston, 1836), 23-25.

37. American Temperance Society, *Fourth Report*, 83.

certain about its own size, guessed at seven thousand societies with 1,250,000 members in that year.[38] The movement built up such impetus that it swept out of the United States over the entire Evangelical world. By 1841 it could claim societies founded in England, Scotland, Ireland, Prussia, Sweden, Texas, the West Indies, South Africa, and Australia. France and Russia were working on it; even in "New Zealand, once noted for cannibalism, the temperance tree has taken root."[39]

Teetotalism catered to the American weakness for extremes, as in the case of Samuel Miller, and it tended to spread to other matters. In 1835 the New York Anti-Tobacco Society focused its drive against "the practice of chewing tobacco in the Sanctuary of Divine Worship."[40] During the previous year the Congregational deputation from Great Britain visited a Methodist church service in Morristown, N.J., where it reported tobacco juice hitting the floor like rain dripping from the eaves.[41] Clearly, the famous sawdust trail, the American's right to chew and spit his way to salvation, was under attack. Threatened, too, was an even more fundamental privilege: it was rumored that ladies in the city and neighborhood of New York were signing pledges "to prevent the design and uses of matrimony in their relation to their husbands."[42]

Along with the tendency to extremes, temperance methods generally conflicted with long-term objectives of the Evangelical united front. The common course of united-front action was to bring together in friendly co-operation people of different views, to smooth over conflicts of class, interest, and opinion, to weaken the forces atomizing American society. For this purpose the requirements to join a united-front organization were kept at the absolute minimum—no commitment of opinion or belief, only a small fee. The average American

38. American Temperance Society, *Seventh Report* (1834), 4, 14.
39. New Orleans Temperance Society, *Temperance, An Address to the Citizens of New Orleans* (New Orleans, 1841), 10-12.
40. *Annual Report* (1835), 3.
41. Andrew Reed and James Matheson, *A Narrative of the Visit to the American Churches by the Deputation from the Congregational Union of England and Wales* (New York, 1835), I, 48.
42. Calvin Colton (A Protestant, *pseud.*), *Protestant Jesuitism* (New York, 1836), 67.

could join a Bible society or a Sunday-school union if he wanted
to, or he could leave it alone.   And, in the early years of the
front, the penalties for the latter course were not too severe.

These circumstances were not true of the Temperance
Reformation.   It split communities and set the factions at each
others' throats.   The situation developed out of the respectable
status of liquor in the public opinion of those days and the
methods which the temperance movement employed.   Lyman
Beecher introduced economic and political sanctions as the
most promising path of attack in 1826: "It is in the banishment
of ardent spirits from the list of lawful articles of commerce, by
a correct and efficient public sentiment; such as has turned
slavery out of half our land, and will yet expel it from the
world."[43]   This was a call to boycott any grocery selling liquor
and throw business to a temperance storekeeper.   If the liquor-
seller remained in business, perhaps he might, for some reason,
lose his liquor license.   And the whole temperance movement
eagerly followed Beecher's lead.

The problem confronted the local storekeeper when temperance came to town: should he set the customary jug of rum
beside the customary jug of water on the counter for the refreshment of his customer friends?   The two had not been, as
a rule, competitive treats; the amount of water a man wanted
in his rum was a matter of personal taste.   Or should he hide
the rum and play up the water?   Or did the accounts on the
books, the competitive situation, and his status in the community indicate that he should sign the pledge and go along?
More people were in the same spot when the temperance group
moved into Sabbath observance in 1828 and began to apply
temperance methods to the freight and passenger business.
Then Evangelical piety became a competitive weapon in the
carrying trade.   A steamboat captain on the Rappahannock
run down from Fredericksburg solved his problem with ingenuity worthy of a Yankee.   A lot of businessmen customers
wanted to make the Sunday trip and save a day.   With much
profanity, the captain nailed up a subscription box to the Epis-

43. *Six Sermons on Intemperance* (New York, 1827), 63.

copal Tract Society, strewed Bibles about the men's cabins, and blew the whistle.[44]

The sanctions employed by the temperance–Sabbath observance people aroused considerable opposition, not all of it as mild as the gentle ribbing of Arthur Tappan, who had just published his modest work on the virtues of frequent holy communion:

> Arthur Tappan, Arthur Tappan,
> Suppose it should happen—
> Mind, I'm only *supposing* it should—
> That some folks in the Union,
> Should take your Communion
> Too often by far for their good.[45]

More frequently, antagonism expressed itself in charges of priestcraft, union of church and state, attack on the liberties of the people, arrogance, and tyranny. So vocal was the resistance that the American Temperance Society, in its instructions for the formation of auxiliaries, abandoned the united-front precedent of calling public meetings for such purposes. The tactics it adopted in 1829 really aggravated the situation.[46] To deny the opposition a chance to rally, promoters were advised to proceed quietly in distributing the Society's literature— "facts"—through the community. Then they should gather a few friends who had already agreed to the plan, draw up a constitution for an auxiliary, with its pledge, and sign it. The group could circulate the constitution among likely prospects to obtain as many signatures as possible and then call a meeting including only those who had signed. Such avoidance of all parliamentary procedure kept the opposition where it belonged —outside. It assured a temperance meeting of undisturbed unity, effectively safeguarded from heavy drinkers or other riff-raff. The town's respectable element was then organized to work for the betterment of the whole community through redemption of its drinking sinners by means of economic sanctions combined with social, religious, and political boycott.

44. Reed and Matheson, *Narrative,* I, 183, 184.
45. *Priestcraft Unmasked,* I (1830), 116.
46. *Third Report,* 31 ff.

This tidy gathering of the better people would include most of those supporting various aspects of the Evangelical united front. The fusion of temperance with religion was so complete that in many communities the pledge was necessary to church membership. For Sabbath observance, the teammate of temperance, the connection with religion was more obvious although less deep. It was natural that both movements should permeate first the tract societies and then the Sunday schools and to a lesser degree the Bible and missionary organizations as well. That is, a redeemed heathen would be one who had signed the pledge.

The relationship of the Evangelical united front to temperance was much the same as the relationship of the group of conservatives who formed the American Temperance Society to Justin Edwards and Lyman Beecher with their radical doctrine of total abstinence. They might not like it or want it, but that made no difference: the thing rose up and swallowed them. Temperance brought to the united front considerable division and contention, to be sure, and some rather poisonous tactics which put a high value on hypocrisy. But it made its contributions, too. After all, hypocrisy is a tribute which weakness usually pays to power, and the Temperance Reformation brought great power to the whole Evangelical movement. Like the Sunday schools, it introduced hosts of new people; it strengthened all of the denominations with new members and a rededication through the sweep of revivals. And it added something that the united front had lacked, except in some aspects of Sunday-school promotion—a militant fanaticism, especially in the North.

Clearly the process of naturalization had altered the character of the united front. British leadership and approval became less important, while both main sources of native strength, the Sunday-school and temperance movements, advanced independently along new lines with a social gospel better suited to American conditions and temperament. What started in the United States as a conservative coalition, intent as in England upon maintaining an ancient order, retained conservative support but acquired radical, visionary, driving forces quite foreign to the united front in Great Britain.

But, curiously, the more distinctly American the movement became and the more engrossed with its peculiar task, the more closely did it approach the united front in Great Britain at the fundamental level of final purpose. Paths to the goal necessarily had to diverge, but the goal remained the same—unquestioned ascendancy of Evangelical ideas and attitudes on both sides of the Atlantic and general acceptance of Evangelical standards of belief and behavior as the norm in both countries and, eventually, in the whole world.

X

THE GREAT OFFENSIVE: THE CITIES, THE VALLEY, THE SOUTH

A GENERAL OFFENSIVE, the major effort of the Evangelical united front in the United States, opened in 1829. A certain rhythm is apparent: the first organized conservative surge followed the election of Thomas Jefferson; the next followed the victory of Andrew Jackson. The earlier one was distinctly British in its inspiration; the second, quite thoroughly American. From the Evangelical point of view, an unchristian nation elected Jefferson; an uncivilized nation chose Jackson. In each case the conservatives sought to repair political defeat by nonpolitical means. However, Evangelical opposition to Jackson was not monolithic. Jackson made his modest play for the Evangelical vote and doubtless got some of it, since the united front had expanded to embrace a much wider range of interests. But the issues which Jackson fought for and the freewheeling democracy which he symbolized were opposed to essential Evangelical aims in much the same sense as the West opposed the East.

In such situations the modern American concept of the relationship between religion and politics developed: only under the strong control of God's government could free institutions be successful. Political prosperity depended upon moral prosperity. The weaker the government, the less power it had to control the passions and interests of its subjects, the more it was endangered by evil customs. The Evangelicals were much impressed by the feebleness of the federal structure, especially since they could not control it. In their opinion the government "has *no* inherent power." Laws derived their character from the sentiments of the people; sobriety and integrity produced wholesome laws, and Evangelical Christianity alone produced sobriety and integrity: "For great, corrupt, and prosperous, it is impossible we should be. . . ."[1]

The year 1829 marked the shift of political power to the West, an event foreseen in the Constitutional Convention of 1787 when a move restricting representation of new states to a par with the old states failed by one vote.[2] That Convention also could predict that the Mississippi Valley might be quite foreign to the East,[3] but only in the sense of being occupied by foreigners. What happened was much better: the West developed strange customs and some hostility to the East, but the fundamental tie remained close indeed. This relationship was especially characteristic north of the Ohio River. The packets of the Erie Canal swarmed with Easterners, who found steamboats waiting for them on the Lakes. Then the trip from Buffalo to Detroit, which had taken three weeks, required only four days. Presently the railroad locomotive, belching clouds of sparks from the roaring pine slabs in its belly, hurtled westward at eight miles per hour. The North was later than the South in occupying the Valley, but it rapidly made up for lost time.

Where, parents of New England, are your homes? Wherever your affections are. Wherever your children are. . . . And where are the children of New England? They are scattered over the whole land. You cannot enter an inlet of Florida, where, if a new city is springing up, you will not find them. There is not a village along the lakes, where you may not meet those who have gone almost from your very door. Through the whole course of the Mississippi, from St. Anthony's Falls to the Balize, there is not a place where business is doing, or to be done, where in the busiest throng you will not constantly hear the familiar sound of New England names.[4]

1. "Review of Reports on Sunday Mails," *Christian Spectator*, I (1829), 159.
2. Max Farrand, ed., *The Records of the Federal Convention* (New Haven, 1937), II, 1.
3. *Ibid.*, I, 182.
4. American Unitarian Association, *Thirteenth Annual Report* (1838), 38-39.

The children of New England and other Eastern areas were not migrating to communities which a conservative Evangelical would approve. It was not that the East was particularly sober and set in its ways. The whole country was exuberant, boisterous in its new strength, ready to try any speculation or utopian experiment. But the West was without sufficient education and tradition to impose even as much discipline upon itself as the East. The lack of discipline was as true in religious matters as in other social relationships, where the gun and the knife were ever ready. In the East the clergy were identified with dignity and education; learning and piety went hand in hand. In the West these two parted company completely. The leading regular denominations were the Baptists and Methodists, neither requiring any special education for its clergy at that time. "We do not, indeed, profess to educate young men and train them up specifically to the ministry" was the position of the Methodist General Conference of 1828.[5] In 1833 the Baptists were trying to raise their standards but complained that their preachers were distinguished for common sense and piety, not for cultivation: "not more than one in fifty of our ministers, until a recent date, have made any pretensions to learning, beyond the rudiments of a common English education."[6] The Cumberland Presbyterians had split from the parent body precisely upon this issue of educational requirements for clergy.

Religious enthusiasm without disciplinary grounding in Christian scholarship of the past thousand years made radical departures inevitable. There emerged the Universalists, mystic Halcyons, Christians, Reformed Baptists, Reformers, and others. An ultra-Calvinist approach to predestination was popular, a "two-seedism" which maintained that the elect were the descendants of Adam and Eve, while the damned were the offspring of a liaison between Eve and Satan. The Baptists were particularly embarrassed, as the rite of immersion appealed to many radicals as a dramatic foundation and point of departure.

5. Nathan Bangs, *A History of the Methodist Episcopal Church* (3rd ed.; New York, 1853), III, 4-6.
6. Northern Baptist Education Society, *Nineteenth Annual Report* (1833), 12.

An example was the Scotch-Irishman Thomas Campbell, a minister of the "Secession" branch of the Presbyterian Church of Ireland. Becoming a Baptist upon migration, he set up a church at Brush Run in Pennsylvania's Washington County. An able man, he founded a considerable sect with churches in western Virginia and all of the new states along the Ohio. Antagonism toward the East was an article of faith with the Campbellites, or "Camelites." The antipathy applied to all Eastern influences, such as education, but was directed particularly against missionaries. The Camelites considered all of the united-front work to be just another Eastern speculation and a fraud at that: the missionaries were high-class beggars out to wheedle money from the poor with a fancy line of talk, and they simply pocketed their collections. Any Camelite church which entertained one of these impostors was excommunicated by that act.[7]

With radical creeds went equally radical procedures. A kind of religious meeting commonplace in modern America arose then to shock Eastern ideas of the proper conduct of divine worship. A Boston Unitarian visiting Dayton, Ohio, in 1826 heard a lot of noise down the street. Thinking several people must be in great distress, he hurried to offer assistance. He found about a hundred men, women, and children at a prayer meeting. They prayed and sang alternately: "While one was praying, others encouraged him with expressions like these, 'O Jesus! how good he prays!' 'An't that right good, Lord!' 'I can conquer a thousand!' 'Yes,' says another, 'and leap over a wall!' "[8] Some laughed, some cried, some cheered while others groaned. To Boston ears it was all quite deafening and shocking. Some worshiped noisily, some in dignity and quiet; many were willing to strike a balance between Sunday morning service and an afternoon of cockfights or horseraces. But the West was also able to muster a vast amount of indifference: "Those, who are pioneers in a new country, are not unfre-

7. I. M. Allen, ed., *The United States Baptist Annual Register for 1832* (Philadelphia, 1833), 196, 197.

8. Account of western tour by the Rev. Moses George Thomas, American Unitarian Association, *Second Annual Report* (1827), 74-75.

quently more engaged in beginning the world anew, than in preparing to leave it."[9]

The West was not the only source of Jackson votes and not the only area of radical hostility to confront Evangelical conservatives. The cities had not solved their problems by 1828. Labor was decidedly restive. Factory workers were putting in twelve to fifteen hours a day at pay from one to six dollars per week under conditions described in some areas as worse than those of state prisons.[10] Strikers were subject to arrest under common law for conspiracy, and other legal remedies were equally stacked against the workers. There were seventy-five thousand in prison for debt in 1829.[11] Skilled workers, who could vote, organized the Mechanics Union of Trade Associations in Philadelphia in 1827 and attained there a certain balance of political power. New York's "dirty shirts" found a stout advocate in Fanny Wright's *Free Enquirer*. And these people could match the Camelites of the Valley spade for spade in calling the turn on the Evangelical united front.

In addition to the problems of the West and the cities, there were those of the South. Before the canals and railroads loosed the westward flood of Northern migration, most of the westward movement came from the South. As the "cradle of the West," the ignorance and violence of the South were held responsible for the conditions across the mountains. Nor did the Evangelicals of the North like the institution of slavery. But their resentment was not so much of Southern slavery as against the ignorance which the South accepted for itself and imposed upon the Negroes by law. The Yankee's conviction that he had to teach the South seems to have antedated his sense of obligation to redeem the South from its "peculiar institution." For that matter, the whole approach of the Evangelical united front assumed a literate public as a fundamental condition.

The general Evangelical offensive which opened in 1829

9. American Unitarian Association, *Second Report*, 78.
10. Harry J. Carman, *Social and Economic History of the United States* (Boston, 1934), II, 57 ff.
11. Selig Perlman, *A History of Trade Unionism in the United States* (New York, 1922), 11.

did not come as a flash out of the blue but developed out of preparatory work during the preceding three years. In this respect the election of Jackson was not a primary force but rather a catalyst of already existing forces. The Mills-Schermerhorn expeditions of 1812-15 tagged the whole region from Lake Erie to the Gulf of Mexico as "the Valley of the Shadow of Death."[12]   But in those days the Evangelical movement was not strong enough to do much about it, and the West was not sufficiently settled to support the social organization that the united front used. The assumption seems to have been that the ordinary process of migration would carry enough clergy to the new country to serve its needs. As the situation developed, the South made no systematic effort to supply its emigrants with ministers, while the domestic missionary societies in the North were content to look after their own people as they moved to northern, eastern, and western frontiers. Of the 127 missionaries employed by the United Domestic Missionary Society of New York in the fiscal year 1825-26, one hundred worked in New York state.[13]

The American Home Missionary Society, another merger of 1826, marked the acceptance of a much broader objective, one that the executive committee of the United Domestic Missionary Society had been thinking about for several years, a conviction that *"a more extended effort for the promotion of 'Home Missions' is equally indispensable to the moral advancement and the political stability of the United States."*[14]   What the merger did was to unite a host of domestic missionary bodies in New England and New York, withdrawing many of them from ecclesiastical control to form one large organization in the familiar pattern of the united front. It used lay leadership and sought as broad a base of support as it could find. This step would have been impossible without the acute recognition of a larger objective. The documents supporting the new

12. Gardiner Spring, ed., *Memoirs of the Rev. Samuel J. Mills* (New York, 1820), 92.

13. United Domestic Missionary Society (New York), *Fourth Report* (1826), 41, 42.

14. Circular announcing formation of American Home Missionary Society, reproduced in *Constitution of the American Home Missionary Society* (New York, 1826), 4.

constitution were more political than religious in their content:
the only way to protect the administration of government from
abuse and the political institutions from ruin was to purify the
twelve million sources of political power and influence.

The concept that "we are doing a work of patriotism, no
less than that of Christianity,"[15] was not new. Beecher had been
promoting "God's government" for some time, and the Holy
Alliance in Europe had accepted the idea as its fundamental
doctrine. The American contribution suggested that the job
could be done by voluntary association working through free
institutions just as well as by autocratic government combining
religious and political functions. What the British Evangelicals
conceived in a vague and general way, the Americans made
precise and practical, as was their custom. Through their
administration of God's government, the American Evangelicals thought that they could attain fairly immediate political
control and turn the United States into a theocracy without
violating a single democratic liberty. An alarmed observer
quoted—quite possibly misquoted—a Vermont clergyman:
"*When all our colleges are under our control it will establish
our sentiments and influence,* so that we can manage the *civil*
government as we please!!"[16]

The repeated expressions of Evangelical political aims were
the principal cause of all the charges of priestcraft and of
church-and-state alliance brought against the united front. The
terms of Ezra Ely's endorsement of Andrew Jackson in 1827
were an extreme expression of the new doctrine, but the American Sunday-School Union took so serious a view of its responsibilities in administering God's government that a frightened
Pennsylvania legislature refused to grant the Union a charter
of incorporation. After the incidents in 1828, extreme expressions of political ambition quieted down, but the essential
doctrine remained to form the broad objective of the Evangelical offensive opening in 1829.

Even with the alluring proposal to turn political defeat into

15. American Home Missionary Society, *Constitution,* 47.
16. Dr. Burton, quoted in "To the Public," *Priestcraft Exposed and Primitive
Christianity Defended. A Religious Work,* I (Lakeport, N.Y., 1828-29), 1.

ultimate victory and with an imposing array of organizations to do the work, the Evangelical united front could not muster the strength needed for a massive offensive without a reorganization of its financial procedures, which had been haphazard and quite inefficient. The societies relied on their agents to arrange special collections for their benefit at church services and to pass the plate again at concerts of prayer. Auxiliaries helped the agents in such efforts, forwarding their meager contributions through proper channels. Some subscribed to life-memberships for their ministers; these and other membership fees helped a little. Sales of printed material were substantial, but since the prices barely covered the physical costs of production, sales were a loss factor, not a profit. A few heavy donations, some bequests, and personal loans to meet crises kept the wheels turning.

At the May meeting of the American Bible Society's board of managers in 1827, Howard Malcom, agent of the American Sunday-School Union, appeared with Dudley's *Analysis of the System of the Bible Society* in his hand and Dudley's motto at his lips: "Not by exactions from the opulent, but by contributions from all."[17] Since Malcom was addressing the opulent, well accustomed to exaction, his persuasiveness may well be imagined. At any rate, the American Bible Society adopted the Dudley scheme of revenue, and other united-front societies did the same, rationalizing the whole system of collections with precise allotment of responsibilities by geographical limits from the states right down to particular houses in particular towns. At each level there were provisions for organizing teams and supplying them with arguments, literature, and all the clerical apparatus needed to make effective reports and records helpful to the next visit. The American Board of Commissioners for Foreign Missions applied Dudley as promptly as did the American Bible Society, hailing the system with great confidence: "It would organize this vast body like a host prepared for war."[18]

17. *Monthly Extracts from the Correspondence &c. of the American Bible Society*, N.S., No. 4 (May, 1827), 50 ff.
18. *Hints to Collectors*, American Board of Commissioners for Foreign Missions (undated but not later than 1833), 8.

The American Board also added to the British apparatus an Americanism completing the modern institution, the "drive." Directions for a trial of the drive by the Auxiliary Foreign Mission Society of Franklin County (Mass.) in 1827 suggested that a week be designated during which collectors would cover their districts and complete their work.[19] The institution of the drive permitted preparation of the public by addresses from the pulpit and other means. It also permitted the allotment of separate times to the several united-front organizations. The scheme proved generally successful in strengthening Evangelical sinews. Putting it to trial immediately, the American Bible Society found by the end of 1827 that towns could contribute as much as whole counties did before. At the same time the income of the American Education Society, closely related to the American Board, doubled. The general application of Dudley's idea marked a significant advance in American social efficiency. It also marked a strong improvement in the financial strength of the Evangelical united front as well as another extension of its influence.

But to the American Tract Society, Dudley meant much more than that. Here was a fine tactical weapon for solving the urban problem. The Society opened the general offensive of 1829 with a tract campaign of a new sort in New York city.[20] The leading spirits were Arthur and Lewis Tappan of the New York Religious Tract Society. The plan called for complete coverage of the city with one tract every month. The Society divided each ward into districts of about sixty families, assigning a team of distributors to each district. The teams were to complete their work by the fifteenth of the month, when reports were due at a ward meeting. Therefore, in March, 1829, *Institution and Observance of the Sabbath* went, with suitable comment, to 28,383 New York families. Only 388 refused to receive this exhortation. Kettredge's *Address on Intemperance* followed in April. May, with its balmy breezes of spring, its

19. Auxiliary Foreign Mission Society of Franklin County, *Fifteenth Annual Report* (1827), 16.
20. American Tract Society, *Fourth Annual Report* (1829), 28, 29, 74, 75.

early flowers, and Anniversary Week, was just the right time for that reliable old tearsqueezer, *The Dairyman's Daughter.*

In addition to district visiting, special committees of the Tract Society covered other assignments. They distributed 146,500 pages of tracts in the markets, 79,000 pages in steamboats. Sunday schools received 239,100 pages of tracts and two thousand copies of the *Christian Almanac.* Additional teams covered the Belleview Hospital and Almshouse, the House of Refuge, Debtor's Prison, Greenwich Prison, the City Prison and Hospital, and some other institutions. The outskirts of the city took 174,000 pages.[21]

Whatever its effect upon the recipients of the propaganda, the plan was an immense success with the distributors, the same kind of success as that of the Sunday-school teaching fad. Anyone who felt the impulse to do some preaching and have immortal souls under his supervision in a parish of his own could go right to work with a host of like-minded fellows. By 1832 these amateur clergy had added prayer meetings to their district activities and, with the help of manuals on the subject, were saving souls with quite professional competence: "in a number of Districts they have selected individuals, whose minds are tender on the subject, as the special objects of their prayers and serious efforts for their eternal welfare. . . ."[22]

Of course such good work could not be confined to New York city. By 1834 it was in full swing in Boston, Philadelphia (two million pages per month), Charleston, Cincinnati, St. Louis, and Pittsburgh. It was a considerable campaign, which tied in with the Sunday-school effort and tended to proliferate in various directions, some profitable, some not. Among the latter, the Magdalen societies tried unsuccessfully to rescue prostitutes by reading them scripture. On the other hand, there was the inevitable relationship to welfare, to general awareness of bad social conditions and popular acceptance of responsibility to help the unfortunate. Here, probably, was the foundation of the modern profession of social worker. On the whole, the campaign accomplished for American cities

21. New York City Tract Society, *Second Annual Report* (1829), 16-18.
22. *American Tract Magazine,* VII (1832), 27.

much of what the British and Foreign Bible Society did for English manufacturing towns with perhaps less unfortunate social side effects.

In the meantime, the whole concept of missionary work had been undergoing a transformation. The Boston Society for the Moral and Religious Instruction of the Poor reorganized in 1834 to form the Boston Home Missionary Society, auxiliary to the Massachusetts Missionary Society. Convinced that the moral-society approach to the city's problems was entirely outdated, the Society recognized that the city and country both had frontiers: the situation was much the same and required the same techniques.[23] While the cities were working out measures to meet their needs, there was also a considerable development of the Western problem, with a corresponding change in the conception of what a Western missionary should be and do.

Early domestic missionary societies developed in New England around 1800 to support efforts which the ministry were already making to serve church members moving to frontiers in Vermont, New York, Rhode Island, New Hampshire, and Maine. These clergy doubled their work at home to relieve some members for extended journeys. Their task was to supply the religious needs of religious people deprived by distance of the services for which they hungered: they yearned for preaching; they had babies to be baptized, marriages to be made or confirmed, sick to be comforted. But such work was largely confined to New England and New York state. The westward movement entirely outstripped it: a generation grew up in the Valley without religious institutions or religious training; the chain of traditional experience was broken. Then the western frontier began to resemble the city frontier. It required a drastic shift of missionary ideas, attitudes, and tactics. The large scale of the task demanded some revision of ideas on financial support; the East could not and would not pay the full cost of converting the West and the South to its point of view. The British had proved that the business of

<hr />

23. Boston Society for the Moral and Religious Instruction of the Poor, *Seventeenth Annual Report* (1834), 10.

paying for one's own conversion was an essential part of the privilege of being converted.

A remarkable person, the Rev. John Mason Peck, Baptist missionary, helped to clarify and systemize both tactics and financial support for the campaigns of the Valley and the South.[24] Peck was working in and around St. Louis, living on faith and a few voluntary offerings. His Baptist board of missions had cut him off. St. Louis was not in Burma; the heathen there were not far enough away to be interesting or near enough to be dangerous. The anti-mission Baptist preachers of Illinois and Missouri had ruined his local support, blocked the charter for his theological school, and probably contributed to his losing his job with the board. At this low ebb Peck received a windfall, a great stroke of good fortune: the Baptist Missionary Society of Massachusetts hired him at the salary of five dollars per week for time actually spent in the field. He could raise that five dollars himself.

Peck made a trip east in 1826, a journey of 4,400 miles requiring nine months and one day, to solicit money for his school. He reached Washington in April, called on President Adams, and looked over affairs at Columbia College. Then, speaking and preaching his way, Peck moved on to visit with his old friends at the American Sunday-School Union in Philadelphia. He made New York in time for the triennial Baptist Convention. There, as chairman of a committee on domestic missions, he had a chance to present his plan for the West. He proposed an enlarged system of itinerant and stationary preaching which the board would support with firm but modest salaries of $100 per year. The missionaries could raise the rest of their income on the ground. The other part of the plan concerned tactics: the missionary's primary task was to organize, and for that purpose he should use the whole united-front apparatus even if it implied downgrading sectarian interests. This plan involved Bible, tract, and Sunday-school

24. See Austen Kennedy DeBlois and Lemuel Call Barnes, *John Mason Peck and One Hundred Years of Home Missions, 1817-1917* (New York, 1917).

work as well as the promotion of education societies and theological schools.[25]

The Convention turned down Peck's plan, but Peck kept on working. He did Anniversary Week thoroughly, talking hard and fast. And there he had better luck. The newly organized American Home Missionary Society adopted his scheme. Much encouraged, Peck went on to New England, where his employers, the Massachusetts Baptist Missionary Society, welcomed him warmly and approved his plan. It seemed only natural that Peck should bring together admirers of Peck, so the American Home Missionary Society added some Baptist support to the Congregational–Presbyterian–Reformed Dutch core of strength.[26]

Peck's tour of 1826 seems to have accomplished much besides dividing the Baptists. For one thing, he gave the leaders of the united-front societies a good firsthand account of conditions in the West and of the missionary problem. More important, he left everywhere the conviction that it was a typical united-front problem, much too big for denominational attack. Sectarian rivalry had best be postponed; nothing but a full-power, united drive would serve. This was his answer to the Baptist Camelites and hyper-Calvinists knifing him in his own territory. In practical terms this idea meant that missionaries and agents who worked for any one of the united-front societies were working for all of them. For example, the American Home Missionary Society had 463 missionaries in the field by 1831, busy promoting Bible, tract, education, foreign-mission, and temperance societies. They organized two hundred Bible classes and more than five hundred Sunday schools, but on such activities they reported directly to the American Sunday-School Union.[27] The Union, in turn, was just as busy founding Sunday schools on which the missionaries could build churches. By 1832 it had 112 missionaries and agents working in the Mississippi Valley, with instructions to make no discrimination among denominations which the people might choose for

25. Baptist General Convention, *Fifth Triennial Meeting, Proceedings* (1826), 28.

26. American Baptist Home Missionary Society, *First Report* (1833), 15.

27. American Home Missionary Society, *Fifth Report* (1831), 56, 57.

their schools or among schools joining or not joining the American Sunday-School Union. The employees of the Union in the Valley were fairly representative of the society's sources of support. There were thirty-nine Presbyterians, twenty-four Baptists, seventeen Methodists, four Congregationalists, eight Episcopalians, two Reformed Dutch, and twelve Cumberland Presbyterians. If the remaining six missionaries had any religious preference, the Union did not know about it.[28]

Thus at this time the primary missionary techniques became those of promotion and organization, and the work in its initial phases was apt to focus on forming united-front auxiliaries rather than churches. The reason is obvious: since these societies imposed no religious tests, they could include many, perhaps a majority, whose attitudes were favorable but vague. Further, the organizations could generate energy and multiply the effect of the missionary's efforts; they gave him social leverage. Churches could not do this work and were likely to be financial burdens, while united-front auxiliaries were units of capital formation. Although sectarian interests were always present and always at work, they tended, for a time, to be swallowed up in the united effort required by the urgencies and conditions of the larger task.

The opening of the great campaign, the "Valley Project," by the American Tract Society, the American Bible Society, the American Home Missionary Society, the American Sunday-School Union, and the American Education Society was practically simultaneous. Delays of a few months were due only to the physical limitations of such leaders as Lyman Beecher and Arthur Tappan.

The American Home Missionary Society led off, as it organized with the Valley specifically in view. On its heels was the American Tract Society, which found the energy to fight on two fronts at the same time—in the cities and over the mountains. At its Anniversary Week meeting in May, 1828, the Society passed a resolution moved by the Rev. Noah Davis, Baptist, of Philadelphia, seconded by the Rev. Jacob Van Vechten, Reformed Dutch, of Schenectady: *"Resolved*: That the

28. American Sunday-School Union, *Eighth Report* (1832), 32n.

moral wants of large portions of the inhabitants of our Country, especially in the valley of the Mississippi; the usefulness of Tracts, and the facility with which they may be diffused, call for prompt and spirited efforts to extend their circulation throughout all our inhabited territories."[29] There was something more than pious lung-power at work. Next day the executive committee considered and adopted a systematic plan for work in the Valley, persuaded the Boston branch to release its corresponding secretary, the Rev. Orman Eastman, and made him general agent for the West. Eastman hurriedly raised one or two thousand dollars in Boston and headed for Cincinnati. The executive committee sent five more agents across the mountains at once to work under Eastman's direction, one each for western Virginia, western Pennsylvania, and southern Ohio, two to cover Louisiana, Mississippi, and Alabama.

The method which the American Tract Society used for its Western drive was basically the same as for city operation; it was the Dudley system adapted to conditions. The agent would ship a box of tracts ahead of him to a central place in each county of his territory. From this supply he sent a small bundle of tracts to some leading man in each of the places where he hoped to form a tract society, and he requested a meeting. If the agent succeeded in organizing a tract society at the meeting, he defined its territory clearly, laid out districts, appointed a collector for each district, and then divided the bundle of tracts among the collectors. He instructed collectors to offer a few tracts even where there were no contributions.[30]

The scheme appears too loose to work well, an operation of the "rat-hole" variety, but actually it did work. With reading matter so scarce, a tract acquired considerable value. Losses through donations were about 10 per cent. The agents were effective and enthusiastic—one reported that he had traveled 450 miles in five weeks and had preached thirty-one sermons. Sometimes he had the whole audience in tears; in two

29. Manuscript, "Minutes of the American Tract Society, Instituted 1825," entry for May 7, 1828.
30. American Tract Society, *Fourth Annual Report* (1829), 24.

or three cases he signed up every man, woman, and child among his listeners as subscribers to a tract society. Sales, as usual, provided the measure of accomplishment: in 1827 about $700 worth of tracts had gone west of the Allegheny Mountains; distribution in that area for the fiscal year 1829-30 was 24,099,800 pages, of which only 2,655,067 pages were donated, and balancing this item were contributions of $941.64. Sales amounted to $13,985.49.[31]

While tears, the Evangelical seal of blessedness, were beginning to flow on the other side of the watershed as a result of tract work, Beecher, Tappan, and others were preparing the American Bible Society and the American Sunday-School Union to join in the general offensive. James Milnor, leading spirit of the Tract Society and member of the Bible Society's board, had tried to stir the American Bible Society to renewed enthusiasm at the May meeting of 1827. He pointed to the growth of the country as far outstripping the Society's efforts and rapped the complacency of auxiliaries in the face of such needs, not only in the West but in cities, towns, and villages. Milnor's eloquence was not as moving as Arthur Tappan's cash, but the situation at the Bible Society required all of Tappan's considerable skill in making a dollar generate energy. What happened there is a special testimony to the urgency of the general situation as the Evangelicals viewed it. The American Bible Society was in no shape to join the Valley drive in 1829. What was offered as a "pleasing reflection" in the report for May must have pleased no one at all. The Society was in trouble with the Methodists. It was $36,000 in debt: it had spent $143,184 during the past year against receipts of $95,668, a deficit of $47,516, and collections were very slow; auxiliaries owed about $30,000. The warehouse was jammed with 200,000 Bibles and Testaments, much of the stock well seasoned and dry.

The answer was to enlarge the plant. The Society proposed to build on adjoining lots a new structure of four floors, forty feet square, to house eight new steam presses with a capacity of 40,000 Bibles per month which would raise total production

31. American Tract Society, *Fifth Annual Report* (1830), 39.

to about 600,000 per year, about twice as much as the bindery could handle. It was an incredible answer, unless one postulates energy of a type and quantity not ordinarily associated with Bible societies and confidence in the over-all power of a combination in which that Society was an important but single unit. In April, 1829, Tappan offered to pay $1,000 above a fair price set by the board of managers to clear the adjoining lots, already purchased, of an encumbering lease. But he would only do this on two conditions: building must start at once, and the American Bible Society must join the Valley drive with a resolution at its May meeting to supply every family in the United States which would buy or accept a Bible. If the resolution was adopted, Tappan would renew an earlier pledge to contribute $5,000 toward that cause.[32] Another $5,000 for the same purpose had been assured earlier in April by a letter from Alexander Proudfit and his friends in the Bible Society of Washington County, N.Y. Pressures were building up.

The May meeting performed according to schedule; the Bible campaign opened with considerable publicity and full equipment of circulars and subscription blanks. To give Tappan's pledge more leverage, a special campaign for New York city opened in June with a goal of $20,000. All of the churches, except some under Bishop Hobart's Episcopal thumb, preached sermons on the Society's resolution, and at a mass meeting at Masonic Hall Arthur Tappan finally surrendered his much-used $5,000.[33] There were similar bursts of activity among the Society's six-hundred-odd auxiliaries. Many of them, like Vermont, pledged themselves to goals they could not attain, but, on the whole, the situation was redeemed. The American Bible Society hit the road with renewed vitality. Its method was the Dudley system, already clarified in 1827, organized at town, county, and state levels. In the first year of the campaign, 23,171 Bibles and Testaments went into Ohio, which expected to be completely supplied by May, 1831. Nearly as many arrived in Kentucky, where three agents were at work; Tennes-

32. Manuscript, "Minutes of the Managers of the American Bible Society," IV, 95.

33. Dorothy C. Barck, ed., *Letters from John Pintard to his Daughter, Eliza Noel Pintard Davidson* (New York, 1940-41), IV, 80.

see's three agents had received more than ten thousand Bibles, but found much to be done. Indiana had a state society but no agents. When the Rev. Isaac Reed undertook to cover nine counties, the home office sent him 14,408 copies. Missouri was in bad shape; there was a little activity in Alabama, especially in Sunday-school Testaments; Mississippi had two auxiliaries, neither of them good for much. Louisiana, where Samuel Mills found Americans who had never seen a Bible or heard of Jesus Christ, was no better off, but agents had gone to work. Arkansas and Michigan territories each had three auxiliaries; at least one of them, in Monroe County, Mich., was quite lively.[34]

In the meantime the American Sunday-School Union was preparing to enter the battle for the Valley. Lyman Beecher started blowing his bugle at the May meeting in 1828. The following year, while the missionary and tract people were already at work and the Bible folks were getting under way, the Union sent agents into the Valley to size up the situation and lay plans. When the time approached for the May meeting of 1830, Arthur Tappan was at Philadelphia with a little more of his hard-working money. If the Union would undertake to establish a Sunday school in every place in the Valley where it was practicable and to do it within two years, he would contribute $2,000 toward the project's cost, estimated at $100,000. And he had another $2,000 ready to encourage work in the field. Up to that limit, if any new Sunday school in the Valley could raise five dollars, he would match it with another five dollars to purchase the Union's standard ten-dollar library.[35] The Union was already selling salvation at bargain-basement rates: it "gives a child a testament and teaches him to read it for 37 cents."[36] Tappan made an irresistible proposition.

Everything was ready for the big moment at the big meet-

34. "American Bible Society," *The Quarterly Register of the American Education Society*, III (1831-32), 137, 138.

35. Edwin Wilbur Rice, *The Sunday-School Movement, 1780-1917, and the American Sunday-School Union, 1817-1917* (Philadelphia, 1917), 196.

36. Speech of Francis S. Key, in American Sunday-School Union, *Speeches of Messrs. Grundy, Wickliffe and others at the Sunday School Meeting in the City of Washington, February 16, 1831* (Philadelphia, 1831), 22.

ing. The Rev. Thomas McAuley made the motion. *"Resolved. That the American Sunday-School Union, in reliance upon divine aid, will, within two years, establish a Sunday School in every destitute place where it is practicable, throughout the Valley of the Mississippi."* Lyman Beecher seconded the motion. There followed speeches by the Episcopalian Rev. Stephen H. Tyng and the Presbyterians McAuley and Beecher. Then the two thousand members rose to pass by unanimous vote a measure "more important in its consequences probably than any previous act of the Society."[37]

There was considerable excitement. The Union held a special session for the Valley project and formally advised the Presbyterian General Assembly, meeting at the same time, of its resolution. There, the same people who made the news received it with proper astonishment and interest. And the General Assembly, too, called a special session on the West, at which an agent of the American Education Society had much to say. Out of this came pledges of about three years' free labor and $12,000 for the Union's project. Then there was a third meeting, presided over by Mayor William Milner, for Philadelphia's especial benefit, which netted more than $5,000. A meeting in New York city came on June 9 in Masonic Hall, Chancellor Walworth presiding. Hundreds thronged the streets, unable to get in. Subscriptions and collections mounted to more than $11,000. The upper-bracket politicians had their day in Washington the following February 16. President Jackson's illness kept him regretfully away, but about everybody else was there. The motion of Francis S. Key called Senator Felix Grundy to the chair; Matthew St. Claire Clarke, clerk of the House, served as secretary. They read the Union's Valley resolution, and there was considerable talk, some of it a little touchy. Elisha Whittlesey, congressman from Ohio, wanted to be sure the resolution was not based on the opinion of Easterners that folks beyond the mountains "are more subject to depravity, or more debased in morals" than other citizens.[38] And $100,000 was a lot of money, enough to build

37. American Sunday-School Union, *Sixth Report* (1830), 3, 4.
38. *Speeches of Grundy, Wickliffe,* 7.

a frigate or twenty to thirty miles of canal. But Daniel Webster had his say, and the meeting closed on a favorable note. There is no record of cash or pledges; if these politicians gave their approval, it was probably all that they were prepared to give.

The special meeting of the Presbyterian General Assembly had requested the American Sunday-School Union to publish a condensed list of arguments in support of its Valley project, and Lyman Beecher compiled his version of such a list for Boston's public meeting on the subject, November 3, 1831. He appealed to the Eastern anxiety at the loss of political power to the West and to the corresponding ambition for indirect political control through imposition upon the Valley of Eastern standards of Evangelical morality.[39]

In response to these arguments the people of Massachusetts managed to scrape together $5,960.95 for the cause. All told, the Valley project produced a total of $60,714.60[40] from its start in May, 1830, to March 1, 1832. The following states contributed heavily: New York, $17,927.77, the major part from New York city; Pennsylvania, $10,066.71; Connecticut, $6,683.93; then Massachusetts. Support from New Jersey, Kentucky, and Virginia was substantial. Every state in the Union and every organized territory gave something. Even Lower Canada and Scotland helped a little.

The financial aspect of the Sunday-school Valley drive would have fared better had it not immediately followed similar efforts by the mission, tract, and Bible societies. For example, Vermont promised $10,000 for Bibles, had trouble raising $1500, and let the Sunday-school effort drop to $158. But the Union's accomplishment in the Valley in this period was significant. During the eighteen months ending March 1, 1832, it established 2,867 schools and visited and revived 1,121 more.[41] Of course the agents and missionaries of other societies of the

39. Beecher's speech as published in American Sunday-School Union, *Proceedings of the Public Meeting Held in Boston, to aid the American Sunday-School Union in their efforts to establish Sunday schools throughout the Valley of the Mississippi* (Philadelphia, 1831), 16-21.
40. American Sunday-School Union, *Eighth Annual Report* (1832), 35.
41. *Ibid.*

united front contributed substantially to this total. The American Bible Society also helped the work along by giving the Union twenty thousand Testaments specifically for use in its Valley drive.[42]

Another unit of the Evangelical united front which joined the Valley offensive was the American Education Society, which was a promotion of the Andover group formed in 1815 as an American counterpart of a similar society in London. It had followed precisely the pattern of the American Tract Society. In the flurry of mergers around 1825 it absorbed the Presbyterian Education Society in New York city and changed the time of its annual meeting from September to May in order to get into Anniversary Week. It seems entirely likely that the tract and education people were substantially the same group in New England and New York city.

The American Education Society established a Western agency at Cincinnati during its May meeting in 1829 and employed the Rev. Franklin Y. Vail as secretary. Vail started work in November, managing to scrape up scholarships for twelve pious young men in Cincinnati. From there, Vail moved on to Hanover, Ind., where he founded another auxiliary.[43]

Although the Valley campaign embraced the New South, the Old South did not receive special attention from the Evangelical united front until 1833. Then the American Sunday-School Union led the assault. The conditions calling the Union into action were much the same as those of the Valley. New England missionaries had been working in the Old South as early as 1819, and their descriptions of religious desolation were as striking as those of Samuel Mills in the Valley. They reported that in a radius of one hundred miles around Beverly, Va., there were 180,000 people without religious instruction of any sort. Educated ministers averaged about one per eight thousand square miles. Of South Carolina's 230,000 people, 201,000 had no regular connection with any denomination.[44]

In response to "loud and pressing calls" from various sources

42. American Sunday-School Union, *Seventh Annual Report* (1831), 38.
43. American Education Society, *Fourteenth Annual Report* (1830), 40, 41.
44. Ebenezer Potter, *Sermon at the Anniversary of the American Education Society, October 4, 1820* (Andover, Mass., 1821), 14, 15.

for increased action in the South, the board of the Union had worked out a plan for vigorous operation and had it approved in the South. So the resolution was ready for the May meeting of 1833, fully equipped with the provisions and hedging which had always marked any approach to Southern susceptibility. Moved by the Rev. William S. Plumer of Virginia, seconded by the Rev. S. K. Talmage of Georgia, it read: *"Resolved, unanimously,—that* the American Sunday-School Union will endeavor, in reliance upon the aid and blessing of Almighty God, to plant, and for five years sustain, Sabbath-schools in every neighborhood (where such schools may be desired by the people, and where in other respects it may be practicable) within the bounds of the States of Maryland, Virginia, North Carolina, South Carolina, Georgia, Alabama, the District of Columbia, and the Territory of Florida."[45]

The Old South came up for action by the rest of the united front during Anniversary Week the following May, but the circumstances were embarrassed by the peculiar institution. The American Colonization Society had been the Evangelical answer to slavery.[46] It offered a bifocal point of view satisfying to politicians such as Henry Clay and to many others averse to to any firm commitment. In the South the Society was pro-slavery; it helped slaveowners by offering to remove trouble-some free Negroes by deportation. In the North it was for the gradual abolition of slavery; it encouraged manumission by providing for the colonization in Liberia of those freed. In both North and South it was a missionary society promising conversion of Africa by sending Christian American Negroes there to propagate the faith.

The Colonization Society, with its feeble settlement in Liberia, probably would never have amounted to anything had it not been for the Nat Turner slave insurrection of 1831. The nationwide increase of racial tension which followed made deportation a solution appealing to many whites, and it made Africa or any other distant place look good to thousands of free

45. American Sunday-School Union, *Ninth Annual Report* (1833), vi.
46. See the author's article, "The Colonization of Free Negroes in Liberia, 1816-1835," *Journal of Negro History*, XXXVII (1953), 41-67.

Negroes. But a counterforce was also at work. The British abolished slavery in the West Indies in 1833, and British example was not without influence in the United States, especially in certain circles. So Arthur Tappan organized his American Anti-Slavery Society. In 1834 he mounted his campaign to whip the American Colonization Society to a pulp, knock it out of the Evangelical united front, and take its place in time to lead the Southern offensive.

On Tuesday, May 6, 1834, the American Anti-Slavery Society held an enthusiastic, noisy, unsegregated meeting in Chatham St. Chapel to the keynote, "We are now attending the funeral of the American Colonization Society."[47] The next day, when Arthur Tappan took his seat with the board of the American Bible Society to prepare for its Thursday meeting, the atmosphere was a little chilly for that time of year. But Tappan played his favorite gambit to bring the American Bible Society into his notion of a proper drive on the South. He would put up $5,000 if the Society would commit itself to spend $20,000 toward providing every Negro family in the United States with a Bible and would do this in a period of two years beginning July 4, 1834. But Tappan's play failed. The board reckoned that less than 2 per cent of the Negroes to receive these Bibles could read them, and it could not see itself sending agents into every hut in the South. It turned Tappan's proposal over to the committee on distribution to keep it out of Thursday's meeting. That committee reported back to the board on June 5, 1834, with a resolution delegating all responsibility for the details of distribution to the auxiliaries.[48] Tappan's term on the board expired with the Thursday meeting; he was not re-elected. This action took the American Bible Society out of trouble and out of any specific Southern campaign. Tappan was stronger with the American Tract Society. There, Milnor managed to tie together the ideas of Tappan and the Rev. William S. Plumer,

47. Speech of the Rev. Ludlow, quoted by David M. Reese, *A Brief Review of the "First Annual Report of the American Anti-Slavery Society"* (New York, 1834), 30.

48. Manuscript, "Minutes of the Managers of the American Bible Society," V, 139, 145-47, 153.

Presbyterian, of Petersburg, Va., with less concession to South-
ern touchiness than the Sunday-School Union had used the
previous year. Milnor offered the resolution: "The American
Tract Society . . . relying upon the blessing of God and the
zealous cooperation of the South, will endeavor WITH THE
LEAST POSSIBLE DELAY, besides the continued circulation of
Tracts, to place ONE OR MORE of the Society's bound volumes in
every family willing to receive the same, in the states of MARY-
LAND, VIRGINIA, NORTH CAROLINA, SOUTH CAROLINA, GEORGIA,
AND THE TERRITORY OF FLORIDA."[49] Milnor argued that the
country faced a crisis; the North and South needed to be
drawn together in closer union. His seconder, the Rev. Plumer,
was much more specific. He said that the work needed to be
done. There might be some opposition, but on the whole
the South would welcome it and pay for it. There was a
"spirit of reading" in the South. The planters did not live in
a whirl of business; they did not spend their days going to town,
because there were no towns to go to. They had a lot of time
to sit around and read, and the books they read were not always of the best kind. The Tract Society's books were good
books with good constitutions: they didn't catch yellow fever
or malaria. Plumer stressed, too, Milnor's theme of North-
South unity.

Thus the campaign for the South got off to a not very
rousing start and did not amount to much. The American
Sunday-School Union accomplished most of what was done.
By 1836 it had raised $5,421.94. More than $4,000 of this came
from Virginia, Georgia, and South Carolina; New York showed
its massive indifference with $172.57; Massachusetts, $25.00.[50]
The major part of the money went to pay missionaries, who
were unsuccessful and did not serve long. It was hard to get
suitable local men for the work; outsiders were suspect. The
Union sold a number of its libraries, but they went to common
and private schools rather than Sunday schools.[51] Probably
the basic trouble was the plantation economy of the South: it

49. American Tract Society, *Ninth Annual Report* (1834), 3-4.
50. American Sunday-School Union, *Twelfth Report* (1836), 22, 23.
51. Rice, *Sunday-School Movement*, 204, 205.

did not provide towns to serve as centers of social organization, and without towns the techniques of the Evangelical united front were fruitless.

Meanwhile the campaigns of the Valley and the cities were going strong. The motivation, especially behind the drive for the Valley, was undergoing a change. Initially it appeared to be shock at the actual shift of political power, marked by Jackson's election, and anxiety to remedy the loss by nonpolitical means. There was fear in 1829, but it was a rational kind of fear, a fear of failure: "the responsibility for the character and influence of our WESTERN POPULATION rests to a fearful extent on the *American Sunday-School Union.* The momentous decision, as to what that character and influence shall be, must be made before our day of effort closes; and if not made on the side of truth and sound morality—a tide of desolation will roll back from their rivers and valleys, before which *Bible, Tract* and *Missionary Societies,* mighty as they are, will be swept away, and with our beloved *Sunday-School Union,* be lost in the overwhelming torrent."[52] The year was a time for sober appraisal of the Eastern predicament, for measuring the work to be done with deep realization of the price of failure. An article in *The Christian Spectator,* published in New Haven, Conn., entitled "Religion necessary to our Political Existence," laid out a line of thought to become standard equipment in the Evangelical united front. The writer argued that the smallest state of the Mississippi Valley was larger than the five states of New England; that the ratio of increase in the population of the Valley was twice that of the East; and that by 1850 there would be forty million people in the states and territories already organized. Where were the colleges, academies, books, reviews, religious publications, schools, churches, and Bible and missionary societies? They were all in the East. In a very few years the Valley would have a majority in Congress: the balance of political power was passing into the hands of those morally and intellectually least qualified to hold it, a "venal and lawless populace." To readers who might consider these the delirious ramblings of a rabid conservative, the anonymous

52. American Sunday-School Union, *Fifth Report* (1829), 10.

writer of 1829 had his answer: "Do we forbode impossible events, And tremble at vain dreams? Heaven grant we may!" He could not see how civil institutions could possibly hold the United States together. Only one remedy might help: "Religion . . . is the last hope of republics. . . ."[53]

As the Evangelical united front started to apply this remedy, the difficulties of what it had undertaken became more apparent. They were formidable indeed. The American Sunday-School Union summed up its troubles in its report for 1832. The Valley was still sparsely settled, families living three-quarters of a mile to three miles apart. It was difficult to get them together; travel took a lot of time. The people were not homogeneous, and there was an embarrassing diversity of views, prejudices, and states of society. Such society as existed was not stable: forms of justice were not established; settlements were continually shifting their inhabitants; and what was favorably regarded one day might presently be disapproved. If a key family moved out, a missionary's painful work could disintegrate overnight. Very few people were qualified to serve as Sunday-school superintendents and teachers; there was so much ignorance that ignorance ceased to be a reproach. In religious matters there was great diversity of opinion, an endless variety of sects; many of them were averse to Sunday schools and some of them, violent in their opposition, had support from the press. The Union Sunday school was the only successful approach, but there was often a disinclination to yield to the general good. Common disregard of the Sabbath and irregularity of public worship were additional handicaps; hostility toward Easterners was such that only one who belonged to this amorphous society could do any good.[54]

By 1830, the size of the task was evident to the American Tract Society:

If ever Christians had a work spread before them, at once of magnitude beyond all that the mind can grasp, and full of promise, in such a work are Christians of these United States now called to

53. "Religion necessary to our Political Existence," *The Christian Spectator,* I, (1829), 165-75.
54. American Sunday-School Union, *Eighth Report* (1832), 26 ff.

engage, and among the rising, forming, giant people within the limits of their own territory.

. . . the Gospel must have a greater prevalence, or millions of souls will be left to perish in the native darkness of their minds; and our free and happy institutions, in the absence of moral principle, to fall under the just judgment of God, and the weight of our nation's iniquities. . . . The Committee would wish the moral state of our country to be seen as it really is. . . .[55]

In the face of such difficulties and deep discouragements, the problems of adequate funds and ever renewed energies to sustain the Evangelical united front in its drive for the Valley became matters of first concern. The appeal to political interest was effective but of itself insufficient. It was not enough to go on hammering the same old balance of power theme. A logical embellishment was a more emphatic appeal to the element of fear. Lyman Beecher's eloquence went to work on this stimulant: "if we do fail in our great experiment of self-government, our destruction will be as signal as the birthright abandoned, the mercies abused and the provocation offered to beneficent Heaven. . . . No spasms are like the spasms of expiring liberty, and no wailings such as her convulsions extort. It took Rome three hundred years to die; and our death, if we perish, will be as much more terrific as our intelligence and free institutions have given us more bone, and sinew and vitality. May God hide me from the day when the dying agonies of my country shall begin!"[56]

Interest compounded with fear, and then it seemed necessary to add hate to the Evangelical brew. The united-front drive for the Valley needed a competitor to excite energies and bring in more funds; that competitor had to be a dreadful foe, precise in form and substance, mysterious in power. Ignorance and sin were too vague and general in nature to provide a satisfactory stimulus. So the Pope, the "Man of Sin," the great "Whore of Babylon," opened his sinister intrigues to move his empire to the Valley of the Mississippi.[57] At least, such was the

55. *Seventh Annual Report* (1832), 33-34.
56. *Plea for the West* (2nd ed.; Cincinnati, Ohio, 1835), 43-44, 46.
57. See Roy Allen Billington, *The Protestant Crusade, 1800-1860* (New York, 1938).

story: "The Pope, and others of congenial spirit, are sending men and money into this country, for the purpose of establishing here, the kingdom of the Beast. And while many may be disposed to laugh at the project as too chimerical to demand a moment's serious attention, it is an actual fact, that in some places, they are acquiring a power which begins to look down all opposition."[58]

Like other emotional symbols of this type, the tale of papal invasion had some slight foundation in fact. Heavy migration from southern Ireland had not yet started, but the Leopold Society was at work in the Valley, founding churches and schools. For example, of four schools in Lexington, Ky., in 1834, three were Roman Catholic, far superior in quality to any native institutions. Americans of the Valley who wanted to give their children good educations with some European refinements eagerly sought out such schools;[59] but at no time did the movement come anywhere near keeping pace with the Protestant drive of the united front.[60] In 1835 the American Sunday-School Union complained that Catholicism was flooding the Valley: "Catholic Europe is disgorging her priests, nuns, and treasures, and extensive and systematic efforts are now making to control education."[61] But two years later, the Unitarians, also considered "intruders and innovators," did not find the Pope offering any competition. What they wanted was "open field and fair play," but they found the whole Valley preoccupied and prepossessed by "forbidding Calvinism" and "repulsive fanaticism."[62]

The strength of the hate campaign lay in the history of bad feeling, abuse, and mutual distrust in Protestant-Catholic relationships generated during the Thirty Years' War and the national rivalries which followed, not in any substantial fact of American history. It received the usual Evangelical form of

58. Vermont Bible Society, *Eighteenth Annual Report*, 6.
59. Andrew Reed and James Matheson, *A Narrative of the Visit to the American Churches by the Deputation from the Congregational Union of England and Wales* (New York, 1835), I, 132.
60. *Ibid.*, II, 77-80.
61. *Eleventh Annual Report* (1835), 4.
62. American Unitarian Association, *Twelfth Report* (1837), 29-34.

organization as the American Protestant Association in 1842, which promoted the publication of anti-Catholic propaganda, invasion stories, and atrocity tales such as *The Awful Disclosures* of Maria Monk, poisoning the atmosphere with hate and falsehood.

During the 1830's the movement was in its early, amorphous stage. Probably not more than 5 per cent of the united-front propaganda used the anti-Catholic theme in any form, and the more vitriolic aspects did not appear at all. Most of the Evangelical leaders were too well informed to believe the invasion story and too honest to publish what they did not believe, although they were willing to accept such advantages as the hate campaign might bring to the Valley project. Lyman Beecher was one of the early promoters of the Catholic competition story as a device to open purses otherwise shut, for it was a theme lending itself readily to his eloquence. There were times when Beecher thought he was telling the truth. On July 8, 1830, he wrote to his daughter Catharine, "the competition [in the Valley] now is for that of preoccupancy in the education of the rising generation, in which Catholics and infidels have got the start of us."[63] And at the time Beecher was preparing to move to Cincinnati to lead Valley education in the right direction. His conviction of the importance of the West was solid enough, but his powers of self-persuasion must have been under severe strain about the competition of the Pope. Only the month before, he had written his son William a letter hinting that the Papal invasion was more useful than dangerous: "the right spirit is awake, and strong to preoccupy the Valley before his Holiness. So much good is to come out of popery, though it meant not so."[64]

63. *The Autobiography, Correspondence, Etc., of Lyman Beecher, D.D.,* Charles Beecher, ed. (New York, 1860), II, 224.
64. Within Point Judith, June 5, 1830, *ibid.,* 221.

XI

WORLD CONQUEST

BEECHER'S KIND OF GOOD certainly came from Beecher's kind of popery, but the Evangelical united front was already drawing upon another source of energy more profound, more honest and genuine, and at the same time more fantastic to a skeptic than any scheme of the "Man of Sin" to capture the Valley and set up there his "kingdom of the Beast"—the vision of world conquest. Not just the Valley, not merely the United States, but the whole earth must fall under Evangelical dominion in preparation for the second coming of Christ. Conviction of the redemption of the world and then its destruction was the touchstone of Evangelical acceptance. The Evangelical doctrine was not simply a profitable personal adjustment to God and to society; it did not bring peace of mind. To the Evangelicals, Christ brought not peace but a sword and a promise: "Only believe and your eyes shall yet see the salvation of our God."

It had been more difficult for Evangelicals to attain this degree of belief back in the 1790's. The conflict between faith and reason was embarrassing to some, especially to scholars such as John M. Mason. He recognized that the idea of world conquest was preposterous, and at the same time he could be absolutely assured that this triumph was inevitable: "On the maxims of carnal wisdom, the fact is, indeed, impossible, and the expectation wild." "This is an undertaking which defies the policy and the power of man." The prospect of success was a matter "of derision to the philosopher, and of sneer to the witling." However, their error rested in their premise that the earthly goal was to be achieved by earthly means: "Their mistake lies in supposing the God who made them to be as foolish as themselves, or as little concerned with the salvation of sinners."[1] However, by the 1830's the contradiction was entirely resolved. The philosopher and the witling had departed, or, if they remained, they did not speak. Or, if they spoke, they were not heard.

Christianity has always been a proselyting faith, not merely in the sense of desire to share a good thing. It goes much deeper: a compulsion to convert others has been an integral part of the basic conviction, and a rough measure of the vitality of Christianity at any given moment has been the amount of aggression it could muster. One cannot escape concluding that the vitality of Evangelical Christianity in the United States was very high indeed during the 1830's. It was Puritan in its intolerance: "The very essence of every system of manners, morals, and religion, not evangelical, is corruption—gross, foul, deep, total corruption."[2] And yet, in a peculiar sense, the Evangelicals of the 1830's were not Puritans at all. The Puritans of the seventeenth century saw themselves as a new Israel; their faith was Judaic, tribal, exclusive. The later Evangelicals wanted to embrace the world. The Puritans lived under the Aristotelian rule of reason: they would have damned the Evangelicals to hell as enthusiasts. The Puritans could scold; the Evangelicals could weep. They could weep in joy, weep in rapture, weep in glory: "O that my head were waters, and mine eyes a fountain of tears!"[3] "Is it not high time for every rational man to say, I lay it down as a maxim of my life, and will hereafter regard it as one of the principles of my con-

1. John M. Mason, *Hope for the Heathen* (New York, 1797), 14.
2. William S. Plumer, *A Call to Personal Labor as a Foreign Missionary*, Missionary Paper No. XIX (Boston, c. 1830).
3. Gardiner Spring, ed., *Memoirs of the Rev. Samuel J. Mills* (New York, 1820), 244-45.

duct, that the world is to be converted to Christ."[4] The commitment was firm and clear to the Evangelicals of the 1830's: "Every one knows, or may know, that the design of Christianity is to bring back this apostate world to God—to reduce the kingdoms and the men of this world to the reign of Messiah— to recover mankind from a state of rebellion against their Maker, to the submissions of obedience—and to make the subjects of this grace holy on earth, and eternally happy in heaven. It is to *reduce* the world, and the whole world, by a system of moral means and agencies."[5]

Aggressive energy was arising with renewed vigor to support political interest, fear, and hate in the Evangelical united-front drive for the Valley as well as its other objectives. Of course there was nothing new about the source of this strength. In the United States, as in Great Britain, foreign missions carried the banner of the Evangelical cause in the forefront of the battle from the very first and served as a constant source of inspiration to all of the other activities. They all envisaged the same final goal. But in the years 1830-37 there was a mighty surge of enthusiasm for foreign missions throughout the East. One measure of the enthusiasm was the yearly income of the American Education Society, which financed the schooling of prospective missionaries and relied heavily on the appeal of the foreign field. In the years 1827-30 the annual income of the Society hung closely to the $30,000 mark. In 1831 it jumped $10,000 and went on climbing to more than $84,000 in 1835. In the same period the income of the American Board of Commissioners for Foreign Missions rose from the $100,000 level to $200,000.

What lay behind the surge was the Temperance Reformation. Wherever temperance went, revivals followed, and temperance went everywhere. By 1831 New England was a burning bush of revivalism; New York state followed about two years later. The effects farther South were of the same order although not so severe. The relationship between revivalism

4. *Ibid.*, 245.
5. Calvin Colton, *History and Character of American Revivals of Religion* (2nd ed.; London, 1832), 28.

and foreign missions was simple and direct. The newly converted were not noted for restraint; they would not accept the
sky as the limit. And their enthusiasm fired their leaders anew.
To a degree the craze for foreign missions was a distracting
competitor of the serious domestic work of the united front.
For example, the American Tract Society complained in 1835,
*"Christians of our country are more ready to contribute dona-
tions for the heathen than to labor in connection with Tract
distribution for souls at home. . . ."*[6] The executive committee
wanted to cut the Society's commitment of $30,000 for foreign
missions to get back on the track of its principal work. But this
competition was superficial; the foreign outlook supplied the
logic and energy of the internal regime. To the Evangelical
domestic missionary of the 1830's fads were nothing new. In
practical terms this one meant that he might find it easier to
found foreign-mission auxiliaries than some other type of
society or it might mean that he should give a foreign-mission
slant to his Sunday schools or other organizational efforts.

There was another relationship between foreign and domestic policy in the Evangelical united front of the 1830's. Before
the middle of the decade the united front could see that it was
winning. A note of confidence and power became quite evident. Victory in the United States was assured; world conquest
seemed less fantastic, assuming the character of an immediate
practical problem, a manifest destiny. The united front had
come a long way since its shaky start in 1797. The marked
change in its estimate of its own strength is clear in two Evangelical outlooks separated by thirty-four years. Alexander
Proudfit delivered his sermon to the Northern Missionary
Society of the State of New York at its first annual meeting in
Troy, 1798, in these terms: "Our situation is awfully critical,
no less than important: do we look at home, infidelity rages;
like a mighty torrent, swelling as it advances, it has broken in
upon our borders, and thousands on every hand are hurried
and overwhelmed in its deadly stream: rising again, as they
rot, they now float upon the surface, and are polluting, with
the contagion of hell, the whole atmosphere of the Church. Do

6. *Tenth Annual Report*, 25.

we look abroad, a field immense and uncultivated opens to our view."[7] On the other hand, Calvin Colton, dealing with the same theme in 1832, had an entirely different appraisal of the situation. According to him, it was quite unnecessary to write another book, make another argument, or preach another sermon "to establish the supremacy of Christianity in the respect of mankind. That work is done, and done for ever." He found the faith so thoroughly entrenched in public opinion that Christians "have only to plant their feet upon this ground, start from this point, and, by one united and vigorous onset, march directly to the conquest of the world, in the use of the simple and naked weapons of evangelical truth. . . . The world is actually hemmed in. It cannot get out of the commitment and surrender, which are made to Christianity."[8]

So, with some confidence, the Evangelical united front faced squarely its responsibility to save more than nine-tenths of the human race from the fires of hell. "The heathen, who are altogether destitute of instructions of the Scriptures, are *literally* in a lost condition, and *must* perish."[9] There were some six hundred million of them; eighteen hundred years had passed, and nobody had done anything to save them. During the last thirty years a whole generation "have gone down to eternal death." Each year six million died without hearing the gospel, "a state of the most agonizing exigency."[10]

There was a notable shift in attitude toward people of other races during the history of the united front. In the late 1790's the influence of the Enlightenment was still strong, even among American conservatives. Then, nature was good, and anything close to nature partook of nature's goodness. It was the day of the noble savage. The heathen were worth saving because they were brothers; "The American Indian, the Pacific Islander, and the African Negro, are shrewd men, whose intellectual capacity will not suffer in comparison with the

7. *A Sermon Preached before the Northern Missionary Society* (Albany, N.Y., 1798), 36.
8. *American Revivals*, 142, 143, 181.
9. *Connecticut Observer*, as quoted by *The Christian Advocate and Journal*, III (1828), 25.
10. *When a Christian May be Said to have Done his Duty to the Heathen*, *Missionary Paper No. VI* (Boston, c. 1830), 1, 2.

uneducated classes of people on the continent of Europe."[11]
This liberal position went down with the rise of the Evangelicals and of their doctrine of man's natural depravity. As a
consequence, the heathen were to be saved, not because they
were essentially good but because they were outragously wicked
people whose sin and misery filled the earth with lamentations.
Besides, Americans owed them something. Fast-sailing ships
were bringing luxuries from the Orient which were not really
a fair exchange for the miserable tradegoods sent there. Equity
demanded "the inestimable treasure of divine truth, in exchange for the wealth which has been wafted to our shores."[12]

In addition to the heathen, the number to be saved included
the Roman and Orthodox Catholics. Foreign missions thus
were connected with the domestic anti-Catholic crusade. As
the story went, many countries nominally Christian had lost
the true light of revelation through human invention and
superstition and had therefore lost the path to salvation. The
Catholics and the Mohammedans were without correct knowledge of God and of God's government as administered by
Evangelicals. They had no proper views of sin.[13]

The Evangelicals were to conquer the world not for love
but for duty. Here, their interpretation of history entered in
full force. The conquest was inevitable, decreed by God;
whether one took part in it, so the argument went, was of consequence only to him. There would come a day of triumph and
then a day of judgment, a counting of noses: "Will anyone care
to assume the responsibility of withholding his aid?"[14] His aid
was not only a personal obligation but a national duty. If
Americans did not choose to engage in the work, other nations
would go forward to be crowned with success, but "we and our
father's house shall be destroyed."[15]

11. Dr. Hardy's sermon before the Society in Scotland for propagating
Religious Knowledge, quoted by Mason, Hope for the Heathen, 41.
12. Evan Johns, A Sermon . . . before the Foreign Missionary Society (Northampton, Mass., 1812), 17-18.
13. American Board of Commissioners for Foreign Missions, Missionary Paper
No. IV (c. 1828), 1, 19.
14. Hints to Collectors, American Board of Commissioners for Foreign Missions (Boston, c. 1833), 4.
15. Spring, ed., Memoirs, 28.

World conquest became a united-front objective in spite of certain serious obstacles, the chief of which was sectarian rivalry. The principal instrument available was the American Board of Commissioners for Foreign Missions, founded in 1810 and incorporated in 1812 with provision for lay participation. The organization was outside ecclesiastical control, but its composition represented the Congregational-Presbyterian collaboration. In 1825 the American Board felt the general impulse for merger and absorbed the United Foreign Missionary Society of New York, withdrawing this Society from the administration of the Presbyterian and Reformed Dutch Churches. With an enlarged board of twenty-four members representing seven states and all the denominations which might be expected to help, it then claimed to be a national institution. Even so, the essential core remained unchanged, and the claim to nationwide character was wide open to challenge by Baptists, Methodists, Episcopalians, and numerous other sects. The only way to make world conquest a truly united-front project—to include all of the major denominations—was to convert the more representative united-front organizations into foreign missionary societies. The transformation was possible, perhaps inevitable, because the foreign-missions movement had rapidly built up the impetus of a fad or craze in the early 1830's.

The American Tract Society, with its insatiable appetite for immense projects, was the first to feel the new foreign-missions impulse and to join company with the American Board. In its May meeting of 1831 the Society passed a resolution extending its operations to the unenlightened of distant lands. To implement the resolution it made a rather extensive distribution of funds to missionaries of various denominations, including $300 to the Baptists in Burma. The next year the Baptists were back for more and they got $1,000. The Rev. Babcock pointed out that Burma had as large a population as the United States; this little sum was no more than the Society spent in supplying two towns or villages in the United States. What the Rev. Babcock lacked in accuracy he made up in enthusiasm, a feeling shared by everyone present. "The audience was large, and a deep solemnity reigned throughout the entire exercises. It seemed to be the general feeling that God had gone before the Society in his providence, that he was now present by his Spirit, and was calling the Society to great and arduous labors for conveying a knowledge of Christ to millions of perishing men."[16]

The distribution of grants by the American Tract Society in 1832 showed how the united front could operate in the world theater through a political division of funds among denominations.[17] In "the BEGINNING of a great work" the American Board and the Baptists fared rather well. The heathen prevailed over the Catholics by more than three-to-two. Letters conveying grants to missionaries requested that the money be used "discreetly" in one of four ways: (1) for the purchase of tracts published by the American Tract Society; (2) for translations of such tracts; (3) for translations of portions of the Bible; (4) for tracts of which English translations should be approved by the publishing committee. The Society also asked its beneficiaries to send in considerable information about their territories: the numbers and literacy of the peoples, the usefulness of tracts for their purposes, and the money needed.[18]

The following year, 1833, the American Bible Society contracted the world-conquest fever. Its prime instigator was the Rev. William S. Plumer, Presbyterian, of Petersburg, Va., active in the American Tract Society and leading spirit of the Virginia Bible Society. He persuaded the latter organization to pass a series of resolutions for supplying the whole world with Bibles. One of these called for a meeting of the American Bible Society's board of managers to consider the proposition "that according to Scripture prophesy, the latter day glory will not be until the knowledge of God shall cover the earth as the waters cover the sea."[19] Knowing that an idea without money would receive scant attention in New York, Plumer induced his Virginia Society to pledge $20,000 to his project and to hire William M. Atkinson away from the American Colonization

16. American Tract Society, *Seventh Annual Report* (1832), 4.
17. *Ibid.*, 32.
18. *Ibid.*, 33.
19. American Bible Society, *Resolutions of the American Bible Society and an Address to the Christian Public* (New York, 1833), 61.

Society to collect it. Then Plumer made the trip from Petersburg to New York by way of Boston, drumming up support
all the way. With plenty of American Tract Society people
on the board, success was assured. Everything went smoothly;
the American Bible Society made the plunge into foreign missions which gave the organization its permanent orientation.
It resolved to co-operate with the British and Foreign Bible
Society, the Protestant Bible Society of Paris, and possible other
Bible societies in supplying the inhabitants of the earth accessible to agents. The time limit accepted was twenty years.

The American Sunday-School Union also heard the trumpet
call to world conquest, although its response was somewhat less
than wholehearted. It managed to scrape up a few thousand
dollars in tribute to the American Board, but it failed to make
global dominion the criterion of Sunday-school success, although not because of any lack of sympathy for the cause. From
their earliest days within the Evangelical fold, Sunday schools
had found foreign missions a source of strength and an engaging field of activity. As early as 1818 they had shown interest
in the education of heathen children. They liked the proposition of missionaries Poor and Meigs at Ceylon, that a school
could pay for the education of a native child at the rate of
twelve dollars per year and have the privilege of naming the
child when he was baptized. But the Sunday-school movement
lacked the tradition of foreign enterprise, once a primary focus
of Bible and tract work. And there were problems of policy.
New England was the hot bed of the world-conquest fever;
more than half of the revenue of the American Board was there.
And New England had always been a difficult auxiliary of the
American Sunday-School Union. The coalition of Congregationalists and Baptists was breaking up, and the future of the
Union in the region was clouded. The Congregationalists
seemed the better bet: what would please them, and how much
would pleasing them cost in Baptist and Methodist support?
Some money therefore went to the American Board, and a
little more went to experimental work to test again the possibilities of the Evangelical Sunday school in Europe, which tied
in with both foreign missions and the anti-Catholic crusade

popular with the Baptists. In the fiscal year 1833-34 the Union spent $500 for translating some of its books into French and $500 more for the general purposes of any Sunday-school association to be formed in France on the principles of the American Sunday-School Union.[20] The experiment never amounted to anything, but the foreign fund carried on with those for the Valley and the South. The collections in 1836 amounted to $2,239.35,[21] more than half from New Jersey. The Union spread the money around in an obvious effort to please everybody, although there was not enough to please anybody very much. It went to missions in India, Greece, Persia, Turkey, China, France, Africa, and the Sandwich Islands and among American Indians. In addition, the Union made donations of books from the general fund to help the work abroad. Some went to the Wesleyan mission in Ceylon, the English mission at Orissa, and the "friends of public instruction" in New Grenada, India, Africa, Russia, France, Nova Scotia, and other places. The Union presented sets of its books to the Prussian government.

Although the American Sunday-School Union could not contribute as much active effort in foreign work as the Bible and tract groups, it could be even more effective at the local level of school support, and the local level continued to be a source of strength to the drive for world conquest. Other agencies contributed what they could. The United States government went into missions in 1820 with an appropriation of $10,000, supposed to go toward the education of American Indians, not their conversion; but since there was no such thing as secular education, deputations of the various foreign-mission societies crowded in to talk with the President and the Secretary of War. There was considerable haggling before each got its share.[22] The federal government also supported the American Colonization Society's project of converting Africa, by turning over the slaves captured in transit, with funds for their rehabilitation in Liberia. The Presbyterian General

20. American Sunday-School Union, *Tenth Report* (1834), 72.
21. American Sunday-School Union, *Twelfth Report* (1836), 26.
22. See Nathan Bangs, *A History of the Methodist Episcopal Church* (New York, 1853), III, 143 ff.

Assembly, rival of the federal government for popular influence and esteem, co-operated with the American Tract Society in proclaiming the first Monday of January, 1835, a day of fasting and prayer for the conversion of the world.[23] The Congregationalists went along and did not stop there: "The church is a missionary society, over which Christ presides. His commission to it is, Go ye into all the world and preach the gospel to every creature. Every one that belongs to this society should obey the Head, and do what their hands find to do for his sake."[24]

As the fever of world conquest climbed, the Evangelical faith assumed an increasingly millennial character. The revivalism following the Temperance Reformation generated energy in the foreign-missions movement, and then the two frenzies fed each other. The result was a rapidly spreading conviction that the whole earth was to be subjugated to Evangelical Christianity in preparation for the second coming of Christ, the glorious day when a believing world would accord Christ the homage denied Him on His first visit. In the 1830's the Evangelicals saw on every hand signs that God had chosen their generation for His accomplishment. The success of the united front was one of these signs, and it was easy to discover more in every technological development: the power of the press, steam navigation of rivers, explorations. The great day was at hand.

Only this atmosphere can make credible the almost fantastic picture emerging from the records of the American Board of Commissioners for Foreign Missions. In a Boston office was the general staff, meticulously plotting the strategy and tactics of world conquest, poring hours upon hours over maps covering walls and tables. Remarkable developments in exploration, geography, and topography in the past few years had provided new, fascinating maps, which in turn fairly begged for military concepts. What were the key centers of communication? Where were the commanding heights to be taken by assault? Which flanking movements promised success? How were the

23. Andrew Reed and James Matheson, *A Narrative of the Visit to American Churches by the Deputation from the Congregational Union of England and Wales* (New York, 1835), I, 257.

24. The General Association of Massachusetts Proper, *Minutes* (1834), 21.

lines of battle to be laid? Here, very probably for the first time in history, was the application of geopolitical thought on a global scale. The army under the command of this general staff numbered 105.[25]

Reliance upon divine aid was certainly heavy, but even in human resources the American Board did not work alone. It had to organize the efforts of the other American societies. A global application of Dudley's method seemed profitable. The Board wanted the societies to stop looking at the job as a whole: let each organization take a well-defined view of the division of the project it should cultivate, calculate the money, men, and time needed to bring its task to completion, and go to work on a realistic basis. The British would do their part; there might be some help from churches in France, Germany, and Russia.

But for everybody to share intelligently in the great project it was necessary to understand the strategy and tactics of the American Board. A fundamental condition for all thinking on the problem of world conquest was the remarkable progress of the past twenty-five years in geography and the art of traveling. Steamboats had made rivers as navigable as oceans; the Niger, Ganges, Indus, Euphrates, Calcutta, Bombay, the Red Sea, Mediterranean, Black Sea—everything was easily accessible. "In all this we notice the wonderworking of the providence of God, preparing the way for his churches to publish the gospel every where."[26]

Getting down to cases, the Board considered Africa. To obtain control of the continent it was necessary to focus attention on central regions and certain points on the western and southern coasts. The Kong Mountains and the Mountains of the Moon, comprising a range running from west to east, really commanded the continent. The Board suspected that a spur came down near the mission at Cape Palmas; an advance up the spur might lead to establishment on the range. Another line of attack struck in from Cape Coast Castle, 450 miles east of

25. American Board of Commissioners for Foreign Missions, *Report read at 27th Annual Meeting* (1836), 115, 116.
26. *Ibid.*, 112.

Cape Palmas, to the Ashantee country and hit the mountain range to the eastward. Steamboats from Liverpool were opening up the Niger River. As soon as they gave speedy annual passage to Boosa, the Board proposed to occupy some upland position thereabouts, twelve hundred miles in a straight line from Cape Palmas, and also the highlands east of the Niger. Another approach to the center of Africa was from the south. The Board could place a mission at Port Natal, nine hundred miles east of Cape Town, and another about four hundred miles from Port Natal in the interior. The proposed line of operations, Cape Palmas to Port Natal, ran about 4,500 miles.

As for Asia, one strategic line began in Macedonia, ran through Constantinople, the northern districts of Asia Minor, Persia, Afghanistan, down through western India to Ceylon. On this line there were stations at Constantinople, two in Asia Minor, one in southern India, and a number in Ceylon; and one missionary was appointed to Rajpootana, higher up the line in western India. Another strategic line started in Greece and passed through southern Asia Minor, Syria, and Palestine.

In eastern Asia the keypoint was Singapore, the geographic, commercial, and religious center of a great area. The Board had a station there (one church with one convert), but plans for the region were not mature. The Board proposed to extend missions up the populous valley of Siam toward China and also the neighboring islands of Sumatra, Java, and Borneo, as well as the coasts of China and Japan. There was already a station in Siam, another at Canton, and one or two in the islands.

Of all the heathen in the world, the American Indians were most in need of conversion, so the Board thought, and they were the hardest to convert. Indian church membership had not yet reached the one-thousand mark, and that part of the work was taking about 25 per cent of the society's resources. The Board's analysis grouped Indians into two classes: those within the limits of states and territories and those beyond the western frontiers. The first numbered about seventy-five thousand; they were moving out and need not be considered. The second class, beyond the frontiers, totaled about 230,000. They, in turn, could be subdivided: about 108,000 who had emigrated from the East were agricultural, settled and partially civilized; the others, about 122,000 of them, were hunters, migratory and savage.

The strategic lines of approach to these western Indians were two. One began to the south with the emigrant Chero-kees, Choctaws, and Creeks, extending to Pawnee country. A tour of exploration during the past eighteen months had sug-gested lengthening the line to a new station among the Flat Head and Nez Perces Indians, then on to the Oregon River. The other strategic line came in from the north with the Mackinaw and Stockbridge Indians. It proceeded from the southwestern shores of Lake Superior through the Objibwa country to the headwaters of the Mississippi River, thence through the country of the Sioux as far as the headwaters of the Missouri River. From there it was to run westward until it intersected the southern line beyond the Rocky Mountains.

To man its key posts throughout the world, the Board reckoned its needs at 1,260 missionaries, twelve times the num-ber at work. Supplementing them, there should be about 420 lay assistants to serve as teachers, physicians, and printers; and it could use a number of female helpers. With the manpower deployed according to its basic strategy, the Board planned to apply the Dudley system on a global scale. Each missionary would have fifty thousand heathen in his district, under his personal care. To be sure, this reasonable assignment would cover only sixty-three million, about 10 per cent of the dusky and the damned, but that 10 per cent would be so strategically located as to apply tremendous leverage, enough to move the whole world.

The key item of the tactics to implement the strategy was the seminary which each missionary was to operate to train native preachers, thus multiplying his own energies. Ele-mentary schools would teach reading and writing to supply stu-dents at this higher level. Natives were to be trained to do their own printing, since there would be much less resistance to propaganda they produced themselves. The seminaries and subordinate institutions might need a little help from the

American Board at the start, but they promised presently to become self-supporting. The wealth-producing characteristics of Christianity were well known; there would be no prolonged financial strain upon the United States.

In 1836 the system was as far as human contrivance could carry its plans for world conquest. In all conscience, it was pretty far. The rest was up to God. All God needed to do was to provide an initial impulse; if He would light just a little fire, He could watch the whole globe burn. If the Holy Spirit should visit only thirty to forty of the proposed seminaries, that would do it.

Such were the hopes and plans of the swelling host of believers. Already their straining eyes could see the dawning day of glory; they were ready in their time to do their part, and it was to be a mighty part. *"Be strong, therefore, and let not your hands be weak, for your work shall be rewarded. Gird thy sword upon thy thigh, O most mighty, with thy glory and thy majesty; and in thy majesty ride prosperously, because of truth, and meekness, and righteousness; and thy right hand shall teach thee terrible things."*[27]   In little more than a generation, so much had come to pass. Old Alexander Proudfit could see in 1836 the shape of the answer to the challenge he had hurled as a young man, back in 1798:

Already the voice re-echoes through the wilderness, *Prepare ye the way of the Lord.* The mountains sink, the valleys rise, crooked places are made straight, and rough places plain. Go through! Go through! Ye ministers of our God, and may the breaker go up before you, even Jehovah our king, upon your head.

Now, "BLESSED BE THE LORD GOD, THE GOD OF ISRAEL, WHO ONLY DOTH WONDROUS THINGS: AND BLESSED BE HIS GLORIOUS NAME FOREVER! AND LET THE WHOLE EARTH BE FILLED WITH HIS GLORY!" AMEN, AND AMEN![28]

27. Letter of Samuel J. Mills to Gordon Hall, Dec. 20, 1809, quoted by Spring, ed., *Memoirs*, 51.
28. *Sermon before the Northern Missionary Society*, 38.

XII

STRAINS OF DISINTEGRATION

BUT IT WAS NOT TO BE. Not then. Even while the general staff of the American Board was mapping its lines of global strategy in 1836, the host marshaled to win the world for Christ was splintering apart. The two concepts, world conquest for Christ and Christian unity, were inseparable. In fact, world conquest was the symbol, the inevitable expression of Christian unity. And before the year 1837 had run its course, Protestant unity in the United States was shattered beyond repair. The collapse of the united front was a cumulative process reaching the crisis in 1837. To a considerable degree, the united front created the tensions which tore it apart; like the capitalism of Marxian theory, it nourished its own murderers. Its greatest failure was its success.

Success particularly effected failure in one of the principal tensions which the united front developed, the pressure to conformity of opinion and behavior. Conformity, after all, was its primary objective. Lyman Beecher stated it clearly in his 1815 speech, so clearly that his words would not be quieted: "The integrity of the Union demands exertions to produce in the nation a more homogeneous character, and bind us together with firmer bonds." What was most needed were "habits and institutions of homogeneous influence. These would produce a sameness of views, and feelings and interests, which would lay the foundation of our empire upon a rock."[1] Pressures to that end were operating with increasing effectiveness. In propaganda the basic document, the Holy Bible, was in abundant supply. The American Bible Society was producing at the rate of 300,000 copies per year by 1829 when it expanded its plant. The Bible cost about fifty cents; the New Testament, in the Sunday-school edition, sold for twelve cents. There was no reason for anybody to lack the essential means of salvation. In 1836, the American Tract Society sold 3,138,392 tracts and 160,454 other volumes, totaling 72,480,220 pages, slightly above the average of its annual production over the past ten years.[2] About the same amount of presswork went out through the American Sunday-School Union during that year: 1,004,852 items required nearly seventy-three million pages. Library books took more than half of these: 701,400 volumes. The rest went into printed supplies: 125,000 volumes of *Union Questions*, 77,592 copies of the *Sunday School Journal*, and 48,000 of the magazine *Youth's Friend*.[3]

Circulation per piece of propaganda was probably fairly high. One estimate, doubtlessly overoptimistic, placed it at forty readers.[4] The three societies mentioned made publication their primary business, but all the other united-front organizations were keenly aware of the power of the press and were using it as best they could. In addition to reports, special notices, and newspaper material, each cause had its magazine or house-organ. The effect was cumulative: a steady, relentless, increasing pressure of propaganda sustained over twenty years.

In America, as in England, the united front was not content merely to present its views to the public through the press. It would brook no competition; it strove to monopolize literature as well as religious instruction for the American people. There

1. Lyman Beecher, *On the Importance of Assisting Young Men of Piety and Talents in Obtaining an Education for the Gospel Ministry* (2nd ed.; Andover, Mass., 1816), 16.
2. American Tract Society, *Eleventh Annual Report* (1836), 20.
3. American Sunday-School Union, *Twelfth Annual Report* (1836), 27.
4. "Sunday School Books," *Biblical Repertory and Theological Review*, VIII (1836), 99, 100.

was a division of labor: the American Sunday-School Union focused on children, while the American Tract Society worked on the adult population. Their weapons against other types of publication were cutthroat prices, expert merchandising, and social pressure. Their campaign was a crusade for truth, preferably divinely revealed truth, but at any rate the truth. Novels were of the devil; all fiction corrupted; one of Sir Walter Scott's stories, so they said, could counteract the good effects of twenty sermons.[5] At least, these were the opinions of the American Tract Society, with its firm ideas of the type of literature to replace Scott, Shakespeare, and Dryden. In the bindery of Tract House a woman was busy folding the pages of a freshly printed tract, *The Last Judgment*. As her hand smoothed the paper, it passed over the dreadful title. Her eyes followed her hand: *The Last Judgment*. Further down the page they caught the finger of accusation: "Depart ye accursed!" She pursued her task: "Depart ye accursed!" She became disturbed: "Depart ye accursed!" "Depart ye accursed!" A fair run for such a tract was 100,000 copies. "Depart ye accursed!" She became terrified: "Depart ye accursed!" "Depart ye accursed!" She did. Convinced and convicted, she departed, "so impressed with the scaredness of her employment, that she felt she must retire from it."[6] Such incidents testified to the quality of the American Tract Society's literary product, the effect that sustained repetition could attain if there were no competing distractions.

It was not necessary for the united front to obtain complete monopoly of literature to achieve its purpose. What it succeeded in doing was to create a literary fashion, a climate of opinion favorable to its reading matter. It became profitable for any writer aiming at the vast Evangelical reading public to write as though his manuscript must pass the publishing committee of the American Tract Society. As a result, once the Evangelical line achieved ascendancy, it began to snowball.

The American Sunday-School Union came much nearer to actual monopoly of children's literature, partly because it

5. American Tract Society, *Eleventh Annual Report*, 40, 41.
6. American Tract Society, *Fourth Annual Report* (1829), 42.

was creating its own market. It was a large market: in 1820 half of the population was under seventeen years of age. As it described its own task, the Union had to make a gradual transition from "silly stories, the very titles of which disgrace the annals of education, to such books as the *Four Seasons, Sketches from the Bible,* and *Anna Ross.* . . . It was a prodigious leap for a child, to pass from the *'History of Robinson Crusoe,'* to the *'Life of Henry Martyn,'* and from *'Mother Goose's Melodies,'* to *'Taylor's Hymns for Infant Minds.'* . . . No Society is known to exist in any part of the world, which attempts to supply the whole youthful population with rational and profitable books. That this is our *professed* object is well understood, and that we have not been wholly unsuccessful in its prosecution, is sufficiently evident. . . ."[7]

In 1836, the editor of *Fairy Book* commented on what had come to pass. "I cannot very well tell why it is that the good old histories and tales, which used to be given to young people for their amusement and instruction, as soon as they could read, have of late years gone quite out of fashion in this country. . . . They are gone—and in their stead has succeeded . . . something half-way between stupid story-books and bad school-books; being so ingeniously written as to be unfit for any useful purpose in school and too dull for any entertainment out of it."[8]

Priced to take the American market by storm, the Union's product invaded England in the mid-1830's. British critics immediately started screaming about "American abominations." "These are works not of amusement . . . but of that half-and-half description where instruction blows with a side wind"[9]—a statement which some might consider an unsporting return, indeed, for America's eager welcome to British tripe.

The most alert and aggressive merchandising techniques supported the united-front drive for American minds. An example was the American Sunday-School Union's effort to extend its domain to the country's elementary school system.

7. American Sunday-School Union, *Sixth Report* (1830), 15.
8. G. C. Verplank, quoted by Rosalie V. Halsey, *Forgotten Books of the American Nursery* (Boston, 1911), 216-17.
9. *Quarterly Review,* as quoted by Halsey, *Forgotten Books,* 222-23.

Ezra Stiles Ely broached the idea in the 1826 report. The succeeding howl of protest from the unregenerate and the charter fight of 1828 blocked the impulse for a while. But in 1833 the Union judged that the situation had cooled off sufficiently to permit another try. The fact that the Southern offensive was putting the Union's books in elementary schools rather than in Sunday schools was quite encouraging. And in September, 1833, the Union's board received a letter from an Albany merchant, John T. Norton, informing the board that there was an effort afoot to pass legislation to tax New York state school districts for the purpose of establishing libraries in each of the state's ten thousand schools.[10] Norton thought that the effort opened an opportunity, and none of his friends in Philadelphia disagreed. Therefore the Union prepared to enter elementary education "on a footing with all other publishers and vendors of books."[11] Its offering comprised 121 volumes, uniformly bound, each numbered according to a catalogue of which fifty copies went with each unit. The bindings bore the letters C.S.L. for the common school library, P.S.L. for the public school, F.L. for family library, or C.L. for the children's library in a factory, as the buyer might wish. The packing case was also a neatly finished bookcase ready to hang on the wall. Its door, lettered "School Library," had a catalogue pasted on the inside and came equipped with a lock and key. The price for the package was $33.00. Such products of imagination, supported by prices covering only physical costs, had also a system of national distribution with district managers, warehouses or "depositories," agents, missionary salesmen, and a house-organ for effective communication. The American Tract Society could match the performance of the Sunday-School Union.

But in calculating the social and intellectual pressure behind this propaganda, one should take into account the way it reached the individual. It was not an impersonal, mailbox

10. Dated Albany, Sept. 28, 1833, printed in American Sunday-School Union, *Sketch of the Plan of the American Sunday-School Union for Supplying a Choice Library of Moral, Religious, and Instructive Books for Public and Private Schools, Families, Factories, &c.* (Philadelphia, 1838), inside front cover.
11. American Sunday-School Union, *Sketch,* 4-6.

or doorstep throwaway affair. The Union had an extensive organization to teach its product to children and to make them learn it; the American Tract Society and the American Bible Society used the Dudley system of systematic visiting and persuading. Their activities carried with them the highest social esteem. Thousands of eager volunteers all used the same materials, the same ideas, the same key words and symbols. They followed manuals especially prepared for their guidance.[12] And visiting was not limited to the distribution of united-front propaganda. Every society used it for collecting funds. It also came into play in rounding up prospects for religious revival; in some cases the means of persuasion extended to physical violence.[13]

Supporting the army of amateur exhorters was the professional branch with its agents, missionaries, and regular clergy to achieve a perfect din of preaching. The pressure came not only from words, written and spoken. Economic and social boycott were the special weapons of temperance and Sabbath observance, but as the Evangelical line rose to ascendancy in public opinion, boycott seems to have been contagious to the point of enforcing general conformity to a certain set of attitudes as well as the use of approved gestures and symbols.

One complex effect was to make religion a special area in American life, to strip it of all privacy, and to render it a matter of public concern. An Englishman visiting the Northern states in 1827 found religious life to be an establishment almost without a priesthood, Martin Luther's ideal come to life: everyone who wanted to exhort and pray publicly was doing it. In stagecoaches, steamboats, shops, barrooms, ballrooms, and at parties, the talk was of sects, creeds, doctrines, and disquisitions, of preachers and people, sermons and so-

12. For an example see Thomas H. Skinner and Edward Beecher, *Hints Designed to Aid Christians in Their Efforts to Convert Men to God* (2nd ed.; Hartford, Conn., 1832).

13. See Andrew Reed and James Matheson, *A Narrative of the Visit to the American Churches by the Deputation from the Congregational Union of England and Wales* (New York, 1835), I, 45-47; II, 17; also Whitney R. Cross, "The Burned-Over District," unpublished Ph.D. dissertation, Harvard University (1944), 194.

cieties, plans and projects, excitement and conversions.[14] On a trip by stagecoach, the Englishman engaged his seat-companion in conversation to clarify his ideas. He inquired why Americans, so businesslike in tackling most personal and social problems, were in such a frenzy about religion. Immediately behind him rumbled a sepulchral voice: "My friend, you are a stranger, I perceive, in this country: I hope you are not also a stranger to the grace of God." The back seat thereupon answered the Englishman's inquiry in terms which he must have found completely satisfying: Americans were excited about religion because they could not stand idly by and see everyone go to hell.[15]

A Frenchman, Alexis de Tocqueville, was even more sensible of the pressure during his visit to this country in the early 1830's, and he noted its peculiar relationship to politics: "Thus in the moral world, all is classified, co-ordinated, foreseen, decided in advance. In the political world, everything is agitated, contested, uncertain; in the one, passive obedience, although voluntary; in the other, independence, mistrust of experience and jealousy of all authority. . . . Far from nullifying each other, these two tendencies, so opposite in appearance, march in step and seem to give mutual support."[16]

More evidence of social pressure appeared in the literature of the period. It was the day of the anonymous publication. People did dare to go to press occasionally with some criticism, but rarely did their courage extend to the responsibility of a signature. As Tocqueville put it, "In America, the majority draws a formidable circle around thought. Within its limits, one is free: but woe to him who dares to break out of it. . . . The master says no more than this: you will think as I think or you will die. . . ."[17] The author of *Protestant Jesuitism* could venture his dim regard for the united-front leaders and give his preview of George Orwell's *1984*: "Their eyes are everywhere; they see and understand all movements; and not a

14. [Orville Dewey], *Letters of an English Traveller to his Friend in England, on the Revivals of Religion in America* (Boston, 1828), 1, 2.
15. *Ibid.*, 65 ff.
16. *De la Démocratie en Amérique* (Paris, 1864), I, 69.
17. *Ibid.*, II, 150-51.

whisper of discontent can be breathed, but that the bold re-
monstrant will feel the weight of their displeasure. The whole
community, on whom they rely, are marshalled and disciplined
to their will."[18] To what degree such expressions accurately
registered pressure to conformity in the 1830's, only further
historical investigation can determine. But the pressure was
severe, severe enough to produce a reaction and also to nourish
other tensions tearing at the fabric of the Evangelical united
front.

A small core of resistance centered in New York city around
a group of liberals who gathered each January 29 to celebrate
the birthday of Tom Paine. Leaders were the Scotch reformers
Frances Wright and Robert Dale Owen. With their paper,
Free Enquirer, they fostered the rising labor movement and
fought for secular public schools and equality for women, and
they challenged the dominant religious influence of the time.
They enjoyed the support of a freethought newspaper, the
New York Correspondent.[19] Fanny Wright's line of attack
upon the united front was to split it by labeling it a strictly
Presbyterian scheme:

> Presbyterian Idol
> Whether it gain its notoriety
> Under the name of Tract Society
> Or Foreign Missionary Board
> The Idol still must be adored.[20]

The story Fanny Wright circulated was pre-Marxian Marx:
there was a secret combination of money lenders, money
makers, and rich merchants with some Christian churches which
promised they would blind the eyes of the people by teaching
them that their misery was by decree of the Christian idol.
They would find their reward in the Christian idol's heaven.
In return for this service the money powers promised the
churches, "We will give ye a tithe of our possessions and we

18. Calvin Colton (A Protestant, *pseud.*), *Protestant Jesuitism* (New York,
1836), 111.

19. A. J. G. Perkins and Theresa Wolfson, *Frances Wright, Free Enquirer*
(New York, 1939), 248, 249.

20. Gilbert H. Barnes, *The Antislavery Impulse, 1830-1844* (New York, 1933),
19.

will build temples for your idol and we will show respect for you. . . ."[21]

Events in Philadelphia gave more real substance to Fanny's claim that she was fighting "a power and influence at war with the spirit of the age, and the genius of the Nation!"[22] The trouble started with the second annual report of the American Sunday-School Union in 1826. Its author was the Rev. Ezra Stiles Ely, a man no more noted for restraint than his friend Andrew Jackson. The report, which must have satisfied the Union's board of managers, took a strong line indeed. "While the committee feel the immense responsibility which they assume in becoming dictators to the consciences of thousands of immortal beings, on the great and all-important subject of the welfare of their souls; while they dread the consequences of uttering forgeries, or giving their sanction to misrepresentations of the glorious truths of the gospel, they are not backward to become the responsible arbiters in these high points, rather than tamely issue sentiments which, in their consciences, they believe to be false, or inconsistent with the purity of divine truth."[23]

The point at issue was not worth all the dust this passage stirred up. The passage had been merely the prelude to a statement that the publishing committee had somehow found the courage to localize or otherwise alter British works rather than reprint them verbatim. Probably the change was a bold venture, but there appears no obvious need to proclaim a dictatorship.

Another paragraph in the report did not help much. It indicated clearly the Union's intention to extend its domain to common schools and to monopolize the publication of reading matter for children: "Your board have felt desirous, therefore, not only of furnishing their own schools with suitable books, but of introducing such books into schools of a different description and of rendering them so abundant as to force out of circulation those which tend to mislead the mind, and to fill

21. Perkins and Wolfson, *Frances Wright*, 263-64.
22. "Opinions of Celebrated Authors," *The Free Enquirer*, IV (1831-32), 66.
23. American Sunday-School Union, *Second Report* (1826), 3.

it with what must be injurious to it in subsequent life."[24]

And on page 93 was still another explosive passage, an extract from a letter of an unnamed clergyman in Connecticut. It was dated July 25, 1825; probably it was from Ely himself before he came to Philadelphia: "These institutions [Sunday schools] may terminate in an organized system of mutual co-operation, between ministers and private Christians, so that every church shall be a disciplined army, where everyone *knows* his place, and where everyone has a place, and a duty, in the grand onset against sin."

The report certainly contained plenty of potential trouble, but it might possibly have passed into oblivion had not the Union applied to the Pennsylvania legislature for a charter of incorporation, which came up for consideration in 1828, as did Ezra Ely's oration of July 4, 1827, proposing a Christian party to support his Christian candidate, Andrew Jackson. While the bill to grant the American Sunday-School Union a charter of incorporation was pending in the Pennsylvania Senate, each member found on his desk one morning a printed broadside bearing the title,

Sunday School Union
or
Union of Church and State

The broadside tied together the whole package, the 1826 report and Ely's oration, to picture the rise of a national religion to capture the political system and snuff out liberties.[25] The *American Sentinel* supported the "Show Bill" with a "Remonstrance" against the "one grand system" which had "spread from Maine to Mexico, and from the Atlantic to the Western Wilderness. Its concerns are managed by men who, both in their public discourses and in private conversation, have not scrupled to avow their determination to subject the consciences and persons of the *free citizens of these United States* to the tyranny of an ecclesiastical domination."[26]

24. *Ibid.*, v.
25. Ezra Stiles Ely, *The Duty of Christian Freemen to Elect Christian Rulers* (Philadelphia, 1828), Appendix, 18.
26. *American Sentinel*, as quoted by the American Sunday-School Union, *The Charter* (Philadelphia, 1828), 10-12.

The attack upon the American Sunday-School Union was well planned; there is every indication that it took the Union completely by surprise. State Senators Powell and Burden picked up the line of the "Show Bill" so vigorously in their speeches that one may suspect some foreknowledge on their part. No senator seems to have spoken in behalf of the Union. Willard Hall, justice of Delaware's supreme court and a vice-president of the American Sunday-School Union, rushed to the defense. He induced the firm of Carey, Lea and Carey, leading booksellers of Philadelphia, to write an opinion that the American Sunday-School Union was helping the trade by increasing the number of readers. Then he persuaded five other booksellers of Philadelphia to subscribe to this opinion and presented his document to the Senate to counter the monopoly charge. However, Senator Burden pointed out that no printers or binders were on the list; they believed that the Union threatened to drive all other schoolbooks out of circulation through price competition.[27]

The Union failed to obtain a charter and did not succeed in getting one until 1845. The source of attack is a little clouded. The Union consistently priced its product below cost, relying upon membership fees and contributions to make up the deficit. These costs, in turn, were based upon mass production with the efficient use of stereotype plates. Since no commercial printer could meet such competition, opposition could come from that direction.

The Methodists offered a more serious source of trouble. The Mississippi Valley was the happy hunting ground for their itinerant and local preachers; the Schermerhorn and Mills reports of 1815, labeling the "Valley of the Shadow of Death," seemed somehow to reflect upon them. Nor had they forgotten Lyman Beecher's use of this report in his speech at the founding of the American Education Society. His plea for an educated ministry hit Methodists where it hurt; their clergy were for the most part uneducated. And Beecher's educated minis-

27. Jesse K. Burden, *Speech in the Senate of Pa. on the bill to incorporate the trustees of the American Sunday-School Union* (Pamphlet), dated *Feb. 7, 1828, 2.*

try was to administer Beecher's notion of God's government. The church-and-state issue was not new when the 1826 report of the American Sunday-School Union revived it.

In the meantime Nathan Bangs had been working hard in New York to build up the Methodist Book Concern. It was a discouraging task against fearful odds. American Methodism was then a religion of the poor. All Methodists were not poor, but those better off apparently trailed along with their economic and social fellows in the great societies. It must have seemed to Bangs that every time the plate was passed among the faithful, the united front took the shillings, leaving only a few pennies and buttons for the Book Concern.

Even after the 1826 report of the American Sunday-School Union, Nathan Bangs could not carry the Methodists with him against the united front. Quite possibly at his instigation, the Methodist General Conference of April, 1827, appointed a committee to investigate the Union. But the report of the committee cleared the American Sunday-School Union completely and found the Union to operate "upon the most liberal principles, and in their spirit and plan of operation are truly catholic and benevolent."[28]

When news of the charter fight reached New York, Nathan Bangs and his cohorts at the Book Concern saw another chance to attack the competition through their newspaper. *The Christian Advocate and Journal* proceeded to hammer the same line as the "Show Bill" and the *American Sentinel.*[29] The attack may have warmed the bosoms of some Methodists, but by no means all. From Philadelphia came a hot rejoinder directed at *The Christian Advocate and Journal,* signed by five Methodists, resident members of the board of managers of the American Sunday-School Union. The counterattack intended to serve a double purpose, to repel the charges of political motives and to blunt the other weapon used by all of the attackers, including Fanny Wright—the insinuation that the united front was solely a Presbyterian scheme, run by

28. American Sunday-School Union, *The American Sunday-School Union* (Philadelphia, 1828), 6.

29. *The Christian Advocate and Journal,* II, No. 24 (Feb. 15, 1828), 93; No. 32 (April 11, 1828), 126.

Presbyterians for Presbyterians. The Methodists suggested that Unitarians and Universalists were behind the attack on the Union.[30] Of course the High Church Episcopalians joined the scuffle,[31] and the unregenerate press was quite vocal. But the American Sunday-School Union received many votes of confidence. The charter fight might have simmered down and eventually passed into oblivion without too much damage to the united front had it not fused almost immediately with another issue. As it was, the battlefield simply shifted from Philadelphia to New York, where Nathan Bangs with his Methodist Book Concern was ready and willing to fight. His resources were a few handpresses, a little weekly newspaper, a load of debts, and a lot of courage.

Undismayed by the friendly endorsement of the American Sunday-School Union in the Methodist Conference of 1827, Bangs organized the Methodist Sunday School Association of New York City into a Methodist Union to withdraw it from any connection with Philadelphia. The Methodist Union was to buy all of its materials from the Book Concern, which offered to meet the prices of the united-front societies on Bibles, tracts, and Sunday-school supplies.[32]

In March, 1828, while the charter fight was still hot and *The Christian Advocate* of the Book Concern was firing its broadsides about church and state, the Methodist Sunday School Union found itself in need of Bibles. It applied to the Young Men's Bible Society of New York City, the stated purpose of which was to furnish free Bibles to the New York Sunday School Union Society, auxiliary of the American Sunday-School Union. Bangs must have known what would happen. The Young Men's Bible Society rejected the petition in rather sharp terms on the grounds that the Methodist Union was sectarian and did not come under the legitimate range of the Society's charity.[33]

Nathan Bangs immediately promoted the rebuff into an

30. American Sunday-School Union, *The Charter*, 24.
31. "American Sunday School Union," *The Episcopal Watchman*, II (1828), 40.
32. Nathan Bangs, *A History of the Methodist Episcopal Church* (3rd ed.: New York, 1853), IV, 8.
33. *Ibid.*, 21 ff.

outrageous affront to all of Methodism. The American Bible
Society stepped in to smooth things over as best it could. Secretary J. C. Brigham wrote to Bangs disclaiming any responsibility
for his Society on the basis that the Young Men's Bible Society
was an entirely separate organization.[34] Technically, he was
probably right: it had been auxiliary to the New York Bible
Society, recently dissolved. Bangs was in no mood to be ap-
peased by a technicality; he explained clearly that it was only
a technicality. Brigham hinted that the real source of trouble
was not the action the young men took but the language they
used. Possibly the hint was true. The societies of the united
front liked to proclaim, "We stand not alone." Possibly, too,
a real source of trouble was the fact that the Rev. Bangs was
looking for it. Several things irked him. Lyman Beecher's
proclamation of God's government to be conducted by educated
ministers was one. The Rev. Ely's indiscretions on behalf of
the American Sunday-School Union were another. A more
serious consideration was the organization of the American
Home Missionary Society with its leadership of the united front
in the drive for the Valley. Since this group drew its strength
almost solely from the Presbyterian–Congregational–Reformed
Dutch alliance, Bangs had some ground to believe that the
offensive was aimed not so much at the Pope and the devil as
at the growing strength of Methodism in the West and South.
Virulent attacks upon Methodism in such periodicals as Yale's
The Christian Spectator and the *Charleston Observer* did nothing to dissuade him from the conviction that the whole united
front was a Presbyterian conspiracy which brought in just
enough representation of other denominations to permit national window-dressing.[35]

Therefore the Rev. Bangs accepted the action of the Young
Men's Bible Society as an open declaration of war by the
Calvinists upon the Methodists. In a gesture of defiance he
organized at once the Bible Society of the Methodist Episcopal
Church. Oddly enough, however, Bangs exempted the Ameri-

34. New York, March 22, 1838, as quoted in *The Christian Advocate and
Journal*, II (1828), 118.
35. Bangs, *History*, III, 9 ff.; IV, 22 ff.

can Bible Society from the general state of hostilities. He said that it was under Presbyterian domination, to be sure, but, perhaps, not of its own fault.[36] That the Book Concern could not print Bibles and Testaments at current prices[37] may or may not have had something to do with Bangs's generosity.

After all the lively exchanges in the spring of 1828, the summer was rather quiet. In July, the Methodist Sunday School Union mustered three thousand children from New York and Brooklyn to celebrate its first anniversary. They met at St. John St. Church in the afternoon for song and prayer, reports and addresses. In the evening they gathered again to hear a little girl from the House of Refuge recite scripture proofs. There was also an examination of a small boy on "Scripture Questions" and an address by a Negro lad from one of the African schools. It had been a successful year; the Union could report 251 auxiliaries, 1,024 schools, and 63,240 students. Geographically, it embraced the nation, but about half of its strength was in New York; Pennsylvania, Virginia, and North Carolina accounted for the rest.[38]

The Book Concern also submitted a report of its work in Sunday-school publication. It listed 10,000 copies of the *Sunday School Hymnal*, 3,500 Bibles, 18,000 Testaments, and 6,000 *Scripture Questions*. Since the organization of the Book Concern a total of 773,000 books had been printed for the use of Methodist Sunday schools. As the Book Concern seems not to have been printing Bibles and Testaments, it may be that the Rev. Bangs was no more averse to a technicality than the Rev. Brigham of the American Bible Society, particularly in the light of Bangs's next serious move the following October. He launched a drive to raise $100,000 to put the Book Concern in competition with the united-front publishing societies. He simply could not meet their prices and was afraid that all of the publications of the Book Concern would be "forced out of circulation." The statement with which the managers of the Bible, tract, and Sunday-school societies of the Methodist

36. "Remarks," *The Christian Advocate and Journal*, II (1828), 137.
37. Bangs, *History*, IV, 21.
38. "Sabbath School Anniversary," *The Christian Advocate and Journal*, II (1828), 178.

Episcopal Church opened the drive for funds expressed in moderate terms the Book Concern's point of view:

For various reasons, repeatedly assigned, we have considered it our duty to decline the proposed "national" combinations which, in our view, threatened for a while to swallow up, and absolutely to annihilate, every other plan of operation in our country. Such a result we still believe would have been pregnant with hazard. This sentiment does not by any means necessarily imply our impeachment of the Christian motives of those who may have differed from us in judgment. Our resistance to the consolidation of denominations, in effect, has had, we believe, a happy influence.

This condition, the managers observed, did not relieve Methodism from obligation to do its part. "But the terms on which Sunday school books, tracts, Bibles, and Testaments are now expected will not admit of this; nor, in the prospect of the vastly increased demand, will it be possible for us in this way, to maintain anything like a fair and honorable competition with other institutions, which were originally endowed with large funds, and are still largely assisted both by regular annual contributions and by occasional donations. . . ."[39]

In another gesture of defiance, Nathan Bangs organized a Young Men's Bible Society of New York, auxiliary to the Bible Society of the Methodist Episcopal Church, to make up for the lack of charity toward Methodism shown by the other Society of the same name.

All of this seemed quite formidable, but it really did not amount to much at the time. Nathan Bangs played his hand to the limit, but it was a weak hand. In Philadelphia, the American Sunday-School Union took a genial view of the Methodist venture and encouraged Sunday schools to join the Methodist Union and to retain their former connection.[40] And undoubtedly these schools continued to enjoy the 25 per cent discount allowed to auxiliaries. The concession would make sure that the price level remained most uninviting to the Book Concern. The Methodist Sunday School Union flourished

39. "Address of the Managers," *The Christian Advocate and Journal*, III (1828), 26.
40. American Sunday-School Union, *The Charter*, 23.

briefly, merged with the failing Methodist Bible and tract societies in 1833, and in 1836 that society, too, dissolved.

Obviously, the united front was too strong for successful attack in 1828. The Methodists were not loyal to their own Book Concern: the drive for the publishing fund of $100,000 failed. There were a number of ten-dollar contributions; a "Friend" made a substantial gift of $3,213.19 in very dubious notes for collection.[41] It took the Book Concern thirteen years to raise $40,000.[42]

What Nathan Bangs with his followers did accomplish in their losing battle was to set a certain line of attack upon the united front useful to any other element wishing to express its rebellion against the mounting social pressure. For example, when the lurid 1832 report of the New York Magdalen Society claimed twenty thousand prostitutes for the city, a protest meeting in Tammany Hall damned the Society as part of a "chain of church and state, sabbath school, Sunday mail, Bible, tract, missionary and temperance party surrounding and inter-woven with the existence of these United States."[43]

Perhaps more important was a side effect of the sharp exchanges between the Book Concern and the united front. They aroused a sympathetic feeling in the bosoms of many Baptists; perhaps the Methodists were fighting for a cause which was really a Baptist cause, too. For instance, in March, 1828, at the height of the charter fight, a Baptist minister sent the Rev. Bangs his two-dollar subscription to the Methodist paper with these encouraging words: "I am greatly pleased with one thing lately observed in your paper, that is, the stand taken against the practice of some to represent all parts of the country as in almost heathenish darkness, unless some of THEIR *competent ministers* are there. Everything, it seems, must be *Americanized,* or it cannot be other than *sectarian* with such, in the worst sense of that term."[44] Clearly, this statement was an expression of class antagonism, one the Methodists shared. These were

41. "Publishing Fund," *The Christian Advocate and Journal,* III (1828), 34.
42. Bangs, *History,* IV, 14.
43. J. R. McDowell, ed., *Magdalen Facts* (New York, 1832), 54-67.
44. "From a Baptist Minister," *The Christian Advocate and Journal,* II (1828), 115.

the denominations for poor people. They required their ministers to be earnest and enthusiastic. They could not pay for an educated ministry, nor did they, for the most part, really want it. Both the Baptists and the Methodists were aware that the prestige denominations held them in low esteem. Foreign observers liked to picture the America of those days as a homogeneous, classless society. True, class lines were not clearly marked and mobility was considerable; but the divisions were there, and increasing class conflict was a growing weakness within the united front, ready to aggravate every other tension.

In numbers, the church populations (communicants plus others who might be expected to attend) of the principal denominations ranked in 1830 about as follows:

Calvinist Baptists	2,743,453
Methodists	2,600,000
Presbyterians	1,800,000
Orthodox Congregationalists	1,260,000
Roman Catholics	500,000
Episcopalians	240,000
Unitarians	176,000[45]

These not-too-accurate figures are subject to different interpretations. The ratio of communicants to church population varied widely, according to the severity of requirements. It was highest among the Presbyterians and lowest in Methodism. In church membership the Methodists outranked the Baptists and showed the fastest rate of growth. Numbers are a convenient but most inaccurate measure of power in this case. The prestige denominations were the Episcopal, Unitarian, Presbyterian, and Reformed Dutch. But the situation was not static. The Presbyterians were gaining rapidly in all categories: power, prestige, and numbers. Their association with the Congregationalists benefited them greatly. Because of its history as a state church in New England, orthodox Congregationalism tended to be catholic rather than class-conscious in its appeal. Its prestige was suffering from disestablishment, but it contained elements of considerable vitality. Under the

45. "Religious Denominations—General Summary," *The American Quarterly Register*, III (1830-31), 227; Reed and Matheson, *Narrative*, II, 60 ff.

Plan of Union of 1800, the two sects agreed not to compete with each other in the newly settled areas of the West but to let each church decide for itself whether it would be Presbyterian or Congregational. In many respects the Presbyterian scheme of government was better fitted to new settlements. It was equipped with a system of jurisprudence—courts to enforce its law and a hierarchy of power to administer it. Where civil power was weak, the Presbyterian sessions could and did serve as governments quite independent of civil law, a system which appealed strongly to the legalistic bent of many Americans and offered a rather intoxicating prospect to Congregationalist clergy looking for ladders to climb. As a result, most of the new churches were Presbyterian.

Solid performance of well-disciplined, tough Presbyterians did as much to build the reputation of the sect as its absorption of Congregational strength. *The Christian Advocate* was quick to pass on to its Methodist readers what was happening in education in 1829: "Of the presidents of 34 [54] of the oldest colleges in the United States, 31 [51] are clergymen and three are laymen. Of the clergymen, *forty are Presbyterians, or Congregationalists,* four are Baptist, five Episcopalians, one Dutch Reformed, and one Roman Catholic."[46] *The Quarterly Register of the American Education Society* was not averse to letting its Presbyterian supporters know how they appeared to Methodist eyes in 1831. It quoted a Methodist minister, the Rev. John P. Durbin: "They are certainly, notwithstanding their doctrinal differences, the most united in enterprise of any churches of the land. . . . Where the center of this unity of action is, I pretend not to know. It may be the General Assembly. . . . The *same schemes* are advocated, and precisely with the *same arguments,* in north, south, and west; by the ministry and the people." The Rev. Durbin went on to observe that the Presbyterian policy in education placed members in powerful positions in universities, colleges, academies, and common schools. They were editors of political, literary, and

46. "Presidents of Colleges," *The Christian Advocate and Journal,* III (1829), 89.

religious papers and were authors, compilers, and editors of the books circulating in the nation.

The inclination to correlate the united front with Presbyterian power and prestige was undoubtedly justified to some extent; but the accompanying tendency to view it as a demonstration of class power was justified to an even greater extent. As Baptists and Methodists recognized the situation more clearly, they reacted: they drew into more tightly cohesive groups, each intent upon emphasizing every distinction which would give it identity and a clear demarcation of insiders from outsiders.

In this experience the Baptists followed a course roughly parallel to that of the Methodists. The Baptist General Convention of 1826 endorsed the American Sunday-School Union;[47] Baptists were also active in the work of the American Bible and American Tract Societies. Nevertheless they started the Baptist General Tract Society in Washington, D.C., in 1824. It was a modest operation: income for the first year was $373.80.[48] The Society struggled along until 1827, when it cut loose from the tangle of Columbia College and moved to Philadelphia. There it began to develop some strength under the leadership of the Rev. Noah Davis. By 1829 the Baptist Tract Society was publishing at the rate of five million pages per year.

Probably such trifling competition did not arouse the American Tract Society to retaliation. The evidence indicates that the Society was intent upon its work in the cities and was preparing to enter the Valley with a massive campaign. It would be perhaps unjust to blame the American Tract Society if its blow aimed at the devil and all his works, especially his published works, counted among its casualties the Methodist Book Concern and the Baptist General Tract Society. Whatever the motivation, in 1830 the American Tract Society cut its list prices from ten pages for one cent to fifteen pages.[49] It was not a full 50 per cent reduction. The Society was taking

47. *American Sunday-School Union,* 5.
48. I. M. Allen, ed., *The United States Baptist Annual Register for 1832* (Philadelphia, 1833), 17.
49. American Tract Society, *Fifth Annual Report* (1830), 21-25, 95.

the opportunity to wipe out a complex system of discounts and to establish a national price list good everywhere in the United States. Only large auxiliaries received discounts, which were not figured as price concessions but as freight allowances to make national pricing feasible. This pricing policy was nearly a century in advance of commercial practice.

There is a curious way to measure the effect of the American Tract Society's price cut of 1830 upon sectarian competition. The effect may not have been a purpose of the cut, but perhaps it was. The Society consistently listed in its reports an item entitled "Sales to Societies and Benevolent Institutions Not Auxiliary," i.e., sales to sectarian societies, quite probably bearing a special imprint on the cover. To what extent the Methodist Book Concern and the Baptist General Tract Society numbered among the nonauxiliary customers, further research may determine. However, such sales had dropped in 1830 to $3,827.25, about 8 per cent of the Society's total business. With the new policy, the item began to climb out of all proportion to the total growth of the American Tract Society. By 1834 it was 25 per cent; by 1836 it had doubled that figure to $16,877.17, or more than one-third of the total output.[50]

Evidently the American Tract Society was not alone in finding a growing market in sectarianism; the same sort of thing was going on in the work of the American Sunday-School Union, which made no distinction as to sectarian interest. In foreign missions the American Bible Society was making specific allotments to denominations. This explains certain puzzling facts. The Methodist Book Concern in 1828 was $12,000 in debt, confessing that it simply could not meet its competition in Bibles, Testaments, tracts, and Sunday-school books.[51] It failed to raise the money it needed, yet remained vigorously in business. In 1830 sales of the Baptist General Tract Society dropped about 50 per cent. The next year the Society met its competition, repriced its stock, and took a loss of $3,241.52,

50. See American Tract Society *Reports*: (1830), 64; (1834), 72; (1836), 112.
51. "Address of the Managers," *The Christian Advocate and Journal,* III (1828), 26, 27.

more than three-fourths of that year's income.[52]   Obviously the Baptists were in no better condition than the Methodists to stay in business, yet sales climbed steadily.

It seems highly probable that price cutting by the publishing societies of the united front obtained for them a considerable monopoly in the printing of Evangelical literature. But they did not press the advantage to the point of eliminating sectarian competition. Rather, they converted those organizations into customers and nourished them, thereby surviving the collapse of the united front in 1837. They had established a solid foundation of sectarian support and no longer depended too heavily upon the spirit of union which gave them birth.

Although the united front inevitably strengthened the sects, it had no intention of strengthening sectarianism. Its activities in that direction were inadvertent but effective. Of considerable importance was the coincidence of the 1826 report of the American Sunday-School Union, featuring Ely's bombastic rhetoric, with the organization of the American Home Missionary Society. The first aroused the latent resistance to social pressure: Ely's words gave the opposition something it could put its teeth into, a threat to political liberty. The second seemed a move to implement Ely's threat and, at the same time, it aroused antagonism to class rule by the Calvinist elite. The American Home Missionary Society, supported only by the Presbyterian–Congregational–Reformed Dutch alliance, lacked a substantial claim to national status. Its adoption of the name "American" could appear to Baptists and Methodists, the most numerous denominations, only as an unwarranted and threatening presumption. The Methodists under the leadership of Nathan Bangs reacted promptly and quite vigorously, as we have seen, but to little effect. However, as Nathan Bangs observed, the reaction "tended to awaken attention to the subject, and led other denominations to look about them, and watch over the welfare of their own institutions."[53]   Many Baptists cheered on the Methodists but were less well organized, slower

52. J. Newton Brown, *History of the American Baptist Publication Society, 1824-1856* (Philadelphia, *c.* 1856), 55, 56; Allen, ed., *Baptist Register for 1832*, 16.
53. *History,* IV, 39.

to move. Their response stemmed from Massachusetts, where Baptists, although relatively few in number, were lively, educated, and aggressive. It started in 1831, when some Boston Baptists, much impressed by all the talk of "spiritual desolation" in the West, sent the Rev. Jonathan Going of Worcester out to investigate.[54] Upon his return, Going reported to the Baptist Missionary Society of Massachusetts. Much excited, that organization sent a deputation to kindred groups in New York and Philadelphia. There followed the familiar pattern of action, pointing toward Anniversary Week of 1832. Out of the Baptist General Convention in New York emerged the American Baptist Home Missionary Society with full equipment of agents, missionaries, and a Valley fund. During its first year the Society made eighty-nine appointments in nineteen states. Its agents managed to collect $6,586.72,[55] a modest sum but to the Baptists of those days a substantial one.

Clearly, the Baptists were aroused, and they had the Methodists to egg them on. The atmosphere of Evangelical fraternity in a common cause began to give way to an era of suspicion and hostility. Methodists and Calvinists had been exchanging shots since 1828. In 1832 the Baptists, often charged with lack of restraint but never with lack of courage, were ready to challenge all the rest, to claim that they and they alone constituted the Christian community. "I am clearly of the opinion that all our ministers should distinctly understand what the Church of God is, and so preach it that their hearers shall have full opportunity to understand the generic difference between that Church and the Paedobaptist community. These two classes of men are completely distinct from each other, and have no fair claim to be called by the same name—yet, taken together, they are erroneously styled the Christian world."[56] This attitude was a far cry from the motto adopted by the American Sunday-School Union in 1824: "The wolf shall dwell with the

54. Jonathan Going, *Inaugural Address at the . . . Granville Literary and Theological Institution* (Columbus, Ohio, 1839), 16; American Baptist Home Missionary Society, *Proceedings of the Convention* (New York, 1832), 25.

55. American Baptist Home Missionary Society, *First Report* (1833), 15, 24.

56. Letter from Daniel Merrill, Sedgewick, Me., Dec. 8, 1832, quoted by Allen, ed., *Baptist Register for 1832*, 51-52.

lamb, and the leopard shall lie down with the kid; and they shall not hurt nor destroy in all my holy mountain: for the earth shall be full of the knowledge of the Lord."[57]

To a considerable degree the clear separation of Baptists from other members of the Evangelical community was an attempt to achieve some kind of Baptist unity. The varieties of Baptists were extremely numerous, and they disagreed upon every topic but one—the place of baptism in the life of the Christian and the proper performance of that sacrament. The doctrine was also the one characteristic distinguishing the Baptists from all other sects. Under such conditions the rite from which they derived their name achieved extreme importance in their minds.

Curiously, the supposed invasion of the Mississippi Valley by the Pope, well publicized by 1832 for the benefit of the Evangelical Valley Fund, encouraged the Baptists to insist upon their peculiarity. The pedobaptist practice of sprinkling infants as a safeguard against original sin was a sacrament of the mother church which had survived the Reformation. Therefore the Baptists might well charge the other Evangelical sects with being really papists, not much better than the Pope who was trying to take the Mississippi Valley. To baptize by total immersion as a seal of conversion was to "defy the Pope and all his laws."[58] Tensions rapidly mounted toward a crisis, especially as the pedobaptists seemed quite unaware of Baptist sensitivity. The explosion was not long in coming. It started in an 1833 meeting of the Baptist board of foreign missions at Salem, Mass.; it instructed its missionaries to use great care with the word "baptizo" and to translate it according to the precise meaning in the original text. During the same year the British and Foreign Bible Society, the American Bible Society, and the Calcutta Bible Society agreed to block further aid to Baptist translators working in the Orient.[59]

A British missionary lit the fuse. W. H. Pearce, employed by the British Baptist Missionary Society in Calcutta, applied

57. Isaiah 9:15.
58. American and Foreign Bible Society, *First Annual Report* (1838), 10.
59. American and Foreign Bible Society, *Constitution of the American and Foreign Bible Society* (New York, 1836), 12, 13, 140.

to the American Bible Society for aid in printing a Bengalese Bible. That was all right; the American Bible Society had appropriated $28,450.75 to aid the Baptist denomination.[60] But Pearce wanted to follow the American Baptists in Burma in translating the Greek word "baptizo" to indicate immersion. The Baptists claimed that the English version, "baptized," was a plot of the papal hierarchy: it was a Greek word, untranslated, in Roman letters with English endings, to permit infant sprinkling, *"a part and a pillar of popery."*[61]

The American Bible Society was in an embarrassing position. It did not want to alienate the Baptists, but the choice was either that or alienate every other denomination. It was slow coming to a decision, probably because correspondence with London took so long in those days. Finally, on the morning of its Anniversary Week meeting in May, 1836, it passed a resolution declaring all applications for aid must be accompanied by a statement that translations will conform to the accepted English version to permit common use by all denominations.[62] The British and Foreign Bible Society took the same position. The board of managers of the Baptist General Convention declared that it could not comply; its British counterpart did the same.

Baptists attending Anniversary Week, furiously angry at the American Bible Society, assembled that very day to organize their own Bible society. On hand were the Baptist ministers of New York city, one from Stamford, Conn., seventeen or eighteen ministers and laymen from upstate New York, and a scattered few from New Jersey, Pennsylvania, and Virginia. Writing a constitution was no problem: all they had to do was add to the usual arrangement a stipulation placing the society under the Baptist Convention. So the next day the job was finished: the American and Foreign Bible Society (version number one) saw the light of day.

Then it was time for all of the other Baptists to be furious with the New York Baptists. It was a good fight; they wanted

60. *Proceedings of the Bible Convention which Met in Philadelphia* (Philadelphia, 1837), 27-29, 29n.
61. *Ibid.*, 18-19.
62. *Constitution of the American and Foreign Bible Society,* 5, 6.

to be in it. So a meeting at Hartford asked for a Bible convention in Philadelphia. That body duly met, although, according to one participant, "it seemed as if brethren hardly knew for what they had come together."[63] This remark from the floor warmed the gathering to a very high temperature. When the shouting was over, the Society organized in New York had been dissolved, and the job done over in style to suit the entire denomination.

It was difficult for supporters of the American Bible Society to comprehend what had happened. The Rev. James Romeyn, leader of the Reformed Dutch, remarked that the American Bible Society had stood alone as an exception to the rising tide of sectarian feeling and denominational action. But now there was a separation; a new organization with "a slight and blinding addition" to the old name was offering a new version of the scriptures "for the sake of the catholic and elegant translation, 'I have a dipping to be dipped with, and how am I straightened till it be accomplished.' "[64]

63. Dr. Wayland's remark on floor of convention, as quoted in "Bible Convention in Philadelphia," *The Biblical Repertory and Theological Review*, X (1838), 421.
64. James Romeyn, *The Crisis, and Its Claims upon the Church of God* (New York, 1842), 12.

XIII

THE COLLAPSE OF THE UNITED FRONT

THE BAPTISTS PROCEEDED to sever any remaining links of co-operation with other denominations. Even before the explosive Anniversary Week of 1836 in New York, they broke up the Massachusetts Sunday School Union, which had embraced both Baptist and Congregational Sunday schools.[1] They exerted pressure upon the Baptist General Tract Society to devote itself entirely to sectarian matters, but the secretary, Ira Allen, refused to yield on that point.[2]

The Baptists were by no means alone in what the Rev. James Romeyn decried as "sectarian feeling" and "denominational action." In the years between 1828 and 1836, the several churches, almost without exception, had adopted the techniques of organization and procedure of the united front to promote sectarian projects in foreign and domestic missionary work as well as the education of young men for their ministry. There was a little sectarian activity, too, in publication, but not much. On the whole, the denominational societies used the publications of the united front.

But the general structure of Evangelical benevolence, or

1. American Sunday-School Union, *Twelfth Report* (1836), 25.
2. Baptist General Tract Society, *Annual Report for the Year 1835* (Philadelphia), 5.

proselyting activity, in 1836 showed a marked change compared
to that in 1828. The total income of American Evangelical
benevolent societies for the fiscal year 1835-36 was $1,014,242,[3]
about triple the 1828 figure. However, there were other interesting aspects. The independent, united-front organizations were still in the lead: their income totaled $668,239. So-
cieties under denominational control collected $346,003. They
had increased their proportion of the total from about 9 per
cent in 1828 to more than 34 per cent in 1836. Only the Congregationalists among the leading sects appeared to rest their
fate with the united front. Investments in strictly sectarian
enterprise appeared as follows:

Baptist	$141,865
Methodist Episcopal	61,337
Presbyterian	60,100
Protestant Episcopal	55,848
Reformed Dutch	16,353
United Brethren	10,500

These figures indicate that while the work of the united front
had tripled during the years 1828-36, sectarian activity had increased tenfold. Many ecclesiastically controlled societies had
failed, especially in the early years, but some survived to create
vested interests in denominational differences and distinctions.
The degree to which they could turn their people away from
the vision of a united, Evangelical Christendom was the measure
of their success. Their success, in turn, nourished the more
conservative element in each church, always favoring ecclesiastical authority as opposed to nonsectarian, lay leadership.

    Another cause of increasing sectarianism was the rapid
growth in membership of the various sects during those years.
The growth was largely the work of the united front, its acknowledged purpose. But it contributed vastly to denominational strength and a sense of power wholly lacking in the
earlier part of the century. With greater numbers at their
command, the clergy regained a remarkable degree of authority
and prestige. Along with this process developed a marked

3. American Tract Society, *The Christian Almanac, 1837*, New York, Connecticut, New Jersey, and Pennsylvania edition (New York, 1836), 31.

change in the focus of Evangelical ideas. In the late 1790's the essential impulse was to close ranks in the face of disaster; by 1836 success had loosened the bonds of alliance. In a favorable climate of opinion the Evangelical sects were strong enough to stand alone, and many members wanted to do so.

But each denomination was deeply divided within itself, largely as a result of its participation in the united front, particularly those denominations national in their geographic coverage: the Baptists, Methodists, Episcopalians, and Presbyterians. The success of the united front focused north of Mason and Dixon's line. Its method of operation required concentration of population in cities, towns, and villages, largely lacking in the South. Virginia had a few small towns such as Richmond and Petersburg; the united front prospered there, as well as in Charleston, S.C., and to some extent in Savannah and New Orleans. But with a plantation economy and scattered population the Southern social unit became the county rather than the town, a hopeless situation for the united front's technique. The Southern drive of 1834 was an almost complete failure.

Thus the four great churches of national extent found themselves attempting to hold in one embrace two distinctly different civilizations, each with its peculiar type of settlement, its distinctive forms of social organization, its own basic ideas, attitudes, and assumptions, and its separate world-view. The united front did not create these differences, but it certainly did much to accentuate the split, to set the North on a dynamic course of social, intellectual, and economic development carrying it away from the South at an accelerating tempo. The essential division created civil war within the churches long before the political schism in 1860. In each denomination a party developed which favored the united front, the new way of doing things, the revolution in social organization. It liked lay leadership and a free-ranging, pragmatic development of religious doctrine. Another party heartily despised all these innovations. Its view was Platonic: in a world of change and decay, its faith stood fast, a symbol of the ideal realm of true being, of purity, an approach to God who showed His perfection by being at rest. That party, like the Platonic idea of God, resisted corruption by resisting change.

Running through all the issues within the churches was a common characteristic: the conservative, clinging to old ideas and traditional customs, glared at the innovator, the enthusiast, the radical. From 1833, the abolitionists adopted the techniques of the united front to press their cause with vigor. They rubbed salt into every gaping wound of division, but the wounds were there before the issue of slavery became critical.

Among the major denominations the Episcopal Church was an exception merely in having a conservative, High Church spearhead as far north as New York city. There, Bishop Hobart fought stoutly and well for ecclesiastical authority, discipline, and strict observance of the calendar and liturgy. He was opposed to revivals and missions; he did not emphasize original sin, although he found no lack of actual sin in his opponents. To the north and west of Hobart, Bishops Griswold of Massachusetts and Chase of Ohio led the Evangelical party of Episcopalians, more Calvinist in doctrine. As in England, the Evangelical Episcopalians liked revivals and extempore prayer; they were likely to be a little careless about the calendar and liturgy. They were enthusiastic about missions and, like Milnor, their only representative in New York city, they did not disdain co-operation with other Evangelicals.

The Methodists divided along much the same lines. Their issue was the authority of the professional preachers, the itineracy, as opposed to that of the local preachers, or secular clergy, allied with their fellow laymen. The laity wished to free the regular, itinerant clergy for spiritual concerns by easing their burden of such mundane cares as church government and control of church property. Also, "they would relieve the preachers of the delicacy of fixing the amount of their own salaries."[4] The itineracy showed little enthusiasm for such assistance, but the laity kept urging the matter. Calvinists egged them on, quoting John Wesley: *We are no republicans and never intend to be. It would be better for those so minded*

4. Nathan Bangs, *A History of the Methodist Episcopal Church* (3rd ed.; New York, 1853), III, 264-65.

to go quietly away."[5]   As the advocates of "republican Methodism" kept pressing their plea to bring church polity more in
line with civil democracy, tension became acute.   The results
were a schism in 1828 and the organization of the Methodist
Protestant Church in 1830.   The principal strength of the
new sect was in Pennsylvania, Maryland, and Ohio.   Obviously,
schism was not a solution.   The problem continued to bedevil
the Methodist Church for forty years.

The Baptists were in worse shape than the Methodists.
They split into Old School and New School parties in 1832.
The Old School, its principal strength in the South and West,
scorned all "inventions of man" in spiritual affairs.   It opposed
education of the ministry, missionary activity, and all forms of
voluntary association for religious purposes.   A Baptist tract,
printed in 1834, explained the difference of opinion in the
form of a dialogue.   Asked to define the word "missionary,"
the Old School Baptist gave his interpretation: "Why, I have
always understood the word Missionary to mean a money-
hunter, or a person going about the country preaching, or rather
pretending to preach the Gospel, when, in reality, he is only
hunting money; and begging people out of their hard earnings,
as he says, for religious purposes, when, indeed, it is only to be
put in his own pocket; thus cheating the people, and carrying
on a great imposition and speculation."[6]

New England began to assume leadership of the New School
Baptists as early as 1823.   In that year, the Triennial Convention passed a constitutional amendment deleting education as
one of its concerns.[7]   The purpose of this move was to free the
Convention from Luther Rice's financial mess at Columbia
College in Washington.   It also disentangled the board of missions, which moved at once to the more congenial atmosphere
of Boston.   There it rapidly built up its foreign-missions program.   New England Baptists, as enthusiastic as the Congrega-

5. "Review of the Doctrine and Discipline of the Methodist Episcopal Church,"
The Quarterly Christian Spectator, II (1830), 485.
6. "A Friend of Zion in Georgia," *A Plain Dialogue between Two Brethren,
A & B of the Baptist Denomination*, Baptist General Tract Society, Tract No.
135 (Philadelphia, 1834), 2.
7. Baptist General Convention, *Fifth Triennial Meeting, Proceedings* (Boston,
1826), 7.

tionalists for an educated ministry, organized similar societies for the purpose. Leadership in domestic missions also stemmed from there. Although geographic lines did not limit Baptist ideas, the New School dominated the North and East. It was the New School Baptists who had co-operated in the united front and had separated from it with such strong feelings in 1836.

Divisions within the Episcopalian, Methodist, and Baptist Churches were a trend which was expressed most dramatically in the Old School versus New School controversy of the Presbyterian Church. The battlefield was the General Assembly, meeting each spring in Philadelphia. It was an impressive gathering, evaluated by Charles Beecher in these terms: "In its relation to educational, charitable, and missionary enterprises, in the appellate jurisdiction of hundreds of local churches, it swayed a power rivaling, if not really surpassing, that of Congress, and affecting not merely the religious, but the civil interests of the nation. . . ."[8] To mention Congress in the same breath as the General Assembly would be enough to identify Charles Beecher as New School in some Presbyterian minds. It would probably be tautological to speak of a "conservative Presbyterian" of those days, but there were degrees of conservatism. In 1831 one branch of the Church, the Covenanters, separated on the question of recognizing the United States government.[9]

The differences between the Old School and the New School may be described as "doctrinal" only if one gives much elbowroom to the term. The Old School's specific complaint was against the "new divinity" and "new measures" of the New School. Doctrine was supposed to be divinely revealed in scripture, free of earthly contamination; but in practice it seemed to arise pragmatically from experience. For this reason it was difficult to separate the new divinity from the new measures, and both were entangled in the united front.

Quite properly, the controversy had to do with the saving

8. Lyman Beecher, *Autobiography, Correspondence, Etc., of Lyman Beecher, D.D.*, Charles Beecher, ed. (New York, 1864), II, 423.
9. Robert Ellis Thompson, *A History of the Presbyterian Churches in the United States, The American Church History Series*, VI (New York, 1895), 102-4.

of Presbyterian souls. The Old School was strictly Calvinist. John Calvin had derived his ideas from St. Augustine, who had experienced a difficult time in his conversion from Manichaeism, a two-year struggle terminating successfully only at the point of utter exhaustion. St. Augustine reasonably concluded that the Holy Spirit, the aspect of the Trinity bringing grace, was quite arbitrary in the matter, and he believed he was entirely without power to influence the result. He was led to believe with St. Paul, "So it is not of him that willeth, nor of him that runneth, but of God that showeth mercy," and "therefore hath He mercy on whom He will have mercy, and whom He will He hardeneth."[10] Jonathan Edwards' careful notes on the revivals in Northampton, Mass., during the 1730's thoroughly confirmed the Augustinian view of the Holy Spirit as a totally free agent, unaffected by human desires or actions.

The doctrine of free grace administered by the Holy Spirit as the only means of salvation was the common core of all Evangelical piety. It distinguished those sects from other churches favoring Christian nurture, rather than emotional experience, as the path of redemption. The Old School, true to its Scotch-Irish heritage, was content to accept the doctrine of free grace and human inability, in the Augustinian tradition, along with the Calvinist interpretation of election, predestination, and the perseverance of the saints. The Holy Spirit would visit them in God's good time. Until then they must be content to preach and pray in hope and patience. The Rev. John H. Rice of Union Seminary, Prince Edward, Va., explained the situation clearly when he applied for help to the American Home Missionary Society in 1828:

Allow me . . . to say in this southern region, we do not want any body, who thinks he has made new discoveries in religion; or that he can account for things, which none before him ever could account for. We hold here that the religion of the Bible is a religion of fact; and it is the part of the Christian to receive the facts which God has revealed, because He has told us of them, and He knows. *How* things are, we do not pretend to explain; and we do not

10. St. Augustine, "Enchiridion," in Franklin Le Van Baumer, ed., *Main Currents of Western Thought* (New York, 1954), 40.

want any body to perplex the people by attempts to do what we are assured cannot be done. In a word, the people here know nothing of the *Isms* which have plagued you all to the North; and we do not wish them to know. But a man, who will preach the Bible honestly and faithfully; and endeavor to make the people understand its meaning, and obey its precepts, will be received, and we hope supported. We should like to receive many such preachers. For want of them the people are greatly mis-led by Arminians [Methodists] and High Churchmen [Episcopalians]. . . .[11]

The North, as the Rev. Rice observed, was different. Yankee Presbyterians and Congregationalists found the doctrine of inability wholly abhorrent and quite unconfirmed by the facts of life. As the Rev. Porter of Andover lamented, "The real gospel, however skilfully preached, if preached clearly, will be opposed. Experience has decided this. If you say that this has resulted from the wrong mode of preaching, I add, God has decided in his Word that 'the carnal mind is enmity against himself.' Christ preached wisely, no doubt, yet to his hearers he said . . . 'You have *seen* and *hated* both me and my father.' "[12] The Yankees may have been more carnal of mind than the Southerners; certainly they were less patient. They had no intention of waiting for the convenience and whim of the Holy Spirit. The notion that "we must wait God's time" they considered an apology for indolence. To their way of thinking, "to wait God's time, in this matter, is not to wait at all."[13] Such sentiments must have profoundly shocked Southern Presbyterians, whose attitude was one of quiet intensity. They expected the Holy Spirit to visit them from time to time; the occasion would be a good sermon. The action of the Holy Spirit was thus related to the Bible: "a *genuine revival* is one which is produced by the exhibition of GOSPEL TRUTH, faithfully presented to the mind, and applied by the power of the Holy Spirit."[14] Southern waiting was much too slow for the North. There, Presbyterians

11. Oct. 31, 1828, W. W. Sweet, comp. and ed., *The Presbyterians, 1783-1840, Religion on the American Frontier,* II (New York, 1936), 664-65.

12. Ebenezer Porter to Lyman Beecher, Andover, Mass., May 22, 1829, Beecher, *Autobiography,* II, 161.

13. Calvin Colton, *History and Character of American Revivals of Religion* (2nd ed.; London, 1832), 5, 6.

14. Samuel Miller, *Letters to Presbyterians* (Philadelphia, 1833), 154.

decided that revivals depended upon man, "at the will of Christians." Yankee thought and practice assumed that the Holy Spirit, like any other natural phenomenon under natural law, was subject to mechanical manipulation. Rational empiricism could discover just how the Holy Spirit operated and put it to work for human benefit through a proper "instrumentalism." Calvin Colton went so far as to suggest that God was Baconian in developing the "economy of the Holy Spirit." He had tried out the old way of individual visitation in the Great Awakening of the eighteenth century, the days of Jonathan Edwards and Whitefield. God, a Yankee as well as a Baconian in disposition, found this method much too slow, if not positively fatiguing, in the face of the host of sinners to be saved. So by further experiment God developed a method for the mass production of saints and trained the Evangelical clergy in the new system.[15] Granted that God, not the Yankee, was doing the experimenting, the Northern Presbyterians could not feel that they were doing any violence to the Holy Spirit with new measures. As Colton put it, "revivals of religion in the United States have grown into a system of calculation, and the means of originating and promoting them are made equally a subject of study, as of prayer, and the ground of systematic effort."[16] "All the preaching, addresses, warnings, entreaties, exhortations, prayers—the time, the place, number, and continuous succession of all meetings—are studiously contrived and applied to the great end—excitement. And when the object of excitement is gained—when public sympathy is sufficiently roused—the most violent measures are employed to urge and press persons to the state of conversion."[17] Undoubtedly such excitement was most welcome to the dull, stodgy, provincial life of Northern villages and towns. There was very little wholesome entertainment and almost no development of painting and music. Libraries were few, and education, even at the college level, consisted in learning to repeat dogmatic assertions by rote. These limitations help to explain how religious doc-

15. Colton, *American Revivals,* 50 ff.
16. *Ibid.,* 58 ff.
17. Calvin Colton, *Thoughts on the Religious State of the Country* (New York, 1836), 178.

trine and controversy, as well as revival, became such absorbing topics of conversation in the America of the 1830's. They may explain, too, the habit-forming nature of revivalism in those days, a periodic catharsis of frustration for both the pastor and his charges.[18] Sometimes the mere rumor that a well-known revivalist was coming to town was enough to start a revival.

To create excitement was one problem; to control and direct it, another. The wild excesses of Presbyterian camp meetings in Tennessee and Kentucky during 1800-1801 gave camp meetings a bad reputation. The Methodists brought the camp-meeting idea east and had it under control there by 1809. They reintroduced it in Kentucky in 1818 with success. The boys threw away their whisky bottles, and everything went well.[19] In the meantime Lorenzo Dow had introduced the camp meeting to England. Methodists there tried it out in 1807 but suppressed it as politically dangerous and "likely to be productive of considerable mischief."[20]

Another trouble spot for the Presbyterians was New York state, where many disorders like Kentucky's appeared in the 1820's. There were snapping convulsions, much groaning and yelling, and numerous people praying and preaching at the same time.[21] Most disturbing to more soberminded Presbyterians was the fact that women spoke and led prayers in mixed meetings. New England Congregationalists and Presbyterians, feeling some responsibility for the Plan of Union area, sent a large delegation there to bring matters under control. They met the Rev. Charles G. Finney, leading revivalist of the region, at New Lebanon. Finney, far from repentant, threatened to scorch New England too. Lyman Beecher, a member of the delegation, promised to meet Finney at the Connecticut state line with artillery.[22] The delighted Methodists suggested the formation of an "American Society for the Prevention of Women's speaking and praying at improper times and places."

18. [Orville Dewey], *Letters of an English Traveller to his Friend in England, on the Revivals of Religion in America* (Boston, 1828), 12-14.
19. Bangs, *History*, III, 77.
20. *Wesleyan Conference Minutes*, quoted by Robert F. Wearmouth, *Methodism and the Working-Class Movements of England, 1800-1850* (London, 1937), 58.
21. Miller, *Letters*, 161.
22. Beecher, *Autobiography*, II, 100, 101.

They proposed to raise a fund of $30,000, send out agents to form auxiliaries, and offer a premium for the best tract on "The 'impropriety' and indecency of a woman's praying before a man."[23]

Apparently, much experimenting went on, possibly not divinely inspired. One Presbyterian preacher with a good voice boasted that he could bring forward fifty converts at any time by singing from the pulpit. Another, after a sermon calculated to move sinners, would ask those impressed to rise and declare themselves, or he might demand that those "whose stubborn will refused to bow" get out of the house.[24]

He was crudely applying the central technique of new measures, the principle of division. The New School found that a skillful application of Cartesian method would serve both to generate excitement and to keep it under control. The basis of division rested solidly upon the recognized psychological steps of the conversion process, a subject under serious study for more than a century. The first stage of the classical analysis, indifference, did not seem to exist in Northern communities. When it appeared evident that a revival was about to strike, a cloud of fear seemed to settle upon the people. For those who relished the experience, it was a curiously exhilarating, exciting sort of dread; those opposed to the revival banded together for mutual comfort and defense. An account of a revival in Hartford, Conn., during the fall of 1828[25] by a perceptive although hostile pen exemplified such a situation. Rumors of a great awakening circulated through the town. A series of private meetings in the churches and societies followed. As tension mounted, some church members even suspended business. A call to Boston brought Lyman Beecher to preach at a special evening service in a large brick church. As the appointed time approached, the big bell took up its rhythmic toll, and people crowded into the pews. They found the church "dark and sepulchral," lamps few and dim except

23. Letter to the editor, signed "A Lover of Propriety," *The Christian Advocate and Journal,* II (1828), 102.

24. Miller, *Letters,* 155, 163.

25. The following description is taken from "Religious Revivals," *The New-Harmony and Nashoba Gazette or The Free Enquirer,* IV (1828-29), 27, 38.

for a blaze of light around the pulpit. Beecher let them sit there for a solid hour with no more comfort to their thoughts than the great bong of the church bell. During all that time there was silence except for the whistle of ropes through the tower and the creaking of pulleys and gears, climaxed by the bursting doom of the great bell. Then came Beecher, "a dark, haggard shape, looking less like a man than like a troubled spirit." There followed a hymn, a lugubrious dirge. Then Beecher extended his long, bony arms to take up the burden of his sermon: "I must rend away the veil of time, and show you the terrors of eternity."

> The roused ocean of deep hell,
> Whose every wave breaks on a living shore
> Heap'd with the damned, like pebbles.

Most of the people at the meeting managed to get home afterwards, but it certainly created an emotional situation which might well have escaped control. The division techniques of the new measures had been at work. In the atmosphere contrived to create emotional tension, individuals started to break; they shook, sobbed, cried out. There was no social disgrace in this—it was a hopeful sign. The pastor or his lay assistants immediately escorted these people to a separate, "anxious" room. If such a room were not available, a portion of the meeting hall, set apart as the anxious seat, would serve. The arrangement made possible a reasonable degree of order in the main congregation while it segregated the better prospects under conditions permitting them to communicate their disturbance and heighten it.

When the anxious room was well populated, the revivalist also retired there to conduct the most important and critical part of the work. He struggled alternately with the group and the individuals, exhorting, threatening, and praying, while within each bedeviled soul the tension and torment mounted toward a climax. The fear was more than a dread of the wrath to come, worse than a fear of death. It was associated with a threatened loss of identity: if God turned his back, one would cease to exist; rather, one would not have existed at all. "I

have seen men in such an agony, as might easily be mistaken
... for the remorse of a murderer or the anguish of a convict."[26]
As Samuel J. Mills described his experience, *"I have seen* to
the very bottom of hell."[27] Intense anger often marked inhabitants of the anxious room. They felt an injustice in their
suffering such torment while others were free and happy. But
the revivalist expected that, too, and knew how to turn anger
inward into self-loathing. Inevitably the tension in each
climbed to a climax of exhaustion, an orgasm of surrender and
release. Then came such joy and assurance as to make the
world a dazzle of radiance glimpsed through streaming tears—
another sinner saved. In this connection, the word "sinner"
acquired a special meaning with no relation to conduct. As a
visiting Englishman marked it: "A sinner with these people
... is one who has not passed through this moral paroxysm."[28]

At this point, new measures required another division.
The convert joined his fellows in another room set apart for
them. From time to time the revivalist reported back to the
congregation upon the success of his labors. Sometimes he
would bring an unusual case to tell the audience of his experience. Usually the newborn saint was more than eager, easier
to start than stop. As the minister returned to his more critical
charges, his lay assistants took up again the activity they had
carried on in his absence. They led the singing of hymns and,
visiting from pew to pew, exhorted and prayed in private
conferences intended to keep the anxious room refreshed.
The newly converted did not rejoin the congregation to provide a source of disorder. Instead, the management of the
revival directed the enormous energies of these eager souls upon
the community in house-to-house visiting. "For the period,
but one object is before them, and it *possesses* them. They have
found mercy, and they thirst to bestow it; they have dishonored
God and they thirst to glorify him. They become missionaries
for the time; and they move about in their families and their
connexions, warning, teaching, and entreating, with tears, that

26. [Dewey], *Letters of an English Traveller*, 6.
27. Gardiner Spring, ed., *Memoirs of the Rev. Samuel J. Mills* (New York,
1820), 13-14.
28. [Dewey], *Letters of an English Traveller*, 43.

they would be reconciled and saved."[29]   It was probably in these visits that instances of violence occurred—the more refractory the sinner, the greater the saint who saved him. Such visitations provided energy to keep a revival going for some time. The need for repeated sessions brought into favor the "protracted meeting," developed by the Methodists in 1827[30] and adopted by the Presbyterians as suitable to their needs. It was a camp meeting without a camp, well adapted to towns. Since the length of a revival testified to its strength, protracted meetings tended to become marathon contests. One ran on for forty days. At the end everyone was so thoroughly converted that the pastor could not muster enough of his flock to constitute a prayer meeting.[31]

On the whole, the process of revivalism in New School hands created a dynamics of its own. Unusual tactics tended to become usual. Young preachers especially, eager to make quick reputations as revivalists, resorted more and more to extreme "instrumentality." The Old School viewed these developments with growing horror and disgust.

The new doctrines evolved inevitably from the assumptions underlying new measures in the North. Nothing so frustrated a revivalist as to enter the anxious room only to find its occupants agreed in Augustinian piety that they were utterly unable to do anything about their own salvation and therefore had no responsibility whatever in the matter.[32] In the face of common religious procedures and the practical needs of the situation, the old Calvinism had to give way. From Princeton, Samuel Miller spoke with dismay:

I feel constrained to add, that when this exciting system of calling to "anxious seats,"—calling out into the aisles to be "prayed for," &c., is connected, as, to my certain knowledge, it often has been, with erroneous doctrines;—for example, with the declaration that nothing is *easier* than conversion:—that the power of the Holy Spirit is not necessary to enable impenitent sinners to repent and

29. Andrew Reed and James Matheson, *A Narrative of the Visit to the American Churches by the Deputation from the Congregational Union of England and Wales* (New York, 1835), II, 16.
30. Bangs, *History*, IV, 52, 53.
31. Reed and Matheson, *Narrative*, II, 31.
32. Beecher, *Autobiography*, II, 75.

believe;—that if they only resolve to be for God—resolve to be Christians—*that* itself is regeneration—the work is already done:— I say, where the system of "anxious seats," &c., is connected with such doctrinal statements as these, it appears to me adapted to destroy souls by wholesale![33]

By the time the New School leaders had adjusted their new divinity to suit their new measures, they had completely swung over from St. Augustine to his outstanding opponent of the fifth century, Pelagius. With him they stood for free will, absolute human responsibility, denial of original sin and total depravity, efficacy of the law along with grace, and the ability of converts to live in holy perfection, free of willful sin.

It seems highly probable that Methodist competition, as well as new measures, was influential. The Methodists had enjoyed a distinct doctrinal advantage in their appeal to the American public, one doubtlessly contributing to their remarkable growth, especially in the Mississippi Valley. Methodism held the human race in very low esteem, lower than Calvinism held it, and this doctrine, curiously, permitted it to advance a back-handed claim to human dignity. Like Calvinism, Methodism believed that man was unable to save himself; any Methodist caught preaching to the contrary faced prompt trial for heresy. A visitation of the Holy Spirit was as necessary for saving Methodists as Calvinists, but in the Methodist view, a person could be so sunk in sin and depravity that he would reject the Holy Spirit. This view opened the door to free will and responsibility, denying predestination. Calvinists taught that the Holy Spirit was an irresistible absolute, foreordained and eternally effective. An elected saint might sin, but he was saved nevertheless. The Methodists, on the other hand, believed that grace cleansed from all sin, enabling its recipient to live the rest of his life in human perfection—not the innocent perfection of Adam or the all-knowing and all-powerful perfection of God, but the ability to live without willful, voluntary sin.[34]

The new divinity of the New School Presbyterians was

33. *Letters,* 165.
34. Cf. Nathan Bangs, *The Errors of Hopkinsianism Detected and Refuted* (New York, 1815), 153 ff.

more outspokenly liberal than anything the Methodists had to offer. By 1836 it had gained sufficient popularity to stop the spread of Methodism in its tracks, especially in the Valley. People who had naturally come to Methodist doctrine, Nathan Bangs admitted, now had other places to go. Not until 1839, when the united front no longer existed, did Methodism resume its growth.[35]

The New School managed to abandon Calvinism for the Pelagian heresy without having to face heresy charges by drawing a distinction between doctrine and what it called the "philosophy" of the doctrine. No New School leaders ever went astray in doctrine; they were as solid there as Jonathan Edwards could wish. But the philosophical interpretation of the implications of doctrine they considered wide open to speculation, and it was there that the revolution took place. The situation became clear in the key doctrinal case before Presbyterian judicatories, that of the Rev. Albert Barnes. Barnes, a graduate of Princeton Theological Seminary, was chosen pastor by the First Presbyterian Church of Philadelphia, a New School church in an Old School synod which rejected Barnes. The General Assembly, with a New School majority, supported him, so the synod tried to charge Barnes on doctrinal matters. For seven years, from the publication of his sermon, *The Way of Salvation,* in 1829, to 1836, Barnes stood trial, but the synod would not try him for heresy. It kept busy trying his publications, the opinions imputed to him, and the implications of the opinions imputed to him. It all came to nothing.

The futility and frustration of the Old School in the face of the New School's elusive tactics was clear in Harriet Beecher's description of her brother George's examination by the Presbytery in Cincinnati in 1834: "One of them got up, and, in the course of his objections, said, with a peculiar solemnity of manner, that 'he did not wish to prejudice any one against the candidate, but, sir, if I understand him, he holds that God has no right to require men to do what they are not able to do. Now, sir, this is an awful error. If God had not the right to

35. *History,* IV, 267, 274, 332.

require things of men which they have no ability whatever to perform, what dreadful consequences would ensue! Oh,' said he, rolling up his eyes, 'they are awful! I will not even name them!' "[36]

The American Home Missionary Society usually managed to free its Presbyterian missionaries from the embarrassment of such examinations when they reached the Mississippi Valley. There were New School presbyteries in the East which cleared their candidates with a minimum of discomfort, especially the Third Presbytery of New York city and the Newbury, Mass., Presbytery.[37] The heart of the Old School difficulty was here evident: Presbyterian doctrine, its teaching as well as its propagation, was beyond its control. Even when the Old School proponents had a majority in the General Assembly it meant nothing, because these matters were beyond Presbyterian control; they were vested in the united front. The New School, supporting the united front, discouraged as sectarian and destructive every attempt of the General Assembly to enter the benevolent field.

There were some ventures in that direction. In 1816 the General Assembly established the United Foreign Missionary Society, proposing to co-operate with the Reformed Dutch and Associate Reformed Presbyterian Churches in its support. But in 1826 that Society joined the American Board and escaped all ecclesiastical control, leaving the General Assembly with no enterprise at all in foreign missions. There was also some early Assembly activity in domestic missions. It put about fifty missionaries at work in the years 1802-3 under the standing committee of missions. In 1816 it organized a board of missions which, lacking any support, continued to exist in name only. In education of young men for the ministry the General Assembly did a little better, but not much. It set up its board of education in 1819; for the first few years the board did practically nothing. The Assembly started to push it in 1825 and by 1829 it was collecting about $1200 a year to aid about twenty beneficiaries. The New School moved to knock out

36. Beecher, *Autobiography*, II, 292.
37. Sweet, ed., *The Presbyterians*, 105.

the board of missions in 1828 by amalgamating it with the American Home Missionary Society. The secretaries of the two bodies agreed upon a plan of union, but the board of missions refused to accept it.[38] The next year, the New School tried again, this time to merge the board of education with the the American Education Society. The proposal brought up the issue of doctrine, raised a great furor, and failed for that reason.[39]

There was considerable justification for Old School fears. The American Education Society co-operated vigorously with the American Home Missionary Society to pump Congregational Presbyterians into the West under the Plan of Union and thus build up New School strength. Lyman Beecher remarked, "The fact is, a Presbytery made up of New England men, raised Congregationalists, is the nearest the Bible of anything there is."[40] There were those who disagreed, as George Beecher discovered during his examination at Cincinnati.

Tensions rose rapidly in the West as Congregationalists moved in with their freshly donned Presbyterian robes, a procedure sanctioned by the Plan of Union. Beneath the robes they were still Congregational, informal and independent. Often they neglected to place themselves under the care of the presbyteries they entered; they wandered into districts jealously guarded by Old School, settled pastors;[41] they sent lay committeemen instead of ordained elders to sit in presbyteries and synods, directly violating Presbyterian law, and even tried to get them into the General Assembly.[42] Exasperated and insulted, Old School men of the West tried vainly to stem the invasion. In 1834 they sent their "Western Memorial" to the General Assembly: "Especially do we complain of, and testify against, what has more than once occurred during the last few years—the ordaining of six, eight, or ten young men at a time,

38. C. B. Goodykoontz, *Home Missions on the American Frontier* (Caldwell, Idaho, 1939), 190-99.
39. "The General Assembly's Board of Education and the American Education Society," *Biblical Repertory*, I, N.S. (1829), 353-55.
40. *Autobiography*, I, 116.
41. Sweet, ed., *The Presbyterians*, 104.
42. Thompson, *History of the Presbyterian Churches*, 141.

most of them just licensed, who have been reared, up from infancy to manhood, in Congregational views, feelings, and habits, and who are thus suddenly, nominally and *geographically*, converted into Presbyterian ministers, before it was possible, in the nature of things, that they could have just and clear views of the nature of Presbyterianism."[43] Since the New School had a majority in the General Assembly that year, the reaction was mild and conciliatory. It requested the Congregational Association of New England to prevent the ordination of prospective Presbyterian ministers by their consociations. The New England bodies concurred.[44] There was no reason why they should not, as they had convenient Presbyterian diploma mills at hand.

In the meantime the drive of the New School with the support of the great missionary and education societies was radically changing the balance of power within the Presbyterian Church as a whole. In the seven years from 1829 to 1837, the New School held majorities five times. Although not larger in membership, it was lively and aggressive; its delegates could get to Philadelphia more easily than those from the South, and they did so.

Once there, they pressed their point of view relentlessly. They opposed sectarianism, whether it was Baptist, Methodist, or Presbyterian. And they proposed to use their control of the Presbyterian General Assembly to knock out Presbyterian sectarianism. As reported by an anonymous member of the Old School,

The most important and startling principle, however, advanced by our new school brethren was, that the Assembly has no power to appoint such a Board [Foreign Missions], or to conduct missionary operations at all. . . .

It is not, however, so much the novelty of this principle . . . which makes it alarming to every true Presbyterian. It effects a radical revolution in the whole church. It not only cuts off the Boards of Education and Missions, but all similar Boards, all ecclesiastical seminaries, and gives up the control of all the affairs of

43. Isaac V. Brown, *A Historical Vindication of the Abrogation of the Plan of Union* (Philadelphia, 1855), 91.

44. The General Association of Massachusetts Proper, *Minutes* (June 24, 1834), 5.

the church, beyond mere matters of discipline, to voluntary associations. And by whom are these voluntary associations controlled? By moneyed men. These men of wealth, so far as we know are good men, but it is not their goodness, but their wealth which gives them their controlling influence. The men who have the direction of the education of the candidates for ministry, and the location and support of these candidates when ordained, have ten thousand sources of influence in the feelings and associations, as well as interests of those concerned, which render them the arbiters of the destiny of the church.[45]

After the New School's rallies of 1828 and 1829, the Old School began to consider seriously some counteroffensive measures. Most appealing was the prospect of re-entering the field of foreign missions in competition with the American Board. The Western Foreign Missionary Society at Pittsburgh, an Old School stronghold in Scotch-Irish Pennsylvania, offered the opportunity. The Society, instituted by the Synod of Pittsburgh in 1805, was a thriving institution, and its constitution stipulated that it place itself under the care of the General Assembly whenever that body so desired. The Old School began to look toward Pittsburgh. Of course the New School reacted vigorously. Having a majority in the Assembly in 1831, it tried to bind the General Assembly "by a solemn act" to stay out of foreign missions except as it cared to support the American Board.[46] The attack nearly succeeded; the best that the Old School could do was to divert it to a joint committee of the General Assembly and the American Board, which was directed to report to the American Board in the fall, then back to the Assembly next year. The Old School moved at once to take advantage of its reprieve. Seven leaders met to draw up a "Secret Circular" to Old School adherents. The object was to rally support for the board of education as well as to obtain full attendance of the party's membership at Assembly meetings. The circular warned

. . . that our theological seminaries are in danger of being revolutionized and perverted from the intention of their orthodox

45. "The General Assembly of 1836," *The Biblical Repertory and Theological Review*, VIII (1836), 436, 438.
46. Miller, *Letters*, 85, 86.

founders; that the property & endowments of our church are in danger of passing . . . into the hands of those who have contributed little, if anything, to their amount: that our doctrinal standards are in danger, either of total disregard, or of a revision and alteration that will essentially change their character; that our supreme ecclesiastical judicatory is in danger of being controlled by delegates unconstitutionally appointed and commissioned, and destitute of every legal claim to membership; and finally, that our boards of Education and of Missions, are in danger of being wrested from the hands of those who wish to make them the sources of supply to the wants of our church in an incorrupted state, and of being rendered subsidiary to the plans and purposes of voluntary associations, subject to no ecclesiastical responsibility, and adopting no formula of faith by which their religious tenets may be ascertained.[47]

In 1832 the joint committee on foreign missions reported to the Assembly the result of its deliberations: *"The American Board of Commissioners for Foreign Missions is, in the opinion of the committee, properly a national institution."* The committee further expressed itself as "fully satisfied that it is wholly inexpedient to attempt the formation of any other distinct organization within the three denominations [Presbyterian, Congregational, and Reformed Dutch] for conducting foreign missions."[48] This conclusion was what the New School wanted, but the time to strike had passed. The situation had developed a trigger mechanism: everyone knew a conclusive move by either side would blow the Church to pieces, and no one was quite ready for that.

The "Secret Circular" had done much to stiffen the Old School attitude, and it seemed to have won support for the board of education. In 1832 that body, borrowing a leaf from the New School book, hired agents and rapidly lifted its income to the $50,000 level.[49] The secondary effects are difficult to measure but unquestionably important. It put men into the field to earn their living by arousing Old School Presbyterians

47. "Secret Circular of 1831," as edited by Sweet, *The Presbyterians*, 829.
48. American Board of Commissioners for Foreign Missions, *Twenty-Third Report*, 183-85.
49. Board of Education of the General Assembly of the Presbyterian Church, *Annual Report* (1836), 4-6.

to the doctrinal dangers posed by New School support of the American Education Society.

And so matters stood, the two parties at bay, opposed in their views of man and of God, in their ways of thinking and solving problems. On the one side was fear and horror of blasphemy; on the other side, contempt. As Charles G. Finney remarked, "These things in the Presbyterian church, their contentions and janglings are so ridiculous, so wicked, so outrageous, that no doubt there is a jubilee in hell every year about the time of the meeting of the General Assembly."[50] On the Old School side of the fence, Samuel Miller was no happier about it. "It is in vain to hope for solid peace in our beloved church, so long as views so discordant and feelings so excited in regard to the relative claims of Ecclesiastical Boards and Voluntary Associations as have recently prevailed, continue to prevail, and to be warmly urged. In reference to this subject there appear to me to be faults on both sides . . . which . . . must keep the church in constant commotion, and ultimately rend her to pieces."[51]

The rending had really begun before Miller wrote. Under a policy of "elective affinity," presbyteries could choose whether they would be New School or Old School. Or, if they could not decide any other way, they could divide and set up new presbyteries. The policy eased no tensions; it simply provided many battlefields and made a jumble of geographical boundaries through the border states. The New School held the line of the Ohio River except for half of Indiana. It had majorities in New York city, northern New Jersey, and the eastern part of Tennessee. Charleston, S.C., wanted to go along with the New School but held back, probably for sectional reasons. The slavery question was a constant irritant, but it did not appear as an issue between the two parties.[52] The debate centered not on slavery or particularly on new divinity and new measures but on the deeper issue of the nature of the Church. The

50. *Lectures on Revivals of Religion* (2nd ed.; New York, 1835), 269.
51. *Letters*, 18.
52. Gilbert H. Barnes, *The Antislavery Impulse, 1830-1844* (New York, 1933), pressed the slavery issue as the prime cause of Presbyterian schism in 1837. However, the New School took the same position as the Old School on this question in 1837, 1846, and 1849. The New School divided on slavery in 1853.

Old School stoutly maintained the traditional, sectarian view of the Church with its ecclesiastical judicatory to conduct all church enterprises and receive all funds contributed to that end: *"it is plainly the duty of the Church, in her ecclesiastical capacity, to undertake and conduct such enterprises; nay, that when she neglects to do so, she is guilty of great injustice to herself, and of direct disobedience to her divine Head and Lord."*[53]

The New School supported its concept of the Church with a quotation from the Confession of Faith: "The visible church, which is also catholic or universal . . . consists of all those throughout the world, that profess the true religion."[54] The concept permitted an atomistic view: "Nor is it necessary that the work should be done by the church, in her ecclesiastical organization, in order to its being done *by the church*, and in a manner acceptable to God. What is the church, but the collective body of Christ's disciples? And what are the conscience and faith of the church, but the conscience and faith of her individual members? What then are the duties of the church, but the duties of the individuals who constitute it?"[55]

But working against the New School was the rage for voluntary association for social purposes. It had overrun itself. Most social objectives had a religious bearing of some sort; all of them used the same method of operation. Agents "like the locusts of Egypt" swarmed over the land.[56] Since the favorite spots to swarm were the churches, pastors found themselves yielding the pulpit much of the time to ministerial agents requesting this courtesy. A reaction set in, probably encouraged in New England by the Andover conservatives, who were no more enthusiastic for the new divinity than was the Old School. In 1836 the General Association of Massachusetts concurred in a resolution already passed by the corresponding Congregational

53. Miller, *Letters*, 70.
54. *The Constitution of the Presbyterian Church* (May 29, 1839), 134.
55. A Member of the General Assembly, *A Plea for Voluntary Societies* (New York, 1837), 23.
56. Calvin Colton (A Protestant, *pseud.*), *Protestant Jesuitism* (New York, 1836), 132.

body of Connecticut. The associations affirmed that liberty of speech and of press was fine, but

> They do not admit an obligation upon the community to hear *all* that associations or individuals may volunteer to speak or print, or an obligation on the pastors of the churches to admit into their pulpits all those preachers or speakers who may desire to address the people. . . .
>
> *Resolved*, That the operations of itinerant agents and lecturers, . . . *without advice and consent of the pastors and regular ecclesiastical bodies*—is an unauthorized interference with the rights, duties, and discretion of the stated ministry; dangerous to the influence of the pastoral office, and fatal to the peace and good order of the churches.[57]

Thus, Old School Presbyterians were not alone in reasserting church authority. But the New School managed to muster a majority again in the General Assembly of 1836 after losing it in 1835. As usual, the two parties caucused secretly and met only to fight in cold fury. The New School pressed its case to the limit, making perfectly clear the restrictions it intended to impose upon the General Assembly's sphere of action. The Old School minority decided that the point of endurance was past; it was time for another circular, not secret this time. It published "An Address to the Ministers, Elders and Members of the Presbyterian Church in the United States," declaring, "whatever else may be dark, this is clear, we cannot continue in the same body. In some way or other, these men MUST BE SEPARATED FROM US."[58] On the New School side, Nathaniel Taylor, Yale's leader in the new divinity, expressed the same idea to Lyman Beecher. He thought that division was necessary, not on the ground of essentials but of expediency, not on the issue of heresy but "as sects differing so much and with such conscience of the *speculative* importance of the differences."[59]

The Old School, with a small majority of the church membership, could still take command of the General Assembly in a crisis, as it did in 1837. It promptly executed its painfully

57. The General Association of Massachusetts Proper, *Minutes* (1836), 8-9.
58. Quoted by Member, *Plea,* 14.
59. March 3, 1837, quoted in Beecher, *Autobiography,* II, 416-18.

considered plans. It abrogated the Plan of Union, thus severing its connection with the Congregationalists, and exscinded five synods in New York state and Ohio to cut out the heart of the New School. Then it erected the Western Foreign Missionary Society of Pittsburgh into the General Assembly's board of missions, thus ruling out the American Board. Finally, it closed the bounds of the Church to the American Education Society and the American Home Missionary Society.[60]

As if Presbyterian schism was not a severe enough blow to the Evangelical cause, the financial panic of 1837 struck with it. "God has 'shaken not the earth only, but also heaven'—not only the world but the church. . . . That golden dream has vanished.—Oh, how suddenly! The wealth which Christians intended to consecrate to Christ, where is it now?"[61]

The united front had ended. Schism changed the character of the New School movement in a flash; its members gathered promptly at Auburn, N.Y., to take up the duties and responsibilities of a denomination. No longer carrying the vision of a united Evangelical Christendom marching to world conquest, the New School became another sect. The forms and habits of co-operation lingered a few years, but the spirit of the united front was dead.

However, the united front did not die before it had accomplished its primary task. It had provided a conservative counterbalance to native radicalism; it had indoctrinated the American people in its ideology; it had provided that "sameness of views" Beecher saw as most necessary to national survival in the face of disintegrating sectionalism. In the nation's most formative years it engraved its message enduringly upon the tabula rasa which was America.

Curiously, the united front did not become a memory. It remained a vision, a hope. Even as it was passing away, it seemed to dwell in the future. "The day is coming and is probably not far distant, when all the professing people of God

60. Thompson, *History of the Presbyterian Churches*, 117.
61. The Central American Education Society, *Twenty-Third Annual Report* (Philadelphia, 1841), 7-8.

will be so united, if not in every point of external reform, yet in spirit, in cordial affection, as to feel that they are 'one body in Christ, and every one members one of another.' "[62]

And so it rests.

[62]. "Abraham Van Dyke, *Christian Union: or the Argument for the Abolition of Sects,*" a review, *Biblical Repertory,* VIII, N.S. (1836), 36-37.

LIST OF SOCIETIES*

AMERICAN SOCIETIES

African Education Society, 1829——.

Albany (N.Y.) Bible Society, 1814——.

American Anti-Slavery Society, 1833——.

American Asylum at Hartford (Conn.) for the Education and Instruction of the Deaf and Dumb, 1816——.

American Baptist Home Missionary Society, 1832——.

American Bible Society, 1816——.

American Bible Class Society, 1827——.

American Board of Commissioners for Foreign Missions, 1810——.

American Colonization Society, 1817-c. 1900.

American Education Society, 1816——.

American Female Guardian Society, 1834——.

American Female Moral Reform Society, 1839——.

American and Foreign Bible Society, 1836——.

American and Foreign Sabbath Union, c. 1843.

American Home Missionary Society, 1826——.

American Peace Society, c. 1830——.

American Protestant Association, 1842——.

American Seamen's Friend Society, c. 1830——.

American Sunday-School Union, 1824——.

American Temperance Society, 1826-36.

American Temperance Union, 1836——.

* This is by no means an exhaustive listing, nor a definitive dating. Terminal dates are often vague or unknown.

American Tract Society, 1825——.

American Tract Society (New England), 1814——.

American Unitarian Association, 1825——.

Andover (Mass.) South Parish Charitable Society, c. 1816——.

Association for the Improvement of the Condition of the Poor (New York), 1844——.

Association for the Relief of Respectable, Aged, Indigent Females (New York), 1814——.

Auxiliary Foreign Mission Society of Franklin County (Mass.), 1811——.

Auxiliary Foreign Mission Society in the Western District of Fairfield County (Conn.), 1824——.

Auxiliary New York Bible and Common Prayer Book Society, 1816——.

Auxiliary Union of the City of Boston for Promoting Observance of the Christian Sabbath, 1828——.

Baltimore Bible Society, 1814——.

Bangor (Me.) Sabbath School Society, c. 1829.

Baptist General Tract Society, 1824——.

Baptist Missionary Society of Massachusetts, c. 1820——.

Bible Society of Charleston (S.C.), 1810——.

Bible Society of Massachusetts, 1809——.

Bible Society of the Methodist Episcopal Church, 1828-36.

Bible Society of Nassau Hall (Princeton, N.J.), 1813——.

Bible Society of the State of Rhode-Island and Providence Plantations, 1814——.

Bible Society of Union College (Schenectady, N.Y.), 1815——.

Boston Home Missionary Society, 1834——.

Boston Society for the Moral and Religious Instruction of the Poor, 1817-34.

Central American Education Society (Philadelphia), 1818——.

Charitable Society for the Education of Pious Young Men for the Ministry of the Gospel (American Education Society), 1814-16.

Colonization Society of the City of New York, 1832——.

Congressional Temperance Society, 1833——.

Connecticut Bible Society, 1810——.

Connecticut Reserve Bible Society, 1814——.

Connecticut Society for the Suppression of Vice and the Promotion of Good Morals, 1812——.

Connecticut Sunday School Union, 1824——.

Connecticut Temperance Society, 1829——.

Delaware Bible Society, 1814——.

Eastern Auxiliary Foreign Missionary Society of Rockingham County, N.H., 1825——.

Episcopal Tract Society, 1810——.
Fairfield County (Conn.) Bible Society, 1814——.
Female Bible Society of Philadelphia, 1814——.
Female Domestic Missionary Society of Philadelphia, 1816——.
Female Domestic Missionary Society for the Support of the Gospel in the Alms House (Philadelphia), 1816——.
Female Missionary Society for the Poor of the City of New York, 1816——.
Female Protestant Episcopal Prayer Book Society of Pennsylvania, 1834——.
Female Society of Philadelphia for the Relief and Employment of the Poor, 1817——.
Female Union for the Promotion of Sabbath Schools (New York), 1816——.
First Day Society (Philadelphia), 1790-1817.
Friends of Public Education, c. 1849.
General Union for Promoting the Observance of the Christian Sabbath, 1828——.
Half Orphan Asylum Society of New York, 1836——.
Hampshire (Mass.) Missionary Society, 1802——.
Hampshire (Mass.) Sabbath School Union, c. 1831——.
Hartford County (Conn.) Sabbath School Union, 1827——.
Haverhill (Mass.) Sabbath School Union, 1825——.
Haverhill (Mass.) Sunday School Society, c. 1820.
House of Refuge of Philadelphia, 1828——.
Hudson County (N.J.) Bible Society, 1846——.
Humane Society of the Commonwealth of Massachusetts, 1788——.
Humane Society of New York, c. 1810——.
Impartial Humane Society of the City of Baltimore, 1830——.
Infant School Society of the Northern Liberties and Kensington (Philadelphia), 1827——.
Ladies Orphan Society (Philadelphia), c. 1818——.
Ladies Society for the Relief of Poor Widows and Small Children (New York), c. 1797——.
Louisiana Bible Society, 1813——.
Magdalen Society (Philadelphia), 1826——.
Maine Branch of the American Education Society, c. 1820——.
Maine Missionary Society, 1807——.
Male Adult Association of Philadelphia, c. 1815-17.
Massachusetts Charitable Fire Society, 1794——.
Massachusetts Domestic Missionary Society, 1822——.
Massachusetts Sabbath School Society, c. 1830——.
Massachusetts Sunday School Union, c. 1828-35.
Methodist Missionary Society, c. 1824——.

Methodist Sunday School Association of New York City, c. 1820-27.
Methodist Sunday School Union, 1827-36.
Missionary Society of Connecticut, 1800——.
Missionary Society of Philadelphia (Presbyterian), 1818——.
Moral Society of Andover (Mass.), 1814——.
Moral Society of East Haddam, Conn., c. 1812——.
New England (American) Tract Society, 1814——.
New Hampshire Bible Society, 1811——.
New-Jersey Bible Society, 1810——.
New Jersey Colonization Society, 1824——.
New Orleans Temperance Society, c. 1840.
New York Anti-Tobacco Society, 1834——.
New York Evangelical Missionary Society, 1816——.
New York Evangelical Missionary Society of Young Men, 1817——.
New York Bible Society, 1810-27.
New York City Tract Society, 1827——.
New York Colonization Society, c. 1820——.
New York Infant Sunday School Society, c. 1830——.
New York Magdalen Society, c. 1830——.
New York Missionary Society, 1796——.
New York Protestant Episcopal Sunday School Society, 1817——.
New York Religious Tract Society, 1812-26.
New York Society for the Information and Assistance of Persons
    Emigrating from Foreign Countries, c. 1794——.
New York Society for the Promotion of Knowledge and Industry,
    1833——.
New York Sunday School Union Society, 1817——.
New York Temperance Society, c. 1830——.
Northern Baptist Education Society, 1814——.
Northern Missionary Society of the State of New York, 1797——.
Northwestern Branch of the American Education Society (Ver-
    mont), c. 1822——.
Ohio Bible Society, 1812——.
Oneida (N.Y.) Bible Society, 1813——.
Penitent Females' Refuge (Boston), 1818——.
Philadelphia Bible Society, 1809——.
Philadelphia Dispensary, c. 1805——.
Philadelphia Home Missionary Society, 1840——.
Philadelphia Missionary Society, 1813——.
Philadelphia Religious Tract Society, c. 1810-24.
Philadelphia Sabbath Association, c. 1840——.
Philadelphia Society for Alleviating the Miseries of Public Prisons,
    1830——.

Philadelphia Society for the Encouragement of Faithful Domestics, 1829——.
Philadelphia Sunday and Adult School Union, 1817-24.
Poughkeepsie Female Bible Society, 1814——.
Presbyterian Education Society (New York), c. 1820——.
Protestant Half Orphan Asylum Society (New York), 1836——.
Public School Society of New York, 1805——.
Revival Tract Society (New York), c. 1830——.
Rockingham Charitable Society in New Hampshire, 1817——.
Seventh Commandment Society (New York), c. 1830——.
Society for the Conversion of Jews (New York), c. 1820——.
Society for Employing the Female Poor (Cambridge, Mass.), 1825——.
Society for Employing the Poor (Boston), 1820——.
Society for the Encouragement of Faithful Domestic Servants in New York, 1826——.
Society for Promoting the Gospel among Seamen in the Port of New York, c. 1820——.
Society for Promoting Manual Labor in Literary Institutions (New York), 1832——.
Society for the Promotion of Temperance in Haverhill (Mass.) and Vicinity, 1828——.
Society for Propagating the Gospel among the Indians and Others in North America (Boston), 1787——.
Society for the Reformation of Morals in Franklin (Mass.), c. 1750——.
Society for the Relief of Half Orphan and Destitute Children (New York), 1836——.
Tract Society of the Methodist Episcopal Church, 1828-36.
Union Society (Philadelphia), 1808-17.
United Domestic Missionary Society (New York), 1822——.
United Foreign Missionary Society (New York), 1816——.
Vermont Bible Society, 1812——.
Virginia Bible Society, 1814——.
Western Foreign Missionary Society (Pittsburgh), 1805——.
Young Men's Bible Society of New York (Methodist), 1828——.
Young Men's Bible Society of New York City, c. 1820——.
Young Men's Domestic Missionary Society (Philadelphia), 1824——.

BRITISH SOCIETIES

Association for Discountenancing Vice and Promoting the Knowledge of the Christian Religion (Dublin), c. 1790——.
Association for Preserving Liberty and Property against Republicans and Levelers, 1792——.

British and Foreign Bible Society, 1804——.
Church of England Tract Society, 1811——.
Church Missionary Society, 1799——.
Constitutional Society, 1700's.
General Society for Promoting District Visiting (England), 1828——.
Guardian Society (London), c. 1820——.
Haddington Tract Society, 1805——.
Ladies Branch, Manchester and Salford Auxiliary to British and Foreign Bible Society, c. 1812——.
Liverpool Tract Society, 1814——.
London Correspondence Society, c. 1790.
London Missionary Society, 1794——.
London Religious Tract Society, 1799——.
London Sunday-School Society, 1785——.
London Sunday-School Union, 1803——.
Prayer Book and Homily Society (London), 1812——.
Proclamation Society, 1787——.
Revolution Society, 1700's.
Royal Benevolent Society, 1812——.
Society for the Promotion of Christian Knowledge (SPCK), 1698——.
Society for the Propagation of the Gospel in Foreign Parts (SPGFP), 1701——.
Society for the Reformation of Manners, 1692——.
Society for the Suppression of Vice, c. 1790——.
Southwark Auxiliary of the British and Foreign Bible Society, c. 1811.
Willow Walk Bible Association (London), 1812——.

BIBLIOGRAPHY

FOR THE CONVENIENCE of the reader, this bibliography is divided into six categories. There is some unavoidable overlapping, but in each case the entry appears under the heading which seems to represent its chief interest.

The first section lists society and church documents. Society reports are of great importance to any investigation of this period. They are extended and rich in detail. Among the more valuable accounts of personal experience is the Rev. Moses George Thomas' story of his western circuit "under very great hardships" in 1826 appearing in the American Unitarian Association's *Second Annual Report* (1827). Thomas was an accurate and articulate observer, whose freedom from obvious prejudice makes him an outstanding source for this period.

The second section treats Evangelical literature published by united-front societies. Competent secondary works on this topic are almost wholly lacking.

The third section lists some periodicals. Of these, the *Quarterly Register of the American Education Society* is by far the most informative.

The fourth section contains books, pamphlets, and articles concerned with the societies and their leaders. It deals with biographical material, society histories, theme histories which involve the societies, and articles about society activities. Lyman Beecher's autobiography is the best of this lot.

The fifth section covers religious ideas and practices. Church histories as well as works on revivalism and theology are here. Nathan Bangs's *A History of the Methodist Episcopal Church* is particularly valuable, as the Methodist Book Concern suffered a serious fire in 1836 which destroyed many early documents. The narrative of Andrew Reed and James Matheson dealing with the visit of these British Congregationalists in 1834 is so informative it should be reprinted.

The sixth and last section is devoted to such social and intellectual background, British and American, as may shed some light on the problem.

Each section containing secondary works lists them separately.

Society and Church Documents

African Education Society. *Report of the Proceedings at the Formation of the African Education Society Instituted at Washington, December 28, 1829. With an Address to the Public by the Board of Managers.* Washington, D.C., 1830.

American and Foreign Bible Society. *Annual Reports.* New York, 1838; Philadelphia, 1839; New York, 1840.

———. *Constitution of the American and Foreign Bible Society.* New York, 1836.

———. *Proceedings at the Convention which met in Philadelphia, April 26, 27, 28 and 29, 1837.* New York, 1837.

American and Foreign Sabbath Union. *Annual Reports.* Boston, 1844-45.

American Anti-Slavery Society. *Annual Reports.* New York, 1834-38.

———. *Proceedings of the Anti-Slavery Convention assembled at Philadelphia, December 4, 5 and 6, 1833.* New York, 1833.

American Baptist Home Missionary Society. *Annual Reports.* New York, 1833-40.

———. *Proceedings of the Convention held in the City of New York on the 27th of April, 1832.* New York, 1832.

American Bible Class Society. *Second Annual Report.* Philadelphia, 1829.

American Bible Society, *Annual Reports.* New York, 1817-37.

———. "Minutes of the Managers of the American Bible Society." There are five manuscript journals of such minutes in the archives of the American Bible Society, New York, N.Y.

———. *Resolutions of the American Bible Society and an Address to the Christian Public on the subject of supplying the whole world with the Sacred Scriptures within a definite period.* New York, 1833.

American Board of Commissioners for Foreign Missions. *Annual Reports.* Boston, 1811-36.

American Colonization Society. *Address of the Board of Managers of the American Colonization Society to its Auxiliary Societies.* Washington, D.C., 1831.

——. *Address of the Board of Managers of the American Colonization Society to the People of the United States.* Washington, D.C., 1832.

——. *Address of the Board of Managers of the American Colonization Society to the Public.* Washington, D.C., 1819.

——. *Annual Reports.* Washington, D.C., 1818-35.

——. *Constitution, Government and Digest of the Laws of Liberia as confirmed and established by the Board of Managers of the American Colonization Society, May 23, 1825.* Washington, D.C., 1825.

American Education Society. *Annual Reports.* Boston, 1824-40.

American Female Guardian Society. *Fifteenth Annual Report.* New York, 1849.

American Female Moral Reform Society. *First Annual Report.* New York, 1840.

American Home Missionary Society. *Annual Reports.* New York, 1827-37.

——. *Constitution of the American Home Missionary Society Recommended by a Convention of the Friends of Missions held in the City of New York, May 10, 1826, and adopted by the United Domestic Missionary Society: together with the Fourth Report of the Last Named Society.* New York, 1826.

American Sunday-School Union. *The American Sunday-School Union.* Philadelphia, 1828.

——. *Annual Reports.* Philadelphia, 1825-43.

——. *The Charter.* Philadelphia, 1828.

——. *Important Considerations Touching the Principles and Objects of the American Sunday-School Union addressed particularly to Evangelical Christians and other citizens of New-England.* Philadelphia, 1845.

——. *Letters on the Design and Importance of the Agency of the American Sunday School Union in New England.* Philadelphia, 1838.

——. *Proceedings of the Public Meeting Held in Boston, to aid the American Sunday-School Union in their efforts to establish Sunday schools throughout the Valley of the Mississippi.* Philadelphia, 1831.

——. *Sketch of the Plan of the American Sunday-School Union for Supplying a Choice Library of Moral, Religious, and In-*

structive Books for Public and Private Schools, Families, Factories, &c. Philadelphia, 1838.

――. *Speeches of Messrs. Grundy, Wickliffe and others at the Sunday School Meeting in the City of Washington, February 16, 1831.* Philadelphia, 1831.

――. *Sunday-School Evangelism.* Philadelphia, 1859.

American Temperance Society. *Permanent Temperance Documents of the American Temperance Society.* Boston, 1835.

American Temperance Union. *Permanent Temperance Documents, II.* New York, 1853.

American Tract Society. *Address of the Executive Committee of the American Tract Society to the Christian Public.* New York, 1825.

――. *Annual Reports.* New York, 1826-43.

American Tract Society (New England). *Annual Reports.* Boston, 1826-50.

――. *Proceedings of the First Ten Years of the American Tract Society.* Boston, 1824.

American Tract Society (New York). "Minutes of the American Tract Society. Instituted 1825." There are several volumes of such minutes in manuscript journal form in the archives of the American Tract Society, New York, N.Y.

American Unitarian Association. *Annual Reports.* Boston, 1826-40.

Arnold, George B. *First Semi-Annual Report of his Service as Minister at Large, in New York.* New York, 1834. (Arnold made his report to individual subscribers.)

Association for the Improvement of the Condition of the Poor. *First Annual Report.* New York, 1845.

Association for the Relief of Respectable, Aged, Indigent Females. *Annual Reports.* New York, 1816-39.

――. *Constitution and First and Second Reports.* New York, 1815.

Auxiliary Foreign Mission Society of Franklin County. *Annual Reports.* Greenfield, Mass., 1826-35.

Auxiliary Foreign Mission Society in the Western District of Fairfield County (Conn.). *Second Annual Report.* Norwalk, 1826.

Bangor (Me.) Sabbath School Society. *Sabbath School of the First Parish in Bangor, for the Winter of 1829-1830.* Bangor, 1829.

Baptist General Convention. *Proceedings, Baptist General Convention in the United States at Their Second Triennial Meeting and the Sixth Annual Report of the Board of Managers.* Philadelphia, 1820.

――. *Proceedings, Fifth Triennial Meeting.* Philadelphia, 1826.

Baptist General Tract Society. *Annual Reports.* Washington, D.C., 1825, 1826; Philadelphia, 1827-40.

Bible Convention. *Proceedings of the Bible Convention which Met in Philadelphia.* Philadelphia, 1837.

Bible Society of Charleston. *Constitution and Address.* Charleston, S.C., 1810.

Bible Society of Massachusetts. *A Circular Address from the Bible Society of Massachusetts with the Constitution, List of Officers, Trustees, &c.* Boston, 1809.

——. *Report.* Boston, 1812.

——. *Reports of the Executive Committee.* Boston, 1812-20.

Bible Society of Nassau Hall. *Semi-Annual Report.* Princeton, N.J., 1814.

Bible Society of the State of Rhode-Island and Providence Plantations. *Statement.* Providence, 1814.

Bible Society of Union College. *Constitution and Address.* Schenectady, N.Y., 1815.

Board of Education of the General Assembly of the Presbyterian Church. *Annual Reports.* Philadelphia, 1832-38.

Board of Guardians of the Poor . . . of Philadelphia. *Report of the Committee appointed by the Board of Guardians of the Poor of the City and Districts of Philadelphia to visit the cities of Baltimore, New York, Providence, Boston and Salem.* Philadelphia, 1827.

Boston Society for the Moral and Religious Instruction of the Poor *Annual Reports.* Boston, 1817-34.

British and Foreign Bible Society. *Annual Reports.* London. 1804-5 to 1839-40.

——. Ladies Branch, Manchester and Salford Auxiliary. *Third Report.* C. 1817.

The Central American Education Society. *Twenty-third Annual Report.* Philadelphia, 1841.

Colonization Society of the City of New York. *Proceedings of the Colonization Society of the City of New York at their third Annual Meeting, held on the 13th and 14th of May, 1835 including the Annual Report of the Board of Managers.* New York, 1835.

Colonization of the Free Colored Population of Maryland, and of such slaves as may hereafter become free. Published by the Managers appointed by the State of Maryland. Baltimore, 1832.

Congressional Temperance Society. *First Annual Report.* Washington, D.C., 1834.

Connecticut Reserve Bible Society. *First Report.* Warren, 1815.

Connecticut Sunday School Union. *Fourth Annual Report.* New Haven, 1828.

Connecticut Temperance Society. *First Annual Report.* Middleton, 1830.

Eastern Auxiliary Foreign Missionary Society of Rockingham County, N.H. *First Report.* Kingston, N.H., 1826. *Third Annual Report.* Portsmouth, N.H., 1828.

Fairfield County (Conn.) Bible Society. *Tenth Anniversary.* Bridgeport, 1824.

Female Bible Society of Philadelphia. *Constitution and Address.* Philadelphia, 1814.

——. *First Report.* Philadelphia, 1815.

Female Domestic Missionary Society of Philadelphia. *First Annual Report.* Philadelphia, 1817.

Female Missionary Society for the Poor of the City of New York. *Annual Reports.* New York, 1817-21.

Female Society of Philadelphia for the Relief and Employment of the Poor. *Report.* Philadelphia, 1818.

General Assembly of the Presbyterian Church in the United States. *The Constitution of the Presbyterian Church in the United States of America.* Philadelphia, 1839.

General Assembly of the Presbyterian Church in the United States. *Minutes.* 2nd ed. Philadelphia, 1835.

General Association of Connecticut. *Proceedings.* Hartford, 1827-30.

The General Association of Massachusetts Proper. *Minutes.* Boston, 1818-36.

General Convention of Congregational and Presbyterian Ministers in Vermont. *Address to Christian Parents of the Churches in Vermont.* Rutland, n.d.

——. *Extracts from the Minutes.* N.p., 1821, 1830-32.

General Convention of Maine. *Articles of Faith.* Portland, 1828.

General Union for Promoting the Observance of the Christian Sabbath. *The Address of the General Union for Promoting the Observance of the Christian Sabbath to the People of the United States.* New York, 1828.

——. *First Annual Report.* New York, 1829.

Half Orphan Asylum Society of New York. *Constitution.* New York, 1836.

Hampshire Missionary Society. *Reports of the Trustees.* Northampton, Mass., 1802-29.

Hampshire (Mass.) Sabbath School Union. *An Address of the Board of Directors.* Northampton, 1831.

Hartford County Sabbath School Union. *Third Annual Report.* Hartford, Conn., 1830.

Haverhill (Mass.) Sabbath School Union. *Constitution of the Haverhill (South Parish) Sabbath School Union.* Haverhill, 1825.

Haverhill (Mass.) Sunday School Society. *Sunday School.* Broadside. N.p., *c.* 1820.

House of Refuge of Philadelphia. *Seventh Annual Report.* Philadelphia, 1835.

Humane Society of New York. I. Van Den Heuvel, Secretary of the Humane Society, to the Rev. John B. Romeyn, New York, Dec. 5, 1811. Manuscript letter in the archives of the New York Historical Society, New York, N.Y.

Humane Society of the Commonwealth of Massachusetts. *The Institution of the Humane Society of the Commonwealth of Massachusetts with the Rules for Regulating said Society and the Methods of Treatment.* . . . Boston, 1788. (Method was resuscitation of nearly drowned persons by infusion of tobacco smoke.)

Humane Society of New York. *A Report of a Committee of the Humane Society.* New York, 1810.

Impartial Humane Society. *Acts Incorporating the Impartial Humane Society of the City of Baltimore.* Baltimore, 1830.

Infant School Society of the Northern Liberties and Kensington. *Constitution.* Philadelphia, 1827.

Joint Committee of Boston Benevolent Societies. *Report.* Boston, 1834.

Ladies Orphan Society. *Annual Report for the Year 1819.* Philadelphia, 1819.

Ladies Society for the Relief of Poor Widows with Small Children. *Constitution.* 2nd ed. New York, 1800.

London Missionary Society. *Report.* London, 1800.

London Religious Tract Society. *Annual Reports.* London, 1800-1820.

Louisiana Bible Society. *Constitution and Address.* N.p., 1813.

Magdalen Society (Philadelphia). *Report of the Managers for 1827.* Philadelphia, 1827.

Maine Branch of the American Education Society. *Report.* Portland, 1823.

Maine Missionary Society. *Twenty-fourth Annual Report.* Portland, 1831.

Massachusetts Charitable Fire Society. *An Address at their Seventeenth Anniversary Meeting by Benjamin Pollard.* Boston, 1811.

———. *The Constitution of the Massachusetts Charitable Fire Society.* Boston, 1794.

Massachusetts Domestic Missionary Society. *Annual Reports.* Boston, 1822-27.

Massachusetts Sabbath School Society. *Descriptive Catalog of Publications.* New ed. Boston, 1841.

Minutes of the Convention of Delegates met to consult on Missions, in the city of Cincinnati, A.D. 1831. Lexington, Ky., 1831.

Missionary Society of Connecticut. *Communications from the London Missionary Society to the Missionary Society of Connecticut.* Hartford, 1803.

――――. *The Constitution of the Missionary Society of Connecticut with an Address from the Board of Trustees to the People of the State and a Narrative on the Subject of Missions.* Hartford, 1800.

――――. *Fifteenth Annual Account of the Missionary Labors directed by the Trustees of the Missionary Society of Connecticut, performed in the year 1813.* Hartford, 1814.

Missionary Society of Philadelphia, Auxiliary to the Board of Missions of the General Assembly of the Presbyterian Church. *First Annual Report.* Philadelphia, 1819.

New England Tract Society. *Constitution and Address.* Andover, Mass., 1814.

New Hampshire Bible Society. *Annual Reports.* Concord, 1812, 1813.

New-Jersey Bible Society. *Address of the New-Jersey Bible Society to the Publick with an Appendix containing the Constitution of Said Society.* New Brunswick, 1810.

――――. *A Plan for the Establishment of a Bible Society in the State of New Jersey.* New Brunswick, 1809.

New Jersey Colonization Society. *Proceedings of the Second Annual Meeting of the New Jersey Colonization Society.* Princeton, 1826.

New Orleans Temperance Society. *Temperance, An Address to the Citizens of New Orleans.* New Orleans, 1841.

New York Anti-Tobacco Society. *Annual Report.* New York, 1835.

New York Bible Society. *Reports* of forty Bible societies in the United States, to 1815, bound in one volume and presented to the American Bible Society in 1818.

New York City Tract Society. *Second Annual Report.* New York, 1829.

New York Evangelical Missionary Society. *Fourth Annual Report.* New York, 1820.

New York Evangelical Missionary Society of Young Men. *A Brief View of Facts which gave Rise to the New York Evangelical Missionary Society of Young men.* New York, 1817.

――――. *Proceedings of the First Anniversary together with the Annual Report.* New York, 1817.

New-York Missionary Society. *The Address and Constitution of the New-York Missionary Society.* New York, 1796.

——. *Annual Reports of the Board of Directors.* New York, 1806-12.

New-York Protestant Episcopal Sunday School Society. *First Annual Report.* New York, 1818.

New York Religious Tract Society. *Annual Reports.* New York, 1813-25.

——. *Constitution.* New York, 1812.

——. *Sixth Annual Report.* New York, 1818.

New-York Society for the Promotion of Knowledge and Industry. *First Annual Report.* New York, 1834.

New York Sunday School Union Society. *First Report.* New York, 1817.

Northern Baptist Education Society. *Annual Reports.* Boston, 1831-40.

Northwestern Branch of the American Education Society. *Annual Reports.* Vermont, 1822-30.

Ohio Bible Society. *Address, Constitution and Subscription Proposal.* N.p., 1812.

Oneida Bible Society. *Constitution, Address and Report for 1813.* Utica, N.Y., 1813.

Penitent Females' Refuge. *Ninth Annual Report.* Boston, 1827.

Philadelphia Bible Society. *An Address of the Bible Society to the Public: to which is subjoined the Constitution of Said Society and the Names of the Managers.* Philadelphia, 1809.

Philadelphia Dispensary. *Account of the Design, Origin and Present State of the Philadelphia Dispensary.* Philadelphia, 1805.

——. *Rules of the Philadelphia Dispensary and Annual Report for 1818.* Philadelphia, 1819.

Philadelphia Home Missionary Society, Auxiliary to the American Home Missionary Society. *First Report.* Philadelphia, 1841.

Philadelphia Missionary Society. *An Address of the Managers of the Philadelphia Missionary Society.* Philadelphia, 1813.

Philadelphia Society for Alleviating the Miseries of Public Prisons. *Constitution of the Philadelphia Society for Alleviating the Miseries of Public Prisons.* Philadelphia, 1830.

Philadelphia Society for the Encouragement of Faithful Domestics. *Address to the Public.* Philadelphia, 1830.

——. *Constitution of the Philadelphia Society for the Encouragement of Faithful Domestics.* Philadelphia, 1829.

Philadelphia Sunday and Adult School Union. *Annual Reports.* Philadelphia, 1818-23.

Poughkeepsie Female Bible Society. "Constitution Adopted July, 1814." Manuscript in the archives of the American Bible Society, New York, N.Y.

Presbyterian Church. *The Constitution of the Presbyterian Church.* Philadelphia, 1839.

Protestant Half Orphan Asylum Society. *First Annual Report.* New York, 1837.

Public School Society of New York. *Twenty-second Annual Report.* New York, 1827.

Rockingham Charitable Society in New Hampshire. *Annual Reports.* Portsmouth, 1818, 1819.

———. *Constitution.* Portsmouth, 1817.

Society for Employing the Female Poor. *Explanation of the Views of the Society for Employing the Female Poor.* Cambridge, Mass., 1825.

Society for Employing the Poor. *Explanation of the Views of the Society for Employing the Poor.* Boston, 1820.

Society for the Encouragement of Faithful Domestic Servants in New York. *Annual Reports.* New York, 1826, 1827.

Society for Promoting the Gospel among Seamen in the Port of New York. *Report.* New York, 1821.

Society for Promoting Manual Labor in Literary Institutions. *First Annual Report.* New York, 1833.

Society for the Reformation of Manners. *Fortieth Annual Report.* London, 1733.

Society for the Relief of Half Orphan and Destitute Children. *Second Annual Report.* New York, 1838.

State Convention of the Baptist Denomination in South Carolina. *Minutes.* N.p., 1833.

United Domestic Missionary Society. *Fourth Report.* New York, 1826.

Vermont Bible Society. *Annual Reports.* Montpelier, 1813-32.

Wardens and Vestry of Christ Church. *A Letter from the Wardens and Vestry of Christ Church, Cincinnati, to the Rev. Henry U. Onderdank, on the conduct of Bishop Hobart towards Bishop Chase.* Cincinnati, 1824.

Young Men's Domestic Missionary Society. *An Appeal to the Citizens of Philadelphia. . . .* Philadelphia, 1824.

EVANGELICAL LITERATURE

Primary Works

An Address by several Ministers in New-York, to their christian fellow-citizens, Dissuading them from attending Theatrical

Representations. New York Religious Tract Society, No. 15. New York, *c.* 1818.

To The Afflicted. London Religious Tract Society. London, *c.* 1809.

The Aged Penitent; or Filial Piety Rewarded. American Tract Society, *Elegant Narratives,* XX. New York, *c.* 1830.

American Sunday-School Union. *Catalogue of Books &c., sixth edition, also A List of Tracts published by the principal Tract Societies together with Miscellaneous Books suitable for Sunday School libraries and general juvenile reading.* Philadelphia, n.d.

———. *Descriptive Catalogue of Books and other Publications of the American Sunday-School Union.* New ed. Philadelphia, 1837.

———. *The Mother's and Infant School Teacher's Assistant.* Philadelphia, 1834.

———. *Union Questions on Select Portions of Scripture from the Old and New Testaments.* 7 vols. Philadelphia, 1831-34.

Anna Ross. American Sunday-School Union. Philadelphia, n.d.

Baxter, Richard. *A Call to the Unconverted to Turn and Live.* American Tract Society, *The Evangelical Family Library,* VI. New York, *c.* 1835.

———. *The Saints' Everlasting Rest.* Abridged by Benjamin Fawcett. New York, *c.* 1830.

Beecher, Lyman. *Six Sermons on Intemperance.* New York, 1827.

Brownlee, W. C. *The Spoiled Child.* American Tract Society, *Elegant Narratives,* V. New York, *c.* 1830.

Catharine Gray. American Sunday-School Union. Philadelphia, 1833.

A Caution against Our Common Enemy. New York Religious Tract Society, Tract No. 28. New York, 1814.

Child, Lydia M. F. *The Mother's Book.* Boston, 1831.

The Christian Traveller. American Tract Society, *Elegant Narratives,* XXI. New York, *c.* 1830.

A Clergyman of the Church of England. *The Cottager's Wife.* American Tract Society, *Elegant Narratives,* VII. New York, *c.* 1830.

Contentment in Humble Life. American Tract Society, *Elegant Narratives,* XIV. New York, *c.* 1830.

Death Bed of a Modern Free-Thinker. American Tract Society. New York, 1828.

A Dialogue between Two Seamen after a Storm. New York Religious Tract Society, No. 43. New York, *c.* 1818.

Doddridge, Philip. *The Rise and Progress of Religion in the Soul.* Exeter, N.H., 1797.

[Edwards, Justin]. *The Well-Conducted Farm.* American Tract Society, Tract No. 176. Boston, 1825.

Ely, Ezra Stiles. *Tracts on Regeneration and Preparation for Death.* N.p., n.d.

English Gentleman. *Mary of Toulouse.* American Tract Society, *Elegant Narratives,* XXIV. New York, *c.* 1830.

The Four Seasons. American Sunday-School Union. Philadelphia, *c.* 1830.

The German Cripple. American Tract Society, *Elegant Narratives,* XXIII. New York, *c.* 1830.

Griffin, John. *Early Piety recommended in the history of Miss Dinah Doudney, Portsea, England.* New York Religious Tract Society, No. 46. New York, 1821.

Hall, Robert. *The Work of the Holy Spirit.* New England Tract Society, I, No. 1. Andover, Mass., 1814.

Hallock, William A. *The Mountain Miller.* American Tract Society, *Elegant Narratives,* XIX. New York, *c.* 1830.

Hendley, George. *A Memorial for Sunday School Boys.* Philadelphia, 1823.

———. *A Memorial for Sunday School Girls.* Philadelphia, 1823.

The Honest Waterman. American Tract Society, *Elegant Narratives,* XVIII. New York, *c.* 1830.

Institution and Observance of the Sabbath. American Tract Society. New York, 1829.

Kettredge. *Address on Intemperance.* American Tract Society. New York, 1829.

A Lady. *Philip and his Friends: or, Cottage Dialogues on Temperance Societies and Intemperance.* Hibernian Temperance Society. Dublin, 1830.

The Last Judgment. American Tract Society. New York, 1829.

A Layman. *The Weaver's Daughter.* American Tract Society, *Elegant Narratives,* XXII. New York, *c.* 1830.

The Life of Col. James Gardiner. American Tract Society, *Elegant Narratives,* XII. New York, *c.* 1830.

The Life of George Washington. American Sunday-School Union. Philadelphia, 1832.

The Life of Henry Martin. American Sunday-School Union. Philadelphia, *c.* 1828.

Lucy and her Dhaye. Sunday and Adult School Union ed. Philadelphia, 1822.

Malan, Caesar. *The Swiss Peasant.* American Tract Society, *Elegant Narratives,* XVI. New York, *c.* 1830.

———. *The Two Old Men; or What Makes Them to Differ?* American Tract Society, *Elegant Narratives,* XIII. New York, *c.* 1830.

Mary of Toulouse. American Tract Society, *Elegant Narratives,* XXIV. New York, *c.* 1830.

More, Hannah. *Parley the Porter.* American Tract Society, *Elegant Narratives,* IV. New York, *c.* 1830.

——. *The Shepherd of Salisbury Plain.* Boston, 1821.

——. *'Tis All for the Best.* American Tract Society, *Elegant Narratives,* III. New York, *c.* 1830.

——. *Two Soldiers.* American Tract Society, *Cheap Repository Tracts.* New York, *c.* 1830.

——. *Village Politics.* American Tract Society. *Cheap Repository Tracts.* New York, *c.* 1830.

——, and others. *Cheap Repository Tracts.* American Tract Society ed. 2 vols. New York, n.d.

The Mother's and Infant School Teacher's Assistant. American Sunday-School Union. Philadelphia, 1834.

Murray, Lindley. *The Power of Religion on the Mind in Affliction and Retirement and at the Approach of Death.* N.p., n.d.

Newton, John. *Eliza Cunningham.* American Tract Society, *Elegant Narratives,* X. New York, *c.* 1830.

Now or Never. New York Religious Tract Society, No. 63. New York, *c.* 1820.

The Only Son. American Sunday-School Union ed. Philadelphia, n.d.

The Orphan. London Religious Tract Society. London, *c.* 1809.

Pike, J. G. *Persuasives to Early Piety.* American Tract Society ed. New York, *c.* 1840.

Plumer, William S. *The Bible True and Infidelity Wicked.* American Tract Society. New York, *c.* 1830.

——. *Early Impressions Reviewed.* Presbyterian Board of Publication, *Tracts for the People,* No. 3. Philadelphia, n.d.

Porter, Ebenezer. *Fatal Effects of Ardent Spirits.* New England Tract Society, Tract No. 125. Andover, Mass., 1822.

The Practical Influence of the Contemplation of Eternity. New York Religious Tract Society, No. 157. New York, *c.* 1821.

The Publications of the American Tract Society. Vols. II and IX. New York, 1826, 1833.

The Publications of the New England Tract Society. Vol. I. Andover, Mass., 1820.

Richmond, Legh. *The African Servant.* American Tract Society, *Elegant Narratives,* VI. New York, *c.* 1830.

——. *The Dairyman's Daughter.* American Tract Society, *Elegant Narratives,* I. New York, *c.* 1830.

——. *The Young Cottager.* American Tract Society, *Elegant Narratives,* IX. New York, *c.* 1830.

Scriptural Lessons in Question and Answer for the Use of Schools. Albany, 1813.

Scripture Questions. New York: Methodist Book Concern, 1828.

Selumiel or a Visit to Jerusalem. American Sunday-School Union. Philadelphia, c. 1833.

Sherwood, Mrs. *History of Little Henry and His Bearer.* New York: Methodist Book Concern, 1828.

――. *Sergeant Dale, his Daughter and the Orphan Mary.* American Sunday-School Union ed. Philadelphia, 1824.

――. *The Wish; or Little Charles.* American Sunday-School Union. Philadelphia, 1825.

Sketches from the Bible. American Sunday-School Union. Philadelphia, c. 1830.

Stowell, Hugh. *William Kelley; or the Happy Christian.* American Tract Society, *Elegant Narratives,* VIII. New York, c. 1830.

The Substance of Leslie's Method with the Deists; and the Truth of Christianity Demonstrated. Sunday and Adult School ed. Philadelphia, c. 1820.

Sunday School Hymnal. New York: Methodist Book Concern, 1828.

Taylor's Hymns for Infant Minds. American Sunday-School Union. Philadelphia, c. 1828.

The Tracts of the Baptist General Tract Society. I, Nos. 1-29. Philadelphia, c. 1829.

Union Questions. American Sunday-School Union. Philadelphia, 1836.

The Village in the Mountains. American Tract Society, *Elegant Narratives,* XVII. New York, c. 1830.

The Warning Voice. Connecticut Religious Tract Society, No. 1. N.p., c. 1814.

The Watchmaker and His Family. American Tract Society, *Elegant Narratives,* XI. New York, c. 1830.

Secondary Works

Fairchild, Hoxie Neale. *Religious Trends in English Poetry.* 2 vols. New York, 1939-42.

Halsey, Rosalie V. *Forgotten Books of the American Nursery.* Boston, 1911.

Meakin, Annette M. B. *Hannah More.* London, 1911.

PERIODICALS

The American Christian Record (New York), 1860.

The American Quarterly Register (Boston), 1830-32.

The American Quarterly Register and Magazine (Philadelphia), 1849, 1850.

American Sentinel (Philadelphia), 1828.

The American Sunday-School Magazine (Philadelphia), 1824-36.
American Tract Magazine (New York), 1826-36.
Baptist Repository and Home Mission Record (New York), 1827.
Biblical Repertory (Princeton, N.J.), 1829.
The Biblical Repertory and Theological Review (Philadelphia and Pittsburgh, Pa.,), 1830-39.
The British Critic (England), c. 1797.
The Charleston Observer (Charleston, S.C.), 1828.
The Christian Advocate and Journal (New York), 1828-36.
The Christian Almanac (New York), 1828-36.
Christian Baptist (Buffaloe Creek, Brooks Co., Va.), 1824, 1825.
The Christian Observer (London), 1803-6.
The Christian Spectator (New Haven, Conn.), 1829, 1830.
Church Register (Philadelphia), 1827.
Columbian Centinel (Philadelphia), 1798.
Commercial Advertiser (New York), c. 1815.
Episcopal Magazine (Philadelphia), 1820.
The Episcopal Watchman (Hartford, Conn.), 1827, 1828.
Evangelical Magazine (London), 1792-94.
The Evening Post (New York), 1835.
The Free Enquirer (New York), 1828-32.
Gentleman's Magazine (England), c. 1797.
Gloucester Journal (England), 1780.
Missionary Papers. Numbered series of undated pamphlets published by the American Board of Commissioners for Foreign Missions. (Boston), c. 1828-34.
Monthly Extracts from the Correspondence &c. of the American Bible Society (New York), 1827-36.
The New-Harmony and Nashoba Gazette or The Free Enquirer (New Harmony, Ind.), 1828, 1829.
New York Baptist Register (Utica), 1823.
New York Correspondent (New York), c. 1828.
The Pamphleteer (London), 1813.
The Panoplist (Boston), 1806-20.
Priestcraft Exposed and Primitive Christianity Defended. A Religious Work (Lockport, N.Y.), 1828-29.
Priestcraft Unmasked (New York), 1830.
The Quarterly Christian Spectator (New Haven, Conn.[?]), 1830.
The Quarterly Register of the American Education Society (Boston), 1827-31.
The Repository or Teachers' Magazine (London), 1811.
Spectator (New York), c. 1815.
Sunday School Journal (American Sunday-School Union, Philadelphia), 1836.

Universal Magazine (England), c. 1799.
Youth's Friend (American Sunday-School Union, Philadelphia), 1836.

BOOKS, PAMPHLETS, AND ARTICLES CONCERNED WITH THE SOCIETIES AND THEIR LEADERS

Primary Works

"Abolition of Negro Slavery," *American Quarterly Review,* No. XXIII (Sept., 1832), 189-265.

An Account of Memorials Presented to Congress During Its Last Session [Sunday Mails]. Boston, 1829.

Action of the Church in Franklin, Mass. in regard to the American Tract Soc. and the American Board. New York, 1834.

Adams, John. "Father Adams," *The Testimony of a Veteran to the Value of the Labours of Sunday-School Missionaries.* Philadelphia, c. 1855.

"Address of the Managers," *Christian Advocate and Journal,* III (1828), 26.

Alexander, Archibald. *The World to be Reclaimed by the Gospel. Missionary Paper No. X.* Boston, c. 1831.

"American Bible Society," *The Quarterly Register of the American Education Society,* III (1831-32), 137, 138.

"American Sunday School Union," *Episcopal Watchman,* II (1828), 40.

Arbuckle, James. *The Sabbatical Institute.* New York, 1828.

Armstrong, Lebbeus. *The Temperance Reformation.* New York, 1853.

Arnold, George B. *Third Semi-Annual Report of his Service as Minister at Large, in New York.* New York, 1835.

Bangs, Nathan. "Remarks," *Christian Advocate and Journal,* II (1828), 137.

Baptist General Convention (1826). *American Sunday-School Union.* Statement on American Sunday-School Union. Philadelphia, 1828.

"From a Baptist Minister," *Christian Advocate and Journal,* II (1828), 115.

Beecher, Lyman. *Address of the Charitable Society for the Education of Indigent Pious Young Men for the Ministry of the Gospel.* Republished. Concord, Mass., 1820.

———. *Autobiography, Correspondence, Etc., of Lyman Beecher, D.D.* Charles Beecher, ed. 2 vols. New York, 1864.

———. *On the Importance of Assisting Young Men of Piety and Talents in Obtaining an Education for the Gospel Ministry.* 2nd ed. Andover, Mass., 1816.

————. *Plea for the West.* 2nd ed. Cincinnati, Ohio, 1835.

————. *A Reformation of morals practicable and indispensable.* 2nd ed. Andover, Mass., 1814.

————. *Six Sermons on Intemperance.* New York, 1827.

————. *Something has been Done, during the Last Forty Years. Missionary Paper No. IX.* Boston, c. 1831.

"Bible Convention in Philadelphia," *Biblical Repertory and Theological Review,* X (1838), 421.

Bird, Isaac. *The Savior's Injunction to his Disciples. Missionary Paper No. IV.* Boston, c. 1828.

Birney, James G. *Letters of James Gillespie Binney.* Dwight L. Dumond, ed. 2 vols. New York, 1938.

Blythe, James. *Speech Delivered at the Anniversary of the Indiana Colonization Society on Dec. 23, 1833.* Indianapolis, 1834.

Boudinot, Elias. *An Answer to the Objections of the Managers of the Philadelphia Bible Society against a Meeting of Delegates from the Bible Societies in the Union.* Burlington, N.J., 1815[?].

————. "Correspondence of Elias Boudinot 1815-1820." There are typed copies of this correspondence in the archives of the American Bible Society, New York, N.Y.

Boyd, George. *Mathew Carey, Esq.* (Circular). Philadelphia, Feb. 20, 1825.

Burden, Jesse K. *Speech in the Senate of Pa. on the bill to incorporate the trustees of the American Sunday-School Union. Feb. 7, 1828.* Pamphlet. N.p.

By the Author of "The Teacher Taught." *Popular Sketch of the Rise and Progress of Sunday-Schools in the United States.* Philadelphia, n.d.

Carll, M. M. *A Lecture on Infant Schools.* Philadelphia, 1827.

"Class Meetings Formed into Tract Societies," *Christian Advocate and Journal,* II (1828), 81.

Clay, Henry. *Speech of the Hon. Henry Clay, before the American Colonization Society, in the Hall of the House of Representatives, January 20, 1827.* Washington, D.C., 1827.

Colton, Calvin (A Protestant, *pseud.*). *Protestant Jesuitism.* New York, 1836.

"Connecticut Society for the Suppression of Vice and the Promotion of Good Morals," *The Panoplist,* X (1814), 17-20.

Considerations on the Foundation, Ends and Duties of the Christian Sabbath, and the late measures for enforcing its observance. Utica, N.Y., 1829.

Dudley, C. S. *An Analysis of the System of the Bible Society.* London, 1821.

Dunn, Thomas. *A Discourse . . . before the New York Society for the Information and Assistance of Persons Emigrating from Foreign Countries.* New York, 1794.

Edwards, Jonathan (the Younger). *The Injustice and Impolicy of the Slave Trade and of the Slavery of Africans. A sermon preached before the Connecticut Society for the Promotion of Freedom, and for the Relief of Persons Unlawfully Holden in Bondage on Sept. 15, 1791.* 2nd ed. Boston, 1822.

Edwards, Justin. *Letter to the Friends of Temperance in Massachusetts.* 2nd ed. Boston, 1836.

———. *On the Traffic in Ardent Spirit.* American Tract Society, Tract No. 125. New York, *c.* 1826.

Ely, Ezra Stiles. *The Duty of Christian Freemen to Elect Christian Rulers. A Discourse delivered on the fourth of July, 1827 in the Seventh Presbyterian Church, in Philadelphia with an appendix designed to vindicate the liberty of Christians and of the American Sunday School Union.* Philadelphia, 1828.

Emmons, Nathanael. *A Discourse delivered . . . to the Society for the Reformation of Morals in Franklin.* Worcester, Mass., 1793.

"Foreign Mission Plans," American Board of Commissioners for Foreign Missions, *Report read at 27th Annual Meeting* (Boston, 1836).

"To the Friends of Religion in New England," *Proceedings of the First Ten Years of the American Tract Society.* Boston, 1824.

"A Friend of Zion in Georgia," *A Plain Dialogue between Two Brethren, A & B of the Baptist Denomination,* Baptist General Tract Society, Tract No. 135. Philadelphia, 1834.

Garrison, William Lloyd. *Thoughts on African Colonization: or an Important Exhibition of the Doctrines, Principles and Purposes of the American Colonization Society.* Boston, 1832.

"The General Assembly's Board of Education and the American Education Society," *Biblical Repertory,* I, N.S. (1829), 353-55.

"The General Assembly of 1836," *The Biblical Repertory and Theological Review,* VIII (1836), 436-38.

Going, Jonathan. *Inaugural Address at the Anniversary of the Granville Literary and Theological Institution, August 8, 1838.* Columbus, Ohio, 1839.

Grimke, Thomas S. *The Temperance Reformation.* Charleston, S.C., 1833.

Gurley, Ralph R. *Letter of the Rev. Ralph R. Gurley on the American Colonization Society addressed to Henry Ibbottson, Esq., of Sheffield, England.* Washington, D.C., 1833.

Hall, Willard. *A Defense of the American Sunday-School Union against the Charges of its Opponents.* Philadelphia, 1828.

Hints to Collectors. Undated broadside bound with *Missionary Papers* published by the American Board of Commissioners for Foreign Missions. Boston, *c.* 1833.

Hints on the Constitution and Objects of Auxiliary and Subordinate Societies. British and Foreign Bible Society. London, 1811.

Hints on the Formation of Temperance Societies. American Temperance Society. *Third Report.* 1829.

Hobart, John Henry. *An Address to Episcopalians on the subject of the American Bible Society.* New York, 1816.

——. *The Beneficial Effects of Sunday Schools Considered in an address.* New York, 1818.

——. *A Pastoral Letter to the Laity of the Protestant Episcopal Church in the State of New York on the Subject of Bible and Common Prayer Book Societies.* New York, 1815.

—— (Corrector, *pseud.*). *A Reply to a Letter addressed to the Right Rev. Bishop Hobart by William Jay.* New York, 1823.

Hodgkin, Thomas. *An Inquiry into the Merits of the American Colonization Society and a Reply to the Charges brought against it with an Account of the British African Colonization Society.* London, 1833.

——. *On the British African Colonization Society to which are added some particulars respecting the American Colonization Society; and a Letter from Jeremiah Hubbard addressed to a Friend in England, on the same subject.* London, 1834.

Jay, William (A Churchman, *pseud.*). *A Letter to the Right Reverend Bishop Hobart, occasioned by the Strictures on Bible Societies contained in his Late Charge to the Convention of New York.* New York, 1823.

Johns, Evan. *A Sermon preached at Northampton before the Foreign Missionary Society, at their first meeting, March 31, 1812.* Northampton, Mass., 1812.

Kimball, D. T., and Lyman Beecher. *Missions will not Impoverish the Country. Missionary Paper No. XI.* Boston, *c.* 1831.

A Layman. *A Letter to the Rev. Lyman Beecher.* N.p., n.d.

Livingston, John H. *Two Sermons Delivered before the New-York Missionary Society.* New York, 1799.

Malcom, Howard. *Hon. E. Everett, U.S. Congress* (Circular). Washington, D.C., Jan. 20, 1837.

Mandeville, Henry. *An Address on the Reflex Influence of Foreign Missions.* New York, 1847.

Marsh, Herbert. "Inquiry into the Consequences of Neglecting to Give the Prayer Book with the Bible," *The Pamphleteer,* I (1813), 93-151.

Mason, John M. *Hope for the Heathen.* New York, 1797.

———. *A Plea for Sacramental Communion on Catholick Principles.* New York, 1816.

McDowell, J. R., ed. *Magdalen Facts.* New York, 1832.

A Member of the Assembly. *A Plea for Voluntary Societies.* New York, 1837.

Miller, Samuel. *Letters to Presbyterians.* Philadelphia, 1833.

———. *Sermon delivered before the New York Missionary Society, April 6, 1802.* New York, 1802.

Mills, Samuel J. *Memoirs of the Rev. Samuel J. Mills.* Gardiner Spring, ed. New York, 1820.

"Moral Society of East Haddam, Conn.," *The Panoplist,* XIII (1817), 252.

Nevins, W. *Do You Attend the Monthly Concert. Missionary Paper No. 23.* Boston, c. 1835.

"Opinions of Celebrated Authors," *Free Enquirer,* IV (1831-32), 66.

Owen, John. *The History of the Origin and First Ten Years of the British and Foreign Bible Society.* New York, 1817.

Perrine, Mathew La Rue. *Women Have a Work to Do in the House of God; a Discourse delivered at the First Annual Meeting of the Female Missionary Society for the Poor of New-York and its Vicinity.* New York, 1817.

Plumer, William S. *A Call to Personal Labor as a Foreign Missionary. Missionary Paper No. XIX.* American Board of Commissioners for Foreign Missions. Boston, c. 1830.

———. To the Executive Committee of the Board of Education of the General Assembly. MS letter dated Petersburg, Va., June 2, 1834, in the archives of the Presbyterian Historical Society, Philadelphia.

———. *Thoughts on Religious Education and Early Piety.* New York, 1836.

Porter, Ebenezer. *Sermon at the Anniversary of the American Education Society, October 4, 1820.* Andover, Mass., 1821.

A Practical Exposition of the Tendency and Proceedings of the British and Foreign Bible Society. H. H. Norris, ed. London, 1813.

Proudfit, Alexander. *A Sermon preached before the American Board of Commissioners for Foreign Missions.* Boston, 1822.

———. *A Sermon Preached before the Northern Missionary Society, in the State of New-York, at their First Annual Meeting in Troy, February 8th.* Albany, 1798.

"Publishing Fund," *Christian Advocate and Journal,* III (1828), 34.

Ravencroft, John S. *A Sermon preached before the Bible Society of N. Carolina, on Sunday, December 12, 1824.* Raleigh, 1825.

Reese, David M. *A Brief Review of the "First Annual Report of the American Anti-Slavery Society, with the Speeches Delivered at the Anniversary Meeting, May 6th, 1834."* New York, 1834.

"Religion necessary to our Political Existence," *Christian Spectator,* I (1829), 165-75.

"Review on African Colonization," *The Quarterly Christian Spectator,* II (1830), 459-82.

"Review of Reports on Sunday Mails," *Christian Spectator,* I (1829), 159.

Rhees, Morgan J. *The Altar of Peace, a Discourse delivered in the Council House at Greenville July 5, 1795 before the officers of the American Army and Maj. Gen. Wayne, to which is prefixed an address of the Missionary Society* [of Philadelphia] *with their Constitution.* Philadelphia, 1798.

Romeyn, James. *The Crisis, and Its Claims upon the Church of God.* New York, 1842.

———. *Plea for the Evangelical Press.* New York, 1843.

Ruffner, Henry. Letter to William S. Plumer, dated Lexington, Va., June 17, 1834. MS in the archives of the Presbyterian Historical Society, Philadelphia.

"Sabbath School Anniversary," *Christian Advocate and Journal,* II (1828), 178.

"Societies vs. Churches," *American Sunday-School Magazine,* VII (1830), 131.

Speeches delivered at the Anti-Colonization Meeting in Exeter Hall, London, July 13, 1833. Boston, 1833.

Spring, Gardiner. *An Appeal to the Citizens of New-York in behalf of the Christian Sabbath.* New York, 1823.

———. *A Sermon preached April 21, 1811, for the benefit of a society of ladies instituted for the relief of poor widows with small children.* New York, 1811.

Stafford, Ward. *New Missionary Field, A Report to the Female Missionary Society for the Poor of the City of New York and its Vicinity.* New York, 1817.

Staughton, William. *A Discourse before the Philadelphia Missionary Society and the Congregation of the Baptist Meeting House.* Philadelphia, 1798.

"Sunday School Books," *The Biblical Repertory and Theological Review,* VIII (1836), 110.

"Sunday School Missionaries," *American Sunday-School Magazine,* I (1824), 48.

"Temperance Society Growth." American Temperance Society. *Seventh Report.* 1834.

"Temperance Pledge." American Temperance Society. *Fourth Report*. 1831.

Tuckerman, Joseph. *A Letter on the Principles of the Missionary Enterprise. Tracts of the American Unitarian Association,* First Series, I (Boston, 1827), 155-94.

———. *The Principles and Results of the Ministry at Large, in Boston.* Boston, 1838.

Tyng, Stephen H. *Forty Years' Experience in Sunday-Schools.* New York, 1860.

Uncle Sam. "National Societies," *Christian Advocate and Journal,* II (1828), 143.

When a Christian May be Said to have Done his Duty to the Heathen. Missionary Paper No. VI. American Board of Commissioners for Foreign Missions. Boston, c. 1830.

Whittlesey, Elisha. *An Address delivered before the Tallmadge Colonization Society, on the Fourth of July, 1833.* Ravenna, Ga., 1833.

Williams, S. P. *Plea for the Orphan.* Newburyport, Mass., 1822.

Wilson, J. L. *Four Propositions Sustained against the Claims of the American Home Missionary Society.* New York, 1831.

Secondary Works

Allen, I. M., ed. *The United States Baptist Annual Register for 1832.* Philadelphia, 1833.

American Female Guardian Society. *Our Golden Jubilee.* New York, 1884.

Appleton's Cyclopaedia of American Biography. J. G. Wilson and John Fiske, eds. New York, 1887.

Bannister, Saxe. *British Colonization and Coloured Tribes.* London, 1838.

Barnes, Gilbert Hobbs. *The Antislavery Impulse, 1830-1844.* New York, 1933.

Billington, Roy Allen. "Anti-Catholic Propaganda and the Home Missionary Movement," *Mississippi Valley Historical Review,* XXII (1935-36), 361-84.

———. *The Protestant Crusade, 1800-1860.* New York, 1938.

Bowen, Clarence W. *Arthur and Lewis Tappan. A paper read before the New York City Anti-Slavery Society, N.Y., Oct. 2, 1883.* New York, 1883.

Brewer, Clifton Hartwell. *Early Episcopal Sunday Schools (1814-1865).* Milwaukee, 1933.

Brown, Isaac V. *A Historical Vindication of the Abrogation of the Plan of Union.* Philadelphia, 1855.

Brown, J. Newton. *History of the American Baptist Publication Society, 1824-1856.* Philadelphia, c. 1856.

Brown, Marianna C. *Sunday School Movements in America.* New York, 1901.

Burleson, Hugh Latimer. *The Conquest of the Continent.* New York, 1911.

Canton, William. *A History of the British and Foreign Bible Society.* 2 vols. London, 1904.

Coupland, R. *Wilberforce.* Oxford, 1923.

DeBlois, Austin Kennedy, and Lemuel Call Barnes. *John Mason Peck and One Hundred Years of Home Missions, 1817-1917.* New York, 1917.

Dictionary of American Biography. Dumas Malone, ed. New York, 1917.

Dwight, Henry Otis. *The Centennial History of the American Bible Society.* New York, 1916.

Encyclopaedia Americana. Francis Lieber, ed. New ed. 12 vols. Philadelphia, 1840.

Forsyth, D. D. *Memoirs of the late Rev. Alexander Proudfit, D.D.* New York, 1846.

Foster, Charles I. "The Colonization of Free Negroes in Liberia, 1816-1835," *Journal of Negro History,* XXXVII (1953), 41-67.

———. "The Urban Missionary Movement, 1814-1837," *The Pennsylvania Magazine of History and Biography* (Jan., 1951), pp. 47-65.

Fox, Early Lee. *The American Colonization Society 1817-1840.* Baltimore, 1919.

Goodykoontz, C. B. *Home Missions on the American Frontier.* Caldwell, Idaho, 1939.

Green, Ashbel. *Presbyterian Missions.* New York, 1893.

Hallock, William A. *Light and Love. A Sketch of the Life and Labors of the Rev. Justin Edwards, D.D., the Evangelical Pastor, the Advocate of Temperance, the Sabbath and the Bible.* New York, 1855.

Historical Sketch of the American Sunday-School Union and of its Contributions to Popular Education in the United States. N. p., 1865.

Lascelles, E. C. P. *Granville Sharp and the Freedom of Slaves in England.* Oxford, 1928.

Logan, Rayford W. "Some New Interpretations of the Colonization Movement," *Phylon* (1943), pp. 328-34.

Lovett, Richard. *The History of the London Missionary Society, 1795-1895.* 2 vols. London, 1899.

McColgan, Daniel T. *Joseph Tuckerman, Pioneer in American Social Work*. Washington, D.C., 1940.

Rice, Edwin Wilbur. *The Sunday-School Movement, 1780-1917, and the American Sunday-School Union, 1817-1917*. Philadelphia, 1917.

Smith, Laura Chase. *The Life of Philander Chase*. New York, 1903.

Spring, Gardiner, ed. *Memoirs of the Rev. Samuel J. Mills. Late Missionary to the South Western Section of the United States and Agent of the American Colonization Society. . . .* New York, 1820.

Stephenson, George M. *The Puritan Heritage*. New York, 1952.

Stone, John S. *A Memoir of the Life of James Milnor, D.D.* American Tract Society. New York, 1849.

The Story of the Benevolent Fraternity of Unitarian Churches. Boston, 1930.

Strickland, W. P. *History of the American Bible Society*. New York, 1856.

Tappan, Lewis. *The Life of Arthur Tappan*. New York, 1870.

Wardle, Addie Grace. *History of the Sunday School Movement in the Methodist Episcopal Church*. New York, 1918.

RELIGIOUS IDEAS AND PRACTICES

Primary Works

Augustine, St. "Enchiridion," in Franklin Le Van Baumer, ed., *Main Currents of Western Thought*. New York, 1954.

Bangs, Nathan. *The Errors of Hopkinsianism Detected and Refuted in Six Letters to the Rev. S. Williston*. New York, 1815.

———. *The Reformer Reformed: or a second part of the Errors of Hopkinsianism Detected and Refuted*. New York, 1818.

Bayard, Samuel. *Letters on the Sacrament of the Lord's Supper*. Philadelphia, 1834.

Bigelow, Andrew. *Signs of the Moral Age*. Boston, 1828.

Bradley, Joshua. *Accounts of Religious Revivals in Many Parts of the United States from 1815 to 1818*. Albany, 1819.

Channing, W. E. *Letter on Creeds, &c.* London, 1839.

Chase, Philander. *Bishop Chase's Reminiscences: an Autobiography*. 2nd ed. 2 vols. Boston, 1848.

Colton, Calvin. *History and Character of American Revivals of Religion*. 2nd ed. London, 1832.

———. *Thoughts on the Religious State of the Country*. New York, 1836.

Duffield, George. *Sermon preached in the Third Presbyterian*

Church, Philadelphia, Thursday, Dec. 11, 1783. . . . Philadelphia, 1784.

Dwight, William T. *Religion, the Only Preservative of National Freedom.* Portland, Me., 1836.

Edwards, Jonathan. *Thoughts on the Revival of Religion in New England, 1740, to Which is Prefixed a Narrative of the Surprising Work of God in Northampton, Mass., 1745.* American Tract Society ed. New York, c. 1845.

———. *The Works of Jonathan Edwards.* Jonathan Edwards (the Younger), ed. 2 vols. Boston, 1854.

Emmons, Nathanael. *Hopkinsian Calvinism.* N.p., n.d.

"Female Religious Behavior," *The Panoplist,* XII (1816), 256-60.

Finney, Charles G. *Lectures on Revivals of Religion.* 2nd ed. New York, 1835.

Hobart, John Henry. *An Address delivered to the students of the General Theological Seminary of the Protestant Episcopal Church, Jan. 27, 1828.* New York, 1828.

———. *An Apology for Apostolic Order and its Advocates.* 2nd ed. New York, 1844.

———. *The High Churchman Vindicated.* New York, 1837.

———. *The Origin, General Character and the Present Situation of the Protestant Episcopal Church in the United States of America.* Philadelphia, 1814.

———. *A Pastoral Letter relative to measures for the Theological Education of Candidates for Orders.* New York, 1820.

———. *The Principles of the Churchman Stated and Explained.* New York, 1837.

Hopkins, Samuel. *System of Doctrines Contained in Divine Revelations Explained and Defended.* Newport, R.I., 1793.

[Mason, John M.]. *The Voice of Warning to Christians, on the Ensuing Election of a President of the United States.* New York, 1800.

Miller, Perry, ed. *Images or Shadows of Divine Things by Jonathan Edwards.* New Haven, 1948.

Monk, Maria. *The Awful Disclosures of the Hotel Dieu Nunnery of Montreal.* New York, 1836.

Muir, James. *A Sermon preached in the Presbyterian Church at Alexandria, May 9, 1798.* Philadelphia, 1798.

Osgood, David. *Sermon delivered May 9, 1798 at Medford, Mass.*

Reed, Andrew, and James Matheson. *A Narrative of the Visit to the American Churches by the Deputation from the Congregational Union of England and Wales.* 2 vols. New York, 1835.

"Review of the Doctrine and Discipline of the Methodist Episcopal Church," *The Quarterly Christian Spectator,* II (1830), 483-504.

Seixas, G. *A Discourse delivered in the Synagogue in New York, May 9, 1798.* New York, 1798.

Sermon III, Traditions of the Elders. N.p., n.d.

Skinner, Thomas H., and Edward Beecher. *Hints Designed to Aid Christians in their Efforts to Convert Men to God.* 2nd ed. Hartford, Conn., 1832.

Sprague, William B. *Revivals of Religion.* 2nd ed. New York, 1833.

Sweet, W. W., comp. and ed. *The Presbyterians, 1783-1840. Religion on the American Frontier, A Collection of Source Matherials,* II. New York, 1936.

Van Dyke, Abraham. *Christian Union: or the Argument for the Abolition of Sects.* N.p., c. 1836.

Viator, "The Anti-Sectarian Sect," *The Christian Observer,* I (1802), 712.

Wilberforce, William. *A Practical View of the Prevailing Religious System of Professed Christians in the Higher and Middle Classes in this Country Contrasted with Real Christianity.* American Tract Society, *The Evangelical Library,* II. New York, c. 1835.

The Young Preacher's Manual. Ebenezer Porter, ed. New York, 1829.

Secondary Works

Bangs, Nathan. *A History of the Methodist Episcopal Church.* 3rd ed. 4 vols. New York, 1853.

Bates, Ernest Sutherland. *American Faith.* New York, 1940.

Cross, Whitney R. "The Burned-Over District, 1825-1850." Unpublished Ph.D. dissertation, Harvard University, 1944.

Dimond, Sidney G. *The Psychology of the Methodist Revival.* London, 1926.

Faulkner, J. Alfred. "The Work of American Societies," *A New History of Methodism,* II, 361-417. W. J. Townsend, H. B. Workman, George Eayrs, F. R. Hist, eds. London, 1909.

Gibbons, Hughes Oliphant. *A History of Old Pine Street.* Philadelphia, 1905.

Johnson, Thomas H. "Jonathan Edwards' Background of Reading," *Publications of the Colonial Society of Massachusetts,* XXVIII (1930-33), 193-222.

Knapp, Shepherd. *A History of the Brick Presbyterian Church in the City of New York.* New York, 1909.

Koch, G. Adolf. *Republican Religion, the American Revolution and the Cult of Reason.* American Religion Series, VII. New York, 1933.

McKenney, William K., Charles A. Philhowen and Harry A. Kniffin. *Commemorative History of the Presbyterian Church in Westfield, New Jersey, 1728-1928.* Westfield, 1929.

McVickar, John. *The Early Years of the late Bishop Hobart.* New York, 1836.

———. *The Professional Years of John Henry Hobart, D.D.* New York, 1836.

Miller, Perry. *The New England Mind: Seventeenth Century.* New York, 1939.

Mode, Peter G. *Source Book and Bibliographical Guide for American Church History.* Menasha, Wis., 1921.

"Religious Denominations—General Summary," *American Quarterly Register,* III (1830-31), 227.

Speer, William. *The Great Revival of 1800.* Philadelphia, 1872.

Sweet, W. W. *The Story of Religion in America.* New York, 1930.

Thompson, Robert Ellis. *A History of the Presbyterian Churches in the United States.* Philip Schaff, H. C. Potter, George P. Fisher, J. F. Hurst, E. G. Wolf, H. C. Veddar, S. M. Jackson, eds. *The American Church History Series,* VI. New York, 1895.

Walker, Williston. *A History of the Congregational Churches in the United States.* Philip Schaff, H. C. Potter, George P. Fisher, J. F. Hurst, E. G. Wolf, H. C. Veddar, S. M. Jackson, eds. *The American Church History Series,* III. New York, 1894.

British Social and Intellectual Background

Primary Works

Babeau, M. *Paris en 1789.* Paris[?], c. 1789.

Barlow, Joel. *Advice to the Privileged Orders in the Several States of Europe Resulting from the Necessity and Propriety of a General Revolution in the Principle of Government.* London, 1795.

Barruel, Augustine. *Memoirs pour servir a l'histoire du Jacobisme.* London[?], 1797.

———. *Memoirs Illustrating the History of Jacobinism.* English translation. London[?], 1797.

Bowles, John. *Antidotes against French Politics.* London, c. 1795.

———. *Hints on Levelling.* London, c. 1795.

———. *Plots found out.* London, c. 1795.

———. *Words in Season.* London, c. 1795.

British Press (1802). "Literary and Philosophical Intelligence," *The Christian Observer,* II (1803), 507.

Burke, Edmund. *Reflections on the Revolution in France and on the Proceedings in Certain Societies in London Relative to that Event.* 9th ed. London, 1791.

A Caution against Drunkenness. Society for the Promotion of Christian Knowledge. London, *c.* 1710.

Chalmers, George (Francis Oldys, *pseud.*). *The Life of Thomas Paine, Author of the Rights of Man.* London[?], *c.* 1792.

Charles, Lord Bishop of Norwich. *A Sermon Preached before the Incorporated Society for the Propagation of the Gospel in Foreign Parts.* London, 1797.

DeFoe, Daniel. *An Account of the Reformation of Manners.* London, 1704.

Emerson, Ralph Waldo. *English Traits. The Works of Ralph Waldo Emerson.* Standard Library, V. Boston, 1884.

George III, His Majesty. *Royal Proclamation against Vice and Immorality.* London, 1787.

Hughes, Lewis. *Historical View of the Rise, Progress, and Tendency of the Principles of Jacobism.* London[?], 1799.

"Jacobism Displayed," *Universal Magazine* (London[?], 1799).

A Kind Caution to Profane Swearers. Society for the Promotion of Christian Knowledge. London, *c.* 1710.

Malthus, T. R. *Essay on the Principle of Population.* London[?], 1798.

Paine, Thomas. *The Age of Reason: being an Investigation of True and of Fabulous Theology.* 2nd Am. ed. New York, 1794.

Persuation to Serious Observation of the Lord's Day. Society for the Promotion of Christian Knowledge. London, *c.* 1710.

Phillips, Richard. *An Account of the management of the Poor in Hamburg since the year 1788.* London, 1796.

Robison, John. *Proofs of a Conspiracy against All the Religions and Governments of Europe carried on in the Secret Meetings of the Free Masons.* Edinburgh, 1797.

Thorburn, Grant. *Men and Manners in Britain; or a Bone to Gnaw for the Trollopes, Fidlers, &c.* New York, 1834.

Wesley, Samuel, Sr. *Letter Concerning Religious Societies.* London, 1699.

Wollaston, Francis. *A Country Parson's Address to his Flock.* London[?], 1799.

Woodward, Josiah. *An Account of the Rise and Progress of the Religious Societies.* London, 1701.

———. *History of the Society for the Reformation of Manners in the year 1692.* London[?], *c.* 1700.

Secondary Works

Brown, Philip Anthony. *The French Revolution in English History.* London, 1918.

Bruun, Geoffrey. *Europe and the French Imperium.* Wm. L. Langer, ed., *The Rise of Modern Europe.* New York, 1938.

Clarkson, Thomas. *The History of the Rise, Progress and Accomplishment of the Abolition of the African Slave-Trade by the British Parliament.* London, 1808.

Cunnington, C. Willett. *Feminine Attitudes in the Nineteenth Century.* London, 1935.

Edwards, Maldwin. *After Wesley.* London, 1935.

Lovejoy, Arthur O. *The Great Chain of Being.* Cambridge, Mass., 1936.

Quinlan, Maurice J. *Victorian Prelude. Columbia University Studies in English and Comparative Literature,* No. 155. New York, 1941.

Overton, John Henry. *The Evangelical Revival in the Eighteenth Century.* London, 1886.

Piette, Maximin. *John Wesley in the Evolution of Protestantism.* J. B. Howard, tr. London, 1938.

Roustan, M. *The Pioneers of the French Revolution.* Frederic Whyte, tr. London, 1926.

Schilling, Bernard N. *Conservative England and the Case against Voltaire.* New York, 1950.

Sherwig, John M. "Subsidies as an Instrument of Pitt's War Policy, 1793-1806." Unpublished Ph.D. dissertation, Harvard University, 1948.

Smith, Edward. *The Story of the English Jacobins.* London, n.d.

Wearmouth, Robert F. *Methodism and the Working-Class Movements of England, 1800-1850.* London, 1937.

Woodward, William E. *Tom Paine, America's Godfather.* New York, 1945.

AMERICAN SOCIAL AND INTELLECTUAL BACKGROUND

Primary Works

The Accounts of the Guardians of the Poor and Managers of the Alms-Houses and House of Employment of Philadelphia from 23rd May, 1803 to 23rd May, 1804. Philadelphia, 1804.

Adams, J. Q. *The Diary of John Quincy Adams 1794-1845.* Allan Nevins, ed. New York, 1928.

——. "Letters of Publicola." *Writings of John Quincy Adams.* Worthington Chauncey Ford, ed. I, 65-109. New York, 1912.

Adams, John, and John Quincy Adams. *The Selected Writings of John and John Quincy Adams.* Adrienne Koch and William Peden, eds. New York, 1946.

Addison, Alexander. *An Oration on the Rise and Progress of the*

United States of America to the Present Crisis. Philadelphia, 1798.

Barck, Dorothy C., ed. *Letters from John Pintard to his Daughter, Eliza Noel Pintard Davidson, 1816-1833.* 4 vols. New York, 1940-41.

Barlow, Joel. "The Columbiad," *The Panoplist,* X (1814), 69.

Beaumont, G. de, and A. de Tocqueville. *Penitentiary System in the United States.* Francis Lieber, tr. Philadelphia, 1833.

Bernard, John. *Retrospections of America, 1797-1811.* Mrs. Bayle Bernard, ed. New York, 1887.

Buckingham, J. S. "Metropolis and Summer Watering-place." *American Social History as Recorded by British Travelers.* Allan Nevins, ed. Pp. 308-29. New York, 1923.

Burritt, Elihu. "Thoughts and Things at Home and Abroad." *American Issues.* Willard Thorp, Merle Curti, Carlos Baker, eds. I, 476-80. Chicago, 1941.

Carll, M. M. *A Lecture on Infant Schools.* Philadelphia, 1827.

Chevalier, Michael. *Society, Manners and Politics in the United States.* T. G. Bradford, tr. Boston, 1839.

Cobbett, William (Peter Porcupine, *pseud.*). *History of the American Jacobins, commonly denominated Democrats.* Edinburgh, 1797.

Colton, Calvin (An American in London). *The Americans.* London, 1833.

[Dewey, Orville]. *Letters of an English Traveller to his Friend in England, on the Revivals of Religion in America.* Boston, 1828.

Dix, Dorothea Lynde. "Memorial to the Legislature of Massachusetts." *American Issues.* Willard Thorp, Merle Curti, Carlos Baker, eds. I, 465-70. Chicago, 1941.

———. *Remarks on Prisons and Prison Discipline in the United States.* 2nd ed. Philadelphia, 1845.

Dwight, Theodore. *Things as They Are—or Notes of a Traveller through some of the Middle and Northern States.* New York, 1834.

Farrand, Max, ed. *The Records of the Federal Convention.* 4 vols. New Haven, 1937.

Godwin, Parke. "Democracy, Constructive and Pacific." *American Issues.* Willard Thorp, Merle Curti, Carlos Baker, eds. I, 412-21. Chicago, 1941.

Grattan, Thomas C. "Observations of a British Consul." *American Social History as Recorded by British Travelers.* Allan Nevins, ed. Pp. 247-61. New York, 1923.

Hall, Captain Basil. "A Naval Officer Sees All Sections." *American*

Social History as Recorded by British Travelers. Allan Nevins, ed. Pp. 139-58. New York, 1923.

Hall, Rev. Baynard R. *Teaching a Science.* New York, 1848.

Hall, Samuel R. *Lectures on School-Keeping.* 2nd ed. Boston, 1830.

Hawthorne, Nathaniel. "Mosses From an Old Manse." *American Issues.* Willard Thorp, Merle Curti, Carlos Baker, eds. I, 484-93. Chicago, 1941.

Higginson, Thomas Wentworth. "Contemporaries." *American Issues.* Willard Thorp, Merle Curti, Carlos Baker, eds. I, 439-42. Chicago, 1941.

Houston, James. *A Plan for the Ladies Fund etc. for the Relief of those Afflicted with Cancers, etc.* Philadelphia, 1804.

Lynn, William. *A Discourse on National Sins delivered May 9, 1798.* New York, 1798.

Mackay, Alexander. "American Culture and American Prospects." *American Social History as Recorded by British Travelers.* Allan Nevins, ed. Pp. 346-70. New York, 1923.

Mann, Horace. "Common School Journal." *American Issues.* Willard Thorp, Merle Curti, Carlos Baker, eds. I, 471-74. Chicago, 1941.

N., M. "Retrograde Movement of National Character," *Panoplist,* XIV (1818), 212.

Ossoli, Margaret Fuller. *Woman in the Nineteenth Century and Kindred Papers.* Arthur B. Fuller, ed. Boston, 1855.

Plumer, William S. *Thoughts on the Religious Instruction of the Negroes of this Country.* Princeton, 1848.

"Presidents of Colleges," *Christian Advocate and Journal,* III (1829), 89.

Richardson, James D., comp. *A Compilation of the Messages and Papers of the Presidents 1789-1902.* Washington, D.C., 1907.

Thoreau, Henry David. "Resistance to Civil Government." *American Issues.* Willard Thorp, Merle Curti, Carlos Baker, eds. I, 494-504. Chicago, 1941.

Tocqueville, Alexis de. *De la Démocratie en Amérique.* 3 vols. Paris, 1864.

Trustees of Allegheny College. *Report of a Committee of the Trustees of Allegheny College on the Manual Labor System.* Meadville, Pa., 1833.

Whittier, John Greenleaf. "Justice and Expedience." *American Issues.* Willard Thorp, Merle Curti, Carlos Baker, eds. I, 452-61. Chicago, 1941.

Wright, Frances. "Of Existing Evils, and Their Remedy." *Ameri-*

can Issues. Willard Thorp, Merle Curti, Carlos Baker, eds. I, 443-51. Chicago, 1941.

Secondary Works

Angell, Robert Cooley. *The Integration of American Society.* New York, 1941.

Barnes, Harry Elmer. *The Evolution of Penology in Pennsylvania.* Indianapolis, 1927.

Brown, Caroline Ainslaw. *The Story of our National Ballads.* New York, 1919.

Brown, Ellsworth E. *The Making of our Middle Schools.* New York, 1903.

Burr, Nelson R. *Education in New Jersey 1630-1871.* Princeton, 1942.

Carman, Harry J. *Social and Economic History of the United States.* 2 vols. Boston, 1934.

Commons, John R., and Associates. *History of Labour in the United States.* 2 vols. New York, 1918.

Cubberley, Ellwood P. *A Brief History of Education.* Boston, 1922.

——. *Readings in the History of Education.* Boston, 1920.

Cunningham, Charles E. *Timothy Dwight, 1752-1817.* New York, 1942.

Fleming, Walter L. "The Slave-Labor System in the Ante-Bellum South." *The South in the Building of the Nation.* V, 104-20. Richmond, 1909.

Gallaher, Ruth A. *Legal and Political Status of Women in Iowa.* Iowa City, 1918.

Haynes, Fred E. *Social Politics in the United States.* Boston, 1924.

Hockett, H. C. "Federalism and the West." *Essays in American History dedicated to Frederick Jackson Turner.* Pp. 113-36. New York, 1910.

Holmes, Oliver Wendell. *The Professor at the Breakfast-Table.* Boston, 1880.

McMaster, John Bach. *The Acquisition of Political, Social and Industrial Rights of Man in America.* Cleveland, Ohio, 1903.

Murray, David. *History of Education in New Jersey.* Herbert B. Adams, ed. *Contributions to American Educational History,* No. 23. Washington, D.C., 1899.

Parrington, V. L. *Main Currents in American Thought.* 3 vols. New York, 1930.

Peers, Benjamin O. *American Education.* New York, 1838.

Perkins, A. J. G., and Theresa Wolfson. *Frances Wright, Free Enquirer.* New York, 1939.

Perlman, Selig. *A History of Trade Unionism in the United States.* New York, 1922.

Poole, William Frederick. *Anti-Slavery Opinions before the Year 1800.* Cincinnati, 1873.

Schlesinger, Arthur M. *Paths to the Present.* New York, 1949.

Schlesinger, Arthur M., Jr. *The Age of Jackson.* Boston, 1945.

Stauffer, Vernon. "New England and the Bavarian Illuminati," *Columbia University Studies in History, Economics, and Public Law,* LXXXII (New York, 1918), 1-374.

Tharp, Louise Hall. *The Peabody Sisters of Salem.* Boston, 1950.

Turner, Frederick Jackson. *Rise of the New West.* Albert Bushnell Hart, ed. *The American Nation: A History,* XIV. New York, 1906.

Van Deusen, Glyndon G. *The Life of Henry Clay.* Boston, 1937.

INDEX